THE CHILDREN'S WAR

Also by C. P. Boyko

Blackouts (2009)
Psychology and Other Stories (2012)
Novelists (2014)

THE Children's WAR

C.P. BOYKO

BIBLIOASIS
WINDSOR, ONTARIO

FIRST EDITION

Library and Archives Canada Cataloguing in Publication

Boyko, Craig
[Short stories. Selections]
    The children's war / C. P. Boyko.

Short stories.
Issued in print and electronic formats.
ISBN 978-1-77196-213-1 (softcover).--ISBN 978-1-77196-214-8 (ebook)

    I. Title.

PS8603.O9962A6 2018   C813'.6   C2017-907307-9
                                              C2017-907308-7

Edited by Daniel Wells
Copy-edited by Emily Donaldson
Cover designed by Gordon Robertson
Typeset by Chris Andrechek

Published with the generous assistance of the Canada Council for the Arts, which last year invested $153 million to bring the arts to Canadians throughout the country, and the financial support of the Government of Canada. Biblioasis also acknowledges the support of the Ontario Arts Council (OAC), an agency of the Government of Ontario, which last year funded 1,709 individual artists and 1,078 organizations in 204 communities across Ontario, for a total of $52.1 million, and the contribution of the Government of Ontario through the Ontario Book Publishing Tax Credit and the Ontario Media Development Corporation.

The author would like to thank the Canada Council for the Arts, which provided financial assistance during the writing of this book.

Part of "Andrew and Hillary" appeared in *The Walrus*, and part of "Infantry" appeared in the 2017 *Short Story Advent Calendar*.

PRINTED AND BOUND IN CANADA

THE CHILDREN'S WAR

—HEY, MATT? THERE'S just one thing I don't understand.

    —What's that?

    —Everything.

    —Let me see. Well, this is a logarithmic equation.

    —I know, but I don't know how to do it.

    —Well, logarithmics are tough. To be honest, I've forgotten just about everything I ever knew about them.

    —But you're the teacher.

    —Yeah, but teachers don't know everything. You know who you should ask? Khaji is good at this stuff.

    —Ugh, but she's such a nerd.

    —Nerds can be cool people too. A lot of my best friends are nerds. I'm married to a nerd.

Matt Roades became a teacher because he never wanted to leave high school. His classmates in teacher college had different reasons: they wanted to inspire, they wanted to ameliorate, they wanted to educate. Matt was appalled by their piety, and they were bemused by his facetiousness. He went from being one of the most popular people in high school to being a loner and a misfit in college. His degree lasted three years. Then he got a job and a classroom of his own. He entered it, that first morning, ready to tear the walls down.

He filed in with the students at the warning bell and sat at one of the desks, which he had arranged in a circle the night before. He propped his feet on his guitar case, opened a novel, and waited. At the second bell a few stragglers rushed in ostentatiously, feigning breathlessness. The hubbub of conversation and insult died down for a minute, then, when nothing happened, rose in a crescendo, till everyone was shouting over one another hysterically. Matt turned the page of his novel.

"Hey, who's the teacher here anyway?"

Matt looked up, smiled, and went back to his novel.

"Hey, dog, seriously: are you going to teach us something or what?"

Matt closed the book. They were all waiting for him to speak, even the ones still chatting, even the ones pretending to be absorbed in their own thoughts. He had, without effort or merit, achieved what he had once had to fight so hard for. He was the center of attention. He tossed his book on the floor. He was going to love this.

"What do you want me to teach you?"

"This is math class, isn't it? You're supposed to teach us math."

"I know what I'm supposed to do. What do you guys want me to do?"

"Teach us math." —"Let us have free time." —"Yeah, independent study!" —"Shit, hoss, it doesn't matter what we want. Don't you know that? You gotta teach us math because it says math on the schedule, and we gotta learn math because we're here."

"What happens if I don't?"

"They fire your ass!" —"And they flunk all our asses."

"Who's 'they'?"

"Come on. You know. The school. Ms. Mowthorpe."

"Who's going to tell them?"

"They'll find out when we all fail the tests."

"Who says we have to have tests?"

"You gotta give tests, or else how do you give grades?"

"That should be easy enough. We can draw lots for grades, or you can give yourselves the grades you want. We can figure that out."

The students who were not taking him seriously shouted that they would take A's. The scholars objected.

"Well, what would be fair?"

"What would be fair would be if Charnise and me gave the grades." —"What would be fair would be if you taught us all math and gave us math tests and the ones that did the best got the best grades." —There was a murmur of grudging agreement.

Matt shrugged. "Is that what everyone wants? Okay, I know voting is lame, but should we put it to a vote or something?"

And so Matt found himself, twenty minutes into his first class on his first day of his first year as a teacher, standing at the board, outlining the approved curriculum from the assigned textbook to a room full of sullen teenagers whose desks all faced the same way and who raised their hands when they wanted to go to the toilet. His had become every class he had ever attended; he had become every teacher he had ever hated. He had offered them freedom and equality, and they had chosen slavery and subjection.

"Hey, Mr. Roades, aren't you forgetting to do roll call?"

"Look, call me Matt, okay?"

"I was here before the bell, Mr. Roades. Everybody saw me."

As the days passed, Matt came to blame the students' abjectness on Dundrum High School itself. The building looked like a prison, and was surrounded by parking lots and chain-link fence. The parking lots were patrolled by security guards and the halls by teachers or student trusties. The entrances were chained and padlocked after hours, and extracurricular entry had to be requested in writing. Caged clocks and loudspeakers were mounted on every wall. The stairwells were festooned with nets to thwart suicides. Some of the windows had bars.

The faculty, too, treated the students like convicts, and spoke of them in the staff room with animosity and contempt. Detentions and suspensions were handed out with vengeful relish. Matt's new colleagues spoke not of inspiration and amelioration, but only of keeping the upper hand. He found this attitude even more repugnant than the idealism of teacher college, which survived here only in the principal's pep talks and the poster over the staff-room door: "They will not care to learn until you learn to care."

There was no one for him to talk to but Gwyneth, and she was too fascinated by the baby to empathize.

"Don't you think she drools too much?"

"I'm sure it's quite normal at that age."

Some nights, as they sat in front of the television, which played soothing mysteries for the baby, Matt cracked Gwyneth's knuckles and told her of his disappointments. Her replies, though brief, were always incisive, and they irritated him.

"Well, after years of being treated like prisoners by their teachers, can you blame them for treating their teachers like jailers?"

"But I'm not like that."

"You'll have to prove it to them."

He tried. When on hall duty, he whistled like a bumpkin and winked at infractions. He plucked his guitar and smiled on discussions in study hall. He ignored raised hands and gum chewing, but acknowledged interruptions, however irrelevant. He sent no one to the vice-principal. He neither outlawed nor demanded any behavior. He called students by their nicknames, or "dog," "bird," and "hoss." He improvised songs about the quadratic formula and the Pythagorean theorem. He digressed, told jokes, burped, and cussed. He lied, and mocked his students' credulity. He asked about their other classes, and joined in their criticism of other teachers. He told them stories about his own high school days.

But nothing worked. Conversations died under his benevolent gaze. The kids groaned at his jokes and sneered at his belches. They fooled around if he tried to teach, and wanted to work if he tried to chat. They threw chalk when his back was turned, until he threw chalk back; then chalk-throwing fell beneath contempt. He revealed that he had been a point guard in high school, and attendance at basketball games dwindled. He admired Ezra Rosales's Buzzcocks t-shirt, and the shirt was not seen again in the corridors of academe. Graffiti, a perennial plague at Dundrum, dried up after Henry McCarnock discovered Matt writing "Fuck The War" on a toilet stall door. Not even sex and drugs were immune to the death-kiss of his approval.

"Shit, bird, no way, drugs fuck you up."

"You're crazy if you'd risk getting knocked up before you're even in college, that's all I have to say."

He belonged to an inferior race. He was an adult. Worse, he was a teacher, and by definition nothing that a teacher said or did could be cool.

"Oh my god, you guys, how uncool are we? Talking to our *teacher* about *dating*. Let's get back to work."

This went on for two months. Matt grew more depressed, and more unsure of himself. Perhaps he really was uncool. Did his students see something that he himself was blind to? He looked at his old, tired, bitter, fat colleagues. Was he doomed to become one of them? Was he already halfway there? It was a terrifying thought. He was only twenty-two; but sometimes he heard himself talking in class, and the voice he heard was that of a thirty-year-old.

Then, in November, the music club was founded, and things began to change.

—Hey, Matt.

—Hey, Taylor. You missed a water fountain.

—Hi, Matt.

—Hi, Parvinder. How's that elbow? Ouch!

—Hey, Matt! Chalmers's uncle'll give him as many two-liters as we want at cost.

—Best. When do we pick them up?

Years ago, in a distant school, a fistfight had broken out in a prom-committee meeting. Since that time, the school district had decreed that every extracurricular club must have one teacher advisor attend all its meetings and ratify all its decisions. These chaperon positions held little appeal for the overworked faculty, and tended to fall to the junior teachers. While students were obligated to join at least one club, teachers were not obligated to act as advisors. But most new teachers did not know this, and those who did found it hard to say no. Some were flattered by the nomination, which came from the students.

—Hi, Matt. What does your shirt say?

—Daisy Chain Gang Bang.

—That'd be a cool name for a band.

—It is a band! Don't you guys know anything?

—Hi, Matt.

—Hey, Matt.

—Hey, bird, hey, dog . . . Damn, since when are those two coupled up?

—Since forever, dog.

—Hi, Matty. Did you get my note? I put it in my test yesterday.

—I haven't corrected them yet. What'd it say?

—Better do your homework, Matty!

The music club was started by two seniors, Judd Haziz and Peyton Almoss. Judd was good-looking, expensively dressed, and sat through all his classes in silent, immobile protest. Peyton was a gawky chatterbox whose classes were always being disrupted by coughs, sneezes, and table tappings of mysterious origin. Matt was flattered by their nomination, which he supposed was due to his own musicality. He later learned that he was the eighth teacher they had approached. And he learned at the first meeting, when the club charter was drafted, that Judd, Peyton, and their friends had little interest in music.

—Hey, Matt! Are you hall cop fifth period?

—Nope. Harris.

—Shit. I was going to skip French.

—And deprive Ta Gueule of your charming presence? Harsh, hoss.

The founders of the music club wanted to throw parties. This seemed too naked a statement of their intent, so, with Matt's help, they translated their aim into officialese. "The purpose of the music club is to promote awareness of the music club. Any activity that promotes awareness of the music club will be considered a legitimate activity of the music club. Legitimate activities of the music club may therefore include, but will not be limited to: producing and/or distributing advertisements for the club, writing or speaking about the club, recruiting new members for the club, and holding social gatherings for members or potential members of the club."

This much was the handiwork of Judd and Peyton, with Matt contributing only a sonorous synonym or two. But when they began concocting restrictions to membership, becoming intoxicated with their exclusivity and increasingly cruel in their exclusions, Matt felt the need to intervene.

"I don't know, I just think our parties will be kind of worst if we don't have as many people as possible."

They looked at him quizzically. In the end, they decided that Ms. Mowthorpe would not let them limit their membership anyway; somewhere there must be a rule that school clubs had to be open to everyone. And so, the final clause of the music club's charter was Matt's: "Every person who chooses to be a member of the music club is a member of the music club."

They all signed it. Matt signed too—not as an advisor, but as a founding member.

"Imagine," Judd said, "if we could get everyone in the school to join. Now that would be a best fucking party."

—Matt! Did you hear what happened to Judd? They're shooting him through the grease for talking in class.

—What the hell! Judd never talks in class. They should give him an award.

—They're going to suspend him probably, so he can't go to the party.

—They can't do that.

—Oh yes they can. The music club is still a school event, so if you're suspended it's off limits.

The music club met opposition from the administration over its first picnic. Every outing, whether curricular or extracurricular, had to be approved at the weekly staff meeting by the Finance Committee. The Committee, consisting of three senior faculty and Ms. Mowthorpe, the vice-principal, contested every excursion automatically. They denied the instructiveness of museums, galleries, and concerts; they viewed the world outside the school as a minefield of liability and litigation. Matt tried to convince them that the music club had no more nefarious designs than to eat hamburgers and play capture-the-flag in the park.

"What exactly does this have to do with music, Mr. Roades?"

"It's a membership drive." Afraid that the self-propagating aims of the club would not bear scrutiny, he improvised: "With enough members, we hope to be able to start a school band."

"We have had bands in this school before, Mr. Roades. To most of us their educational value was not, shall we say, manifest."

—This is total bullshit.

—It's just revenge. They can't shut down the party so they're going to harass as many of us as possible.

—You better watch out, Matt.

—The hell I will. I'm going to talk to Bartleman.

Nevertheless, the picnic was permitted, after the Committee made clear to Matt that he would be held solely accountable for any crimes committed or injuries sustained by his charges while outside the school walls. When all fifteen students who had attended the picnic came to class on Monday morning, apparently intact and no more inattentive than usual, a precedent was set. The Committee groused and stonewalled at every new application he submitted, but they could find no reason to forbid the music club from holding its meetings.

—There's not a heck of a lot I can do, Matthew. You know I don't concern myself directly with discipline.

—I got the kids to clean up their parking lot, didn't I? You owe me one, Trevor.

—Perhaps if you hadn't been quite so eager to make enemies . . .

Though Matt portrayed it that way to the students, not everyone on the staff was against him. Some of the younger teachers, those who had tussled with Ms. Mowthorpe themselves, showed by their silence in staff meetings or their smiles in the hallways that they supported Matt's rebellion. And Trevor Bartleman, the principal, apparently confusing him with other teachers he had known, said he was in sympathy with Matt's philosophy of pedagogy, and treated him like an undercover agent.

But when Matt proposed to host a meeting of the music club at his own house, everyone objected. They all agreed that it could not be done. Maybe twenty years ago, but not today. Not today, when merry-go-rounds had been removed from playgrounds and teachers were forbidden to shake their students' hands for fear of lawsuits. It might be different, someone said, if Matt were a woman, but, unfortunately . . .

"My wife will be there. And my ten-month-old daughter. What do you think is going to happen?"

The Finance Committee scoured the school district's bylaws, but could find no prohibition against students being inside teachers' homes. Next they tried to bury the proposition beneath paperwork, but Peyton Almoss retaliated by holding an open workshop on forgery during detention period, which drew record numbers and supplied the music club with enough permission slips for years to come.

—Lyle Harris is complaining that some of the students are calling him by his first name.

—That's not necessarily a sign of disrespect—nor is 'Mr. Harris' necessarily a sign of respect. Nor is a noisy classroom necessarily a disordered one. Or sneakers necessarily a sign of diseased morals.

—Rules become very confusing for the teenage mind if they do not apply universally, Matthew. It's only a matter of time before one of the students asks why, if you're allowed to wear sneakers, it's not all right for them.

—Rules become very confusing for the teenage mind, and not just the teenage mind, if they don't make any sense, Trevor. Good reasons make good rules.

Nearly one hundred students crammed into Matt and Gwyneth's house for three hours of board games, darts, dancing, gossip, and pizza. At ten-thirty there came rumor of a knock at the front door. On Monday morning, the entire student body was talking about Matt's showdown with the police.

"It's okay, I'm their teacher. We're not being that loud. And it is a Friday."

"Well, just be sure to shut it down by midnight. This is a residential area."

By the time school let out on Monday, the music club's membership had exploded to over three hundred, and they were forced to look for a bigger venue for the Christmas party.

—I'm on your side, Matthew. But there is a great deal that is out of my hands.

—What happens if Judd Haziz comes to the party despite being suspended?

—Well, if it got back to the Disciplinary Committee— he could be expelled.

—That's what I thought. Thanks a lot, Trevor.

THE DAY AFTER the Christmas party was the last before holidays, when the administration, knowing that no learning would be interrupted, distributed evaluation forms. These were to be filled out anonymously, in the absence of the teacher, and under the eye of a student invigilator who was instructed to seal the evaluations in an envelope and deliver them to the office. This ceremony was largely meaningless, since the teachers were allowed to review their evaluations and could identify most of their students' handwriting; but it lent a solemnity to the proceedings that most of the students responded to, and their dignified postures as they completed the questionnaires suggested effort, precision, and justice.

Matt tried to dispel this gravity with mock fear, mock threats, and mock bribes, but no one was amused. They waited sullenly for him to leave the room so that they could begin writing about him. In the hallway he exchanged mock grimaces with the other exiled educators, some of whom told him not to worry: the evaluations were just a formality for the school's insurance policy. But the atmosphere remained portentous.

He had not enjoyed the party. He had arrived late, with untamed cowlicks, on Gwyneth's bicycle, because she would not let him drive the car, with its faulty signal, after dark. The decorations were already up, the punch and cookies already out, and the first round of Dance Lotto tickets already drawn. His official job that night was DJ, and to avoid being tied to the stereo, he had put five hours of his favorite songs on a disk; but after half an hour, someone put on a Polly Pringle record of staggering mediocrity—and no one even noticed the change. It seemed that in every room he entered, the laughter was just ending and a game had just begun. He stood for twenty minutes by the pool table, munching cookies and making sarcastic commentary, and though Hollis Turanti was playing without a partner, no one asked him to join. Searching for Anita Paulstone, who by note had asked to talk to him tonight, he found only Devlin's parents, who mortifyingly thanked him for helping bring their son out of his shell, and asked his advice on consolidating the boy's social and academic gains.

Then, just when he had insinuated himself into a game of Monopoly, Devlin himself tapped him on the shoulder.

"Hey, Matt. Judd just showed up."

Everyone looked up, looked at each other, looked at Matt to see what he would say.

"Well, what do you want me to do about it?"

"I don't know. Shouldn't somebody say something to him?"

"If he wants to risk getting expelled over a stupid party, it's his decision."

The Monopoly game fizzled, and Matt again went looking for Anita. As the search wore on, it seemed to grow in importance. Anita was surely one of the most attractive, well-dressed, and popular girls in the school. She had a little bow-tie mouth and a laugh like an eraser skidding across a desktop. When she was displeased with someone, she showed them not her middle but her pinky finger; and she cursed like a sailor in her high sweet voice. She was constantly grooming herself, adjusting her hair, her skirt, her bra. In class, when asking a question, she insisted on raising her arm, supporting it with her other hand and leaning forward in a way that flaunted her cleavage. When she brought her notebook to his desk he could smell her perfume, and her long hair sometimes brushed his shoulder.

"Hey, Matt. Can I talk to you?" It was Peyton Almoss, looking distressed.

"What's the matter?"

"Well, Jen C. told me Palm-Wine saw Elton and Alitz go into a bedroom upstairs."

"Okay."

"Don't you think that's a problem? I mean, the school could shut us down if they found out, couldn't they?"

"I guess Elton and Alitz never thought about that."

"Well, should we do something?"

"What do you want to do? It's Devlin's house. Talk to him about it."

Matt did not know what Anita really felt. In the halls and parking lot she hardly acknowledged him. Was she made shy by her infatuation, or did she only flirt with him in class out of cruelty? Nothing could ever happen between them, of course, and not only because he was happily married; but it was delicious to imagine her in love with him, and to rehearse the gentle, complimentary words he would use to tell her he was unattainable. He studied her note for clues, but the words were noncommittal.

Khaji handed him a glass of punch, and he found himself wishing that someone had had the guts to spike it.

"It's not a very good party, is it?" he said.

"No! I think it's great."

"When I think of some of the parties we threw back in my high school . . ."

He was still lost in remembrance when Anita Paulstone poked him in the ribs.

"I've been looking all over for you, Matty."

"And I've been looking all over for you, Neetie."

Khaji moved away.

"I wanted to talk to you."

"Let's find someplace quieter."

But every room was crowded, and in every room someone shouted his or Anita's name. They did not reply, and the others' eyes followed their progress knowingly. Before they could find a suitable refuge, Devlin grabbed Matt by the arm.

"Hey, Matt. I think we got a problem. Some guys just showed up that I don't think they're in the music club. In fact I don't think they even go to Dundrum."

"So charge them a ticket."

"Well, the thing is, they sort of brought some beers."

This news was announced during a lull in the music, and several faces turned their way. The faces showed disappointment and appeal; and Matt imagined that the disappointment was directed at what they expected him, as a teacher, to say, and the appeal at what they hoped he, as one of them, might say.

Realization dawned in him. The party was dull because he was there. His presence made it a school function. At none of the parties he had enjoyed in high school had a teacher been present. And at all of them, without exception, there had been alcohol.

He smiled and spread his hands. "I'm not going to say anything if you guys don't."

"Forget it," said Devlin. "I'll talk to Peyton."

The music started again, and the faces turned away—Anita's too.

"You wanted to talk to me?"

"I wanted to ask you something, but I think I know what you'll say."

"Well, ask anyway. Maybe the answer's not what you think."

She tucked hair behind her ear and adjusted her belt impatiently. "I was going to ask you if you'd ask Peyton if he likes me, but you would've said I should ask him myself, right?"

All the times she had ignored him in the hallway or in the parking lot: Peyton had been with him.

"I don't know," he said. "I guess I might have asked him for you."

"That's okay. I guess I'll probably just ask him myself. That's probably the grown-up thing to do."

TAYLOR MEDAVAL CAME out of the classroom, clutching the envelope of evaluations importantly. He was reluctant to relinquish them.

"I'm supposed to take them to the office myself. It says right here."

"That's just so they get there, dog. Do you think Ms. Angeles cares, or even notices who puts them in her box? Come on, I'll save you the trip. I'm going there anyway."

"Don't you need to be in class? There's still fifteen minutes left."

"I'm putting you in charge."

The boy's eyes became glazed with visions of prepotence, and his grip on the envelope relaxed.

Matt secured himself in a toilet stall, tore open the envelope, and riffled through the forms, reading at random:

"Mr. Roades needs to take more care when he writes on the blackboard." —"It was often difficult to concentrate in Mr. Roade's class because of all the talking going on all the time." —"We should of spent more time on preparing for the final exam and not so much time making decorations and planning for the music club, when some people in class were not even in the music club (not me) although I did enjoy the preparations a lot. But not the party itself, for reasons that I will be mum about here." —"Matt seems to have

some teacher's pets in this class, I will not say who though."
—"Hard to get anything done in this class." —"Spent
too much time talking about himself (but we all liked
it)." —"Mr. Roades is rude and forgets people's names."
—"Some of the things talked about and the language used
in this classroom was not always appropriate." —"I learned
a lot in this class but I couldn't help the sneaking suspicion
that I could of learned more: That is to say, if the teacher
(Mr. Roades) had not spent so much time helping the more
'challenged' students catch up to the level of the rest of the
class (like 90%)." —"With Matt's brains and education he
could get a lot of jobs better paid than a teacher." —"There
should have been more structure to this class." —"Matt tries
too hard."

He searched in vain for the praise and gratitude that
he'd been expecting, then for some explanation for his students' treason. Their comments purported to be objective,
and even hinted at sorrow for having to be so blunt, but
much of what they said was nonsense. He knew all his students' names. He did not teach to the bottom ten percent,
but rather, if anything, the top ten. If there was too much
talking, whose fault was that? He wrote on the blackboard
perfectly legibly.

Waves of anger and sadness passed through him. Did
they really believe what they had written? If so, why had no
one ever asked him to write more clearly or to talk less? Why
had none of them ever said, "It's too loud in here," or "Let's
move on to the next problem already"? And even if some of
them had spoken up (*had* some of them?), what did they
think that he could, or should, have done about it? Did they
really want another teacher who told his class to shut up and
sit down and turn to page sixty-seven?

No, he decided that the feedback was not sincere, but ad
hominem slander. These must be the words of the unpopular students, the quiet students who had been too timid

to join the music club, the ugly students who resented the attention paid him by their attractive classmates, the stupid students who had been unable to grasp the coursework. Under the cover of anonymity, they were venting their spite. He was able to entertain this hypothesis until he came upon an evaluation, proudly signed, by Khaji, who may have been quiet, but was not stupid, ugly, or, since joining the music club, unpopular. He read her words with bewilderment and pain, and stuffed the sheet of paper in his pocket before returning the others to the envelope and delivering them to Ms. Angeles, the school secretary.

"To be truthful to begin with, I would not recommend it (the teacher or the program) to other people. I am in twelfth grade now and therefore naturally I have experienced every different kind of teaching math, but the way Matt did it here would be for me the bottom of them all, really."

The music club called no meetings in the new year, and eventually its constitution lapsed. It was revived, two years later, by four students interested in starting a school band.

"I will however put forth the opinion that Matt (he preferred to be called Matt) can be very likeable, but that might not be what we needed above all. It can help to keep people paying attention (I mean when you are charming and talk well and are funny) but not everyone. I am afraid that many people get left out under that method. Maybe a few don't like the humor, and a few don't like the math. In either event, if you make it optional to learn, a lot of people will not bother. Would that be their fault? They are the people I can't help but feel regret for."

Judd Haziz was never expelled, because no word of his having defied suspension ever reached the Disciplinary Committee. No teacher heard him speak again in class, and he flunked out of high school with dignity.

"What can you do for them? I don't know, but it would have to be individualized. You can't treat the whole roomful of people like one good, attention-paying, wanting-to-learn pupil. People are all different. Give too much freedom, and you give people the choice to fail. But failure can't be an option, a good teacher would believe. You are in my opinion being undemocratic toward the people who don't care if they fail."

A year later, one of Matt's students accused him of abusing his own daughter. No one really believed it, but several of Matt's colleagues muttered that they were not surprised: it was the sort of thing that came of fraternizing with teenagers, who, after all, hadn't yet learned to master their emotions.

"Another point: It can be nice to be nice, and maybe a bad grade can feel like a penalty, but when people know for a certain fact that they cannot get a grade below maybe a C, they will quit trying if they ever tried to begin with. Therefore again I think trying to be helpful rendered Matt actually unhelpful."

The scandal soured Matt on teaching and cast a shadow over his career, but he did not quit. He didn't know what else to do, and was afraid of the unknown.

"Next, I hope I will be permitted to opine that external to the educational context Matt could learn a thing or two, too. I am talking now about the oh-very-popular club with the puzzling name. You know the one I mean. Here too he didn't do the job required of him. And the outcome? Everyone who attended will be embroiled in a web of concealment and deceit till their dying day. Thank you once again, Mr. 'Matt' Roades. Sincerely, Khaji Ji DuPreane."

As the years passed, his classes gained structure, and his evaluations improved.

—Hey, Mr. Roades? There's just one thing I don't understand.

—Let me see. Oh. This looks like you're getting into matrices.

—I just don't understand why you can't divide a matrix.

—Yeah. Huh. You know, I wouldn't worry about this stuff. You won't have to know anything past chapter twelve.

—But if you can multiply a matrix, why can't you divide it?

—Honestly, I wouldn't worry about it. You don't need to know that.

A GIRL SAT in the motel parking lot, reading a book too large for her and keeping an eye on her two younger sisters playing in the dirt. She was still learning to read and many of the words were strange to her, so the page appeared rather like this:

> The best eye on its own would be puviqkirr if it did not hold the ends of immaliqable niqti foziqs that pick up the ssolako set up by the light qaemse. Huvitiq, the many millions of niqti foziqs would be voqsaekly superfkauar if there were not certain areas in the brain specially dirofmed to rirnumc to the cgilobek and electrical riebsoums of these foziqs. It is here that the ilnqirroum produced by the pgusums on the light-simrosoti layer of the eye first becomes *light* and *color.* The light we sannuricly see with our eyes is not born in this layer nor in the niqti foziqs. It first comes into eworsimbi in the brain. Light and color are tgiqiduqi not outside us: we carry them within ourselves, for the world around us is blacker than the most ssxfoem night.

She looked around in surprise. Sunlight lay upon everything, causing the grass and trees to shimmer, the pavement to sparkle, the church and factory spires to glow, and the flags of the car sales lot to scintillate in the distance like an ocean. She could not believe that all this existed only in her brain, or that the world was in reality dark even when the sun shone. The idea seemed foolish: one had only to open one's eyes and *look* to see that the light and color were out there, in the things themselves, and not in her head. Disappointed with herself for failing to grasp the book's truth (she was too young to doubt that books contained only truths), she reread the page, pausing to stare balefully at the words she did not know, as though a more concentrated attention might divulge their meaning.

A boy sat in the shade of the motel, sniffling and feigning absorption in toy soldiers, but in fact mesmerized by the three girls, especially the smaller two. He had many older siblings, some of whom pampered and some of whom tormented him, but he had encountered few children smaller than himself, and never without adults around. These two babies constituted an exciting new field in which to exercise and expand the operations of his will. He looked at the windows of Number 5 and Number 9, and found neither his mother nor his sister Nance watching him. He increased the violence and the noise of his soldiers' maneuvers until they had all died in agony twice over, but the girls did not even glance his way. Finally, he stomped over to them peevishly, like an ill doctor called to the bedside of a hypochondriac in the middle of the night.

"Well, this is my parking lot—but you can play in it. For now."

He awaited some recognition of his largesse, having been taught by his mother and certain of his siblings that sharing was a virtue, and being accustomed to receive praise and rewards for virtuous behavior. The girls, however, contemplated him in puzzled silence.

"Are you in school or something?" he asked the girl with the book. —"Yeah. When the summer's over. Then I start." —"Me too. I don't want to go."

Hillary, who could not understand this reluctance, said nothing. She was looking forward to school as an escape from the baffling arguments and volatile silences of home. At the same time, she did not know who would take care of her sisters while she was away. Anticipating missed lessons, she already felt herself to be behind her classmates, and was studying hard to catch up.

She and the boy exchanged names, ages, and other vital data, such as their stance on dogs (Hillary was for them, Andrew against) and whether or not they had ever seen a dead squirrel with a stick sticking out of it (Andrew had, Hillary had not).

"Where did you get those babies?" —"They're my sisters." —"I'm not a baby," said Prudence, and Gillian, the baby, blinked defiantly and crinkled her chin. —"Sh," said Hillary. "Be polite." —"Do they do everything you tell them?" —"I don't know. I guess." In fact, the girls had learned that the best way to avoid being smacked or yelled at was to obey their sister, who was usually able to translate their parents' incomprehensible demands into concrete tasks.

Andrew said, "Tell them to . . . hit themself." —"I don't know," said Hillary. "I don't think they'll do that." —"Hit yourself," Andrew instructed them.

The girls looked at Hillary with large, liquid eyes, but their protector did not meet their gaze. They burst into tears of abandonment.

This was nearly as satisfying to Andrew as if they had struck themselves, and he looked about, arms akimbo, in search of anyone who dared challenge his newfound omnipotence.

But the babies would not stop crying long enough for him to issue a new command, and he was overcome with awe and envy at their surrender to hopelessness. He grew nostalgic for his own infancy, which seemed to him, compared to his present austere maturity, an era of voluptuous egoism.

"I wish I was a baby who could cry like that," he said—meaning that he wished he could cry like that without his father or certain of his siblings making him feel he was too old for such behavior.

Hillary again could not comprehend this sentiment: she wanted more than anything to grow up—to be tall, and smart, and beautiful, and competent, and powerful, and old. But she was too polite to disagree, and anyway suspected that, as with the book, her failure to understand was due to some shortcoming of her own.

"Come with me," said Andrew. "I want to show you something." He did not know what he wanted to show them, but felt a strong desire to impart some wisdom. He walked a few feet, the girls following at different speeds, and stopped before a large rock. He explained that large rocks could be turned over—but a demonstration had to be abandoned. He showed them how poles could be swung around, sticks broken in half, ants stepped on, and trees kicked. Then he was tired and hungry, and, without another word, he went inside Number 5 in search of food.

When he had eaten all the sandwiches his sister had put before him, Andrew's interest in the girls revived, and he stood watching them through the window, sniffling and muttering plausible dialogue for them as if they were toy soldiers. He realized with amazement that they played without toys of any kind. He thought of his own toys; his consciousness expanded into the rooms around him, reached into the closets and crannies where his and his siblings' old toys lay, until the trucks and robots and guns and dolls seemed part of him, like so many limbs and appendages to his own body.

"Why don't you invite your new friends inside to play?" said Nance.

"No!" he screamed; and his body swallowed his sister and continued to grow, crushing the life and light out of everything it encompassed, until he was as large as the universe, the owner of all the sandwiches, and in control of all the televisions.

Andrew's disappearance left Hillary and her sisters diminished, as if a hole had been rent in the fabric of the day. He had not taught them anything extraordinary, but he had bestowed his information with a condescending benevolence that was irresistible. Hillary tried to fill his absence by telling her sisters about the sun and the niqti foziqs, but the story was too abstract for their weak and literal minds. She felt that her authority had been undermined, and she looked for an opportunity to reassert herself. When their father arrived home from work and called them inside to wash for supper, she scowled at her sisters and told them that they were dirty, filthy babies. They did not object to this slander, which made her even angrier, for in failing to recognize injustice they showed themselves ignorant of the usual justice and gentleness of her rule.

The girls went inside Number 37, where no supper was in evidence, and where their parents spoke in semaphore, cut the curtains with scissors, wore plants on their heads like hats, repeatedly dismantled and reconstructed the telephone, and took turns weeping in the empty bathtub. Hillary understood nothing, but gave her sisters admonitory and reassuring glances as though she understood everything.

That night, lying in bed, she thought sadly of Misha, whom they had left behind at the old place. Then she thought of Andrew, with his easy familiarity and his glorious bossiness, and she wondered if she had found a new friend.

HILLARY WAS WEEDING the flowerbed, and questioning the weediness of weeds, some of which were just as beautiful as any flower, when an urgent message reached her from the Candy Ninja.

Her brother Ben handed her a piece of paper. "Andrew told me to give you this."

She looked at the paper, which Andrew had not even taken the trouble to fold, for the message was in code.

Gregarious, Matinee Principal.
Theater Cane Ninny island real toad movie.
Youth hem island needeled.

She slipped the paper into the front pocket of her dress, put her sister Prudence in charge of the younger siblings, and went inside the house. She could decipher most of the message by sight, and in any case could guess its gist, but half the fun of having a secret code was going through the process of decoding it, and then destroying both the translation and the original. She entered the bedroom she shared with her sisters, withdrew from its hiding place beneath her and Judith's mattress a pocket dictionary, identical to one that

Andrew owned, and silently locked herself in the bathroom. On a fresh piece of paper she wrote down the word that alphabetically preceded each of those in the message.

> Greetings, Math Princess.
> The Candy Ninja is ready to move.
> Your helter-skelter is needed.

The code, while simple, was not infallible. As usual, Andrew had skipped a word when encoding: presumably it was her help that was needed. She was also amazed that he could misspell a word ("needled") even in the act of copying it out of the dictionary. Nevertheless, the Candy Ninja had other assets that made him an excellent secret agent. She thought almost affectionately (agents could little afford such luxuries as affection) of his speed, his ingenuity, and his strength. His capacity to endure the cold and rain was as legendary as his capacity to withstand torture. And there was, of course, his ninjutsu.

She began to compose a reply, then realized that he would have to return home to decode it. She tore all the papers to tiny shreds and flushed them, and returned the dictionary to its hiding place. She found Andrew in the back alley throwing stones at a plastic bottle, an activity from which she was able to distract him only with difficulty. He had a tendency to drift into trances, which irritated his teachers and most of his family, but which Hillary respected, for she knew that he was dreaming about candy.

"Do you have any money?" he asked her, according to formula.

"No," she replied, according to formula, "but I wish I did."

Having thus established her identity and her abiding commitment to the cause, he went on, "The people in Number 147 just moved out."

Sometimes guests at his family's motel left behind a dollar or two, in seeming absentmindedness (neither Andrew nor Hillary was yet familiar with the concept of tipping).

"How will we get the key?" —"Grandpa is at the desk. If he's not sleeping, you'll talk to him while I sneak around back." —"He'll hear you." —Andrew reminded her that he was a ninja. —"I don't know. I'm supposed to weed the flowerbed." —"Okay. I'll help." —"I don't know." She remembered the time he had helped her roll coins for her parents. He had stuck the rollers on his fingers like claws and run around the room growling, he had built towers of coins and brought them crashing down, he had devised embezzlements that involved buying coin-sized washers from the hardware store, but he had not actually rolled any coins. "It can be hard to tell the weeds from the flowers if you've never done it before."

"Pay your brothers and sisters to do it." —"Pay them! With what?" —"With some of the candy we'll buy with the money we find." —"What if we don't find any money?" —He shrugged. "Then you'll be in debt."

The word froze her soul. From the way her parents used it in their arguments, she had come to think of debt as synonymous with muddle, illness, and disgrace. Suddenly she saw how easy it was to fall into dishonor, criminality, even death, and how thin was the crust of civilization beneath her feet.

But she feared that she had already raised enough objections to make Andrew doubt her allegiance. She made an offer to her sisters and brothers, who accepted as happily and gratefully as if the payment were already in hand—for they were not accustomed in that family to being compensated for their chores. Hillary reflected, with fright and excitement, that she and Andrew simply *must* find money in Number 147; if they did not, her siblings would never trust her again. They might never trust anyone again.

Andrew and Hillary walked their bikes the seven blocks to the motel by back alleys, where life was messier and richer. They saw mysterious animal tracks preserved in concrete, a car bumper like a disembodied smile, a herd of ants carrying a leaf, and a paint can half full of gelatinous paint.

."Wrong color," said Andrew. —"Wrong color for what?" —He grinned. "Camouflage."

When they reached Andrew's room, Number 15, he closed the curtains, handed her two black markers, and took off his clothes. "Start with my feet," he said.

She understood immediately. Andrew often undressed before performing physical feats like climbing trees or jumping ditches; he claimed nakedness gave him greater agility, and Hillary could well believe it. As a ninja, however, he had to be dressed in black in order to blend with the shadows. Here was an elegant solution. She began blackening his toes.

"That tickles." —"This is gonna take forever." —He took one of the markers and colored the other foot with rapid back-and-forth strokes, as if he were shading a foot in a coloring book. —"I'm not doing your doink," she said. —He took his penis in hand and colored it with rather more care. They both paused to admire his handiwork.

Andrew quickly lost interest in the task, and the markers ran out of ink before Hillary had finished his legs. Nevertheless, he was pleased with the result, and moved around the room liberally and in demonstrative silence.

"Now we're ready."

His grandfather was asleep in the office and the keys to Number 147 lay on the counter, but Andrew managed to invest his acquisition of them with a great deal of ninjutsu. On their way back to his room, however, he and Hillary were spotted by Andrew's brother Roger, who was smoking in the doorway of Number 12.

"Hey, Andrew, why the hell aren't you wearing a shirt?" He did a double take. "Why the hell aren't you wearing any *pants?*"

"I was just going to put some on," said Andrew graciously.

They ducked inside Number 15 and Andrew got dressed. Then, moving with conspicuous stealth, they let themselves into Number 147.

The room smelled moist and tangy, like the underside of a rock, and was in a state of magnificent disarray. There were bedclothes in the bathroom, towels on the bed, lamps lying on their sides; the telephone was out of its cradle and the television was turned to the wall; newspapers and the residue of meals were strewn across the floor.

"Boy," said Andrew, "it's worse than my room."

They found much treasure, which they divided equitably, including a cardboard box with a flip-top lid, part of a watch strap, a marble, a battery, and several elastic bands— but no money. Hillary dropped into a chair and succumbed to gloom, while Andrew rummaged through the fridge in search of sweets.

"Hey, have you ever had this?" He held up a jar of instant coffee. —"I don't know." —He said that it must be good, because his parents and most of his brothers and sisters drank it all the time. —"What's it taste like?" —"You know," he shrugged. "Like coffee."

She found and washed a cup, into which he poured coffee crystals and hot water from the bathroom tap, stirring the concoction with a corner of the shower curtain.

"You first," he said.

"Ugh. It smells like burnt toast."

"Ugh. It *tastes* like burnt toast."

But they drank it all, while standing around in efficient and preoccupied poses like adults.

"Do you feel any different?" he asked. —"No," she lied.

They couldn't stop giggling. They ran outside, as if expecting to see snow or a parade passing through town. The sky was purple and the horizon piled with kingdoms of cloud. The trees in blossom smelled as sweetly perfumed as uncooked hotdogs. A soft breeze carried intimations of else-where. Andrew remembered the time he had thrown a frog on top of the school. Hillary imagined herself a girl in high school, carrying a purse and with her hair in a braid. The world was brimming with adventures. Every solid object concealed spaces where candy might be found.

"Come on!"

"Let's go!"

They hopped on their bikes and pedaled away.

"Andrew," a voice called after them, "have you delivered your paper route?"

"Shut up, Nance!" he screamed. "I *said* I'll do it later!"

They raced up Hawk Hill, but Hillary was laughing too hard to catch her breath. They coasted down the other side all the way to Main Street, flying over potholes and past stop signs, car horns blaring a salute to their fearless inde-pendence. Andrew turned in to the bank parking lot and slammed on his brakes, pivoting on one foot and spraying gravel. Hillary came to a more sedate stop, which she embel-lished by remaining upright for several seconds before hav-ing to put a foot down.

"Hey, would you look at this!"

The poster had been on the telephone pole for weeks, and they had both seen it many times—but now it seemed to glow with significance.

MISSING: Our beloved cat
Answers to "Mr. Whiskers" or "Charles"
Last seen down by the lake
Needs meds

There was a picture of the cat looking surprised, and the offer of an exorbitant reward.

"Do you know how many Tongue Lashers we could buy for that much money?" said Andrew.

The question was not rhetorical, and Hillary did some calculations, the results of which left her flushed and dazed. "Enough to fill your fort."

Andrew's fort (which was also, unbeknownst to one another, the fort of several other kids) was an abandoned garden shed in a vacant lot. It was not large, but it could hold a lot of candy. Andrew went into a brief trance.

"I've seen that cat," he said finally. "I *know* I have. Come on!"

They rode out to the lake at top speed, standing on the pedals and pulling hard on the handlebars for leverage. When they reached the picnic area, they jumped off their bikes without braking, and the bikes rolled several feet before they wobbled and collapsed in the grass.

Catherine and Caroline, two girls from their class, were there with their families, and Hillary waved. Andrew batted her hand out of the air.

"Don't. They're—dorks." He had been about to say "girls." "Plus they'll want to join us and share the reward."

Hillary saw that he was right.

They moved down to the beach and began searching for clues, while striving not to appear to be searching for clues. There were, if anything, too many clues; the area was teeming with them. A bottle cap, a broken sand shovel, a half-buried plastic bag—all these suggested to their imaginations conflicting scenes of abduction, escape, scuffle, chase, injury, fugue, and drowning.

Andrew asked Hillary whether, if she had to drown, she would take a breath or let out a breath first. —"Take a breath," she said, after consideration. "Although I guess you'd probably let it out in the end." —"Yeah. It'd probably be over faster if you let out your breath. But I'm the same as you," he said. "I'd take a breath."

"Here, kitty, kitty," said Hillary softly. "Here, Mr. Whiskers." —"That won't work. The owners would have tried it already."

An idea brought her up short. "Maybe he didn't *want* to come. Maybe he ran away." —Andrew concealed his surprise, but not his admiration. "My thoughts exactly."

They moved along the shore, away from the swimming area and out of sight of the picnickers, to where the beach became rocky. No longer spurred by observers, they allowed their search to become relaxed, almost luxurious. They hopped from stone to stone, choosing their steps carefully to avoid booby-traps. They plucked foxtails and chewed them contemplatively.

"Theeth theedth thtick in your mouth." —"Turn them around. They only stick one way—like fishhooks."

Hillary discovered a pool filled with algae and tiny crayfish, but Andrew, who disliked bugs and muck, found something better. Among smooth rocks the size of apples and tennis balls, he found a doorknob.

He tried to pick it up, but it was stuck. He moved some stones and found that it was attached to a piece of wood.

"Maybe it's a whole door," said Hillary, and helped him clear away rocks.

It was a door. But it did not appear to have washed up or been dumped there. It was free of dirt and slime and was well preserved, neither warped nor rotten. And it was embedded firmly in the ground, flush with the earth around it. It looked, indeed, like a cellar door, still in regular use, that someone had taken the trouble to conceal.

"But who would put a cellar *here?*" —"Maybe it's a bunker," said Andrew, "or a hideout."

They looked around to make sure they were not seen; then Andrew turned the knob and lifted the door open—revealing a long stone stairwell dimly lit by strange, flickering lamps.

"Well," said Andrew, "now we know where Mr. Whiskers got to."

Hillary hesitated—thinking of her siblings, the flowerbed, her homework, her teachers, the laundry that needed to be done for tomorrow, the three books she was reading, even her parents.

"Maybe it isn't safe," she said. "I mean, maybe we should bring along Duke and Burchett and those guys." —"Naw. They won't come. They're mad at me." —"Why?" —"Just 'cause I wanted to play Burchett or Birdshit." He explained. "You say either 'Burchett' or 'Birdshit' really fast and they have to guess what you're saying. It's great. It's almost as good as Quack or Whack."

He and Hillary played a few rounds of Quack or Whack; Andrew won, 4-3.

Then, because she had hesitated, Hillary forced herself to go first down the stairs.

She took two steps. "Something's weird." The stairs seemed to be repulsing her feet, and at the same time tugging at her heels. She took another step with difficulty, feeling as if she were wading in water against a current. Then she realized what was unusual about the lamps along the walls: their flames pointed not upwards, but horizontally. Finally she understood.

"The stairs *look* like they go down, but they don't—they go up!"

She backed out and got down on her hands and knees, this time taking the stairs head first, so that when she passed through the plane of the door and gravity shifted by ninety degrees, she found herself clambering up the stairs on all fours.

Andrew watched in amazement as she stood upright: she seemed to be sticking out from the stairs like a board that had been nailed to them. He followed her example, feeling dizzy for only a moment as his head passed through the door. Then he too found himself crawling up a staircase, and it was a simple matter to stand and continue upright. Neither could remember why they had experienced any difficulty; it seemed as if gravity had always operated in this direction. They laughed and looked over their shoulders with fond condescension, as though at their own childhoods, and were startled to see, through the door at the bottom of the stairs, only empty sky.

At the top of the stairs was another door, which Andrew opened slowly and poked his head through. They found themselves in a long stone corridor lined with identical doors, and whose walls disappeared in darkness overhead. The air was cool and smelled like the woods after rain; the walls looked damp in the lamplight. There was no sound, but the silence was busy and varied, like the blackness behind one's eyelids.

"We should mark this door," Hillary said, "so we can find our way back out."

They searched their pockets but found nothing capable of leaving a mark, so Andrew reluctantly placed one of his elastic bands on the doorknob.

The corridor curved to the right in either direction, like an S, with no end visible. They went right. They passed 173 doors, by Hillary's count, before the passage began to curve to the left.

"Well, at least we're not going in circles."

"Unless it's a really big circle."

Finally, Andrew threw open a door at random—and they stood looking out on a grassy plateau that rolled gently downhill to the horizon, where a white haze betokened a distant sea. Clouds tumbled across the sky, casting undulating blankets of shadow over the plain; lush grasses and edible-looking flowers rippled and bristled in the wind. And everywhere were horses: horses single and in pairs, horses cantering, galloping, and grazing, horses flicking their tails and fluttering their manes in contentment and exhilaration.

"Wrong door," said Andrew, and tried another.

They saw a dark, narrow, winding alley between brick tenements that was clogged with food stalls, nests of rags and cardboard, and heaps of garbage. Dogs of all shapes and sizes roamed through the shadows; sniffed the air and one another; shat, hunched and quivering, or pissed, one leg cocked, in corners; and rooted in the trash like shoppers hunting for bargains.

"*Dogs*," said Andrew, and slammed the door.

The next door opened onto a vast atrium filled with warm, candy-colored light. Sunshine streamed like stage spotlights through high stained-glass windows, igniting clouds of lazy motes that glowed as brightly and briefly as sparks.

"Now this is more like it."

The floor was covered with languorously sprawling cats—cats dozing, yawning, stretching, preening, purring, and snoring.

"Excuse me," Hillary addressed a nearby tabby. "We're looking for a cat." —The tabby gazed up at her with steady indifference. —"His name is Charles," said Andrew. —"Charles Whiskers." —"Although he might be using an alias." —"An alias is a different name."

The tabby yawned, waited a moment to be sure that another yawn was not coming, then said, "Can't say as we have much use for names round here."

Hillary was perplexed. "Then what do you call one another?"

The tabby smacked his lips reminiscently, as though memories had taste. "Don't recollect as we call one another much of anything at all."

Hillary began outlining the inadequacies of this system, but Andrew interrupted her to describe the cat they had seen on the poster.

"No," said the tabby, "afraid I never was much of a one for faces. Mind you, I know just the cat you might should ask. He knows everycat hereabouts."

"What's his name?" said Hillary. "I mean, what's he look like? I mean, where can we find him?"

The tabby licked himself thoughtfully. "No," he said at last, "won't claim as I'm much good with directions."

They approached another cat, a Siamese who looked at them intelligently as they explained their problem, then said, "Might one inquire as to your *rank*?" —"Rank?" —"That's what one *thought*: visitor-class. Well, permit one to be the first to inform you that cats of the visitor-class, when addressing cats of the superior-class—and one is a cat of the superior-class—are required to look at three points before making eye contact."

"We're not cats," said Andrew.

The Siamese nodded. "Apology *accepted*. Just remember that the rule applies all the way up the line: you must look at four points for cats of the outstanding-class, five for cats of the distinguished-class, six for cats of the exalted-class, and of course seven points for King Charles himself—though one hardly supposes you'll find yourself in the king's company. It is rather less unlikely in one's own case; and naturally a cat of the superior-class is required to look at only four points before meeting the gaze of the king."

"The king's name is Charles?" said Hillary. —"Well, *yes*, but a cat of the visitor-class would address him as Lord Admiral Whiskers The Most High." —Andrew said, "That cat over there told us you didn't use names." —"That cat over *there*," said the Siamese, "is no doubt a cat of the eminent-class. One need scarcely say more."

"How does one—how does a cat of the visitor-class get an audience with the king?" said Hillary.

The Siamese assured them that it was difficult, unheard of, fraught with peril; but when they pressed for details, pledging their commitment and intrepidity, he was unable to supply any definite facts or guidance. Gradually they realized that he knew nothing about the king besides his name and rank.

They asked other cats, but none of them knew or would reveal the king's whereabouts. Eventually Andrew and Hillary gave up and went in search of the king on their own.

They passed through cavernous galleries, parlors, courts, annexes, antechambers, hallways, and halls; everywhere cats lay basking in pools of sunlight.

"They don't seem to *do* much here," said Hillary. —"I know. Isn't it great?"

At last they found the king in yet another stuffy ballroom, enjoying no regal distinction other than a dusty palanquin, which looked no more comfortable than the flagstone floor.

"Hello, Your Kingness," said Hillary, bowing, curtseying, and looking at seven or ten points around the room, "I mean, Lord Admiral Whiskers The Most High."

The cat from the poster blinked benevolently and looked at Andrew, who had gone into a trance and was staring at him hungrily. Hillary pinched Andrew's arm, and he wagged his head but did not take his eyes off the king.

"Who," said the king in a voice of ominous softness, "is this boorish cat who fails to observe the court etiquette?"

"I'm not a cat," said Andrew. "I'm the Candy Ninja. This is the Math Princess. And you're Mr. Whiskers. We've come to rescue you."

The cat king's face puckered in what Hillary took to be wrath; the muscles in her legs tensed, preparing to flee the royal death sentence. But then King Charles laughed.

"I like this cat," he said. "He flouts the etiquette, and he calls me 'mister'—something that you bunch of lickspittles would never dare do, am I right?"

Without lifting their heads, the cats around him agreed obsequiously that they were all terribly obsequious.

"But what makes you think I'm in need of rescuing, kitten baby? I'm perfectly content where I am." The king stretched and yawned.

"But your family misses you," said Hillary. "They've been looking all over for you."

"Don't talk to me about *family*—those fat cats were my slave-drivers. They took me for endless footslogs—on a leash! They wouldn't leave me alone: always pushing me outside or calling me back in. They weren't happy unless I looked busy. They thought a cat should always be on the prowl, hunting for its supper—even when the cupboards were full of tuna! No, pussycat, I'm never going back to that gulag, thank you very much."

Andrew muttered sympathetically.

"But your medication," said Hillary. "Don't you need to take your medication?"

"That poison!" The king waved a paw contemptuously. "There's nothing wrong with me that a little nap won't fix."

Hillary looked glumly at Andrew, but could not catch his eye.

"Well, if we can't persuade you," said Andrew in a bright voice, "I guess we'll just be leaving, then."

"Aw, kitten, I was going to make you a minister. Your friend, too, maybe."

Hillary would have liked to hear more about the positions they were declining, but Andrew was already asking for directions home.

"Your world," said the king, "has few exits, but plenty of entrances. Try that door there, and if not that one, the next one. You'll get there eventually. You can't really miss it."

"Goodbye, Your Highness . . ." Hillary bowed and genuflected, but Andrew was already walking out the door indicated.

They found themselves emerging from a blackthorn bush at the bottom of Main Street. Looking back, Hillary was amazed: the foliage appeared unbroken; no one would ever guess that there was a door there. Indeed, as soon as they had taken a few steps, she doubted whether she herself could say for certain where they had come out.

She sighed. The adventure, which had begun so promisingly, was over.

"I guess we better walk back and get our bikes," she said.

"Not till we've collected our reward," said Andrew.

He lifted his shirt and revealed a hissing, wriggling Mr. Whiskers.

"But how!"

He reminded her that he was a ninja.

Her joy and admiration were quickly superseded by scruples. "But you kidnapped him!"

"Technically he belongs to his owners, so technically we're returning him. Ow! Stop scratching!" He held the cat at arm's length as he hurried up the street. "Besides, he needs his medicine. You said so yourself."

Hillary trailed behind, too overwhelmed by doubts to keep pace, yet moving too fast to think clearly. By the time they reached the owners' front door, she had resolved to do the right thing, but was no closer to knowing what the right thing was. Andrew told her to ring the doorbell, and her amorphous thoughts dissolved into a jumble of amorphous feelings. She rang the doorbell.

The door opened.

"Hey lady, we found your cat."

A woman whose many chins gave her the appearance of perpetually recoiling in disgust stood glaring at them.

"That's not our cat," she said. "Our cat came home last week."

With a violent convulsion, the cat king escaped from Andrew's grasp and ran away down the street. The woman offered to let them each pick an apple from the tree for their trouble, and closed the door.

Andrew and Hillary parted at the sidewalk with few words, Andrew slouching vaguely homeward and Hillary going to retrieve her bicycle.

The sun was low in the sky, there was a chill in the air, and the picnic area was vacant. The sight of her bicycle, lying twisted and forlorn in the grass, filled her with shame; she pushed it home, feeling unworthy to ride it. All the excitement of the afternoon had drained from her, leaving only despondence and dismay. She winced as she remembered each of her misdeeds: abandoning her siblings and her work, stealing the room key, drinking coffee, ignoring stop signs, jumping off her bicycle, snubbing her classmates, abducting a king. And, worst of all, she had nothing to show for it, nothing with which to pay her brothers and sisters for their labor. Not that any amount of candy could ever have justified her behavior. How had she allowed herself to do all those things? First she blamed herself, but that made her unhappy. Then she blamed Andrew, but that made her feel mean. Finally she blamed the coffee, and vowed never to use drugs again.

Her brothers and sisters sat through supper in a state of restless agitation, eager to show Hillary what they had accomplished in the garden and anxious to receive their reward. They were sure that their older sister's sullenness was feigned, concealing some delicious surprise. They all, even the littlest ones, helped clean up after the meal without bickering or bargaining, prompting their father to cynically express his astonishment.

Prudence, acting as guide, drew Hillary's attention to the yellow flowers like goblets, the pink flowers like dripping wax, the white flowers like folded napkins, the purple flowers like splashes of paint, each nestled in splendid isolation in its black bed of freshly turned soil.

Hillary just shook her head.

"What's the matter?"

"Don't you know anything?" She kicked one of the purple plants. "These are weeds," she said, and stomped back indoors.

Each of the children looked to their next-older sibling for some explanation; Prudence stared at the beheaded flower. —"Why is Hillie mad at you?" asked Gillian. —"Be quiet, you *child*," said Prudence. She kicked one of the purple weeds and went inside. —"Why did Pru tell you to be quiet?" asked Ben. —"Shut up, you *boy*," said Gillian, and, kicking one of the yellow flowers, followed her sisters inside. Alan cried, and Judith sang a song about butterflies.

Andrew, on his way home, stopped at the house of Mrs. Willoughby, the most senile of the customers on his paper route.

"Is it that time again already? I always lose track. My goodness, when I think of how the time—"

"Thirteenth of the month," Andrew confirmed, picking a number at random.

She rummaged in her purse for money. "Your brother Lawrence was just here with the paper. It's wonderful how the whole family pitches in."

Andrew felt neither gratitude nor surprise at this information. He had learned that if he could avoid the job long enough, either his mother or one of his nice siblings would deliver the newspapers for him. He could then count on his father or one of his nasty siblings to chastise him for his laziness, but he was used to that.

"Thanks, Mrs. Willoughby. See you next month."

Mrs. Willoughby watched him saunter down the street till he disappeared first from view, then from her imagination, her heart warmed by the sight of a boy so young carrying so much responsibility so lightly. She never read the newspapers he brought, her eyesight not being what it used to be, but she cherished his visits.

Andrew bought twenty Tongue Lashers and five chocolate bars at the grocery store. Then an idea occurred to him. He would share his spoils with Hillary and her little brothers and sisters. He was touched by his own generosity, and daydreamed about their tearful gratitude. When he reached Hillary's street, however, he was appalled to discover that he had already eaten all the candy. He could not even remember what it had tasted like, and the pangs of loss were compounded by remorse.

ANDREW SEARCHED THROUGH Nathan and Claudia's medicine cabinet, trying to recall if he had ever taken any of these drugs before. Methotrexate, amoxicillin, hydroxyzine, bepridil hydrochloride. The names did not look familiar, but he would hardly have recognized the names of his own prescriptions. Ignoring their indications, he scanned their side effects. "Dizziness," "headaches," and "malaise" held little attraction. "Stomatitis," "pruritis," and "enteritis" were kinds of inflammation and probably best avoided. "Thrombocytopenia" and "telangiectasia" sounded foreboding; "epistaxis," "syncope," and "paresthesia" had a pleasant ring . . . Then he hit the jackpot. Hidden by a row of vitamins were expired bottles of "insomnia," "tachycardia," "cognitive dysfunction," and "mood alteration." He washed down two insomnias and a mood alteration with a swig of beer, flushed the toilet and ran the faucet for a few seconds, then returned to the living room—where Connie and Bruce were getting ready to leave. Andrew remonstrated.

"Work tomorrow," Bruce apologized.

"That never used to stop us!"

This claim was debated, which led to further reminiscence of their college days. Connie, who had not been at school with them, noticed that all their stories seemed to revolve around Andrew doing, or inciting others to do, stupid, illegal, or dangerous things while intoxicated. She could not understand or share in the laughter these memories generated, and to combat feelings of isolation, she allowed herself to feel haughty and disdainful towards her husband's friends. She was, however, not immune to Andrew's charms—he was tanned, languid, and unabashed—and she feared a night like the ones they described: a night of recklessness, loss of control, and joy. When Andrew waved his hands, deprecating the past, and proposed again that they all go out and make new memories, she squeezed Bruce's arm, hard.

"How long are you going to be in town this time?" he asked Andrew. —Andrew didn't know. "A week," he said at random. —"Then we'll make memories on Saturday."

When they had gone, Claudia yawned and asked Andrew if he needed a place to sleep. Nathan began tidying the glasses, and did not offer him another beer.

Andrew said no, he was staying with his brother Roger.

"That reminds me," said Claudia. She handed him a stack of mail. "Your folks forwarded it. I guess they figured we'd see you before they did."

Among the bills and the bank statements was a letter from Hillary.

He would not let them call him a cab. At the door, he hugged them goodnight absentmindedly, and went out into the night.

In bed, Claudia asked Nathan, "How do you think he looked?" —"Pretty haggard," he admitted. —"What did he get up to all this time in India?" —"Who knows. It doesn't seem to have done his asthma any good."

Claudia tried to imagine Andrew's life, failed, and shook her head to clear it of the effort. "It must be awful, not having anything to live for." —"Or anyone," said Nathan, putting his arms around her. —"He just never grew up . . ." —"Of course that's what I always liked about him . . ."

But they were already half asleep, and their words were merely reflexive. In broad day they would have been embarrassed by these sentiments, because pity, condescension, and bemusement were the conventional responses to Andrew's unconventionality, and they did not believe that close friends should treat each other conventionally.

Andrew sat at a coffee-shop counter and read Hillary's letter; his face assumed as many different expressions as that of a baby digesting, and finally settled, when he had finished, between admiration and defiance.

Hillary was his oldest friend. They had grown up together; he could not remember a time before he had known her. They had built forts and explored woods together. They had done each other's homework. (She was good at math and history—anything involving memorization or following rules; Andrew was good at writing essays and generating hypotheses—anything requiring originality or opinion.) She had relieved him of his virginity. They had criticized each other's lovers. They had cut each other's hair.

But they had not seen each other, and had hardly spoken on the phone, for three years. Now she was a doctor in the army, and had been sent to the island. Now she was at war.

I know you are against this war and disapprove of the army in general. He could recall but no longer recapture this attitude of his youth, and was appalled that they had become estranged over anything so abstract. *But I believed that doctors were needed here more than perhaps anywhere on earth, and now that I am here I believe it more than ever.* She was forgetting or ignoring the fact that the army had paid for her education. That was the real reason she had enlisted, and the real reason she and Andrew had argued: he could not understand why, if she needed money, she had not come to him—or, what amounted to the same thing, his parents. But she was too proud to borrow, or to ask anyone for help. The idea of her self-sufficiency was too precious to her. Some of his old anger resurfaced. To be hung-up about *money*, of all things! He remembered how in college she would stay at home, not because (as she claimed) she needed to study—she knew more than any of her professors—but because she couldn't afford to come out. Though she never drank, and never ate much, she didn't like to buy *nothing*, and would never permit anyone to treat her to so much as a cup of tea. In his mind was a picture of her, a vegetarian on Wing Night, nursing a diet soda that was already paid for, while her friends ran up tabs in search of satiety and oblivion.

The soldiers do not match your idea of them as leering, macho sociopaths. He doubted that he had ever put it so crudely. *They are all different: shy, polite, clownish, brash, thoughtful, clever, simple, kind. They are tall and short, scrawny and stout, handsome and homely. They come from all over. They miss their farms, schools, cars, dogs, pianos, girlfriends, and brothers. They get their legs and fingers and faces and lungs pierced, torn, and blown apart by bullets and shrapnel and mine fragments, and some of them are never shy, polite, or clownish or anything ever again. They come to us hurt or dying, but none of them complain.* She neglected to mention that these shy, polite boys were busy piercing and blowing apart other shy, polite boys; that they were being paid—had signed up—to kill; and that some of them, surely, must enjoy it.

The waste of life is awful, but I was prepared for that. I was not prepared for the waste of character, of personality, of unique minds filled with unique memories spilled forever like water from a smashed vase. He found himself thinking of friends who had died: Blake Burchett, who had been hit by a car while bicycling down Hawk Hill; Paul LaMoz, the best chess player Andrew ever met, who had run out of gas on the highway one winter, walked into town, and died a week later of pneumonia; Debbie Lorenzo, who had a birthmark shaped like a duck on the small of her back, who spoke like a radio announcer when she was drunk, and who had died of some disease whose name Andrew had never committed to memory. But unlike Blake, Paul, and Debbie, Hillary's soldiers had courted death. Perhaps they did not deserve to die, but they had at least known what they were getting into.

But then Hillary, too, had known what she was getting into.

The doctors, nurses, and orderlies I work with are equally varied. There followed a series of pen-portraits: the surly doctor, the sentimental doctor, the flamboyant surgeon, the sardonic anesthetist. Andrew felt himself growing jealous of her dedicated, competent, tireless colleagues, and began even to envy the soldiers their ills and injuries. He wished that he were a doctor; he wished that he were dying. He wished that he were in charge and knew just what to do; he wished that someone else were in charge and that he need do nothing.

The ambulance drivers I have met are especially inspiring. As volunteers, they work completely without supervision, yet night and day they drive into the most dangerous areas, nonchalantly braving mortar shells, mined roads, sniper fire, and ambush.

How foolish, how ostentatious these volunteers seemed, risking their lives to save others! Were their own lives worth so little to them? Were their existences so meaningless?

He put the letter away. After a minute of jaw clenching, he clapped his hands as if accepting a challenge, ordered another coffee, swallowed two tachycardias and a cognitive dysfunction, and went to the payphone in the foyer, where he began dialing numbers from his address book.

He called several friends and former girlfriends before calling Regan, but he pretended to himself, and made her believe, that she was the one person he had most wanted to see. Because her husband was out of town, she invited him over, telling him not to ring the doorbell when he arrived because her kids were sleeping. He forgot, and a little girl answered the door promptly. Though in pajamas, she did not appear to have been sleeping.

"Oh," he said. "I thought you'd gone to bed."

He disliked people who spoke to children in cloying, condescending voices, and who bribed them with candy and piggyback rides. He respected children (in fact, he was a little in awe of them), and addressed them as equals; consequently children did not like him much.

"You're not company," said the girl. "Mom said company was coming." —"I don't know what you've done with Regan, but I'm coming in now, so step aside and no sudden movements."

Andrew and Regan sat drinking wine in the kitchen, but the little girl and her little brother kept peeking through the doorway, so finally Regan bribed them with a glass of juice and a quick game of hangman with Andrew. "But then straight to bed."

The girl chose a word three letters long. He soon guessed the first two, "B" and "E," but the girl denied, with obvious disingenuousness, that the third was "D." Nor was it "G" or "T," and no other solution made sense. He guessed "X" and "Z" and "Q" and "7."

"That's it," he said. "I'm hanged. You win." —"No, I still have to draw your toenails. Guess again."

The figure beneath the gallows became increasingly ornate as he worked his way through the alphabet. When at last she permitted him to lose, she declared that the final space had been blank: the answer was "BE." She was overcome by mirth at her cunning; Andrew and Regan could still hear giggles coming from her bedroom half an hour later. Andrew plotted revenge.

They drank wine and talked about themselves. Each seemed to be what the other, at that moment, wished to be. To Regan, Andrew's life sounded dramatic and gloriously unfettered; to Andrew, Regan's life sounded rooted and luxuriously comfortable. Andrew did not remember his girl-friends so much as he remembered himself, the way he had

been, with his girlfriends: with Sandra he had been ingrati-
ating, with Tabitha domineering, with Kasuko a child, with
Pari a professor; with others louche, lazy, or clingy, a monk,
a rebel, or a philosopher. (With Hillary, that first time, he
had been a client, a suppliant—a patient.) With Regan he
had been a connoisseur. They had traded esoteric recom-
mendations of artists, books, and music, believing that their
tastes were indices to their characters, their preferences virtues. Now he told her about the galleries he had visited, the
concerts he had attended, the masterpieces he had discovered, the poets he had drunk absinthe with.

Regan was envious and amazed. Her own history seemed
a series of irrevocable decisions, none perhaps regrettable
in itself, but each depriving her of countless alternatives.
Andrew, on the other hand, seemed miraculously to have
avoided decisions; he had shed none of his possibilities, and
could still be or do anything. She began devising futures for
him, as his friends and family members did constantly—but
she felt none of their anxiety, only excitement. She asked him
why, if he loved art so much, he did not become an artist?
He shook his head and replied with honest humility that he
wouldn't know what to make. Even if he decided arbitrarily to
become a painter, say, he would need a lifetime just to determine his influences. There were more great paintings in the
world than he could ever look at, and more being produced
every day. Until he had seen them all, how could he imagine
that he might do something better, or different? And then
another lifetime would be needed to learn the craft. No, to be
an artist required ignorance and arrogance. He was content
being an art lover; that was job enough for him.

They had migrated to the floor, and sat with their backs
against the cupboards. He looked at Regan, and a wave of
pure nostalgia, without reference to any memory, washed
over him like a breeze, and he felt that his life was sad, priceless, and larger than his understanding.

"Why did we ever break up?" he asked, moving closer to her.

Regan snorted. "Are you kidding? We weren't ever really together. We had sex that one time, then I didn't hear from you for months." She said it lightly, but at the time she had been hurt, bewildered, and angry.

He ignored this. "Remember how we said we'd get married when we were forty, if we hadn't found anyone else?"

"We were twenty then. And I *am* married."

Nevertheless she let him kiss her—because she was drunk; because, arrived from nowhere after so many years, he did not seem quite real; and because he would be leaving town again soon, so nothing was irrevocable.

They had sex, quietly and in the dark, and as soon as it was over his mood plummeted. Now he saw himself quite clearly: he was a failure, a vagrant, and a callous philanderer who would say, who would temporarily *believe*, anything to get a woman into bed. He harbored no affection for Regan; they had hardly known each other years ago, and they had nothing in common now. Her body pressed against his was as strange and repugnant as a corpse. He broke out in a sweat. He had to get away. He escaped to the bathroom and got dressed, then reflexively searched the medicine cabinet.

He was drunk, he was restless, his heart was racing, his emotions were altered and his cognition dysfunctional, but he believed that he felt normal. As always, some core part of him remained unchanged, and he desired to be altogether changed, if only for one night, if only for an hour.

Perhaps he had taken all of Nathan and Claudia's drugs before, after all; perhaps he had already developed a tolerance to them. He remembered Hillary warning him against increasing the dosage of his asthma medication. But if the old dose gradually became ineffective, what else could one do? For some reason, he remembered the medical term for habituation: tachyphylaxis. He filled his pockets with Regan's medication and left the house.

This time, she was not hurt, bewildered, or angry. She considered this progress.

At a bowling alley, Andrew told one woman that he was a painter, another that he was a photographer, a third that he was a poet. At a billiard hall, he confided to another woman that he needed a place to sleep, and her boyfriend pushed him. Andrew laughed. He ordered a beer for himself and an elaborate, fruity cocktail for the man who had pushed him. He swallowed two dizzinesses and a syncope and challenged someone to a game of pool.

He telephoned his friends. Most of them sounded concerned, so he reassured them. He visited his brother Roger, who gave him coffee and urged him to visit their sister Nance in the morning. "She's been worried sick about you." Andrew batted the air dismissively.

In the street again, he stumbled, then hollered in triumph at having not fallen. He shared a taxi with someone. He took money out of a bank machine. He bought a round of appetizers. He remembered a trick he used to play on his sisters, leaving one of two hallway light switches half-on, thus breaking the circuit and rendering the other switch inoperative. He tried to tell a woman seated on a banquette about this, but the significance of the anecdote eluded her. Someone disparaged the war, giving reasons why it was unnecessary, unwinnable, and unjust. Andrew told them to shut their face.

In the morning, his brother Lawrence's wife, Beth, nudged him awake. She winced teasingly at his hangover, and told him that he had a visitor.

At the front door was an irate taxi driver, who insisted on Andrew's taking total and immediate responsibility for the puddle of vomit that had been left in the taxi's back seat.

Andrew agreed, apologized, sympathized, shook the man's hand, invited him in for breakfast, asked his name and where he was from, and smiled winningly through his hangover when he discovered that he had, in his travels, visited the man's hometown.

SHE LAY ON her rack but did not sleep. She felt guilty for
not sleeping: she needed sleep; she had been ordered to
sleep; but sleep wouldn't come. She hadn't slept for seven
or eight days—she didn't know how long exactly. She
could only count back four days before she began to doubt
her chronology. Some days blended together, too, especially those joined by all-night sessions working on mass
casualties in the operating or preponderant rooms. She had
last slept, she believed, the night that the massive chest
trauma had suddenly expired, presumably from an embolism. Had she remembered to put him on anticoagulants?
She didn't know, and his chart had left with his body for
interment registration by the time she'd started her ward
rounds in the morning. She had no reason to think she
had forgotten anticoagulants, and the orderly or the nurse
might have ordered them even if she had forgotten—it was
done routinely in nearly every case of major trauma—but
she would never know. That had been either seven or eight
days ago, she knew, because the next afternoon Hartner
had scheduled a demonstration operation (canceled at
the last minute due to mass casualties), and he only did
demonstrations on Tuesdays or Wednesdays. She could ask

someone what day it had been; but they might not remember either. Was a record kept somewhere? Would Hartner know? It didn't matter.

Seven or eight days, then. It didn't sound possible: she'd read studies in which subjects deprived of sleep for seventy-two hours began to show signs of psychosis—paranoia, hallucinations, aggression. Her symptoms were less colorful, but given her responsibilities, just as grievous: exhaustion, emotionality, mental fogginess, forgetfulness, and consequently a breathless oppressive feeling of self-doubt that undermined her every decision. In medical school she had functioned adequately on nine hours' sleep every two days, and as a resident had often got by on less. But no sleep for a week? As far as she knew, it was not humanly possible. Therefore she must in fact have been sleeping some, without realizing it; or else lying awake thinking was giving her enough of what sleep and dreams usually gave people. What did sleep give people? Rest. Well, she was getting that. What did dreams give people? She tried to recall what she had read. Freud believed dreams were a kind of wish-fulfillment, the dramatization of our unmet desires. Jung thought dreams were a sort of pressure-release valve—the exercise yard of our criminal shadow-self. Crick and Mitchison said that dreams were an active forgetting, the neural network's way of disburdening itself of superfluous information. Roffwarg said the opposite: that dreams were the brain reinforcing its connections. None of these theories described her own absurd, discursive dreams very well, and none could account for the efficacy of her night thoughts. She was inclined, rather, to think that dreams were what they seemed: the byproduct of a dozing, reorganizing brain; the disjointed and only half-aware efforts of the mind to review and absorb the events of the day and thus prepare itself for tomorrow.

And so she lay awake, listening to the distant, echo-swaddled rumble of mortar fire, and methodically evaluated her day. When memories flashed into her mind randomly, she suppressed them, or rather deferred them, restricting herself to a sequential, and therefore dispassionate, review. (She refused, for now, to think about the unexploded grenade; or Hartner's formal complaint to Major Witte about Latroussaine; or the boy without a face (blunt cranial trauma); or the collapsed lung that had sent the decompression needle flying out of her hand; or the boy who had bled to death (exsanguinating hemorrhage) before they could find his wound; or the self-inflicted foot wound that she had cleaned and dressed, then reported to the military police; and she refused to think about Andrew.) The problem was that by night she could only remember about half of what had happened each day; and it was always the worst moments— the biggest blunders, the goriest injuries—that jumped the queue and forced themselves upon her attention.

Mostly she lay with her eyes open, because when she closed them the imagery of her thoughts became distressingly vivid—oversized and palpable, as if pressing against her face. Whenever particular images haunted her, she used words as a disinfectant, describing or naming the terrible thing in clinical terms.

Sometimes, after following long chains of internally consistent and seemingly logical thought, she suddenly stopped herself, realizing that her premise was nonsensical or an analogy corrupt—as when her arm falling asleep under her had seemed a problem of trigonometry, or when she had visualized the dose titration of fentanyl as the revolving door of a hotel she had once stayed in back on the mainland. These lapses terrified her, like omens of insanity, but she reassured herself that she was only tired, and half dreaming.

That morning she had first gone for a jog; every morning at dawn she ran four times around the compound's inner perimeter in her combat boots, dodging revetments and pallets but not puddles. Then, sweating and hungry, she had visited the wards, intending only to pause on her way to breakfast and the showers. Nurse Anwar, who was friendly with Latroussaine, refused to write her name on the board before she was on shift. Hillary did not insist. She sought out her patients of the day before, scanning charts for her signature. She was looking for her mistakes, and inevitably found some; but she also found other doctors' mistakes, and the night staff's oversights, and unaccountable delays in treatment, and waking soldiers who were thirsty or in pain or hypotensive or simply in need of reassurance; and she dealt with these matters too. Nurses, orderlies, and other doctors circulated as well, but there was always too much to be done. By the time she had completed her first superficial rounds, breakfast was over and her name was on the board.

She flushed with saline and rebandaged a suppurating knee, which its owner kept picking at, then she wasted five minutes failing to convince him that most wounds were best left open, and left alone. She rewrote triage numbers on the foreheads of two gas gangrenes who had sweated the ink off in the night. She sent a land-mine amputation to the operating room to have his remaining femoral artery reapproximated, something that should have been done as soon as he'd stabilized—six or more hours ago, according to his chart. Now he would probably lose the other foot. The mandible fracture had again panicked in the night and snipped the wires holding his jaw shut. "I thought I was going to puke," he apologized. She reconnected the upper and lower arch bars and put the wire cutters away in a drawer, reminding him to use them only in an emergency. She piggybacked a sedative onto the IV of a crushed trachea whose chin had been sutured to his chest to prevent further injury, and who had been thrashing and shouting in his sleep. She examined and spoke soothingly to a fractured clavicle who feared syphilis. She put a collapsed lung with hyperglycemia on five units per hour of insulin. She cleaned and reattached an ileostomy bag that had been dislodged by gas buildup, pretending not to hear the man's questions about when the bag could be removed. The answer was never, of course: he was missing a colon and a rectum. She injected a small amount of furosemide into a multiple fragment wound whose urine output was low. She put a heatstroke with low sodium on a free water restriction and added seven hundred milliliters of saline to his IV. She stopped a transfusion on an abdominal through-and-through who was spiking a fever with chills and back pain. Suspecting a blood-type reaction, she injected adrenaline and ordered liver function, clotting time, and complete blood-count tests. The donor unit said O positive, and the patient's chart and dog tags said A positive, which should have been fine, but there was no record of a crossmatch being done, and the dog tags were often wrong. She supposed it could be septic shock, but his blood pressure was normal and his extremities were cool, showing no sign of vasodilation. She sent him to the NPR for observation and saline from a fresh IV, then filled out a medevac tag for transport to the mainland. Was she saving his life, or wasting the taxpayers' money? She'd never know; whether right or wrong, she'd never hear about it. She avoided the cranial fracture with blood in his eye, because he was on bed rest and was not allowed to read and would want to talk to her about the reasons for the war. (What the hell was he doing thinking about these things only now? It reminded her of Andrew.) She also avoided the forearm amputation who two days earlier had been accidentally given a sub-therapeutic dose of ketamine (Orderly Parungao had used the wrong syringe) and who consequently was convinced that his spirit had left his body. In proof of his newfound immortality, he said that he could still feel the "spirit" of his missing arm. No amount of explanation of the physiology, of the fine nerve fibers in his arm or the interdependent network of neurons in his brain, could convince him otherwise. It was none of her business, anyway. Besides, was she so certain that her understanding of the body—as a delicate, interwoven complexity leaving no room for spirit—was the superior one? To patients who asked her point-blank if they were going to die, she always answered, "Not if I can help it," even when she could not. And for patients who saw through this bravado and asked what would happen to them after they died, she had no answer at all. This soldier could at least have told his dying comrades that their spirits, equipped with arms, legs, and heads, would survive elsewhere. And how could she know for sure that he was wrong? Perhaps she and the other doctors should give all their anticipatory casualties a shot of ketamine and let them decide for themselves. Finally, she checked on the islander who had refused a blood transfusion the day before. Though he wore no uniform, he was presumably an enemy soldier, and had been handcuffed to the bed till he could be moved to the prisoners' ward. Now he was too weak to resist, so she started him on fluids, antibiotics, and packed red blood cells. At this moment Hartner appeared at the bedside, tall and groomed and ruddy, healthy and fed and rested. He was with Baltin and Martoskif, his favorites. Although he made no comment, Hillary blushed with shame. Two days earlier he had screamed at Latroussaine for sending a jinkie into his preponderant room when he knew for a fact that there were mainlanders, dying combatants, still waiting to be triaged.

"Have you eaten, Doctor V.?" When she hesitated, Hartner sent a passing technician for coffee and buttered rolls. "We can't have you rarting on us, now can we, Doctor?" He was in a good mood. He used the slang term with comfortable clumsiness, like an old man tossing a softball. Hillary smiled at the notion that Hartner could ever be thought a fogey—though she herself did not approve of words like "gork," "crump," or "rart," humorous terms for such unhumorous conditions as coma, deterioration, and death. Martoskif had popularized "rart," which meant to rapidly assume room temperature—that is, to die, or to be dead. He sometimes wrote it in capital letters on charts or on casualties' feet. It had even gained currency among the soldiers: she'd overheard someone in the mess call the powdered eggs "completely fucking rarted."

"Join us in the anticipatory room, Doctor?" said Hartner. "Let's see what kind of mess our friend the senior triage officer has left things in, shall we?" He too was looking for yesterday's mistakes: Latroussaine's.

She ate her rolls with a surgical clip while Hartner went from bed to bed, checking pulses, blood pressures, and pupil dilations. Occasionally he addressed a question, in which the answer was contained, to her or Baltin or Martoskif. Did she manage to reply intelligently? Her mind was forever going blank in Hartner's presence. Probably she was still awed by him. He was, after all, forceful, handsome, a captain, and a brilliant surgeon in the classic mold: poised, dexterous, unhurried but unhesitating, and domineering. Many nurses and orderlies thought him cold and overbearing, but Hillary found his confidence reassuring, his mere proximity a relief. When he was in charge there was little for her to do but appear attentive and follow orders. Perhaps that was why she sometimes sank into a trance: her mind was taking the opportunity to rest.

Then again, she thought, munching in memory her stale bread, maybe she was not sleep-deprived so much as malnourished. Maybe she was not getting enough protein? She quashed that hypothesis. Granted, she often skipped meals, but when she ate she ate heartily enough. Besides, she knew there was enough protein in even the potatoes, rice, and chocolate bars that were her staples; indeed, there was probably a day's worth of protein in the bread she now ate, the butter, the cream in her coffee. So where did such worries come from? A lifetime of vegetarian guilt; years and years of friends, family, and colleagues (even doctors!) showing solicitude for her health.

"Let's get another pillow under this handsome exoph-thalmic head of yours, private. There we are. A simple thing, but surprisingly effective, eh? Check back in an hour, doctors, and see if his ICP hasn't gone down. A little trick we might all keep in mind."

She sipped her coffee with distaste—she would not herself have added cream—and thought of the cow she had adopted in high school. Hillary's sponsorship had rescued Millicent from a factory farm and transplanted her to an animal sanctuary nestled among rolling, verdant hills. But even this recollection carried guilt, for in her first year of medical school the sanctuary had suddenly doubled its fees, citing the rising cost of feed, and Hillary, who had barely enough money for textbooks, had been forced to withdraw from the program. Dolly, her cynical roommate, tried to cheer her with the suggestion that there never had been any such cow as Millicent, that it was all a scam. But Hillary knew better; she had seen pictures.

For a vertiginous moment, she could not remember what ICP stood for.

Of course, the chocolate bars she ate had milk in them.

Even if she *was* malnourished, she was still healthier than eight-tenths of the world's population. Indeed, it was as shameful today to be well fed as to be rich. (Andrew's family's lack of embarrassment had always amazed her.) Most of the islanders, certainly, both combatants and civilians, were underfed. Outwardly they were a tough, wiry people, but she saw signs of malnutrition every time she opened one of them up. Spongy bones, jellylike marrow, shrunken livers, inflamed bowels, soft tissue that bruised and bled easily. Last week she had tried to repair a torn colon in a pelvic fracture, and the sutures had cut through the intestine like cheese. The mainland forces' bullets, too, whether by design or shoddy manufacture, seemed to have a greater tendency to fragment, ripping tortuous and jagged holes through the locals' softer bodies—wounds that were almost impossible to trace and debride fully, and thus were particularly susceptible to gas gangrene. As a result, and because they were triaged last, most islanders were sent directly to the anticipatory room (where casualties were anticipated to expire). Often there were more islanders in the AR than mainlanders. There certainly were now. Hartner ignored them.

The nurses and orderlies who dreaded working with him had to acknowledge that, unlike many brilliant surgeons, Hartner had an excellent bedside manner. Baltin and Caltavos and others, who were general practitioners, said that he should have been a general practitioner. Even here in the anticipatory room, where one's tact and empathy might be expected to lapse, Hartner was at his warmest and most personable. He spoke directly to any casualty who was conscious; he asked them how they felt and what they had been through and whether there was anything he could do for them; he placed a gloved hand on their forehead or shoulder while they spoke, and he never appeared impatient with their replies. When he looked at their chart, he held it in their view, treating them, in effect, like a consultant on their own case—although, had they been able to decipher the notations on that chart, they would have discovered that they were expected not to survive, and were only being made comfortable while they fulfilled that expectation. When Hartner discussed the real prognosis or the true extent of the casualty's injuries with his entourage, he employed the usual medical euphemisms and abbreviations, but he spoke so loudly, openly, and cheerfully that no casualty could doubt they were convalescing. None of them ever had to ask Hartner if they were going to die, or what would happen to them afterwards. His manner was like clean and sterile sunlight, neutralizing fear.

At last he found what he was looking for: a casualty whose prognosis appeared incongruously favorable. Private Reingold had arrived at the triage tent yesterday morning in the middle of a spate of mass casualties, all from the same platoon, suffering from mortar-fragment, land-mine, and blast injuries. Reingold had been mistaken for one of them, though in fact he was from a different battalion altogether. His medevac helicopter had been diverted for the emergency; in the confusion his chart was misplaced, and the evac tag on his wrist went unnoticed. Apparently unconscious, with an arched back and rigid arms and legs, and covered in someone else's blood, Reingold had been sent to the AR as brain damaged (decerebrate). Today, however, he was awake, and showing no signs of brain damage, or indeed injury. Hartner guided him patiently through the reflex, balance, and attention tests. Reingold was able to tell him that he had not been in any firefight, but had been sent to the rear with a fever and headache. Light and noise bothered him, too, and his jaw and fists kept clenching of their own accord. —"Any cuts or scrapes in the last week or two?" —"Just my right foot. Damn blisters keep opening up on the rivets in my boots." —Hartner looked to Baltin, who asked Reingold if he'd ever been immunized against tetanus. —"When I was a kid, I guess." —Baltin ordered the blood tests, Hartner requested diazepam for the muscle spasms, Hillary gave separate injections of tetanus toxoid and immune globulin, while Martoskif, with dictation from Hartner, updated Reingold's chart, drawing a large quarantining box around the old incorrect diagnosis. All four doctors signed. —"We'll put you in the officers' tent," said Hartner. "It's quieter." It was an unusual journey for any casualty to make. The clerk had to be called from across the room to mark his entry, and was duly amazed. —"Miracle cure, huh?" —Hartner chuckled. "Sure. Sometimes Latroussaine makes us look good, too."

71

Passing through the PR, they were hailed by Caltavos, who wanted a second opinion. A casualty who had come in three days earlier with apparent influenza had returned in much worse condition. Hillary peered at the chart over Hartner's shoulder and was relieved to see only Caltavos's name on it. —"She came into the NPR pallid, diaphoretic, emetic—" —"She's a combatant?" asked Hartner. —"Private with the Seventh Rifles." —"What was the triage assessment?" —"Oh, the same: probable flu. So I put her on antibiotics and kept her hydrated and the next day she was feeling better so I sent her back to her company." —"And now?" —"Crumping like crazy. Puking again, pain in her upper right quadrant, low urine output, jaundiced . . . Christ, you name it: low sugar, lactic acidosis, bleeding gums, bruising. Haven't got the clotting times back but, well, to the unaided eye she's not clotting so good. I'm afraid to take more blood for tests." —"So what's your impression, doctor?" —"Well, her liver's fucked. I mean, her hepatic vein and artery are sticking out an inch." —"Is she a drinker?" —"She says not. But I can't hardly do a biopsy with her blood this watery." —"No. How else could we rule out cirrhosis? Doctor V.?" —She felt a pang of gratitude that the question was easy. "An ultrasound might show edema." —"Sure," said Caltavos, "but what I'm wondering is, what's left to rule in?" —"Oh, it could be just about anything," said Hartner. "Hepatitis, Wilson's disease, Budd-Chiari." —"Sure. But we're not exactly equipped to test for any of that." —"We'll do what we can. Is she awake?" —"Some hebetude. Keeps forgetting where she is." —"Okay. Let's talk to her."

Hillary stood as far from Private Shibiatisu's bed as possible without drawing attention to herself. The girl's face was a grayish yellow. Droplets of sweat stood out like plastic beads on her forehead. Hartner squeezed her shoulder. She smiled up at him weakly but as if with full recognition. —"Hiya, doc." —"Hello there, private. How are you feeling?" —"Not too good, I guess." Hillary could smell the sweet, fruity odor of the girl's breath from where she stood. Her blood was already saturated with ammonia. (She reminded Hillary of Andrew. But why?)

A mortar exploded miles away, reverberating like an excerpt of thunder. Hillary wished it would come closer.

Lying in bed with her eyes open, she realized that she was wrong. Hartner had not examined Private Shibiatisu that day, but earlier in the week. Gratefully she pushed the memory from her mind and groped to recover the correct thread.

Someone was shouting, "Mass casualties! Twenty twenty-eight and ten. Mass casualties! All medical staff to the PR. Twenty twenty-eight and ten mass cas!" She rolled off her rack, laced up her boots, and stepped, blinking, into bright sunlight. Had she slept all night and all morning? "Sorry," said a voice, and the light went out. "Sorry." It was Nurse Hashmi, coming off shift. —Hillary was up on her elbows. "Mass casualties . . . ?" —"Naw, it's slowing down. Go back to sleep."

Someone was shouting, "Mass casualties! Twenty twenty-eight and ten!" Hartner and the others headed toward the scrub station outside the preponderant room. —"Well, doctors," said Hartner, smiling grimly. —Baltin said, "Here we go." —Table ten needed a doctor; Hillary hurried over. Nurse Thota and Orderly Mills were trying to place an IV in the arm of a writhing, kicking, groaning boy with a shattered head (blunt cranial trauma). Where his nose had been was a bleeding knot of crushed cartilage; one eye was swollen shut and the other was split open and aimed vacantly at the ceiling; his upper lip, torn diagonally in a grotesque sneer, hung in a flap on his cheek, revealing smashed teeth oozing pulp. He looked as if he'd been hit in the face with a sledgehammer. According to Mills, it had been a rocket-propelled grenade—a dud. Hillary did not know where to begin (what would she do with his eye? pry it out with a spud? suck it out with the aspirator?), but she could at least place an IV and secure an airway. She gave him a shot of succinylcholine in his thigh to relax him enough to allow Mills to insert the IV. Now, lying awake hours later, she stiffened in horror: succinylcholine increased intracranial pressure, which, given the state of his cranium, was probably what had killed him. Nor, given the state of his mouth, could it have been a good idea to intubate him. She should have gone in through his cricothyroid membrane. Well, it hadn't mattered. They'd placed the IV, oxygenated him, sedated him, and she had just slid the laryngoscope over his tongue when Nurse Thota observed that the patient had expired. "Space on ten!," Mills shouted, waving. Perhaps it wasn't her fault. Probably he would have died anyway. Triage should probably have sent him straight to the AR. The next casualty's clothes and hair were dark with blood; blood suffused his gurney and dripped onto the floor as the clerk's orderly pushed it across the room. —"Where's the site of injury?" —Nobody knew. —"Why hasn't his wound been pressure-dressed?" —No one knew. They hoisted him onto the resuscitation table and cut open his sodden uniform. His eyes were rolled back in his head and his breathing was rapid and labored, sounding sometimes dry and sometimes wet. She told Mills to get a transfusion ready, while she and Nurse Thota searched for the injury. With dozens of laparotomy pads they wiped blood from his abdomen, chest, legs, face, and scalp, but as soon as they had moved to a new area the old area was glistening with fresh blood. He seemed to be exuding blood from his pores. —"Help me roll him onto his front." —"Forget it, doctor." —"Help me roll him over!" —"It's no use, doctor. He's kaput." —She never did learn where he was bleeding from. (Now, lying in bed, she felt a stab of anger: there must already have been two liters of blood in a pool on the gurney by the time he got to her; he too should have been sent directly to anticipatory.) Mills came back and changed the table cover. "Space on ten!" Next came three or four major abdominal injuries that blurred together in her memory: at least one from multiple gunshots, one from a bounding mine, and one from what was probably a fragment of mortar shell. They had all lost too much blood to undergo sedation or the extensive surgery required. In every case Mills started IV blood and fluids while Hillary and Nurse Thota stopped the bleeding by packing the abdomen with bowel bags and laparotomy pads. Then, covering the viscera with another bowel bag, they placed chest-tube drains and stapled them to the skin, filled in any gaps with sponges, and covered the entire wound with a drape and an IV bag, leaving the skin open. Then they sent the casualty to intensive care to stabilize, at which point a more comprehensive operation could be undertaken. In the middle of one of these packings, Hartner, behind Hillary on table eight, called to her. She hesitated for a moment, then told Nurse Thota to take over. At Hartner's table, Nurse Glauberzon was standing a few steps away and scowling. —"Doctor V.," said Hartner, "with your skilled and steady hands will you kindly hold this clamp in place?" —"Should I rescrub?" —"No, don't bother." —She took the handles from him but could not see what she was clamping: the chest wound that he was working in was filled with blood and grayish-pink froth from a ruptured lung. How had he been able to see enough to place the clamp? How could he see now what he was doing? —"That's it. Thank you, doctor. I think we'll manage from here."

(Hartner told Private Shibiatisu that her liver might be damaged. He asked if she often drank alcohol, or whether she had drunk a lot four days ago. She said she never drank: it didn't agree with her. Then, without further prompting, she asked him softly if her sickness might have something to do with the pills she'd taken. —"What pills were those, private?" —She looked away, abashed. "Headache pills." —"Did you have a headache?" —"No, sir." —"How many did you take?" —She closed her eyes and pursed her lips, as if she would not answer. Then she said, "I couldn't take any more." —"Any more pills?" —She shook her head. Sweat ran down her face like tears. "Just any more." —"How many pills did you take, private?" —"Two bottles." —"How many pills were in the bottles?" —She didn't answer. Her face became blank, her eyes vacant. She'd forgotten they were there. —Hartner repeated the question. —"All of them. They were new bottles." —"Ah, fuck," said Caltavos, "fuck me." —"I didn't want to go out again. I couldn't go out again." —"All right, private. Get some rest." —"I'm sorry, doc." —"Don't you worry about it. You'll be all right." —"Don't tell Sergeant Psorakis, will you? He'd shit down my throat." —They moved away from her bed and Caltavos said, "I asked her. I asked her three days ago when she came in if she'd taken anything, if she was on anything. Ah, fuck, I should have caught it." —"Well," said Hartner, "there's not much we can do now but make her comfortable. Let them know in the AR exactly what she's in for, and maybe they'll make her properly comfortable. She hasn't got much to look forward to now but hemorrhage, multiple organ failure, and coma." —"I should have caught it three days ago and we could have done something." —"It's not your fault, doctor. The triage assessment misled you. It could have happened to any of us." —"But, Christ, you don't *expect* the triage assessment to be right." —Hartner sighed. "Not in this field hospital, you don't.")

"Incoming mass casualties! Eighteen twenty and four mass cas!" —"Christ," said Martoskif, who had been at the front, "I wish they wouldn't shout 'incoming' like that." —Hillary's next casualty was awake and couldn't stop talking. His ears were leaking blood, and his face, scalp, and shoulders were covered in a pox of tiny puncture wounds, some with slivers of shrapnel still protruding. "Shit—I'm lucky we overload our air-burst shells, or I'd be dead right now. Fucking short round came down right on my fucking head! I don't know what the hell happened to my helmet. Must've knocked it off when I hit the ground. I guess they'll give me a new one, won't they? You know, aside from some ringing in my ears I feel great. Yeah, all that powder we put in them just rips those shells to shreds, thank God. How soon till I can go back?" He was pale, his extremities were trembling, and he started whenever they touched him. She was worried about central nervous damage caused by the blast, but since he was awake and his pupil reaction was normal she could not justify spending more time on him now. She sent him to the NPR to have the shrapnel removed, his wounds cleaned, and his ears flushed. She ordered antibiotics and magnesium and recommended an eventual X-ray of his head. (Had she missed something? Why had triage sent him into the preponderant room at all?) Next came the screamer. She had heard him outside in the triage tent, but without realizing that she was hearing him; his screams had become background noise, like the helicopters landing outside, the artillery fire in the distance, the hissing of respirators and aspirators and the clacking of metal instruments on metal tables. Now, at close range, his wails of agony, interrupted only for breath, penetrated her skull. He had been shot in the shoulder. She peeled away the medic's pressure-dressing. The wound was not severe, though the bullet had pierced the suprascapular nerve. —"Mills, how about a little sedative?" —"I've just given him a 150-milligram push of ketamine, doctor." —"Oh. That's rather a lot, isn't it?" —"I sure hope so." —"Well, let's give it half a minute." —They stood and waited with their hands on the patient, less to soothe him than to constrain him. But he continued to bring up from deep in his belly deafening howls of anguish, as if he were being burned and flayed simultaneously. Nurse Thota giggled. —"Okay," said Hillary, "that's enough. Let's try some etomidate." —"Thirty milligrams?" —"On top of the ketamine? Are you kidding? Maybe ten." —"Fifteen?" —"Okay, fifteen." —Caltavos and Baltin looked over from their tables in awe and consternation. The man continued to scream. —"Are you sure you're in a viable vein?," Hillary asked. —"Well," said Mills, "it's going *somewhere*." —"Give him another fifteen of etomidate but let's put in a new IV while we're waiting for that to kick in, just in case." —Nurse Thota said, "Maybe he's immune to ketamine and etomidate." —Hillary shook her head; she'd never heard of any such thing. The second dose of etomidate had no effect, so they tried a hundred milligrams of propofol in the new IV, then another hundred. Hillary said, "I'm afraid he'll expire before we can sedate him." —"Well, his heart's still racing, so I wouldn't worry about that." —Martoskif came over and suggested they try thiopental. —"No," said Hillary, "not on top of everything else. First let's try another 150 of ketamine." —"In which IV?" —"It doesn't matter." —The second dose of ketamine seemed to have some effect; at least, the breaths he took between screams lasted longer. —"Okay, another one-fifty in the same IV." —Smiles were seen all around the preponderant room when, at last, the man's screams diminished to groans and finally, after another injection, to whimpers. —"This guy's a fucking sponge," said Mills admiringly. "He can't be more than eighty kilograms, either." —Hillary debrided, flushed with hydrogen peroxide and saline, and dressed the wound, then sent him to the recovery ward with a note on his chart: "Resistant to sedatives." She looked over her shoulder. Hartner was still working on the same casualty. "Space on ten!" Intensive care sent back a major abdominal injury who was not stabilizing: they could not get blood and fluids into him fast enough; he needed a central venous catheter. Hillary had performed several of these during her residency, all under supervision and all successful. Since arriving on the island she had bungled four, all unsupervised, and now dreaded them. The procedure was done percutaneously, without an incision, and was therefore considered elementary; but it was this fact, that she could not see what she was doing, or where exactly her needles and wires were going, that inflamed her imagination with visions of ravaging error. A guidewire was threaded through a large-bore needle into the subclavian vein of the shoulder, around a corner, and down into the superior vena cava, just centimeters above the right atrium of the heart; the needle was then removed, the puncture enlarged, and the catheter slid into place over the guidewire, which was then withdrawn. The main danger was entering instead the artery, which ran alongside the vein just below the clavicle. Usually one knew when one had done this, because the blood that entered the syringe was bright red and pulsating; but in casualties with low blood oxygen, low blood pressure, or (like this one) low blood volume, venous and arterial blood were not always easy to distinguish. Hillary, Mills, and Nurse Thota began by placing drapes, leaving exposed below the shoulder a square of skin which they scrubbed for a minute with povidone-iodine before injecting a small amount of lidocaine. Then, placing her left index finger on the sternal notch below the trachea and her thumb on the middle of the clavicle to guide her, she inserted the needle at a shallow angle into the groove between the deltoid and pectoral muscles. She advanced it carefully in the direction of the sternal notch, pulling back lightly on the plunger of the syringe with her thumb. The needle went in five, seven, nine centimeters, but still no blood entered the syringe. "Must have missed it," she said, and tried again, this time half a centimeter closer to the clavicle, and therefore to the artery. This time she struck blood after only four centimeters. She felt a gust of panic, for though the blood was dark, almost purple in color, it seemed to be entering the syringe in spurts. She withdrew the needle; but now blood welled and spilled from the site slowly and steadily. Nevertheless, she applied pressure to the spot for five minutes (as one would do with an artery puncture), then tried again (as one would not do with an artery puncture). This time the blood was dark and did not pulsate. She advanced the needle another half centimeter and unscrewed the syringe, placing her thumb over the hub of the needle to prevent air from entering the vein. Nurse Thota handed her the curved guidewire, and Hillary fed it a centimeter at a time through the needle and ostensibly into the subclavian vein. This guidewire, unlike those she had used on the mainland, had no length markings, so she stopped when she guessed she had reached seventeen centimeters— eighteen being the textbook standard. However, while she was removing the needle, sliding it back over the guidewire, which she held as steady as possible, Mills noticed an arrhythmia on the heart monitor. She must have pushed the guidewire all the way into the heart. Then Hartner was addressing her, and for a moment she believed he was chastising her for her mistake.

"Doctor V., will you please come with me?"

"Of course," she said automatically, but looked down at her bloody gloves holding the guidewire—a guitar string emerging from a disembodied shoulder.

"Doctor V.? We need to talk to the senior triage officer right this instant."

Martoskif and Baltin were with him; so she dropped the wire and followed them out of the preponderant room.

There were only four casualties in the triage tent, and they were all islanders. —"Where are the rest of the casualties?," Hartner demanded. —"This is what's left," said Latroussaine. —"I thought there were thirty-eight non-walking wounded altogether." —"Yes. Two were retriaged nonpreponderant, and two self-triaged." (By this he meant that they had died while awaiting treatment.) "Your staff has dealt with or is dealing with the rest."

From their conversation, and from movements around her in the PR of which she had been half aware, Hillary understood that the casualty Hartner had been working on for over an hour had expired, and that Latroussaine had sent him an islander as a replacement.

"Oh," said Latroussaine, feigning afterthought, "there is one mainlander left. But I thought it best to leave him till last. I'm sure you'll agree."

But Hartner did not agree; and after ordering the triage clerk to fetch someone from ordnance disposal, he led his three doctors outside to the empty sandbagged shed where the soldier with a grenade in his belly lay alone.

He was conscious and in pain, and aware of his plight. Gripping the sides of the gurney, the tendons of his neck popping out like cables, he warned them not to enter. "I'm likely to blow up."

"Nonsense," said Hartner, laughter in his voice. "If it wasn't a dud, it'd have gone off already. Right, private?" He sent Hillary and Martoskif for gloves, eyewear, anesthetic, an instrument cart, and a resuscitation box. "But nothing else. No heart monitors or ultrasounds or anything fancy with an electronic signal, all right?"

They crossed the dusty, sun-drenched compound in silence.

The soldier reminded her of Andrew. Why?

Returning with the equipment, which rattled and yawed across the macadam, Martoskif said, "Hartner's a crazy old bird, isn't he?" There was amazement, and admiration, in his tone.

Later, back in the PR, Martoskif and Baltin were exuberant, like naughty boys who had escaped punishment; they spoke loudly, laughed, and struck doctorly poses over their resuscitation tables. But Hillary felt no exhilaration—only a hollow remorse, as if she had left matches in reach of a child. While debriding wounds that afternoon, she kept expecting something to detonate every time her metal hemostat clicked against a metal fragment. Her belly tingled for hours afterwards, the skin there still quivering with the expectation of being ripped open by bursting shrapnel. Why her belly, and not her equally exposed chest or face? For some reason, she had pictured the grenade exploding in a horizontal fan, like a bounding mine—perhaps because the casualty himself had first been cut open by a bounding mine, before being penetrated by the rocket-propelled grenade while he lay on the ground bleeding. Was she identifying with the casualty, then? She recalled Hartner's words of weeks ago: The operating table is no place for sympathy; sympathy is the response of the layman, who can give nothing else. Had she been reduced to sympathy?

The operation was over quickly, before the ordnance-disposal technician could return with flak vests, which he had at first forgotten. Baltin injected a sedative and muscle relaxant intravenously, and lidocaine locally. Hillary and Martoskif stood with their hands on the casualty's arms, less to soothe him than to appear useful. Hartner extended the edges of the wound with a plastic scalpel, reached into the abdomen with both hands, tugged three times, paused, tugged three more times, then pulled the grenade free. It was covered in blood and smaller than she'd imagined; for a moment she feared he had removed the bladder by mistake. He placed it in the containment receptacle and lowered the lid. Then he straightened, peeled off his gloves, and said, "I believe this soldier has just been retriaged."

They rolled him back to the preponderant room but did not stop there. Hartner led them to the command hut, and asked to see Major Witte.

Witte promptly called in Communications Lieutenant Pastrick as a witness, and ordered his secretary to take notes. He listened to Hartner's allegations intently, almost without blinking, and Hillary sensed that there was impatience, even distaste, in his show of grave efficiency. With a giddy flash of impiety, she decided that she did not like the man. She stood at attention, her eyes moving alertly from man to man, ready to confirm or elucidate any detail. But Hartner was accustomed to giving dictation: his words were well chosen; his breath-length clauses followed one another in limpid sequence; even his pauses were eloquent, his periods distinguishable from his semicolons, his semicolons from his colons. No clarification was required. Neither she nor Baltin nor Martoskif were addressed at any time; she supposed their presence was corroboration enough.

When Hartner had finished, Major Witte, off the record, asked whether he had given any thought to who should replace Latroussaine, should matters come to that.

Hartner made a gesture of indifference. "If not for the perennial shortage of surgeons, I'd volunteer myself. However, literally anyone would be an improvement. Any one of these doctors, for instance, would do an excellent job."

She had thought little of this at the time, but now, lying awake in bed, she curled up in dismay. She could not do Latroussaine's job; she could barely do her own. The difficulty of the senior triage officer's job became suddenly apparent to her. Faced with thirty or forty casualties at once, you could but examine them one at a time. You sent the first casualty to the preponderant room; but the second one was in even worse condition, so you sent him too. And so on, till all the tables in the PR were full, and you realized, with the next massive trauma, that you had not been performing proper triage at all. Or vice versa: expecting worse, you sent the first several casualties to the nonpreponderant room—and all the casualties that followed proved to be less injured. Or, simply, the last casualty you examined had already expired—and should have been the first you examined. Indeed, it seemed necessary to triage all casualties first to know what order they should be triaged in. The only feasible method she could think of was to have on hand as many skilled and experienced triage doctors as incoming casualties; each could immediately shout out their assessment to the senior triage officer, who could then turn to the most urgent cases. But the triage tent had only five or six staff on duty at any given time, and only two of these were doctors. Suddenly Hillary went from despising Latroussaine to pitying him. His task was obviously an impossible one. Why couldn't Hartner see that? And how could he imagine that she would do better?

By the time they returned, the PR had emptied. Hartner sent them for lunch, while he himself went to the operating room. Neither Mills nor Nurse Thota were in sight, so Hillary visited the intensive care room. There she found their last casualty, his central venous catheter neatly in place. Perhaps another doctor had assisted; perhaps Nurse Thota had seen the procedure done enough times to finish it herself; the chart did not say. Whatever the case, it proved to Hillary what she had long suspected: that she was not necessary here; that she would be more useful at the front, where soldiers were actually being wounded, where people were dying.

Her mind turned again, inevitably, to Andrew, who was driving an ambulance somewhere at the front. She had been suppressing thoughts of him all week, but she was sick of not-thinking about him; the effort was exhausting, and anyway ineffective: everywhere she looked she encountered reminders of him. Very well: she decided finally to deal with him directly, to put him under the microscope of her full attention, to cauterize with the intensity of her focus the part of her mind that would not ignore him. She would think everything that could possibly be thought about him. Once and for all, she would solve the problem of Andrew.

She recognized in her feelings towards him several elements, among them anger, pity, and guilt. She was angry because he had acted impulsively, as usual. One simply didn't run away and join a war as though it were a circus. She remembered him as a child, hurtling down Hawk Hill on his bicycle, laughing as cars braked and honked; in high school, being the first to hand in an exam, never pausing to double-check his answers; in college, sleeping with women before he knew anything about them. Most annoying was the delusive facility with which he justified even his most irresponsible behavior, giving it a heroic, romantic, or otherwise self-serving interpretation. Thus, he had sex with a woman because he was deeply, poetically in love with her—never mind that she was fatuous and shallow. He was exempt from traffic laws because he was a skilled cyclist—never mind the bruises on his knees, the scabs on his palms. He handed in his exams first because he was the smartest in the class—never mind what the grades showed (and never mind the students who followed him to the teacher's desk, having modestly waited for someone else to stand up first). He could always find good reasons for everything he did, for anything he wanted to do, and the war was no different. He had managed to convince himself that he'd always wanted to drive an ambulance, that he'd always been fascinated by ambulances; he had even manufactured memories to support this idea. In his letter, he claimed to recall that one of his earliest memories was of an ambulance siren. He'd asked his mother what it was; she'd told him, and explained what an ambulance was. He'd said, "But why does it sound so angry?" This question was allegedly repeated to his brothers and sisters, who found it amusing, much to his exasperation. An ambulance *did* sound angry; and peremptory; and powerful; and that was why he'd always wanted to be an ambulance driver. Never mind that this was the first, surely, that anyone had ever heard of it.

She felt guilty because he was at the front and she was not; and because she was responsible for his being there. She could hardly recognize herself in the portions of her letters that he had quoted back to her. (They were riddled with spelling mistakes, for one thing; but she knew that Andrew was quite capable of misspelling a word even while copying it from the dictionary.) She supposed that she had exaggerated the virtues of her colleagues to forestall his criticism of their presence on the island. In her letters home to her family she had a similar tendency to gloss over anything unpleasant; but with them she was motivated by consideration: she didn't want them to worry. With Andrew, apparently, she had been more zealous, probably because she had been expecting an argument. She remembered the Christmas at his parents' house when he had picked a fight with his sister Chloe's soldier boyfriend—a fight aimed at Hillary herself, of course, who had just enlisted in the army's medical program. He had made an ass of himself, angering everyone— but she had said nothing. Perhaps in her letters to him from the island she had been trying to atone for that silence. And trying too, perhaps, to convince herself that she was doing the right thing. Well, it seemed she had convinced not just herself; and now she regretted it. Why?

Because he didn't belong here. Because he would not survive.

Where did that thought come from? There was no reason, aside from his atrocious driving habits, to think that he would do a poor job. And in fact, his fearlessness and aggression behind the wheel might even be assets to an ambulance driver here. (By his own account, they were.) Some people thought he was lazy, but she knew that when he found something that interested him he could apply himself to it fully, with prodigious, effortless industry—at least until he grew bored. (She recalled the time that, inventing a charity, complete with letterhead, he had wheedled most of the town out of their recyclables. And the time that he had stood on one foot for two full days, even while asleep, in pursuit of a world record. And the time that he had watched every Taiwanese movie ever subtitled, seeking evidence for some thesis for a film-studies paper; the research had continued for months after the end of the course, which he had failed.) She could only hope that the unpredictability, the drama, and the danger of driving an ambulance at the front would keep him interested and alert for as long as he chose to do it.

But she did not believe that they would. He had only rarely taken jobs, because his mother and several of his siblings could not resist lending him money; but every one of those jobs had ended badly, with acrimony on his part, on his employer's part, and on the part of the friend who had recommended him for the work. Hillary herself had regretted providing him a reference on more than one occasion; and now she feared that she would be given much greater cause for regret. Indeed, though she knew it wasn't rational, she could not shake the feeling that he was going to die in this war. She was overwhelmed with pity for him, a doleful pity beyond the correction of intellect. Her exhausted mind, coming untethered from language, reeled through images of Andrew, grieving in flashback the way mourners do in films and almost never do in life—memories being just what one does *not* lose when a loved one dies.

In fact, what she took for memories were actually inaccurate reconstructions, absurd and discursive dramatizations of her feelings of pity, anger, and guilt—in a word, dreams.

In one of these dreams, Andrew was an adolescent; she was much older. They had broken into the school at night and were exploring the halls and classrooms, all fascinatingly transformed by darkness and silence. They left oracular messages on the blackboards in disguised handwriting; they switched the left and right drawers of Mrs. Allard's desk; they locked toilet stalls from inside and crawled out under the doors. Andrew became excited by these depredations, and was breathing heavily. Afraid that his pranks would become destructive or cruel, she challenged him to a game of basketball in the gym. The balls were locked in the equipment room, so instead they built with gymnastic mats a fort, which they took turns leaping into and rebuilding. Finally, sweating and out of breath, they lay on their backs and stared up at the ceiling, and talked. His tone, as usual those days, soon became aggrieved. He criticized her friends; she defended them vaguely. —"What do you see in those guys anyway?" —She found it hard to put in words. —"All they're interested in," he said, "is driving up and down Main Street, getting drunk, and getting laid." His contempt for these things was absolute, though he had never done any of them. This made him difficult to argue with. —She asked, "What do you have against driving up and down Main Street?" —"It's boring!" —"What do you have against drinking?" —"Are you joking? It makes people stupid, and even more obnoxious than they already are." —"Well, what do you have against getting laid?" —Now he struggled to find words, and the struggle made him vehement. "It's disgusting," he said finally. —She sighed. She knew that he had recently written several long and fervid love letters to Stacey Minto, a girl who wore a lot of eye makeup, who waved her cigarettes around at arm's length, who called everyone "earthling," and who was mortified by Andrew's protestations of everlasting devotion. In Hillary's opinion, Andrew's problem was his virginity: he was sexually frustrated. —"You know," she said, "sex isn't really anything special. It's a bodily function, is all. Like drinking a glass of water." —He snorted, as if to say he could name a more pertinent bodily function; but after a long pause he sighed, and in a voice quavering between derision and appeal, he said, "Well, since you're such an expert—just what *is* sex, exactly, anyway?" —She showed him.

In another dream, Andrew was a young man sitting in a bar, surrounded by friends; Hillary was at home studying. At that age, he was the cynosure of any group. Men loved him for his joviality, his irreverence, his mischievousness, women for his aristocratic languor, his self-deprecating grin, his scruffy cuddliness, and his innocent self-absorption—the way he was constantly asking others to tell him what they really thought of him, what he was really like.

He was the cynosure of the group, though he pretended not to be: he solicited others' opinions and preferences so that he could defer to them, he broke off muttering in the middle of an anecdote if he was the only one talking, he disappeared to the bathroom or into the street for an hour at a time, or even went home without telling anyone. But tonight he suddenly thought of Hillary, and decided that she should join them. After much discussion, a delegation was elected and sent to collect her. As they neared her apartment, Andrew paused to inspect an untied shoelace, so Bruce pressed her buzzer. In one voice, they clamored for her to come down. —"I can't," she said. "I have a test on Friday." —The group dissolved, leaving only Andrew standing there in the cold, hopping from foot to foot and blowing on his hands. "Can't I come up?" —"No," she said; but somehow he got inside. —"I won't make a peep, I promise. I'll just lie here on the bed until she calls." Apparently he had given by mistake Hillary's phone number to a woman at the bar. Hillary scoffed. He shrugged, forgiving himself. "A common error. Who calls their own number?" —She sat down at her desk and lowered her head into a textbook the size of a suitcase. He began telling her about the woman at the bar. —"You said you were going to be quiet." —"So I did. And I shall!" His mouth clacked shut; soon the bedsprings were creaking beneath the effort of his self-control. She slammed her book closed. They had an argument. —Why did he come here just to disturb her? —Why did she always work so hard? —Why was *he* so lazy? —Why was *she* allergic to having fun? —Why did he sleep with sluts? —Why did she only date men she hated? —"Because they leave me alone when I tell them to!" —Finally he left. Too angry to work, she lay down on the bed, which, she discovered, he had muddied with his boots.

In another dream, Andrew was scattering breadcrumbs for a gaggle of geese. She seized his arm and pointed to a sign that read, "Please do not feed the birds." Together they roamed the park, confiscating food from well-meaning visitors and burning it. Their campaign was successful: all the birds starved to death. "Don't worry," said the park warden. "This happens every year."

In another dream, Andrew was a child with scabs on his knees. He was lying on a gurney in the preponderant room, pleased to be ill and being cared for. He had swallowed a bottleful of grenade-shaped pills; they were bursting inside him. Blue light spilled from cracks in his abdomen, and he pointed to these boo-boos proudly.

The blue light of dawn was coming in through the cracks around the door. Hillary rolled off her rack, laced up her boots, and stepped, blinking, into the morning. The compound was still, but already noisy with the buzzing generator, the roar of approaching helicopters, and the rumble of distant mortar fire.

She jogged four times around the perimeter, then, on her way to breakfast and the showers, she stopped at Major Witte's hut.

He had a telephone to his ear, but motioned for her to speak. She stammered a few words of humility and apology, expecting at any moment to be interrupted by Witte's phone call. When Witte realized that Hillary was not there on behalf of Hartner, he became friendly, sending his secretary out of the room, inviting her to sit down, and offering her real coffee. Major Witte held conservative opinions about women in the military, but these opinions did not extend to nurses. (He believed that Hillary was a nurse.)

The focus of her resolve blinded her to his flirtation and condescension. With effort, fighting feelings of betrayal and ingratitude, she asked that she be removed from consideration for the post of senior triage officer.

Witte made a gesture of curtailment. "No need to fret. I've given that little bailiwick to Doctor Hartner. He seemed to be brimming with ideas on how better to run the show. So." —"But can the OR and the PR spare him?" —Witte smiled benevolently and a little sadly, like one about to dispel superstition. "The doctor is not quite as indispensable as he would have us believe. Just between you and I, his staff management leaves much to be desired. His use of steroids in brain injuries is positively medieval. And his on-table triage is woeful. He simply refuses to give up on a casualty, no matter how hopeless."

Hillary's allegiance to Hartner was provoked. "But he shouldn't be getting sent hopeless cases!" —Witte made an elaborate gesture of uncertainty amid a multiplicity of opinions. "In any case, we have several surgeons arriving next week, two of them outranking Doctor Hartner. So his petition was not untimely. And I for one think he will do a fine job. Don't you?" With the phone still to his ear, he sipped his coffee and glanced meaningfully at hers, which remained untasted.

"What about Doctor Latroussaine?" —"To make the good doctor happy, we're sending Latroussaine to Pastor's Hill. Well, to be quite honest, it was time to rotate somebody out." —"To the front, you mean?" —"It's an enemy-proximate installation, yes, if that's what *you* mean."

"I'd like to go with him."

"With Latroussaine?"

"What I mean is, I'd like to request permission to be transferred to an enemy-proximate installation, sir." —"But not Pastor's Hill in particular, with Latroussaine in particular." —"No, sir." —His face showed a struggle, but his hands were still. "Might I ask why?" —"I'd like to do more for the effort, sir." —"You don't feel you're doing enough here?" —"No, sir. I mean—I feel that I could do more good at the front."

Major Witte looked at her closely. So here was another of these masculine women who were so keen to be treated as equals, not just at home, at work, and in the street, but everywhere—even in the ugliest, fiercest, dirtiest, and most dangerous places on earth. They must be equal in abjection as well as in glory. Very well.

His interest in Hillary evaporated; he could no longer even find her attractive. He hung up the telephone.

"All right, you're rotated to Pastor's Hill. That's your helicopter outside; you might want to run. Talk to Captain Augello when you get there and tell him I need him to send me back the paperwork. First, let me give you a little piece of advice, my dear."

But his telephone rang before he could give it.

AFTER RETURNING FROM the island with a bullet in his thigh, Andrew worked for two years as an ambulance driver on the mainland—by far the longest he had ever stuck at one job. Though not nearly so thrilling or glorious as the driving he had done in the war, the work was fun when he was busy, and when he was not, he relished the inactivity: he loved the idea of being paid to sit around the staff room and play poker with the EMTs, watch television, read a book, or sleep. Some days he was even paid to be on call—paid simply to *be ready* to work!—and though he had to stay sober and close to a phone, the constraint gave him a feeling of responsibility and importance. His family and friends were impressed, too. His only complaints were directed at the bureaucracy of the large medical organization of which he was a part. He had to attend meetings every week; his mailbox was always overflowing with inessential memos; he was constantly being required to fill out forms. He bristled at this treatment, and rebelled in small ways: by not paying for the coffee he drank in the staff room, by not ironing his uniform, by drinking *a little* when on call, and by going on shift a few minutes late and going off shift a few minutes early.

The week before Andrew's two-year review was scheduled, his supervisor invited him into his office for a chat. Patrick was jovial and chummy with his staff; he never gave them orders, but asked favors; he cadged their cigarettes and bought them donuts. Andrew disliked him, seeing his easygoing bonhomie as a ruse by which he elicited obedience. How little he actually cared for his staff was epitomized, Andrew felt, by his habit each morning of taking the fresh newspaper into the bathroom for half an hour, and returning it to the staff room with its pages rumpled, disordered, and faintly polluted.

To show Andrew that there was nothing to fear, he left the door to his office open and straddled his chair informally. After several minutes of small talk, in which he demonstrated a knowledge of Andrew's hometown, favorite beer, and penchant for movie-going, he asked if Andrew was happy in his job.

Here it comes, thought Andrew. "Happy enough, I guess." —Patrick peered at him shrewdly. "I sure hope you're not sweating about this little review coming up." Andrew made the verbal equivalent of a shrug. Patrick disparaged the seriousness of the review process for a while, then grew pensive. "Of course, the best strategy is always to be prepared. You don't want to go in there and get blindsided." Andrew agreed; and after a few more minutes of reassurances and truisms, Patrick admitted that the review board would *probably* broach the subject of speeding.

Andrew bridled. Some months earlier, Patrick had (in an even more roundabout, noncommittal, and apologetic way) reprimanded him for not using his turn signals to their full advantage. There had also been a memo reminding drivers to obey all posted speed limits—a memo that he now felt certain had been directed at him especially. (It had been.) He realized that he was the target of a prolonged campaign of intimidation and harassment. He started coughing—his asthma being often triggered by indignation.

"Am I fired?" —Patrick, who was terrified of the union, back-pedaled furiously. To show Andrew just how far he was from being fired, he outlined all the steps that would have to be taken before Andrew, or anyone, could be dismissed from his job: an official warning, in the presence of a union steward; an official correction, subject to dispute and appeal; and, finally, three official demerits, with not less than three months' probation between them, giving the employee time to mend his or her ways.

Andrew did not receive this information in the spirit in which it was offered; rather, he took it as a threat, expressed in Patrick's mealy-mouthed fashion. Patrick was the arresting officer outlining to the malefactor the months in court that would lead nevertheless inevitably to his conviction and incarceration. Either Andrew must submit, or all the weight of the system would descend upon him and force him to submit. The choice was the same, whether he made it now or three demerits from now: he could toe the line, or he would be fired.

"Of course, I'm not giving you shit here or anything," said Patrick. "I'm just giving you a heads-up. If it was up to me, I'd say speed all you want. I mean, if you've got your lights and your siren on and your way is clear, I say absolutely, drive as fast as conditions and safety allow. But unfortunately, it's not up to you or me, is it?"

Andrew emerged from this meeting in a mood of anguished despondency, for he knew that he must quit his job. Only by quitting could he expose the enormity of this injustice. But he was not ready to quit. Now that he was faced with leaving it, his job acquired a noble, heroic luster. But how could he go on under these conditions? All his life, all he had ever wanted was to be an ambulance driver. But an ambulance driver who was not permitted to drive fast? An ambulance driver prohibited from saving lives? It was too absurd; it was an outrage.

That night, over many beers in several bars, as he wove together the threads of his resolution, hardening his heart with anger and disgust, he arrived at the conclusion that he was not, after all, making a great sacrifice, or playing the role of martyr. He was not relinquishing anything precious, because what he had once cherished had already been lost. It was his time on the island, he decided, that had been the real adventure, his true life's calling. There he had been brave, and dogged, and clever, and necessary. These past two years on the mainland had been nothing but the dazed sloughing of a dream. It was time to wake up.

ANDREW'S MEMORIES OF the island were perhaps incomplete, but they were not altogether inaccurate. His work there had at times been glorious and thrilling; he had occasionally been tenacious or daring. But he had a nostalgic tendency to leave out of his memories the dull and the inglorious, with the result that his past always looked to him a little better than it actually had been, its passing always a little more poignant than it was. This feeling of loss, this sense of premature endings, pushed him constantly to seek new beginnings—and consequently he was, although unwittingly, among the happiest of beings.

He had forgotten, for example, the difficulties he'd faced even getting to the island. As soon as he made the decision to go, he told everyone he knew. After a couple of weeks spent basking in what he believed was his friends' and family's diminishing astonishment and growing admiration, he at last took himself to the airport like a soldier reporting for duty. His momentum was soon checked, however, when the ticketing agent asked for his passport, which had gone missing somewhere in India and which he'd neglected to replace after returning home under a temporary one. He could not believe that this was an insuperable obstacle; surely once his flight was paid for they could hardly turn him away. He told the woman behind the counter that it was buried deep in his bag, but not to worry, he would produce it when he reached customs. —"I'm afraid I can't issue a ticket without your visa number." —Visa? —"It's probably stapled in your passport. That is, if you did get a visa . . .?" —He recovered quickly: "Yes, of course, it's stapled in my passport. But do I really need to pull it out now?" His tone was humorous and collusive. —The woman liked Andrew, she didn't know why, and wanted to help him; and so the distress she felt was acute. "I really honestly can't even print a ticket if that field is empty. The system won't let me." She didn't know for a fact that this was so, but it stood to reason. She had once forgotten to enter a passenger's first name, and the computer had let her go no further till she'd rectified the oversight. Andrew, who was complacently ignorant about computers, believed that their rules were as arbitrary and flexible as people's. He asked the woman—her name was Olivia—to try.

Now Olivia became quite miserable. If she tried and succeeded, she would be revealed as a liar. Furthermore, she would be guilty of having issued a ticket without a visa number, an act which, if not impossible, was certainly against protocol. Who knew what far-reaching repercussions might follow? For her, the consequences would probably be negligible: she could always claim that she had merely made a mistake. But what if the matter was more serious than she realized? What if the visa numbers she collected were submitted to airline headquarters, to the airport transit authority, to the government? What if a missing visa number triggered some silent alarm? What if a missing number caused the computer system to crash? Her total ignorance of the reason for requesting the numbers provided a breeding ground for terrifying hypotheses. In fact, she might well be risking her job, and her supervisor's job; she might be undermining the airline's reputation; she might be, for all she knew, endangering diplomacy between the island and the mainland. And there was a war going on! There must be a reason for collecting those visa numbers, and no doubt a good reason. The passenger little realized what he was asking her to do. How dare he suggest she flout protocol! Her distress became anger, and her anger made her hard.

"I'm afraid you'll just have to find your passport, sir."

Andrew sighed—not impatiently, but absolvingly—and asked to speak to her supervisor.

"Certainly, sir." Now she disliked him, for there remained the possibility that Kathy, her supervisor, would be obliging, would waive the visa-number requirement, and thus by contrast show Olivia to be finicky, inflexible, and inconsiderate of her customers' needs. But she needn't have worried: Kathy supported her, with adamant authority. The passenger would produce his visa if he wanted to fly.

Andrew started coughing violently in his frustration and disbelief. What did they care if he had a visa or not? It was not their job to check his papers but to sell him a seat on an airplane! Petty tyrants!

Later in the day, Olivia saw him at another ticket counter, talking to another agent and her supervisor. Her eyes widened with understanding and her chest tightened with loathing. He was trying to fly to the island without a visa! She had half a mind to call security.

Finally forced to admit his oversight, Andrew took a taxi downtown. He sat in the front seat to signal his hurry, choosing to believe, in order to sustain his enthusiasm, that the visa was a mere formality, and that he would still reach the island today. Everything at the passport office, however, conspired to disabuse him of his enthusiasm. There were queues to get into queues, and paperwork to be submitted requesting paperwork. His soul shriveled under the fluorescent lights, and by the time he was called by number to an interview carrel, he was in a belligerent, anarchistic mood.

The agent, seated behind glass, perused his application with patient bewilderment, while Andrew fidgeted, nervous and resentful. "It's a passport-replacement application," he explained. "And a visa request for travel to a provisional protectorate," he said, borrowing the jargon from the form itself.

When at last the agent spoke, her voice was muffled by the glass. "To where are you traveling." —Andrew told her. —"And why." —The woman's impassive face and robotic voice, in these stern surroundings, told Andrew that she would be even less sympathetic to his prospective heroism than his family had been. "Holiday," he said. —"What kind of holiday." —He was nonplussed. "For relaxation," he said. —The agent moved papers around like a florist arranging a bouquet. "You know, of course, that there are some excellent and affordable holiday resorts right here on the mainland." —Andrew feigned a polite interest, and was given several brochures featuring patriotic slogans splashed across photographs of laughing actors in colorful locales. "I'll keep it in mind," he said, "for next time."

The agent looked at Andrew candidly. "I always find it strange, all the people I meet everyday, who are actually trying to leave the greatest country on earth—when so many thousands would do anything to get *in*." —Andrew shrugged. "The grass . . ." —The agent sighed and looked around her, as though seeking assistance. "You go on holiday often." —"I like to travel, I guess." —"The travel ministry, you realize, cannot guarantee our nationals' safety on the island at this time. You have heard about the insurgent activities." —He was stunned for a moment by the euphemism. "Yes, but I gather it's not so dangerous in the cities."

"Are you a journalist." —"No. Why?" —"Are you in the employ of any foreign power." —"Definitely not." —"Have you ever been indicted for a crime against mainland national security, or against the person of the president." —He swallowed his incredulity, and said only, "No." —"Is this

application invalid for any reason." —"Not that I know of."
—"Would you like to cancel your application at this time."
—"No, I don't think so." —"You would like to proceed."
—"Yes, thank you."

Between long, reflective pauses, the agent began signing and stamping documents. "The assessment will take six
weeks," she said at last, "or four and a half if you'd like to pay
the expeditement fee."

He left the office coughing. Four and a half weeks! There
had to be a faster way.

After a greasy meal that he did not taste, he took a taxi
down to the quayside and stood looking at the boats lit like
lanterns in the sifting dusk. Choosing a squat freighter that
appeared seaworthy, he walked down the pier and hailed a
couple of men doing something with ropes on deck. They
climbed down and joined him.

"We're in dock for two days," said one of them, "and
anyway we never go out that far. What do you want to go
to the island for?" —"Never mind," said the other quickly.
"None of our business. But we might know someone who
could help you." —"We do?"

Two hours later, after a series of costly introductions performed with a furtiveness that Andrew found stimulating,
he was shown into a dim cargo hold no bigger than a garage
that was cluttered with wicker furniture, old motors, new
refrigerators, and hundreds of empty pails. He made himself
comfortable on two wicker chairs, and fell asleep.

In the middle of the night, ignoring the sailor's injunction to stay hidden, he climbed out onto a narrow grated
deck, and, gripping the railing, leaned into the void. The
mist on his face, the creaking rumble of the ship, and the
starlit plain of water that rose and fell like a sleeping giant's
chest, presented to his imagination a thrilling picture of
adventure. He felt himself on the margin of the world,
where no one else cared, or dared, to go.

As the first light of dawn appeared in the sky, he discerned the outline of the island. It was larger than he had expected—there seemed no end to it. Lights twinkled along the coast, and blue hills faded with distance into the sky. There was no movement, no sound. It might have been any coast anywhere. He went back to the hold, and to sleep.

"Who the fuck are you and what the fuck are you doing on my ship?"

The engines were silent, and full morning poured in through open doors. The man addressing him had a beard, and for some reason this fact disposed Andrew to trust him. Standing and smoothing the wrinkles from his clothes, he confided that he had come to the island to be an ambulance driver.

This revelation had no effect on the bearded man, who wanted to know how he'd got on the ship. Andrew said that he'd sneaked on board without assistance. The bearded man expressed his doubt, naming several likely conspirators.

"I'll deal with them; but what the fuck am I supposed to do with you?" He soon answered his own question: "I can't have you fucking up my permits. I'll have to turn you over to the port authority."

Andrew did not mind the sound of this. Half a night's rest had restored his confidence, and he did not think that any harbor official would actually send him back to the mainland now that he was here. Indeed, they might even be able to direct him to a recruitment office.

The bearded man hollered some orders, then escorted Andrew off the ship and onto a crowded, clamorous wharf where pigeons and gulls dodged stevedores driving trucks the size of golf carts pulling trailers the size of trucks piled with crates of fruit, cigarettes, and electronics. He was so blinded by so much colorful activity, so distracted by so much picturesque disorder, that he hardly heard the bearded man's portentous apologies. He didn't know if the scene reminded him more of Mumbai, Singapore, or Constanța—and decided finally that it was unlike any other place on earth.

The captain, meanwhile, was having difficulty extracting a bribe from his stowaway, who did not seem at all concerned by the prospect of his imminent arrest. The captain's threat was also undermined when the first customs station they came to was vacant, the second was impeded by a long, unmoving queue, and the third, to which they were eventually pointed, proved to be up the hill in the town center. The captain took some steps in that direction with now unconvincing determination, then pretended to soften.

"Listen," he said, "maybe I shouldn't ruin your life."

Andrew reassured him.

"I mean," said the captain, "maybe we can come to some other arrangement, you and me."

With a shrug, Andrew gave the man the last of his mainland dollars, happy enough to be rid of their symbolism. Then, bag slung over one shoulder, he walked up the hill into town alone, whistling as he went—but sadly, to politely disguise his joy.

And indeed, the first thing he noticed about the islanders was their grumpiness. Everyone in the street, whether on foot, on bicycle, or in a vehicle, seemed to be scowling. Of course, this was perhaps not odd in a people at war. On the other hand, he saw no signs of the war—no tanks in the streets, no bombed-out buildings, no rabble-rousers in the squares. Here was any morning in any seaside town: the birds sang, the sun shone, and the buses ran. He reflected on the remarkable resilience of nature, and of mankind—not realizing that this truism rather contradicted his initial observation. In any case, he soon saw some men laughing, some children playing, and a church in disrepair, and his first impression was followed by a second impression, and a third; new generalizations displaced old ones, but so gently and continuously that he was never made aware of the uselessness of generalizing.

He went inside a restaurant—noting with approval that the restaurants here were nothing like the sterile, cavernous restaurants of the mainland—and ordered breakfast, then explained while eating why he could not pay for it. The proprietor was too exasperated to listen to any offers or promises, and shooed him outside. Andrew concluded that the islanders were tetchy; then, as the fact of a free meal sank in, he concluded that they were in fact generous and agreeable.

"Mainland army scum," said the proprietor, and spat for the benefit of any partisans in the room.

Andrew strolled through the town, smiling at women whose responses defied generalization. Some frowned, some blushed, some leered, some looked away, some merely stared. His clothes betrayed him as a mainlander, and consequently, depending on their allegiance—the accidents of their upbringing and acquaintances, their circumstances and their luck—they viewed him as either a rapacious mercenary or a regal liberator. And some liked the mercenary; and some hated the liberator.

Eventually he paused to ask the way to a hospital, and was given well-meaning but contradictory directions. When at last he found the place, which was more a clinic than a hospital, the puzzled nurses said that they had no ambulances, and suggested that he try at the next town, which was larger. On the bus, he explained to the driver and the passengers why he could not pay the fare, and was given money. Everyone donated for different reasons, but primarily because he was a mainlander, and recent experience had led them to believe that when a mainlander asked you for something, you really had no choice—and also because they wanted him to shut up, and the bus to get moving. One woman gave a dollar because she thought he was a brave boy.

The bus reached the next town without mishap.

While searching for the hospital, Andrew heard a shrill, cantankerous wail in the distance. He asked a fruit seller what it was.

The man looked at him incredulously. "You do not know? It's an ambulance."

Andrew was taken aback. "But why does it sound so whiny?"

Nor was the hospital what he had expected. It was clean, modern, and very quiet. Having unwittingly come in by the emergency entrance, he was received with lively interest, which was modulated but not dampened when the staff realized that he was not ill. They took turns explaining that there were no jobs available, that the hospital already had more drivers than needed. Andrew said that he was not looking for a job; he wanted to volunteer. The staff were bewildered; more doctors and administrators were called and consulted. Eventually, after much confusion and some embarrassment on both sides, Andrew's worldview was partly communicated to the staff, and the facts partly revealed to him. This hospital, though financed through mainland contributions, was operated locally and had no affiliation with the occupying (some said "peacekeeping") forces, or with the domestic army, or with the war effort at all, except incidentally. After some heated deliberation, the staff decided that Andrew's best hope was the base just outside town, which some of them thought had a field hospital. He thanked them and set out on foot, leaving much emotion and speculation in his wake.

Private Mann and Private Sloane were on watch that afternoon when a man came into view on the road from town. They debated fiercely, in whispers, whether or not to shoot him. They were both jumpy, for only yesterday a grenade had been tossed over the wall during their watch. This had been on the opposite side of the base, which overlooked a swampy field where the latrines were emptied. Originally, for aesthetic and sanitary reasons, the latrines had been dumped farther away, but the soldiers assigned to this detail had, inevitably, tripped landmines and been shot at by snipers; and so the dumping ground had crept closer and closer to the base, till it lay right outside the western gates, reeking beneath the sun and churning beneath the rains. Soon, however, local farmers were drawn to this valuable fertilizer; and when they realized that the shots fired at them were only warnings, they paid them no more attention than horses pay flies. And when the soldiers realized that the islanders—mostly children, women, and old men—could not be driven away, an unofficial truce was effected, and the locals were permitted, without much harassment, to cart away the mainlanders' dung.

Then, yesterday afternoon, some partisan had taken advantage of the soldiers' benevolence to lob a grenade at them, thus bringing the ceasefire to an abrupt end. The grenade had been a dud, and perhaps only intended as a joke or a gesture of defiance. Nevertheless, Private Mann and Private Sloane had both been shaken by the incident— Private Mann because the CO had bawled them out; Private Sloane because he had shot in the back a woman who may or may not have been the perpetrator, but whose body, in any case, had been left lying in a twisted heap, half sunk in feces, as a warning to other would-be guerrillas.

The man on the road appeared to be unarmed, but he carried a bag that could have been filled with explosives. He was dressed like neither a soldier nor a farmer, so Mann deduced that he must be a guerrilla. Sloane disagreed: guerrillas always disguised themselves as soldiers or farmers.

"Then what the hell is he? And why is he coming here?" —"I don't know. Could be a civilian, come to sell cigarettes." —"Could be a fucking jinkie rebel disguised as a citizen." —"Could be an advisor. Could be a journalist." —"Walking?" said Mann, his voice breaking with disbelief. "Walking all the way out here without a fucking vehicle?"

—"Could be his car broke down." —"Could be just about any fucking thing, according to you."

Sloane's radio was malfunctioning again, so he shouted down to the gatehouse. "We expecting any journalists?" —Lance Corporal Aberfoyle made an elaborate and sarcastic reply. Meanwhile the man on the road came nearer. —Mann said, "I guess we just let him walk right in here and blow the whole damn place up."

". . . All right," said Sloane. "Shoot him."

"What? Why me? *You* shoot him."

Sloane wanted to say that it was Mann's turn, but he could not bring himself to refer even indirectly to the woman he'd killed. "You're the one who wants to stop him so bad, go ahead and stop him."

Mann lifted his rifle and took aim, muttering, "All I can say is he better not be no fucking journalist."

A minute passed.

"What are you waiting for?" —"I'm just going to give him a little old warning first." —"All right. Sure. And see what he does." —"That's right, and see how he reacts."

Andrew's body reacted automatically, and with all the flinching, shrinking signs of guilt; but his mind reacted with ingenuous astonishment. "What the hell was that for?" he cried, waving both hands as if flagging down a speeding truck.

Meanwhile Lance Corporal Aberfoyle was on the radio, demanding to know who had authorized Mann to fire his weapon. The two privates suddenly felt sheepish, the fear of a moment ago seeming to them now strange and irrational. Abandoning their post, they climbed down to the gatehouse to explain themselves, and to receive the visitor.

Because Andrew was a mainlander, and because he had been shot at, he was admitted to the base with unusual briskness. Before he could tease Private Mann for his mistake, he was sent by Lance Corporal Aberfoyle to report at the aid station to someone whose name Andrew immediately forgot. He strolled approximately in the direction indicated, looking avidly all around him. This was his first time inside a military base. He was impressed by its size, its clutter, and its monochromatic filthiness.

He found the mess hall, where he asked for and was given a meal. He sat down with some officers who, having ascertained that he was not regular army, were amused by his audacity, and welcomed him with avuncular roughness.

"First day in the country," he said, "and I've already been shot at!" Then, overwhelmed by this astounding fact, he lapsed into a daydream in which he replayed the incident from different angles, ostensibly searching in memory for details, but in fact searching in imagination for dramatic embellishments. By the time he finished eating, he half believed that he had been shot at, not once but five times, by hooded guerrilla snipers whose bullets had exploded in the dust at his feet, and that he had performed a rolling tumble off the road and crept behind cover to the base's gates, where miraculously he had guessed the password.

The officers straggled out and the enlisted men and women filed in, so Andrew queued for another meal. The food this time was worse, all of it coming directly out of large aluminum containers, but a can of warm beer was also placed on his tray. He toasted the soldiers around him at the table, who toasted him.

"You just get off leave?" —"Nope, just got here." —"What outfit you with?" —"The ambulance outfit." —They toasted him with more gravity; one private gave Andrew his beer. "You guys saved my buddy's life." With increasingly maudlin solemnity, they shared anecdotes attesting to the heroism of medics and ambulance drivers. Andrew was given more beer, which he accepted courteously.

He proposed to buy a round, and was told that the beer was rationed to two cans per person per day. The only way to get drunk was either to hoard for a few days—and then you risked inspections—or to donate to the beer pool, whereby one quarter of the participating privates received, every fourth night, the beers of the other three quarters. Andrew nevertheless managed, with the coins he'd received on the bus, to bribe two extra beers out of the commissary staff. He gave these away, and was toasted.

He wandered around the compound as sunset turned to dusk; the air smelled of oil, dust, shit, and some nutty blossom that seemed to remind him very strongly of something that he nevertheless could not identify. He stared at a khaki-colored tank. He kicked an empty ammunition barrel. In amazement he placed his hands on an armored vehicle, which looked to him like a garbage truck with mounted guns. He could hardly believe that thirty hours ago he had been sitting in the passport office. If only his mother, and Nance, and Roger and Maria, and Lawrence and Beth, and Nathan and Claudia and Bruce, and Hillary, and Pari could see him now!

A helicopter roared down out of the blue-orange sky, whipping up a cyclone of dust and trash. He watched as hunched silhouettes unloaded a gurney and two cumbrous duffel bags. The gurney was received by other hunched silhouettes, who pushed it inside a sandbagged metal shed lit with fluorescent lights so white they seemed purple. The bags were left outside, and the helicopter roared back into the sky. Andrew's imagination eventually revealed to him the contents of those bags.

He had found the aid station. With some misgiving, which he represented to himself as eagerness, he went inside.

He had never been awake inside an operating room before, and was mesmerized by the sight of four adults subduing and stripping naked a fifth who lay writhing on a table. A nearby voice asked if he needed help. Without looking away, Andrew replied, "I was told to report here." —"What's your complaint?" —"Huh?" —"What's wrong with you?" —"Oh. Nothing." —"Then why were you told to report here?" —"Oh. Right." He looked briefly at his interlocutor. "I'm here to help." To this there was no response, so he elaborated: "I came to drive an ambulance." —"Hal?"

One of the doctors leaning over the operating table straightened. "Yeah?" —"This guy's here to drive ambo." —"Great. You from UPESCU?" —"I don't think so," said Andrew, alarmed that the man had stopped what he had been doing. —"What outfit you with?" —"No outfit, per se. I'm freelance, I guess you'd say. I just got here." —The doctor shrugged. "Even better. Less paperwork. You find a bunk yet?" —"Uh, Hal?"

"What." —"We don't have any vans to give him." —Now one of the women at the operating table took a step back and placed her bloody hands on her hips. "There's got to be six collecting dust in the motor pool as we speak." —"They've all been requisitioned by Knob Grange." —"Then what are they doing here?" —"Nobody to drive them."

The casualty kicked the doctor named Hal, though not apparently on purpose.

"How'd you say you got assigned here?" —"He's freelance, Hal." —Andrew said, "I can go wherever I'm most needed, I guess." —"Knob Grange sure as shit could use drivers. From what I've heard, they've been getting walloped."

Hal looked thoughtfully out the doorway. "I wish I could keep you, but—well, you want to take one of them vans to Knob Grange?"

"Sure."

"All right. Thanks." —"Good luck." The doctors returned to their patient.

The orderly asked Andrew if he knew how to get to Knob Grange. "Oh, sure," he said. And because he remained standing there, she asked if he knew where to find the motor pool.

The guard at the motor pool was conscientious enough in his duty to know not to care who Andrew was or which ambulance he drove away in: the vehicles had been requisitioned—he had a paper to show it—and were therefore no longer his responsibility. They were taking up space and should have been removed days ago.

Andrew sat in each of them. The newer models seemed to have revolving lights but no sirens, so he selected a somewhat battered wagon with no lights but, as he proved, a powerful, angry siren.

"Now cut that out," said the guard.

His ambulance, like some of the others, had the steering wheel on what he thought of as the wrong side. He could not now recall on which side of the road he had seen vehicles driving that day, but trusted his ability to detect and adapt to convention. He was equally sanguine about the manual transmission, which he had never used before. He started the engine, gave it gas, tooted the horn, turned on the headlights, and tested the windshield wipers; then, his heart in his mouth—he turned off the engine.

"Say, what's the best way to Knob George this time of night?"

"You mean Knob Grange?" —"That's the one." —"Well, shit. You got to get to Knob Grange *tonight*? Alone?" —Andrew nodded grimly. —"Well, shit. For starters, turn your fucking lights out. At least you got some moon, or should have." With thoughtful deliberation, naming many roads and towns that meant nothing to Andrew, the guard outlined a possible route, from which Andrew gleaned little more than the predominant direction the guard's hand gestured—west. —Andrew thanked him, and restarted the engine. —"And try to get behind some other car if you can, even if it slows you down. Them milk trucks are best: we call them minesweepers. Otherwise, change your speed a lot, and avoid any straight and open roads. And don't stop for nobody, not even a little girl with her leg trapped under a bus. She was probably put there by a fucking rebel who's only too happy to hijack you or kidnap you or shoot you or all three. Yeah, even an ambulance driver. No shit. Welcome to Jinkie Land."

Andrew sent the ambulance forward with a lurch, but the guard came running after him. —"Shit, I almost forgot. You mind stopping at Poplar Junction? It's on your way." —"Sure, no problem." —"Great. There's a little package I need delivered. Hold on."

The guard at the gatehouse requested a similar favor, and Andrew gunned the engine anxiously while some private was sent to the commissary for another little package—which, like the first, also proved to be a large crate. This was placed beside the first atop the collapsed gurneys in the back, Andrew was given more money and handshakes, then finally the gates rattled apart and he was free—grinding in first gear in a westerly direction down a washboard road that he could hardly see. After a mile or so of this, he turned on the headlights, failed to shift into another gear, switched on the siren, and, pretending the crates he was transporting were wounded soldiers, pressed the gas pedal to the floor and raced the tattered moonlight across the dark, rolling landscape.

FIVE WEEKS PASSED before Andrew reached Knob Grange. His first deliveries led to others, till soon he was transporting goods back and forth—along with the occasional soldier bound for a better hospital on one of the larger bases along the coast or back home on the mainland. These passengers were mostly amputees, and mostly sullen. None of them seemed very glad to be going home or getting out of the war, which, considering how eager all their comrades were to be off the island, struck Andrew as ungracious. He found these casualties difficult to talk to, for he had not seen enough of the war to understand or even ask intelligent questions about their experiences. He felt more heroic when they were unconscious.

As for his other cargo, he quickly discovered (by opening the boxes) that liquor, canned goods, and manufactured items flowed west, while meat, dairy, and fresh produce flowed east. He was astounded by the prices the latter fetched: a dozen eggs were equal to a bottle of whiskey, a head of cabbage worth its weight in coffee. Finally, he could not resist going into business himself, trading with (by preference) farm girls for wheels of cheese or onions or, one time, a pig, and with quartermasters for tobacco and sugar and, one time, a violin. Within a very few days he would find himself quite rich, and would take a week's holiday to divest himself of the burden. He then bought drinks for many officers and soldiers, and fell in love with several local women.

Eva was tall and fair and had a dimple in one cheek, as if she were always hiding a sweet, or a secret. She demonstrated in bed that sexual arousal was governed by the parasympathetic nervous system; she lay there like someone digesting a good meal.

Mol was thin and lithe, her face a permanent pout. She flicked her head in little jerks, like a bird, to keep the hair out of her eyes. She never stopped moving—not fidgeting, but dancing to some wandering tune that only she could hear. She talked a lot about the future: she wanted three children, and money. She kissed him with probing virtuosity, like a saxophonist testing a saxophone in a shop.

Hallie was short and dark, with luminous brown eyes. He took her to movies, to restaurants and bars, and for drives in the ambulance. She never made a suggestion of her own, but consented to all of his with a sly and playful smile, as if she were preparing a surprise that she knew he was going to like. She did not let him touch her.

He saw little but telltale evidence of the war, such as sabotaged bridges and destroyed roads. The eastern and mainland forces cratered roads to impede the movement of the guerrillas, while the western and guerrilla forces barricaded the same roads to harass the eastern and mainland armies. Andrew could not grasp this distinction, so any roadblocks he encountered he ascribed to generic, impersonal "military tactics." Indeed, he had trouble keeping straight who exactly was supposed to be fighting whom, and why—and in this respect was not unlike many of the soldiers and civilians he talked to. He believed that he was neutral; but since most of the people he dealt with were mainlanders or profiteers, it is not surprising that the roles of villain and bogey occasionally required by his imagination were played by the unseen, unknown partisans.

One night, driving at a constant speed down a stretch of straight and open road, he found himself swerving and mashing the brake as a thundering geyser of dirt and light appeared in the road before him. He came to rest half in the ditch, his headlights illuminating some stalks of corn and a swirling cloud of dust. Blinking, he got out of the ambulance and staggered down the road towards the site of the explosion. Some mine must have detonated, perhaps triggered by the vibration of his approaching vehicle. Wonder percolated through him slowly. He might have been killed! Good thing he wasn't! "Ha!" he shouted, and shuffled forward in the dark to investigate the size of the crater. Then from the ambulance came a noise like pistons popping out of the engine; at the same time a crackle of fireworks sounded from somewhere beyond the cornfield. "What the fuck?" The crackle was repeated; one of his headlights shattered, and twangs like snapping cables whistled past him through the night. Bullets.

"Hey!" he cried angrily. More bullets.

He loped back to the ambulance, hunching his shoulders but refusing to move quickly. He was an ambulance driver, a neutral; he was *him*. What were they thinking? He'd never done anything to *them*. He spun the vehicle around and drove back in the direction he'd come. The next day some soldiers explained that the mine had also been intended for him, and that only poor timing or the unreliability of the electronic fuse had saved him. They too assumed that the attack had been conducted by partisans.

When at last he met some of these partisans face to face, he did not, however, find them greatly fearsome. One afternoon he came upon what from a distance looked like just another crater-filling party, but which proved to be a barricade-building party. Men, women, and children were singing as they tossed broken furniture and cinderblocks and scrap metal pell-mell from trucks into the middle of the road. Teenagers with rifles motioned superfluously for him to halt, and a mustached man wearing a faded camouflage jacket hopped down from one of the trucks and gestured at him to roll down the window. Instinctively, Andrew became affable, contrite, and a little stupid—the same persona he adopted when pulled over by the police.

"Where are you going?" —"Just over to Pokeshole. I guess the road's closed?"

"And where are you coming from?" —"A place called Turnip Flats. Do you know it?"

"I know there's a mainland army base there." —"That's where I came from all right."

"You're working for the mainland army?" —"Not exactly, no. I go where I'm needed."

"You're needed in Pokeshole?" —"There's some sick people there."

"And now, you're carrying sick people?" —"No, sir."

"What're you carrying now?" —"Oh, a bit of just about everything, I guess."

"You're not carrying weapons?" —"No."

"No bombs?" —"No bombs."

"You won't mind if we take a little look?" —"Not at all. It's just foodstuffs and stuff. Canned peaches and condensed milk, mostly. A few cartons of cigarettes."

"For the sick people." —"I'm not sure who all gets what, to tell you the truth. I just carry whatever I'm asked to, if I have the space."

"You're being paid to do this work?" —"No, sir. I'm a volunteer."

"Like us." —"I guess that's right."

"Only without political convictions like us." —"I'm neutral, if that's what you mean."

"You have no opinions about the war?" —"No."

"It's neither good nor bad?" —"Well, I'd have to say that it's mostly bad, from what I've seen."

"But like the weather, no one's to be blamed for it." —"I'm sure it's plenty complicated."

Throughout the interview, the mustached man had been looking carefully all around Andrew, as if registering evidence of his ideological decadence. Now he looked briefly in Andrew's eyes.

"You are in fact a rather despicable character, aren't you? With your shady hithers and hences and your total indifference to the struggle of the oppressed." —Andrew shrugged. "I think I'm doing what I can to help." —"Sadly, we at this moment in history are enlisting the help of even unscrupulous and despicable characters of such unsavory type as yourself. Seeing as how you're utterly devoid of principles, you I predict will have no objection to our taking these medical supplies, of which we're currently in desperate need." —"Help yourselves." —"Of course you don't mind. You'll always be able to get more at Pokeshole, or at Turnip Flats, or at Pastor's Hill, am I right?" —"I guess so."

"We'd have great need of those also. So great a need, in fact, that we'd happily pay for them. And pay also, retroactively, for these we take now—to show that we, at least, have some scruples. We aren't communists, you know. We're not opposed to profits, if they're earned in a just cause." —"I'm not sure when I'll be back this way, but sure, I can try to bring more, what is it? Bandages, iodine, stuff like that?" —"Simply everything. Medicines especially. All kinds. I am not a doctor." —"I'll see what I can do." —"Thank you. Also, we're taking the peaches and canned milk this time. For these we'll pay now." —"Okey-dokey." —The man with the mustache withdrew some bills from a wallet. "This a fair price?" —"Sure," said Andrew. (Later, when he counted it, he was disappointed.)

"We cannot dismantle this roadblock now, you understand. You'd not mind going the long way?" —"Not at all. So long." —"Farewell. Also, I should mention, we've taken the cigarettes."

They had taken the gurneys too, and not only the medical kits but the cabinets containing them, and a flashlight, and a pair of shoes for which Andrew had just traded a box of batteries. He had now no reason to continue to Pokeshole, and a reason positively not to return to Turnip Flats. He had been staying in Whitefield with Hallie's family, for whom he'd been selling butter, but they were acting oddly: Hallie had begun petting him and speaking to him cloyingly in sentences that dissolved in baby talk; her mother, who'd doted on him, had become aloof; her father, who'd never concealed his disdain, had become warm and solicitous; her brother had with significant silence shown him a pistol and a box of grenades; and her younger sister, Cassie, had begun looking at him imploringly and trying to get him alone. Now the interview with the mustached partisan had left him obscurely disgruntled. He did not like the man's implication that he, an ambulance driver and volunteer, was some kind of crass opportunist. He decided that it was time to go to Knob Grange.

At Knob Grange his ambulance was re-equipped, a medic was assigned to him, and he was sent in a convoy to retrieve the corpses of twenty soldiers killed the night before in a skirmish. The site of the battle was the scorched and writhen remains of a sorghum field; the farmer's family watched the operation from the shadow of a smoking barn. The wounded had been evacuated by helicopter; a sergeant had stayed behind to direct the salvage team. He was not much use. He recounted the ambush of his patrol in disjointed fragments, but did not know or could not remember where all the bodies lay. Andrew and the medic rummaged through a swath of tangled grass, sending swarms of crickets into the air. At last they followed a trail into a grove of swaying poplars.

"Well," said the medic, "*he's* dead."

Andrew agreed. The soldier was sprawled upon the ground like a climber across a cliff face. Despite the strained posture, the body was obviously lifeless—as limp and inert as a mannequin. Andrew was surprised by his own lack of surprise. The smell was bad, however.

They fetched a gurney, and the medic suggested they flip a coin for the feet. —"I don't care," said Andrew, "I'll take the head." —The medic removed the soldier's belt, dispersing a cloud of flies, and fastened it around the calves, while Andrew, following instructions, loosened the cartridge belt and stuffed the hands and arms inside it. "Ready?" The medic crouched and gripped the ankles, and Andrew hooked his hands into the armpits. —"Should we turn him over first?" asked Andrew. —"What for?" —As they heaved the body up and slammed it face-down onto the gurney, a grey porridge spilled from the man's skull onto Andrew's shirt. The medic guffawed mirthlessly. "Next time you'll flip," he said, and began removing the soldier's boots, which were in good condition. Due to the shortage of adequate footwear among the rank and file, an injunction had recently been issued against burying the dead in their boots; but no provision had been made to collect or redistribute them. So the thief was technically following orders.

As they trundled a second body back to the ambulance, Andrew muttered, "This isn't exactly what I signed up for." —The medic could not understand his complaint. "We're not under fire, are we?" —Another ambulance driver agreed. "I'll take clean-up over rescue any day. And this is a good clean-up as clean-ups go. It's the fights we lose that you need to worry about fucking booby traps." —"And snipers," said the medic, "and potshots from howitzers. No thanks." —Andrew, looking around at the field and the ambulances filled with corpses, snorted. "We won this one?" —"Fuck," said the driver, "we scared them off, didn't we?" —The medic said pettishly, "You heard the LC: we bagged at least a dozen of them." —"Then where are the bodies?" —The driver flapped his hand dismissively, signifying distance. —The medic said, "Not our problem, is it?" —Another medic said that the partisans were always sneaking off with their dead before you could get a proper count of their casualties. —"They eat them," said the driver. The medics laughed, but the driver assured them it was true. "They eat their own dead—like wasps."

Andrew did not like driving in convoy; and he did not like the medic, who was cynical and spoke of casualties as of meat. Nor did he greatly care for the other drivers, who lounged around the barracks, playing poker and roughhousing and half-listening to the radio for distress calls from patrols, but who seemed relieved when medevac helicopters were dispatched.

That night he drove back to Whitefield, still smelling of death. He was stopped on the way by a group of partisans.

"You're working for the army?" —"Yes," he said. —"Carrying their wounded to the hospital?" —"And their dead." —"Daisy! You like that job, then?" —"Not much." —"You won't mind if we take a wee peek to be sure you're not carrying any contraband or explosives or anything nasty?" —"Go ahead."

". . . That's all right, then. Thank you, brother. Now off with you to bed. I'm guessing you'll need all your winks." —"You're not going to confiscate my supplies?" —"I wouldn't dream of it, me. Your soldiers'll need them themselves, I'm thinking."

Andrew had instinctively adopted throughout this interrogation the weary cynicism of the medic. Now the attitude persisted; he prolonged and embellished it, till he was hunched over the steering wheel, bowed by disgust and nihilism and fatigue. He felt pity, envy, and a little contempt towards Hallie and her family, who did not know what war was really like.

There came into view on the western horizon a flickering glow, like sheet lightning but more colorful. He slowed and rolled down his window, and heard a sizzling and popping like grease in a hot pan.

A firefight. At this distance it was beautiful—a pulsating sunset. He groaned, flicked on the siren, and turned west at the next crossroad.

The noise of the fight grew louder exponentially; soon the nearly continuous thunder of artillery completely drowned the siren and the rattling of the ambulance over the road. The cacophony shook the earth and caused the air to buckle. At last he pulled over, climbed out of the vehicle, and simply stood there looking about him in amazement that anything could be so loud. The ground beneath his feet bucked as the shells came whooping dementedly out of the sky and crashed down, still a mile or more away, beyond a wooded rise. The sky above was filled with smoke that writhed garishly as yellow and green flares sank slowly through it. He got back in the ambulance and drove a few meters farther before a shattering concussion seemed to land right on top of him. But he was all right; he drove on.

He passed a burning farmhouse and was temporarily blinded by the flames. Still he drove on, feeling for the edge of the road with his tires. Then a flare ignited high overhead, illuminating the landscape like a sickly, quivering moon. In a pasture a hundred meters away, black figures crouched, gesticulated, or scrambled back and forth. He pressed the brake; were they partisans? Slowly, taking shape out of the skittish shadows, a helicopter lifted into the air, pivoted uncertainly, and again alighted. So they were not partisans. He turned onto a rough track and continued toward them.

Here the explosions were literally deafening—so loud that he could not hear them, only feel them. Climbing out of the ambulance, he did not even bother covering his ears. He could not keep from ducking, however. In between the shells he heard terrific ripping sounds like a gigantic canvas being torn, rasping splintering sounds like trees falling, and a deep underwater throbbing sound. All this noise must have been originating somewhere in the woods beyond, for none of these people were firing weapons. They shouted at each other and into handsets and were apparently understood. One of them shouted at Andrew.

"What?" —"Durm fad vuggith lizem onv!" —"What!" —"TURM FAD FUGGITH SIZEM ONF!" —"Oh." He turned the siren off; the soldier went away, cussing.

He asked two soldiers what was happening, and received two lengthy, frantic, but incomprehensible answers. Then a couple of medics bearing a soldier on a stretcher emerged hobbling from the trail out of the woods. Others assumed the burden and loaded it onto the helicopter, which immediately took flight, just as another landed.

Andrew shouted into the ear of a lance corporal, "Can't the choppers get any closer to the casualties?" —Modulations in the shelling rendered the lance corporal's reply intermittently intelligible: "Fey'n dzych, but the only bolliter brail do buck down is completely seezoach im-om tie fa vuggith kithea'ce mortars. We've lost two zvickis arsecky, amsh fa uffiz byruld won't risk it. Not that I fucking traing feng."

Andrew pointed at his ambulance and said that he would go in and get some of the casualties. The lance corporal gave him directions to the most seriously injured, and told him to bring them back as far as the helicopters. Andrew nodded, though most of this was garbled, and what was not garbled, excitement prevented him from heeding.

Entering the woods was like entering a dim underground corridor: the branches formed a low, arched ceiling that screened the light, and the thick foliage muffled the noise of the shells and the guns. He turned on his headlight—just in time to avoid running over two medics carrying a stretcher. The trail was deeply rutted and the ambulance swayed and shuddered as he progressed.

It was almost with relief that he emerged at last into a clearing lit like a fairground by flares, burning trees, tracer bullets strung like fairy lights, and the red-hot, white-hot flash of bursting shells. Other than the convulsive light, nothing moved. Humps that might have been bodies, hiding or dead, dotted the ground. And there, ten feet from his front bumper, slowly flailing one arm, lay a wounded soldier.

He pulled forward, hopped out, and knelt down. "Hi, pal! Can you walk?"

Private Jeremy Faulkin could not walk. In fact, he could not feel his legs. A strange indigestion-like pain originating approximately in his pelvis had expanded down into the space his groin and legs had inhabited, and continued expanding until he and his pain seemed to be twelve feet long. His body was suddenly strange and awful to him; he sensed its limitless capacity for disfigurement and transformation, and was terrified, less of death than of what he might become. He did not trust himself to speak.

Andrew dashed in a crouch to the next soldier, knelt, and touched their shoulder. It was a girl. She was dead. Her eyes were fixed thoughtfully on the distance, her mouth pursed uncertainly. He moved on to the next hump. "Hi, pal! Can you walk?"

A boy with a pale face looked up at him with eyes like open mouths. "Sure I can walk!" —"Then come with me! I need your help!"

There was a lull, or diminution in the shelling, and, as they ran back to the ambulance, Andrew could hear bullets all around him, buzzing like angry bees. He felt that he was dodging them; and when a mortar shell exploded nearby, sending him briefly to his knees, he felt that he had ducked a deadly fan of shrapnel at exactly the right moment. Private Lorrie Spack, who had been following him, was not so agile, and was hit in the neck with a fragment. He fell to the ground, clutching his throat, only a few feet from Private Faulkin. "Shit," said Andrew.

He heaved a gurney out of the ambulance. —"Nuh-uh," said Private Spack, his voice glutinous with blood, "I can walk!" And without taking his hands from his throat, he rolled onto his knees, stood, and showed that he could indeed walk, by walking to the ambulance and clambering inside.

Andrew rolled Private Faulkin onto the gurney and winched it up, but he could hardly move it over the rough ground. Luckily, a soldier came bounding out of the trees, and, hoisting the other end of the gurney, helped load it into the ambulance. Then, without having uttered a word or made eye contact, he bounded back to his cover.

Andrew jumped in and slammed the door, and the ambulance became his body. Tensing every muscle against bullets and shrapnel, steeling himself to ignore injury and roll through every obstacle, he hurtled down the trail and out of the woods, bounced past the officers and medics scurrying about the pasture, and leapt up onto the road. He turned off his headlight, turned on his siren, and ratcheted his transmission into second gear, where he left it. They were on their way.

"Twenty minutes to Pokeshole!" he said—though it would be longer if he avoided the direct route, which was all straight and open road. He decided to stay on it, but to continually change his speed in order to make himself a difficult target for the landmines. He pumped all three pedals as if he were operating a loom, but with ingenious irregularity, weaving an intricate pattern of patternlessness. The ambulance lurched like a wild horse. "Hope you guys buckled your seat belts!"

Private Faulkin kept blacking out. He had lost a lot of blood and was dehydrated. His tongue was wooden, and he could feel its every bump and cranny, all the way back to his epiglottis. His hands felt hot and swollen to the size of oven mitts; his fingertips were sensitive, so that touching anything, even his own palms, was stiflingly overwhelming. The pain in his pelvis was trailing several feet behind the ambulance, twisting and shrieking like a wraith. He couldn't see anything, not even darkness; he couldn't see.

Private Spack was concentrating on his breathing. Blood or mucus trickled into the back of his mouth faster than he could swallow it. He felt an overpowering urge to clear his throat, but was afraid of tearing or dislodging something. He exhaled, swallowed, inhaled, spat, exhaled, swallowed, inhaled, spat. He made snoring and wheezing and burbling sounds when he breathed but so far he had not inhaled much blood. He was afraid of what coughing would do to him. He felt no pain, only a creeping black panic, as if his head and chest were slowly filling with rubber.

Andrew was exhilarated, and sought channels into which his exhilaration could flow. These soldiers—they were great. The mainland army was great. Even the enemy was great. War was great. The islanders were great. Hallie was great. Oh, God—Cassie was great! He pictured her barefoot in the yard, laughing and taunting and dodging the clods of dirt her brother threw at her. He remembered how he had longed to chase her, to wrestle with her. The way her body moved seemed to invite it, as if she knew that all life was play. She carried herself with the graceful indifference to grace, the comfortable clumsiness of an experienced middle-aged woman at home in her own skin. He loved her; and the astonishing, wondrous thing was that she loved him too. That was what she had been trying to tell him all week; and that was what he had taken such pains to avoid learning. The proximity of so great a happiness—happiness was

123

great!—had daunted and paralyzed him. But now he would act. He would never fail to act again. His alacrity was translated to speed as he gradually stopped making use of the clutch and brake pedals.

"I can't see," said Private Faulkin. —"There's nothing to see," Andrew reassured him. "It's nighttime. I can hardly see the road myself!" —"I'm blind. I can't see." —"You're okay. It's just dark out. There's no lights. You'll be okay. We'll be there soon." —But exhaustion and pain had finally deprived Private Faulkin of all restraint. He succumbed to a wave of self-pity; tears spilled from his unseeing eyes. He recalled what he had been only an hour ago—his ideal self, the self he presented to his mother in his letters home: clean, well fed, healthy, and relaxed; friendly, funny, and popular; a good man and a good soldier; young, handsome, and whole. Now he was wrecked, and no use to anyone. No one would want him like this, not even his mother. It wasn't fair. He sobbed softly, "My eyes are shot. I can't see."

"Your eyes are fine, boss," said Andrew. "Here, look: I'll turn on the light for a second. See? You're all right." Then the steering wheel jumped through his hands and smashed his chin.

The soldiers naturally assumed that they had been shelled again, but Andrew knew what had happened as soon as he came to. He was unconscious only briefly but completely, so that everything that followed had a stark and tremendous quality, as if he'd been wakened in bed by an earthquake.

He had driven into a crater at full speed.

He could not open his door. The interior lights no longer worked. The siren was silent. He smelled gasoline, heard it glugging from the tank. "Are you guys okay?" He climbed into the back and scrabbled over cabinets and limbs to the doors, which he threw open to fresh air and moonlight. "Come on, we better get you out of here. This thing could blow at any second."

Private Spack followed him out but Private Faulkin remained where he lay, crumpled between the passenger seat and his gurney. From the edge of the crater, Andrew reached down into the ambulance and began pulling out and throwing aside whatever his hands encountered, clearing the debris from his path to Faulkin. Private Spack started to ask for bandages, so that he could pressure-dress his wound and free his hands to help, but air bubbled out through his fingers when he tried to speak. He rummaged through the scattered contents of a medical kit with his feet.

Andrew lowered himself back into the vehicle and shook Private Faulkin roughly. "Come on, big guy. You awake?" —"Leave me," said Faulkin. "I'm no good anymore. Just leave me." —"Oh, cut it out. Come on, put your arms around me. Good, now hold on tight." —"I can't." —"You can." —"I can't," he continued to say, even after Andrew had lugged him out of the ambulance and dropped him onto a gurney; "I can't." —"You did!" Andrew ruffled his hair; the young man's whining helplessness only amplified his own feeling of masterful competence. Now he turned to Private Spack. "Let's get that wound of yours bandaged, soldier." He wrapped three rolls of gauze around Spack's neck and told him to keep it elevated. Spack nodded and sat down by a tree. Although slightly strangled, he did feel better. His moist, irregular breathing sounded like a man trying to get the last film of dish soap out of the squeeze bottle.

"Okay. Are you guys all right here for a few minutes? I've got to go get us a new vehicle." Private Spack nodded, but Private Faulkin, with the hopelessness of a child who knows he will be denied, pleaded for painkillers. Andrew rifled through the detritus for pill bottles, which he held up to the moonlight. He was astounded: codeine; morphine; dexedrine! He knew what these pills did, all right. He realized that he had not taken a single pill for nearly six weeks, not even his asthma pills—nor had he needed them. He did not stop

125

to ponder if he needed these pills now; his only reflection was that six weeks' abstinence meant six weeks' reduced tolerance. He gave Faulkin a couple of morphines and himself chewed a dexedrine and a codeine, feeling all the nervous anticipation of a neophyte. Then he clapped his hands, and to Private Spack's amazement, turned and without hesitation sprinted across an empty field, over a hill, and out of sight.

Hunger and boredom returned to Private Spack, and, with them, resentment. To be hit with artillery while picking cabbages! There must have been rebels in the barn they'd passed. Why couldn't the jinkies have waited five minutes, till after he'd eaten? His mind lovingly fabulated the salad he had been about to enjoy: crisp cucumbers; tender carrots; chives and radishes and shredded beets; leaves of lettuce as robust and fibrous as palm fronds; all drizzled lightly— so lightly!—with a lemon rosemary dressing. And on the side—a potato! Oh, what he wouldn't do for a baked potato. Even a butterless, boiled potato. Even a raw potato—even half a raw potato! He would happily kill any number of jinkies for half a raw potato. For a baked potato, he would choke Private Faulkin to death, twice. The night was chilly; he snuggled nearer to the image of his baked potato. In the distance he heard the sarcastic cry of a peacock, and wondered elaborately what peacock tasted like.

Andrew soon returned, pedaling a bicycle, which he had purchased at gunpoint from a groggy and unsympathetic farmer. He was breathing heavily and eating an apple, most of which he exhaled. Only now that he was facing the prospect directly did he realize that the bicycle would never carry all three of them. His mind raced through considerations. Faulkin seemed to be in worse condition and so should probably be helped first. On the other hand, he would, in his weakened state, be more unwieldy; what if he couldn't hold on? Perhaps Spack should ride the bicycle, and Andrew could carry Faulkin? No; even in his exalted state he realized that

Pokeshole was still too far to walk. It would be better to send an ambulance back for the second soldier. Would it be faster altogether if he simply rode to Pokeshole alone and came back with an ambulance? What if there weren't any available? Perhaps he should instead ride the bicycle to the nearest town and steal a car. No; he wouldn't leave his casualties alone again. "All right," he said, "who wants to go first?"

"Leave me," sobbed Faulkin. "I'm useless."

Private Spack looked at him with disgust. At last he gestured that Andrew should take Faulkin first.

They lifted Faulkin onto the seat side-saddle, wrapped his arms around Andrew's chest, and tied his hands together with his belt. Andrew saluted Private Spack, who saluted him; then, pulling hard on the handlebars for leverage, he pedaled away at top speed, Faulkin's feet dragging behind in the dust.

Private Spack watched them till they were out of sight. Then, dreaming of apples, he started out across the empty field and over the hill.

Private Jeremy Faulkin died in surgery. Private Lorrie Spack survived, eventually being operated on by a local non-partisan doctor. A year later he married an islander, and was arrested and court-martialed for desertion when he tried to bring her back to the mainland with him.

Hallie's father, seeing Andrew return the next morning covered in blood, decided not to denounce him to the rebels when they entered the town (they never arrived), but instead warned him to get away. Andrew asked Cassie to come with him; startled, she said no—and always regretted it. He spent three more months on the island, driving ambo at Knob Grange and other enemy-proximate installations, before he was shot in the leg, and flown home at the taxpayers' expense.

Captain Augello had been killed by a mortar, and no replacement had yet been sent. Major Jenkman knew nothing of the medical corps, and wanted to know nothing. He gave Doctor Vadilevaniakis and Doctor Latroussaine free rein, and told them to do their best.

Hillary, uneasy in this vacuum, thought that one of them should assume command temporarily. As an army doctor, she had the higher rank, but Eric had more experience, both since and prior to being drafted. They flipped a coin. He took command.

At first, Eric liked Pastor's Hill very much. He had no one to report to, and nothing to do. Once a week he spoke to Major Lopez on the radio, and asked for supplies that he knew would not be sent. He had no duties, for the casualties wounded on patrols were evacuated by helicopter directly to the field hospitals at Hard Top River or Poplar Junction; anyone seriously injured by the incessant mortar fire was also evacuated, because the medical hut contained little more than an instrument cart, resuscitation box, and a cabinet of expired antibiotics. He soon grew accustomed to the shellings, and ceased even to wonder why the air force didn't simply raze the forest surrounding the base. He had enough money for whiskey, and time enough, at last, for Pascal—the only book he had brought with him from the mainland. His French was poor enough to render the text richly unfathomable. He could daydream entire afternoons over such teasing obscurities as (in his own translation), "We are so miserable that we cannot take pleasure in a thing designed to make us angry if used badly," or "When everything moves, nothing seems to move—like in a something; when everyone moves towards the something, no one seems to move towards it." His leave had twice been canceled, and was three months overdue. Now, instead of leave, he had been sent to the front. So he had no qualms—at first—about treating Pastor's Hill as a holiday.

The only problem was Doctor Vadilevaniakis. She did not know how to relax, and her vigilant industriousness made it difficult for him to relax. He found some reassurance in his newfound rank, telling himself that, naturally, the subordinate should handle most of the routine tasks, leaving the superior free to address crises, should such arise. At other times he reasoned that there was not enough work for even one of them, and he was doing Doctor Vadilevaniakis a favor by letting her keep busy. She had more to learn, and was learning.

But these rationalizations were less effective at alleviating disquiet than whiskey; and when he was drunk, solitude made him maudlin. So he drank with the privates, who were friendly and boisterous, but with whom he felt little rapport. For one thing, they were all a decade younger than him. For another, unlike him, they were not on holiday: they went out on patrols most nights of the week, from which some of them, sometimes, did not return. Consequently, every few days, Eric got up from the mess table where they drank, bullshitted, and gambled, and carried a bottle to the medical hut, where he attempted to persuade Doctor Vadilevaniakis to unwind, to cut loose, to have a little fun.

Hillary was sitting at the desk, rubbing her scalp and watching flakes of dandruff fall tumbling through sunlight to the page below. She was vaguely surprised that her hair was almost long enough to twist around a finger; but otherwise her mind was empty. When Doctor Latroussaine entered, she stiffened with shame. She stood and saluted him, though they had agreed this was not necessary.

"Fuck off, Doctor. As you were. Have a drink."

"Thanks, but fuck you all the same, Doctor. I don't drink when I'm on duty."

"Are these sterilized?" —"They were this morning." —He poured whiskey into two graduated cylinders, but set both before himself. He proceeded to sip from one with demonstrative relish. "Sure you wouldn't like a taste?" —"Quite sure, thanks."

Aside from the fact that his conversation was sometimes repetitive, Hillary did not mind these visits from Doctor Latroussaine. Though she felt guilty whenever they were in the same room, as if they could best serve the base's medical needs only by spreading out, she did stop worrying, when he was here, about what she should be doing. If they were idle, it was his decision—his order.

"What's that you're laboring over?" —"Oh," she said, putting it away, "just a letter to my brother." —"Which one?" —"Ben." —"Ah yes. Ben. 'Ben.' How is Ben?" —She told him how Ben was. Sweet, imprudent, and naive, Ben had married a harpy, who he now realized was a harpy. He wanted to know why no one else had noticed, or if they had, why no one had warned him. Hillary was torn between explaining exactly why nobody had thought fit to tell him that the woman he was in love with was a bitch, and encouraging him to make the best of a bad situation. So far, after five hours, she had written a paragraph of greeting.

Eric, however, was impressed, and contrite. He had not written to his mother in over a month. "You don't believe in divorce?" he asked. —"My family doesn't. My brother doesn't, I don't think. Anyway, they've only been married a year." —"I was married five years, and I wish someone had told me to get the fuck out after a year." —"What happened?" —"The short story, I guess, is that I was a workaholic. Do you want to hear the long story?" —"If you want to tell it."

He told her the long story.

She commiserated, and refrained from pointing out what he might have done differently.

"That's probably why I'm here," he said. "Probably I wanted to get away from everything—her family, all our friends. Otherwise, wouldn't I have fought the draft a little harder?" —Hillary sighed. "You didn't fight the draft because deep down you knew it was your duty to your country."

Eric denied that one had any duties to one's country; countries had obligations to their citizens, not the other way around. Indeed, one had a duty to flout one's country, to practice civil disobedience, if one disagreed with its policies. One must obey only good laws, and fight only good wars. —Hillary, borrowing from her father an opinion she at other times had repudiated, said that it was attitudes like his that were causing them to lose the war. "Nobody likes war. So if you send over a bunch of cameras and journalists to show the average person what the war is really like, of course they are going to object." —"What's your alternative? Censorship and propaganda? A mushroom electorate, kept in the dark and fed on shit?" —"The time for discussion is before the decision is made. Continuing the debate, protesting the decision, just hamstrings everybody and undermines all our efforts. You see it all the way down the line. Why can't we get a fucking cardiograph in this room?" —"I don't . remember any discussion. I don't remember being asked if we should go to war." —"It's called a representative democracy. They're not going to consult you personally on every matter. And anyway, it's too much to ask that every civilian be informed on every matter. Don't you think it's too much to ask every private here to search his or her heart every morning after reading the newspaper and to decide whether or not the war is still a just one? Isn't there enough pressure on them already? You'd have them held responsible for the president's decisions. You'd have them subjected to being spat on and called murderers when they come home." —Eric made violent clearing gestures, as if he were climbing through cobwebs. "The truth is that war *is* murder. Neither the generals nor the populace should ever be allowed to forget that. If we're going to bomb a village, we'd damn well better have a TV crew on location to interview the survivors and show the carnage. That'll keep us from making the decision lightly. And if soldiers are spat on as murderers, they'll be damn careful about choosing their wars. They *should* be spat on." —"You don't really believe that." —"Fucking right I do." —"All those privates you carouse with, all those men and women whose lives you've saved—they're all murderers?" —"Yep." He laughed bitterly. "No. I don't know. They're just a bunch of dumb kids." The crash of exploding mortars drowned out their conversation for several seconds. Automatically, they climbed down from their chairs and sat on the floor, their backs against the desk. "All I'm saying," he continued, "is that at least we have the decency, while fighting a pointless and unjust war, to hamstring ourselves. At least we're doing this fucking thing half-heartedly. You can say that much for us."

"And what about you?" she asked. —"What about me?" —"By your own logic, and given your scruples, shouldn't you be refusing to participate? Where's your civil disobedience?" —"I, Doctor," he said, taking a sip from his graduated cylinder, and retrieving the other and placing it on the floor beside Hillary, "I am in the process this very moment of incapacitating the occupying forces' medical personnel."

—She slid the glass back across the floor till it rested against his leg. "Shouldn't we get the fuck out? Aren't we contributing to the problem?" —"Aw, hell," said Eric. "We're here. We've made our decision. Now we've got to live with it."

The conversation had been vehement; now it grew lugubrious as they each acknowledged the validity of the opposing view. Hillary admitted that the war was immoral, that the eastern government was a repressive regime, and that his and her work here, making soldiers fit for more fighting, was indefensible. Eric replied that they were too close to the war to judge it objectively, and that their duty was to follow orders, and to save lives. "Besides," he said, "you can never know whether the private you patch up today will go on to kill more civilians, or fly home to their four kids tomorrow. You're no more responsible for their future crimes than you are for the reporter's future slander or the lawyer's future embezzlement. These people need medical attention. We give it to them. End of story."

Far from having its intended effect, Eric's thesis only made Hillary feel culpable for all of her patients' future crimes, and made her doubt, for the first time, the worthiness of the medical profession. She overlooked an abyss: what if doctors actually did more harm than good?

"We all do about as much harm as good," said Eric. "Even our good does harm, and our harm good. The trick is to do the best one can in the circumstances, and to enjoy oneself in the meantime." He climbed to his feet to elaborate on this theme, but quickly sat back down as an exploding shell rattled the walls and rained debris like hail on the metal roof. "The world is in as bad a state as it ever was—" —"Worse," said Hillary, and cited examples. —"All right, worse than it ever was, despite (I'll not say 'because of'!) hundreds, despite thousands of years of attempts to improve it. So the best any of us can do is take pleasure where we can find it." And he sipped whiskey. —"Hedonism," muttered

Hillary. —"No; utilitarianism: the greatest happiness for the greatest number. But you can't make others happy. So it's a moral imperative to enjoy *yourself*—that's the only certain way to increase the total happiness on the planet."

His argument mollified Hillary, less by its convincing-ness than its bravado. She admired the sanguine ingenuity with which he defended his hedonism; and she was touched, too, by his self-contradictory attempt to win her over to this hedonism, and to make her happy.

"If you, at this moment," he went on, "are healthy and well fed, it is a sin not to rejoice—even if, *especially* if, some-one somewhere else is miserable. If we don't get into the habit of enjoying ourselves now, while the world is a mess, we'll lose the capacity for it by the time the world is put in order." —She smiled. "I thought the world was never going to get put in order." —"Exactly!" he cried. They laughed at his inconsistency. "The bottom line being," he said, "that you should seize the day, *carpe felicitatem*, and have a god-damn drink with me, Doctor."

—"I think you drink too much, Doctor." In fact, she liked him better when he drank—he was friendlier—but she worried about his health. However, she did not have time to elaborate. —"On the contrary," he declared, "I drink too little. To prevent habituation, I should really drink more, less often, and less more often. But I'm weak; I like being fuddled too much."

Climbing onto his haunches, Eric delivered a paean to drunkenness, pacing and gesticulating as expansively as his posture allowed. Drunkenness was light; drunkenness was wisdom. Drunkenness allowed one to see the truth: that the world was a garden of delight teeming with plants and animals as lovely and various as colors, as dense and numerous as stars, as vivid and insubstantial as sparks, each one itself comprising a dense, vivid, and various universe of cells, every cell in turn a bogglingly fine-tuned society of organelles, which were themselves made of intelligent proteins, and so on. He spoke almost angrily, for the vision was one that he cherished, but seldom possessed.

Hillary, reluctant to acknowledge the beauty of any system revealed by inebriation, agreed that the human body was a complicated machine, but reminded him that that very complexity was a liability: the machine often malfunctioned, and was all too easily broken. "And frankly, I find the microscopic view rather depressing. All that intricate technology, and look what we do with it! Playing solitaire, collecting stamps, washing dishes, buying shoes. It's like using a supercomputer to hammer nails." She confessed that sometimes, listening to two ordinary people converse, so clumsily, so trivially, she was appalled to think of the sophistication and tireless heroism of, for example, their immune systems. "If we're galaxies, we're transmitting inanities in morse code across light-years of emptiness."

"But that's just what makes our communication so precious! Every conversation, however stupid, however inarticulate, is as momentous, as miraculous, as worthy of celebration and awe as interstellar contact with an alien intelligence. Maybe we do only touch at a point; but how amazing that we touch at all."

And he touched the tip of her knee with the tip of his finger; and to their mutual surprise, something nontrivial was communicated.

Private Bicyk entered, and Hillary scrambled to her feet. "Is everyone all right?" —"Huh? Oh, sure." —"What's the matter, soldier?" asked Eric, lifting himself onto a chair.

Private Bicyk had come to ask Doctor V. for pills, but was obscurely discomfited to find Doc Eric there. He sensed, first, that he was interrupting. He felt, too, that it would be immodest, even obscene, to be treated by two doctors at once. Besides this, he had steeled himself to confess to one person, and found his will now insufficient to face two.

And finally (though he was unconscious of this), he did not like the idea of revealing his weakness to a man whom he drank with, and whom he considered a friend.

His platoon had been picked to go on patrol that night; the route would take them through the minefield. Private Bicyk was terrified of mines. More sudden than mortars, more impersonal than sniper fire, they filled him with the kind of primal dread that he felt in dreams towards snakes and deep water. He was certain that, without some kind of nerve pill, he would be unable to cross the field this time; and the thought of delaying the patrol, of being physically unable to move while the others pushed and screamed at him, was more tormenting, because more tangible, than the thought of injury, pain, or death.

"Oh, nothing, really," he said. "I'll come back later." And, neither crouching nor hurrying as the sky retched another barrage of mortars, he walked back out the door.

When the explosions had dwindled to an intermittent roar, Eric, again seated on the floor, said, "You know, I think the privates find you a little remote." This was not quite true. Eric had noticed Private Bicyk's discomfiture, and was eager to attribute it to some cause other than himself. —"Remote?" —"You know: Distant. Unapproachable." —Hillary was aghast. "I certainly don't mean to be." She fell into a reverie of self-interrogation. Was it true? How had it happened? —Embarrassed by the effectiveness of his pretense, Eric now tried to restore levity. "It's only because you never drink with us," he joked. —Hillary looked at him beseechingly. "You know I'm not a prig. I can't drink when I'm on duty, and I'm always on duty." —"You don't need to be. Nothing ever happens." —"But if something did!" —"We'd evac them." —She shook her head; but she had already conceded much. Finally, by promising to stay sober himself, Eric persuaded her to come to the mess hall the following evening.

The soldiers were honored, and nonplussed, by her presence there. They were formal and solicitous, and pressed food and drink on her. Hillary was charmed by their kindliness, and though she drank little, she was soon pleasantly and unwittingly intoxicated. Eric acted as master of ceremonies, encouraging conversation and eliciting old stories and favorite anecdotes. But the privates' esteem for Doctor V. was an obstacle to intimacy; and some were constrained by the memory of infections or rashes she had treated. Some, like Private Bicyk (who had crossed the minefield the night before like everyone else), were abashed to think how close they had come to confessing to her their worst fears. And her own feelings of goodwill were not untainted by condescension. They were all so young, and so adorable—even the unhandsome ones. Every face seemed to glow with its own uniqueness; she felt that she could read in each one an eloquent expression of its owner's character, desires, and passing emotions. She enjoyed watching them and listening to them speak, but felt no inclination to confide in them. To Eric's chagrin, the talk repeatedly stalled; he began drinking surreptitiously. At last Private Maldau suggested they play a game.

There was an implicit consensus that the doctor would not care to gamble, so card games were ruled out. With the enthusiasm of nostalgia, the privates named different games they had played as children: Mumblety-peg, Lapjack, Hot Buttered Beans, Mother May I, Follow the Leader, Bloody Murder; but the only game they all knew was Hide and Seek. Private Patello was elected to be "it," because his resentment could be relied on. "Aw, fuck you guys," he whined, and everybody laughed. The ammunition shed was chosen as safehouse, the entire base was ruled in-bounds, and Private Patello began counting down from one hundred. Everyone scattered.

Hillary crossed the base briskly and squeezed between a concrete revetment and the wall of the motor pool. Someone was revving an engine inside; she could not hear

Patello's count. Then the noise ceased. She listened intently, but could hear only the wind rattling an aluminum roof panel and the chirring of cicadas in the tall trees beyond the perimeter fence. The evening was warm, the air soft, the sky a lingering lilac. A tiny beetle with legs like wire brushes clambered onto her left index knuckle, then seemed to pause to catch its breath. She realized that she was holding her own breath, and let it out slowly, stirring the dust between her fingers. Her face felt strange. She was smiling.

Eric found her at last, and joined her noiselessly, crawling forward on his belly till their foreheads almost touched. "Where is he?" she whispered. He mouthed the words: "He's coming," and every muscle in her body tensed, making her feel like one solid unit of poised readiness.

Eric scrutinized her face in the darkness with an attentiveness bordering on anxiety, as if he were memorizing an escape plan. He too was smiling, but painfully. His only thought was one recurring word: "Fuck. Fuck. Fuck."

Then from the woods, closer than either of them had ever heard it, came the familiar *fwump, fwump, fwump* of mortars being fired, followed a few seconds later by the screaming falling shells, and then all around them the shuddering explosions. They did not have to move to take cover, and this novelty made them feel absurdly safe, as if all the world were a hammock cradling them. Eric stopped worrying that he would have to kiss her, and simply lay there, riding the earth like a raft downstream. And Hillary's happiness was so great that it frightened her; suddenly she felt sick and dizzy and disgusted. Her imagination provided a reason: someone was hurt, and she could not help them, because they could not find her! And she had been drinking, and could not do her job properly. Doctor Latroussaine too had been drinking, she knew, but this only made her angrier at herself: she had smelled whiskey on his breath, and ignored it. The great hammock was now a suffocating cage. She climbed to her feet, and, oblivious of the bombardment, which twice threw her to her hands and knees, hurried to the medical hut. There she sat on the floor, writhing with dismay and willing herself sober, and awaited the casualties.

In fact, no one was hurt; the shelling ended, and the game continued. Eric, assuming that she had made a bold dash for the safehouse, was filled with admiration. When finally he realized that she had simply quit, he made excuses for her, then for himself, and retired to his bunk and stared for hours at the meaningless code of Pascal.

THE NEXT DAY, Hillary visited the village of Pastor's Hill— something that none of the soldiers would have done alone, never mind unarmed, for the village was known to be held by rebels. Eric was organizing a rescue party when she returned in the late afternoon, carrying a somewhat depleted first-aid kit. He harangued her for taking unnecessary risks, and she harangued him, and, by extension, all the mainland forces, for ignoring the plight of the local populace.

"If we only treat our own people, we're not a medical service, we're a military one. Besides, I thought part of our mandate here was to win the islanders over to our side." —Eric spluttered, able to sense but not to identify the contradiction in these two statements. "Look, you can't just hand out meds to a partisan village. That *is* a military act." —"I saw no evidence of any allegiance to the partisans." —"They aren't going to stand up and announce their allegiance!" —"No, but we can't assume every islander is a rebel, either. Most of these people just want to be left alone—by both sides." —Eric sighed and rubbed his eyes. He admitted that most islanders were probably nonpartisan, but he could not see how a unilateral withdrawal would benefit anyone but the partisans. "The more we leave them alone, the less the rebels will." —But Hillary was not, at the moment, advocating a withdrawal, or even addressing the larger morality of the war. She granted him that most of the locals probably *were* partisan, but that was no reason to deny them medical attention. "We do our job. End of story."

She argued the more forcefully for the abstract good, because the specific good was in this case somewhat hazy. That day, she had been welcomed warmly enough into several homes, but none of the villagers would admit to any ailment more severe than psoriasis. Nor did they seem to be suffering from malnutrition: cauldrons of stew bubbled in many kitchens, and the larders she caught glimpses into were crammed with canned goods. She thus felt some misgivings when Doctor Latroussaine finally capitulated. The next day, with Major Lopez's authorization and Major Jenkman's blessing, Hillary returned to Pastor's Hill in a jeep, accompanied by Doctor Latroussaine and three jumpy privates acting as bodyguards, among them Private Bicyk.

To her relief, the village bore a very different aspect twenty-four hours later. Now no food of any kind was in evidence, and all the villagers, even the children, complained of headaches and stomachaches, fevers and chills, insomnia and fatigue. The change was puzzling, but too gratifying to analyze. She supposed that they had been shy, and that now they trusted her. She and Doctor Latroussaine did what little they could with what supplies they had. They swabbed and sterilized; they palpated and massaged; they auscultated; they bandaged. They dispensed salt tablets and their least expired metronidazole pills. Mostly they took notes and made plans to return, to see if the oddly elusive symptoms persisted.

In fact, the villagers were shamming. The local partisan militia—that is, all the boys and most of the girls aged fifteen to twenty-five—had instructed their parents, grandparents, and younger siblings to defraud the mainland doctor of as much food and pharmaceuticals as possible, which could then be sold back to the mainlanders stationed or on leave in the cities. In the same way, partisans across the island had found it more profitable to sell their produce, dairy, and meat than to eat it—the occupying forces' need for these things being great, and their dollar being worth so much more than the island currency. And the partisans, who were young and zealous, happily subsisted on canned rations—which were for them, indeed, a delicacy, because foreign and machine-produced. Besides, they could always raid a nonpartisan town if they wanted to eat, say, a carrot. (Although, to be sure, this practice had a discouraging effect on the farmers, and had helped contribute to the food shortages—which, happily, raised the prices of what remained.)

Mrs. Karla Zapolitz refused to participate any longer in this scheme. She sensed that her grandsons, profiting by the presence of the very army that their rebellion had drawn here, had no intention of ever allowing the war to end. But she, for one, was fed up with the guns, the bombs, and the deaths. With heroic defiance, she told the doctors that there was nothing in the world wrong with her. "I am perfectly healthy!" she shouted out the window. "And am not the least bit hungry!"

To most of the thirty young partisans in hiding around her house, this declaration seemed merely odd; but it filled one young man with consternation and anger. Her grandson, First Cadet Ice Sword, who was crouched just outside the window, recognized her defiance, and realized that she was betraying the militia's presence to the enemy. She was a traitor to the rebellion. He hesitated only a moment.

Everyone inside the house—Hillary, Eric, Private Bicyk, Private Talomey, and Mrs. Zapolitz—watched the grenade roll on the floor in diminishing circles until it came to a stop. Then Private Bicyk threw himself on it.

Still no one else moved. Slowly the grimace on Private Bicyk's face slackened; eventually he opened his eyes. The grenade was a dud.

Private Talomey took charge. He shouted to Private Allgood, posted outside the door, that they were under attack; he shrugged the radio off his back onto the table and began tuning it; he advised the doctors and Mrs. Zapolitz to get low and out of sight; and he told Private Bicyk to toss the fucking grenade back out the fucking window already. This was done—and instantly there came a tearing burst of semi-automatic fire. The militia, who had not been expecting three soldiers and a jeep, were jumpy too. Bullets raked across the walls of the house; a porcelain jug in the kitchen exploded. Private Allgood somersaulted inside, and everyone got low and out of sight. Mrs. Zapolitz muttered phrases of amazement and disgust to herself. Eric and Hillary exchanged a glance, each finding comfort in what they took to be the other's look of calm reassurance. Meanwhile, Private Bicyk squirmed on the floor in a puddle of blood. He had been hit.

The gunfire ended as abruptly as it had begun. Voices outside screamed questions, accusations, and orders. Hunched over Private Bicyk, Hillary and Eric worked obliviously, cutting away the collar of his uniform and stanching the blood that poured from the hole behind his ear while simultaneously trying to determine the extent of the wound. —"Don't see an exit, and I don't see the projectile." —"Looks small caliber, at least." —"But it could have got anywhere." —"Doesn't seem to have interfered with his airway. Give me a deep breath, private." But Private Bicyk wouldn't open his mouth. "Through your nose. Excellent." —"You're going to be all right, soldier." —"How long till we can get an evac helicopter in here, Private Talomey?" —Private Talomey swore, slammed down the radio headset, and immediately picked it up again to resume negotiations. "The fuckers say they can't land with the rug this hot." —Private Allgood, with one eye above the windowsill, said, "I'd say the rug has cooled down some."

In fact, the militia, expecting retaliation, had already retreated to the woods, leaving the village to its fate. They all rebuked one another for starting a firefight so close to home; but their bitterness was alleviated by the romantic prospect of building a new community in the treetops, or underground.

Private Talomey said, "What they really mean is they won't drop into a partisan village. The best they can do is Hill 70." —Hillary objected, "That's halfway back to base!" —"We'll have to run for the jeep," said Private Allgood. "Can he move?" —"Ask him," said Eric, pressure-dressing the wound. —Private Bicyk, by narrowing his eyes and clenching his jaw, seemed to nod.

"Bullshit," said Hillary. "Can't we get an ambulance out here?" —"Driver shortage," shrugged Private Talomey. —"Bullshit. I am going to shit down someone's throat for this." But she helped Eric get Private Bicyk to his feet, and together they supported him as far as the door. Then, at Private Allgood's signal, they staggered from the house—leaving Mrs. Zapolitz to fend for herself. Half an hour later, still grumbling, she stood, dusted herself off, and surveyed the damage desolately.

In the jeep, Hillary kneeled next to Private Bicyk, who lay on the back seat. Eric sat in the front, wedged between Private Talomey, who drove, and Private Allgood, who aimed his rifle at the trees hurtling past.

"We don't necessarily need to stop," said Hillary tentatively. —"What do you mean?" —"At Hill 70. We can just keep going, back to base." —Eric turned around; his eyes grew wide with understanding. "Oh, no. No, no. This soldier needs to be medevacked. He needs blood and fluids, and a full exploration of the wound and a radiograph to rule out hematoma, and—" —"We've got ultrasound, and we've got two units of packed red cells, which will surely tide us over till we can tap the walking bank." By this she meant that they could draw blood from other soldiers—the 'walking blood bank.' —"How on earth are we supposed to do a crossmatch?," Eric asked disingenuously. —"White tile method." She went on quickly: "What if there's a backlog at Poplar Junction? He's going to sit in the triage tent for an hour. Meanwhile, we could be debriding and exploring and repairing. If we find nerve trauma or hematoma, which I don't think we will, we can still call in the medevac, and our chart'll push him to the front of the queue." —Eric chewed his lip. "We don't have the resources they have." —"But we've got the time and the personnel, which they may not have."

The helicopter came into view. "What are we doing?" asked Private Talomey. "Stopping or going?"

"Come on, Doctor." Hillary's eyes said what she did not: that this was her fault.

"I'd feel a lot better," Eric murmured, "if we knew the trajectory of that projectile."

"Oh, we know that," she said. Private Bicyk, who was afraid of crying out, was grinding the bullet between his teeth.

"Stopping or going, Doc?"

"Going," Eric sighed. "Fast."

OVER THE DAYS that followed, all of Hillary's energy, anxiety, and compassion found an outlet in Private Bicyk. She confined him to bed and prohibited him from trying to speak until his wound had fully healed; and his mute immobility made him seem as helpless and needy as an infant. Twice daily she redressed his wound (which, aside from a shattered tooth, was not serious); she sponged and shaved him; she emptied his bedpan; she improvised a feeding tube from a nasal trumpet and an infusion pump, with which she sent a continuous diet of mashed rice, potatoes, and bananas directly into his stomach; and she gave him morphine for his pain. She slept on a gurney in the medical tent to be near him at night.

Eric took over her neglected duties—treating the cuts, abrasions, ulcers, and sexually transmitted infections that appeared sporadically on the base. He was still left with much free time, which he spent less often in the mess, and more often with Hillary at Private Bicyk's bedside.

Together they soothed and entertained the patient with tales, riddles, and simple children's games; occasionally Eric read a few pages of Pascal. "It's not necessary to have a very elevated soul to realize that there is no true and solid satisfaction here, that all our pleasures are only vanity, that all our evils are infinite, and that in the end death, which menaces us at every instant, must inevitably, in a few years, place us under the horrible necessity of being either eternally born, or eternally unhappy." Finding some of these passages rather bleak, Hillary asked Eric to refrain from translating them.

But mostly the doctors gave Private Bicyk lessons—for they believed that conversation was salubrious, and they found it easier to talk about biology, chemistry, and physics than about themselves. Since he could not tell them what he already knew, nothing was extraneous. Every object around them, every spoken word, every invoked concept suggested new topics for their lectures. One would tell him everything they knew, everything they could remember, about spiders; or glass; or dust; or the water cycle; or white blood cells; or static electricity; or carpentry; or harmonics; while the other, acting on Private Bicyk's behalf, would play the role of naive interviewer, posing the endless series of "why" and "how" questions that are the despair of so many overtaxed parents. But Eric and Hillary were not overtaxed, and their unhurried investigations, rather than leading to frustration or annoyance, ended only in wonder and delight. They looked at everything with the fresh, inquisitive intensity of children, and admired everything with the adult's capacity for understanding and awe. They imagined that they were seeing the world through Private Bicyk's unclouded eyes, and that they had him to thank for this vision of glory.

But in fact, when Bicyk was not voluptuously stupefied by morphine, he was alternately bored and mortified. He was appalled at having so much attention paid him, and his shame was only aggravated when his friends came to visit. He could not demonstrate his strength or his stoicism while lying speechless in bed, and his injury was not horrible enough to constitute its own heroism; so he resorted to implying—from his bearing, or his gaze—that he was in a great deal of pain, which he was withstanding manfully. Doctor V. detected these hints more readily than his fellow soldiers, however, and was always quick to administer another dose of painkillers—thus depriving him of both the means and the desire to continue miming distress.

On the day that Captain Augello's replacement finally arrived, Eric and Hillary took Private Bicyk for a walk around the base. They had a wheelchair, so they used it. This humiliation was more than Private Bicyk cared to bear; he allowed Hillary to conclude that his tooth was hurting him. With the morphine in his body, he was content to be rolled around like a well-fed baby in a pram, absorbing sunshine and oxygen. It had rained heavily the day before, and the slimy puddles lying everywhere prompted Hillary to tell him all about freshwater algae.

"Most of them are too small for us to see individually, and in a mass they often just look like green scum. But when you view them under a microscope, you discover that there are actually more different kinds than there are species of plants in a rainforest. The algae are plants, too, of course—at least, they convert sunlight directly into nutrition like plants do—but some of them swim around like little fish. They're as varied and colorful as tropical fish, too. Even the single-celled ones come in dozens of shapes and sizes. Some are spherical, some long like needles, some crescent shaped; some are like balloons, some like canoes, others like jellyfish, others just blobs; some are smooth, some spiny; some look like S's, or C's, or J's; some are triangular, some cubical, and some are perfect pentagons. And sometimes they get together in colonies, or many-celled bodies, which in turn can take the form of discs, or globes, or sheets, or rods, or cogwheels, or even branched filaments, or broad leaflike fronds. Unlike plants, though, they don't actually have leaves, or distinct stems, or even proper roots. And they don't grow fruit, and they don't have seeds!" —"How do they reproduce?" asked Eric. —"All kinds of ways. Sometimes they just split in two. Sometimes two cells come together to make new cells. Some give off spores, which are tougher and simpler than seeds, and can survive indefinitely—through freezing cold, or drought, or even fire. There are spores everywhere, which is why a rain puddle that wasn't there yesterday can be flourishing with life today. And some spores can swim—even those of certain stationary algae. Imagine if an apple tree dropped apples that could walk!"

But Private Bicyk, who was an amateur photographer back home, was more interested in the way the reflection of the sun shrank and expanded on the rippling surface of one puddle, but without growing brighter or dimmer. He realized that the sunlight was falling equally on every part of the puddle, indeed on every inch of the earth, and that with just the right combination of waves, the entire ocean could become a blinding spotlight. "The light's nice," he murmured, and gestured at the puddle. Immediately, Doc Eric launched into a lesson on the physical properties of color.

"The funny thing about color," Eric concluded, "is that it's what's *rejected*. The redness of the rose is due to the fact that the petals absorb blue and yellow frequencies of light radiation, but can do nothing with red. Red gets reflected, and that's what reaches our eyes." —"So," said Hillary, "it's almost like what we *see* is the opposite of what really *is?*" —"Exactly!" And, searching for a dramatic illustration, he became somewhat fanciful: "Take the darkness of the night sky, the blackness of deep space. It's actually brimming with sunlight; a rainbow shower of electromagnetic waves pours through it constantly. But nothing stops it, nothing deflects it—except occasionally a planet, or a comet, or the moon."

Private Bicyk smiled and nodded, hearing in this description a beautiful echo of his own unexpressed idea.

BUZZING OF THE INTERCOM, followed by knocking at the door. Two janitors, a man and a woman, enter. Noise from the factory floor while the door is open.

Male janitor. "Ain't here."

Female janitor. "Good. Maybe we'll get done on time for a change."

They relax, taking possession of the room. It is a plush office, with a view of the factory's vast ceiling through the window.

Male janitor. "I don't mind overtime."

Female janitor. "A born janitor, all right."

Male janitor. "What's that supposed to mean? Don't muss those papers."

She shifts some papers on the desk. "A born slave."

Male janitor. "I just happen to like getting paid time and a half's all."

She sits in the chair behind the desk. "They throw you some scraps, you forget you're a dog."

Male janitor. "Aw, don't start. Janitor's a good clean job. —You know what I mean."

Female janitor, reading a page. "Seven thousand dollars for transportation!"

Male janitor. "Transportation of what?"

Female janitor. "How should I know? Of him, probably. Him and his secretary. All over God knows where and back again."

Male janitor, sitting at the conference table. "Boss gotta travel, I guess."

Female janitor. "Ever hear of a telephone?"

Male janitor. "What do you think it's like, being boss? Running meetings. Organizing things. Bossing."

Female janitor. "Degrading. Shouldn't even be offices like this. All this for one person!"

Male janitor. "Aw. I think'd be fun."

Female janitor. "Seven thousand dollars." She stands, covertly replacing the papers. "I'll tell you one thing you don't know. This might be the last time I ever clean this office."

He stands and begins tidying and dusting. "I don't see you cleaning it now."

Female janitor. "And I do know what you mean: you mean it's honest, necessary work. Like farming, and cooking, and teaching, and building—and cleaning. So how come everyone looks down on us?"

Male janitor. "Aw, don't start."

Female janitor. "You're part the problem: a dog who wants to be master. A slave who only wants his own slaves. Your hope's what fuels the whole apparatus. When you gonna wake up? We need to get rid of slaves and masters and dogs and bosses altogether."

Male janitor. "You sound like a churchman." Laughs. "You sound just like a Church man."

Female janitor. "At least Matheson Church and the union's willing to fight for our rights."

Male janitor. "Bite for 'em, you mean—the hand that feeds."

Female janitor. "And you sound just like Babcock. At least coming from him it's self-preservation. You, you lick the foot that kicks you. A foot-licking lackey, that's what you are."

Male janitor. "I ain't gonna let you rile me up."

Female janitor. "Exactly your problem."

Male janitor. "I ain't gonna get riled up. It ain't healthy."

Female janitor. "Working in these conditions—"

Male janitor. "I don't know if your union's gonna do any good, or it's just gonna get us all fired. One thing I do know. Getting riled up ain't healthy for a life. Since the union came in, you all look sicker and unhappier. And uglier."

Sid Babcock enters. The janitors start.

Sid. "You can leave."

Female janitor. "Yes, sir."

Male janitor. "Should we come back, or—"

Sid. "Straightaway! There's a shareholders' meeting begins in five minutes!"

Male janitor. "Yes, sir."

Sid. "Take the garbage at least!"

Female janitor. "Yes, sir." They take the garbage and go out.

Sid paces, muttering and gesturing. He uses the intercom on the desk.

Receptionist. "Yes?"

Sid. "Can you bring me the recentest quarterlies, please?"

Receptionist. "Yes, sir."

Sid. "Oh, forget it, I've got 'em."

Receptionist. "All right."

He flips through papers, then again uses the intercom. "Get me Pensilby."

Receptionist. "Just a second." Pause. "Uh, she's not at her desk at the moment."

Sid. "Where in hell is she at?"

Receptionist, after a pause. "I'm not sure, sir."

Sid. "Inexcusable." He disengages, then again engages the intercom. "Daize is around, I suppose? There's a couple of things that I'd like to review with her. Well? Are you there?" There is no answer. "Why the hell in the name of the holy today is this happening here?" He goes to the door and throws it open. "Is there anyone working today? Where is Daize?"

Daize Glied enters, papers in hand. "Sid?"

Sid. "Close the door. Did you finish the list?"

She hands him a sheet of paper. "Here are the thirty-one names."

He glances at it. "Which is what we decided?"

Daize. "Other things equal, that brings us by year-end to ten and a quarter."

Sid. "All our youngest employees?"

Daize. "Leaving out those with dependents."

Sid. "Is Renfrento not union?"

Daize. "So is Parhada, and others. We don't want to look like we're playing at favorites."

Sid. "Take them off. We don't need to give Church an excuse to start rousing the rabble again. And besides, our apparent collusion with them will make them seem complicit with us in the layoffs. With luck, we discredit 'em." He hands the paper back, and watches over Daize's shoulder as she sits at the conference table, making changes. "Good. Then tomorrow we'll hand out the first of the slips at the afternoon shift-change. On their way out the gate."

Daize. "Might it be better to mail them?"

Sid. "Well, perhaps. I suppose if they're all in one place when receiving the news, there's increased chance of trouble. We'll deliver them during the day. We can use the new courier service."

Daize. "Sure."

Sid. "Then that's everything now."

Daize begins to stand.

Sid gestures for her to remain seated. "You can stay for the meeting. For taking the minutes." He looks at his watch and begins pacing again. "I won't bend over backwards to kiss owner ass for one tenth a percent. We'll reach ten twenty-five by year-end. They should know the ordeal that we've had. Even getting these bums to all work a full day has been, lately, a feat. For the union I need not apologize. Maybe it seems a concession, but it cost us no money. And now they just tiff with themselves. If they can't get a raise, it's not me, it's the union to blame. I perhaps should myself have imposed it: that haven of sinecure; nest of red tape and committees fissiparous; creep-hole of delegates, stewards, and cronies! By God, I detest them, the unions! Their members deserve them, the knobs. To be asking for raises, with sales low as this? Their delusion's astoundingly deep. Course, the owners, those glorified land-lords, are worse. They want ten and a quarter percent, while still more competition from all the world over, obtuse to the industry's glut, yet comes slithering in every month. I can't *give* the shit hardly away. My old buyers are ordering less, and they ask me for discounts on top. And those pinchfart suppliers, and the shipping consortiums, they live in the same world of dreams, renegotiate contracts at twice what inflation is. We have accomplished no less than a miracle, all things considered. So no, I won't grovel, nor will I abase myself; no, not for tenths of percentages. Ten twenty-five! We did less than that last year."

Daize. "Less overall, and in any one quarter."

Sid. "They perhaps will opine that I earlier should have resorted to layoffs. But those are my kin, in a manner of speaking; my people. I feel I'm responsible for 'em. They've some of 'em been with the company longer than my twenty years. Unashamed, I admit that I care. If mistake I have made, it's I've been insufficiently cruel. I'm old-fashioned—outmoded, perhaps. If I'm hard as a boss, if my thumps I don't curb, if my words I don't blunt, it's because I know people improve under pressure. But deep in my heart, I'm a softy. A director directs, but he also protects his employees. Commanders command, but they don't send their men to their deaths for no reason. Dismiss me, court-martial me, over a tenth a percent, if you must. I'd take positive pride in so gross an injustice; I'd wallow for years; I could gnaw on the marrowy bone of my martyrdom through to my dotage, with relish. So fuck 'em. I care not one shred what they think. They know nothing about how to superintend. They can suck out the shit from my ass. Am I right?" The intercom buzzes. "Right; all right. Thanks, Daize." He answers the intercom. "Yes?"

Receptionist. "Ms. Ottavia Farr-Mp, the shareholders' representative, is here for the meeting, sir."

Sid. "Send her in, by all means." To Daize. "You can stay; take the minutes."

Daize. "Sure."

The receptionist opens the door for Ottavia Farr-Mp, who enters.

Ottavia. "Good afternoon. Well?"

Sid laughs. "It's a pleasure to see you again, Miz Farr-Mp. You remember Daize Glied . . ."

Ottavia. "I'm sure that I must."

Daize. "How do you do."

Ottavia sits at the head of the conference table. "If you're quite ready."

Sid. "Well, perhaps we should wait just a few minutes more till the others arrive."

Ottavia. "This is everyone."

Sid. "Were the owners not able to come, then?"

Ottavia. "They sent me; I'm their representative. I speak for them all."

Sid sits. "And Rebecka, and Tonio, and Glen—how've they been?"

Ottavia. "If their personal well-being is what you refer to, it's no business of mine, and still less of yours. If their financial well-being, it is no business of yours, except insofar as it pertains to this factory, which is what we're here to discuss, starting now, or so I do hope."

The intercom buzzes.

Sid. "But of course. Just one moment, please." He crosses to the desk and answers. "Yes?"

Receptionist. "Matheson Church and some others here to see you, sir."

Sid. "We're just now in the midst of the shareholders' meeting. They can wait till tomorrow."

Receptionist. "Yes, sir."

Sid. "No more calls, interruptions, or visitors, please."

Receptionist. "All right."

Sid returns to the table. "My apologies."

Ottavia. "Now perhaps we can with the pleasantries dispense, and proceed to matters fiscal." She withdraws a page from a folder. "Ten point sixteen net percent profit is point zero nine net percent short."

Sid. "I'll explain."

Ottavia. "The figure alone speaks with adequate eloquence, thank you. I'm not here to chide you, or to shrive you. I'm no shareholder, but I doubt that they have any interest in explanations or in excuses. I'm here to tell you— it won't take long—that you've done yourself a disservice. Ten and a quarter was a waymark only, not a destination. You have neglected it to your own cost. You'll find it harder now to reach ten and a half by year-end."

Sid. "And a half!"

Ottavia. "Correct, by year-end. That is, and has been, the shareholders' goal."

Daize. "In the fourth quarter, you mean?"

Ottavia. "Most certainly not. For the total year."

Sid. "That's impossible."

Ottavia. "The shareholders, I gather, believe it to be possible. In any case, your failure to reach it will not prove that it wasn't; it only will prove that *you* weren't able to do it."

Sid. "It's undoable. No one could do it. This product, this equipment, this staff! If you'd any idea what we've struggled with lately—"

Ottavia. "I'm not remotely even curious. It is you who is responsible for operational considerations; it's what you're paid for. It bores me even to say this out loud. Do your job, or the shareholders appoint somebody who will. That's all there's to it." She closes the folder, leaving the paper on the table.

Sid. "Let me get this thing straight. You are threatening me with replacement . . ." The intercom buzzes. "Goddamn it." Sid crosses to the desk.

Ottavia. "It's not a threat, just a statement of fact."

Sid speaks into the intercom. "Wha'd I say? Hold my calls! We're'n the middle of this."

Ottavia. "We can end it here."

Sid. "Now just hold on a minute or two. I have been with this company twenty-plus years, I have built from the ground up this factory; now you intend to replace me because some fantastical margin which can never be met won't be met?"

Ottavia. "You don't understand; communication only flows one way between you and me. I'm the shareholders' representative to you, and not your representative to the shareholders. Talking to me is a waste of your breath. Hearing you's a waste of my attention. As for the product, we know of this-size factories reaching eleven point five."

Sid. "You don't surely mean this year."

Ottavia crosses to the door. "This year, this world, this industry, this life. Though it's not my job to say so, you should try to do better."

Sid. "But why didn't they say to begin with that ten and a half was the goal?"

Ottavia. "I'm sure I don't know. But if you would like a piece of advice, which comes not from the shareholders, but from me as a private individual, you might consider making a habit of exceeding the expectations you're given, instead of underperforming, making excuses, and hoping to be forgiven, like a schoolboy who shirks as much homework as he dares. Goodbye, and see you again in six months."

As she opens the door, Matheson Church, Lea Pensilby, the receptionist, the female janitor (still holding a bag of garbage), and others stumble into the doorway.

Sid. "If you'd wait just a minute . . . Oh, out of her way, you damn fools!"

Ottavia. "Excuse me. Goodbye." Ottavia exits.

Sid. "Now you all can get out of my office."

Matheson. "We have some things to say first, Mister Babcock."

Sid. "You can say them tomorrow. The morning. Now buzz."

He pushes them out the door and closes it. He and Daize exchange a look. Knocking at the door.

Sid. "For the sake of the holy!" He yanks the door open. "The hell do you want?"

Matheson. "We've come to say the union membership's decided that the time has come for us to take job action—to proceed to strike."

Sid. "You're not serious."

Lea. "If demands aren't met. We've come to read you our demands first."

Matheson. "We've suffered long enough indignity, abuse, and inequality. A dawn begins to newly rise; we workers, these, the people, are its flaming harbinger—the sun's first gaudy, not-yet-scorching rays. But full ungentle noon will straight succeed this soft matutinal diplomacy, if this time you don't give us what we want."

Lea. "Matheson, just read 'im the demands now."

Sid, to Lea and the receptionist. "It's not possible; tell me that *you* haven't joined."

Lea. "We are representing sixty-seven—sixty-eight percent of clerical, of janitorial, and support staff."

The receptionist nods.

Janitor. "That's right."

Sid. "It's outrageous to me. What complaint in the world could you possibly have?" To Matheson. "As for you, I allowed you your union, and this is the way I'm repaid?"

Matheson. "You gave us nothing. Unions form, they aren't bestowed. They coalesce, self-organized. They swell up from the poisoned ground, don't drop from out the toxic sky. They're nature's force, immunological reactions to oppressiveness. We made the union from ourselves, we made ourselves the union. No one could have stopped us—least of any, you."

Sid. "I most certainly could've!"

Matheson. "The tide has turned, and leaves exposed what was submerged: our power. History is on our side. Inexorable gravity—"

Lea. "You permitted them to form a union, but what good is it? Negotiations stall. Two months already passed, and still no closer to a contract. Small surprise, when you refuse their each and every asking."

Sid. "I refuse them because they're ridiculous, Lea."

Lea. "Oh, just read 'im the demands already."

Matheson consults a piece of paper. "The first of our demands is this. We ask—insist—that management and foremen will begin to treat us with respect."

Sid groans. "And just how are you measuring that?"

Matheson. "From this point on, they'll tell us what needs doing, not what to do. Our supervisors will assist, and guide, and supervise, not spy, and reprimand, and punish. They will treat us not like children, but like colleagues. And for every word correcting us, we want two words of praise. They will address us by our first names. As for us, we find the *sir*s and *ma'am*s demeaning, and we will not use them anymore. The same applies to all those deferential honorifics: *Miz*, and *Missus, Mister*. We will smile when we are smiled at, or we feel like smiling, not on your command. We'll be allowed to go to toilet as the need arises, too."

Sid. "It's a line of assembly! It cannot be stopped for a piss!"

Lea. "Forewomen and foremen can cover for 'em."

Matheson. "Respect. That's first, our item number one."

Sid. "Is this really your goal with the union? To make of politeness a law? And to legislate craps?"

Lea. "Go on, Matheson."

Sid. "Oh, continue, I beg."

Matheson. "Demand the second is democracy. From now on, every worker's thoughts, ideas, opinions, views should be solicited on every matter bearing on our work environment, production quality, our work hours, hiring, firing, benefits and holidays, and company direction . . ."

Sid. "You, in short, want to manage the place by yourselves."

Lea. "No. Discussion. Input. Contribution. Take into account our attitudes, and give consideration to our judgements."

Matheson. "We want an end to hierarchy, want decisions made collectively. There's not an inessential person here; we each have part to play, and·each unique perspective. We want to see this fact substantified in votes for every man and woman. No pronunciamentos, edicts, or decrees, but surveys, referenda, plebiscites, and factory-wide consultation shall henceforth determine our directive bulk."

Sid. "So the helmsman should ask of the cooks in the galley and the engine-room stokers what way he should steer."

Matheson. "Allowing for analogy, why not? We're all upon the selfsame ship, which not one knot of speed achieves, indeed, which naught—N-A-U-G-H-T—that's nothing—yes, which nautically *naught* achieves without the all of us aboard. Why shouldn't we have all some say about the course we plot?"

Sid. "There was never a ship in a mutinous state that so much as left port. And desist with the tub-thumping demagogue's word-pyrotechnics. You're not on the soapbox."

Matheson. "My righteous indignation is a fuel that feeds my fiery eloquence. Could I control me, modulate me, bowdlerize or summarize me, I would be revealed the panderer you paint me. All unchecked, uncheckable, my logorrheic rage escapes me left and right, at night or day, at work or play, in public or alone. So long as our demands remain unmet, I'll vomit speech like birds at dawn belch song."

The others have come further into the office. The receptionist wipes dust from a framed certificate. The janitor peers at the sheet of paper on the table. Daize snatches it away.

Sid. "Keep your hands to yourselves! This is my office still!" To Matheson. "So it's mutiny, anarchy, chaos you want; duly noted. Now finish your spiel and be done."

Matheson. "A common misconception. Anarchy's not lawlessness. It's only bosslessness. We're done with rulers, masters, potentates . . ."

Sid. "But you cannot have rules without rulers! You need to have orders for order! And men do no work without foremen! The boss, like adversity, brings out the best in employees. For each self-propeled, independent, industrious worker, there's ten would-be shirkers—those scrimshanking, goldbricking, dog-fucking, featherbed slobs you must constantly watch, and who need to be goaded, and threatened, and yes, sometimes punished. —Your speechification infects me, goddamn you."

Matheson. "It's there you're wrong. When freed from tyranny—"

Sid guffaws. "When from tyranny freed!"

Matheson. "The worker, when from their oppression freed, does, like a cramped and pallid flower from which a stone's been lifted, stretch and grow towards the sky in natural, productive self-expansion. What makes work work? Outside force imposed—it may be duty, hunger, fear— that makes work necessary. Do but lift that pressure, render optional what was obligatory, and your work becomes your play—and no one ever tired of play. We shall work better, harder, for sheer joy, when work's a choice and not an odious chore."

Sid. "You're deluded! You really think anyone comes for their shift if they don't need the money? What keeps the world turning's not actualization of selves, but the hunger of stomachs."

Janitor. "Next thing, he'll say he's doing us all a favor keeping us hungry."

Sid. "It's a factory, not the soul's playground or gym. I've no clue why I even am listening to this."

Matheson. "Because you must. Our fourth demand is noise reduction."

Lea. "Third. You missed the third demand."

Sid. "Two's enough. I'll begin by reducing *your* noise. You can vacate my office now. Out! I will talk to you all—or to three, at the most—in the morning."

Matheson. "We're not yet done. You know what happens if we leave."

Receptionist. "Mr. Babcock . . ."

Janitor. "It's a job action."

Sid. "I'm not calling a vote here! Vamoose!"

Matheson, to Lea. "Let's show him."

Sid. "No one listens and everyone talks. Noise! Noise! Noise! That's democracy for you. If any of you'd ever served on committees, or sat on a board of directors, you'd know that it's noise, not decision, that's collectively made. Because everyone speaks, no one hears, and the loudest shouts carry the day. Yes, democracy's only disorganization. What the hell are you doing?"

Lea has slid open the window. Noise from the shop floor. Matheson steps to the window.

Matheson. "Maltreated, unappreciated drones! You toiling, abject, subjugated throng! Suppressed by equals, and by lesser men surpassed, you slaves in all but name, arise!

Defy! Throw off the half your shackles, so to show it can be done—to show they're made of mind, not steel!"

He makes a grand slicing motion. Some of the machinery grinds and clatters to a stop.

Sid. "What the fuck have you done? Ignoramuses! Fools!"

Lea. "That's reminder why you're listening to us: because our strike is really ready."

Sid. "It's been years those machines were last stopped."

Matheson slides the window shut. "We haven't finished."

Janitor, to the receptionist. "Straight hot how! We're just getting started."

Sid, muttering. "Pack of Luddites. Benighted, ungrateful, uncaring . . ."

Lea. "Read the rest."

Matheson. "Our third demand is safety."

Sid. "What on earth here's unsafe?"

Lea. "Everything!"

Matheson. "I'll itemize. The ceiling fans should be replaced. Last week, in the propellant room, a blade fell, nearly killing Radar Houghpt."

Sid. "Was he wearing his helmet?"

Matheson. "We want to see installed some cages round annealers, guardrails round conveyor belts, and by the gangway, barriers, before an arm is lost, or someone's burned, or falls and breaks their neck. The oldest crimpers, too, are operating hot, which yet'll cause autoignition, costing eyes—or lives."

Sid. "I need help understanding. You're saying you want to be treated like adults, but still you want Dad to protect you from harm. Keep your arms the hell out of conveyor belts. Shit! Don't collide with annealers. Wear your goggles! Be careful. Remember the sign: Stay alert, stay alive. We can upgrade machines, we can pack every man in excelsior, shield each sharp corner with bubble wrap, but if you flout regulations, you're careless, you're stupid, the whole goddamn factory could, any minute, explode. Every life's on the line at all times! If I dreamed there was anyone couldn't be trusted, I'd fire 'em; I wouldn't have hired 'em. It seems that I've got more respect for you all than you do for yourselves."

Lea. "Sure, when money's to be saved."

Sid. "There's no money to save! As accountant, you know that we're struggling to hold what we've got, that we run at full pelt to stay put. Were there money to spare, I would buy you all platinum wristwatches, teeth made of gold, electronic fur coats, pearls of string, and convertible aerodynamical hats for your feet, but there *is* no more money unless there's more sales! And repairs, yes, cost money! That's math!"

Matheson. "And Lea, as our accountant, also knows the factory makes ten point sixteen net percent in profit."

Daize. "That is a little misleading . . ."

Sid. "That is none of their business. That's none of your business! What the hell do you know about profit, percents, net or gross? D'you suppose that it goes in my pocket? It keeps this place running. Materials, freight, and the rent, electricity, payroll . . . It's profit that keeps you in jobs. If it's oxygen, we're short of breath—and I'm wasting my own. In this industry, ten sixteen's nothing. It bores me to say this out loud. It's a waste of attention to listen to you. Twenty years I have fought on behalf of you stumps, and you don't even realize; you make me fight *you*! Mister Matheson Church, who has worked here three years—on the floor! And Lea Pensilby! After thirteen in the office you ought to know better! And you! I gave all of you livelihoods!, paychecks!, intent! Your ingratitude's second to ignorance only."

Matheson. "We're still not finished, Mister Bab-cock—Sid."

Sid. "I don't care. Have it framed, have it hung on the wall. Roll it up, shove it up your collective behind. I've been here twenty years, long as any of you puny glorified janitors; longer than them, bloated glorified landlords. I've tripled our sales and I've doubled our staff. Just the person to oust, with a job action looming. Delightful. Divine. —Go on strike? Great idea! See how *you* like it: *I'm* goddamn going on strike. Yes, we'll see who the hell's indispensable. I fucking quit. I concede, as director outgoing, to every demand. And I grant all your wishes; worse, power to grant all your own. I bequeath to you infinite rope; may you fashion a noose to contain every neck. Yes, the factory's yours; may it crush you. Get out of my way. You can all go to hell. With your net percent profit." He pauses on the threshold. "Go shower yourselves with my shit." Sid exits.

After a stunned pause, the janitor returns the garbage bag she has been holding to the garbage can.

Janitor. "And you can take out your own garbage from now on, too."

Lea. "What just happened?"

Matheson. "It's over. We have won."

The janitor hugs the receptionist.

Lea. "We weren't finished reading the demands yet."

Matheson. "There's now no need. They're all accepted." To Daize. "Or's there anything that you would like to say?"

Daize. "What do you mean?"

Matheson. "The charter, my associate tells me, lists as vice-director one Daize Glied."

Lea. "Not the charter . . ."

Daize. "That was a joke, I assure you, of Sid's. Or a gesture, quite empty: a title in lieu of a raise, or more duties, or perks. I am only, was only, director's assistant—his helper or personal aide sort of thing, it was."

Matheson. "You're not allegiant to our former boss, or loyal to the status quo?"

Daize. "Only to what is the best for the company. Not that it matters what *I* want. It's *you* who's in charge now, apparently."

Lea. "We who are. And you as well are."

Matheson. "And yet, it seems to me we hardly need, with no executives, executive assistants anymore. Perhaps the best thing for the company would be for all superfluous employees to resign."

Lea. "Don't be vengeful, Matheson. For crying skies, it's not a coup or revolution. Let's not start with purges, reigns of terror, or beheadings."

Matheson. "You're right, of course. At least today, this hour of triumph, shall no stain of bloodshed see."

Union member, at the door. "Hey, Matheson, what's going on? We saw Mister Babcock storm stomping out of here in a huff. Are we going on strike, or what?"

Matheson. "I'll tell you all together; first you'll shut down everything, and gather round below."

Union member exits, shouting: "Shut it down! We're going on strike!"

Lea. "That decision should've been a joint one. They're already treating him like he's the new director."

At a nod from Matheson, the janitor slides open the window. The last machines wind down and stop, leaving a warm, ticking, echoing silence.

Lea. "Shouldn't we discuss first what you're saying?"

Matheson. "I'll know what's in my heart when out it spills across my tongue, but not before. I feel it's much; its swelling spate distends my throat with ache like tears unshed. I'll shout; I must. —My brothers, sisters, friends! Accomplices and colleagues; partners, comrades, kin—rejoice! We've overcome! The factory is ours! The tyrant's left the plant—for good. The threat of our consolidated might, the sight of our united wrath, sufficed to cow, dishearten, overpower him. Our matchless force in solidarity prevailed. We hardly dared to hope for such complete success. My joy's a measure of my proud amazement; gratitude betrays surprise; but shouldn't I have known that we would be victorious? For it's only when divided that we're conquered; only when disorganized exploited. Conquest, though, and exploitation sow revolt; stung pride, balked need, and desperation unify inevitably, joining all against their common enemy: the profiteers who sell sweat-labor cheap—and, worse, treat cheap, to justify their victimizing bent, the ones whose sweat they sell. From this day forth, we'll set our price ourselves, and reap our own rewards. Let this day mark the birth of our cooperative! There much remains to do; with freedom comes responsibility, and with responsibility comes work, and sacrifice. But, unlike former pains, which smarted like a whip inflicted, these shall make us pleased and proud, as muscles sore from voluntary exercise are felt as promise, growth, and strength incipient. We have shed the rank excrescence; here's to clean and streamlined health! The dictatorial head is lopped; long live the body! Now we walk in tandem, not on one another's backs. We chatter not in raucous counterpoint, but sing in one harmonious unison!"

Matheson leads the workers in song. "We'll smash the system, break the bars, the apparatus blast; no longer will we be content to be the least and last!

"You'll keep us down no longer, for together we're much stronger! You'll keep us in no fetters, for together we've no betters!

"We're the best! You're the worst! You're the last! We're the first!

"Your power, this very hour! Give it us!"

Matheson speaks over the singers. "We'll celebrate this breaking dawn with toasts and tippling! To the pub! Let no one treat, but all one tab divide! Come, Lea, and Daize—no more 'Miz Glied'—teetotaling's forbidden. Intoxicating triumph we'll enhance with ale—or simulate with ale, perhaps, until it's felt for real?"

Lea. "Everyone can't leave at once. There's safety regulations for a shutdown, surely. Stations to secure, machines to power off, and doors to lock, at least? I hardly know; it's never happened, to my knowledge."

Matheson. "We'll leave all that to those responsible. Assume each person knows their job. You're not in charge, remember? No one is! Besides, we're not abandoning the factory completely, I should guess. Let's not forget the thirty-two percent of clerical, custodial, and support staff who withheld support, and whom you do not represent. Let them hold down the fort!"

Daize, rummaging in the filing cabinet. "I'll stay behind and ensure that procedures are followed correctly."

Lea. "I'll stay too. I'll join you later, Matheson. Promise. After all, there's still so much we haven't figured out . . . The fifth and sixth of our demands, for instance, which we never thought he'd grant us . . ."

Matheson. "Tomorrow's soon enough to change the world. Let's leave things as they are for one day more." Matheson exits with the others, singing.

Daize withdraws papers from the cabinet. "Here. And a copy for you."

Lea. "Right. What's first?"

Daize. "First is the coolant controller, which hopefully someone's already put into its standby mode."

Lea. "What a mess."

As they exit, Daize begins to shut the door behind them, but on second thought leaves it open.

THE OFFICE HAS become a workers' lounge, as evidenced by disarrayed chairs, and clothing and scraps of food and garbage lying about. The desk has been cleared of papers, which have been replaced by a chessboard and microwave. The filing cabinet hangs open, as does the door. A poster on the wall reads CLEANLINESS IS NEXT TO SOLIDARITY. A worker in overalls sits at the conference table, eating from a plastic container. The two janitors enter.

Male janitor, to the worker. "You here for the quarterly meeting?"

The worker makes a sarcastic gesture towards his meal.

Male janitor. "Well, there's gonna be a meeting in here in a few minutes, so you maybe gonna want to leave before it starts."

Female janitor. "Leave 'im alone."

Male janitor. "Aw, I'm only saying."

The worker finishes eating without haste, and exits.

Male janitor. "Pull yourself a chair up. We're first ones here. Maybe they let me take the minutes."

Female janitor. "I gotta say, I find your newfound enthusiasm a little hard to digest."

Male janitor. "Heh. Get me a few new marketable skills and take me to someplace maybe where they pay me more."

Female janitor. "You're the worst kind of opportunist! You shouldn't been allowed in the union."

Male janitor. "I ain't had me a raise since this hullabaloo started."

Female janitor. "That was only three months ago! And before that, when did you ever see a raise? Besides, that wasn't a raise. That was wage equalization. Some folks lost money."

Male janitor. "And they should've taken themself elsewhere—like what I plan to do."

A couple of workers enter, laughing and chatting. "Thing took hold of his entire arm, right up to the shoulder there! No shit!"

Female janitor. "You all here for the meeting?"

Worker. "You kidding. Another fucking meeting?"

Male janitor. "This one's the quarterly. Wanna get here early and get a good seat."

The workers exchange a look and exit.

Female janitor. "What I'd like to know is where your loyalty's at. They ain't been training you around in different jobs just so you can take your trained-up ass someplace else. And you think they're gonna ask your opinion or give you a vote at some other company?"

Male janitor. "They sure maybe might, if they know I been asked for my vote in the past. That's called resumé. And I'm getting me some steel-shiny resumé."

Female janitor. "You never should've been allowed in. You and all the other latecomer bandwagon-jumpers looking out for themself. Sometimes I don't know what Matheson Church is thinking."

Male janitor. "I could be loyal maybe to these bonuses he been talking about."

Female janitor. "Those're gonna be for the hardest workers—not you. It's another kind of equalization, actually. Some work's harder than other work, even if you do put in the same number hours."

Male janitor. "Way I hear it, it's the union will decide who works hardest."

Female janitor. "So? Who else would decide?"

Male janitor. "Well, I'm union now, ain't I? So maybe I decide it's *I'm* who's working hardest."

Female janitor. "And maybe I joined the union before you, and maybe I got a different view on the matter."

Male janitor. "Aw."

Female janitor. "Anyway, you're half right. Janitor's among the hardest work there is, and people still treat us like second-class. Probably I wouldn't doubt it's the harder you work, the more the soft and lazy people gotta look down on you—way to try and maintain their own self-respect. Only way to fix that's to pay us a little more. Get some of that prestige up. Should be called prestige equalization, really."

Male janitor. "All I know's buy me some nice new shoes. These getting pretty ratty. No prestige in that."

Lea and Daize enter.

Lea. "It's projected loss, until we're out of stock. It's maddening, however. Really aggravating. Aren't we all supposed to be this unified collective, working for each other, for ourselves? A happy family?"

Daize. "Sid used to say that too."

Lea. "That's because he saw himself as father, with a father's power, and infallible. All paternalists think they're paternal. There's a grain of righteousness within the adolescent's peeved rebelliousness, when taking little somethings from the old man's wallet. But to pilfer from your siblings? From yourselves? It's lunacy, obtuseness."

A worker enters.

Lea. "You here for the meeting?"

Worker. "Oh, is that now?"

Lea. "Starting in about five minutes. Will you come back then?"

Worker. "Oh, I can't in five minutes, sorry."

Lea. "Never mind. But close the door behind you, will you?" To the janitors. "And're you here for the meeting?"

Male janitor. "Sure as sharks eat fish!"

Lea. "Wonderful, but will you let us have the room until it starts? We've got some things that need discussing. I appreciate it."

Male janitor. "All right, no problem, can do." The janitors exit, closing the door behind them.

Lea. "Nine point ninety-seven's not so measly. We have fallen under ten, four other times, four other quarters, over five years. Thus, this quarter's round the twentieth, twenty-fourth percentile. But you go back ten, it's right around the average. Not so lousy. I should even say it's quite within the range of normal fluctuation. Taking in consideration all the drastic changes we've experienced, the upheaval undergone, the transformation we've been able to achieve these past three months, one's bound to say that it's a miracle we've done so well. I'm not ashamed of nine point ninety-seven—though I do wish it were better. —Did you talk to whatsisname, the guy who never cared for Sid, your contact at Horizon Techware?"

Daize. "Selton Faraj. Yes, this morning, at length. Says they won't place an order unless we can drop down to fifty a case."

Lea. "Has he lost his reason?"

Daize. "All the departments, he says, he supplies, have been downsized, or will be, or worry they soon will be. Money is scarce these days."

Lea. "Isn't crime increasing? What's the matter with this country?"

Daize. "That's the perception, in any case. Violence in crime is apparently down, though, according to him. Law and order's unpopular just at the moment, he says. Individual freedom's the catchword right now—independence, autonomy. So the departments're feeling the squeeze in their budgets."

Lea. "What we need's a thumping civil war. —Of course I'm only joking."

A worker enters. "Oh."

Lea. "Hi. You coming for the meeting?"

Worker. "No thanks." The worker exits.

Daize. "Maybe I could've persuaded him better in person."

Lea. "Can't afford to fly you clear across the continent whenever there's a contract needs negotiating. Makes us look a little desperate, too, I'd think. It's better, surely, to appear unneedy, and a little bit aloof. Suggest to him that we've less need of him than he has need of us. Besides, we can't go low as fifty. It'd set a precedent."

Daize. "You've the decision to make."

Lea. "Or you don't agree? If your opinion's we should sell at fifty, I'll present both sides and bring it to a vote."

Daize. "Anything sold'd reduce excess stock—though the thieving is doing that too—and help transfer some numbers to ledgers' black sides."

Lea. "Yes, I'd feel much better if our books looked better. But I'm hopeful we can get to ten point ten by end of year. The owners cannot hardly be displeased with that. And with the workers happier, the future of the company is solider than ever. Anyway, they've tasted freedom, and are dead against all interference. No, the owners wouldn't dare appoint a new director, risking costly turmoil, if we manage ten point ten, or somewhat better, overall, and by year-end. Or don't you think so?"

Daize, hesitating. "May I speak frankly?"

Lea. "Naturally. I value— Your opinion's always valued."

Daize. "Really you shouldn't put every least question to vote. It's confusing to people, and tiring, and leads to these meetings interminable, which is why they're so clearly unpopular."

Lea. "There are still a couple minutes left yet."

Daize. "You're in a better position than anyone, nearly, for making decisions: you're expert, and knowledgeable, and your vision is clear. But you open instead every matter to endless and fruitless discussion. The average employee knows nothing, moreover cares nothing, of selling a case at fifteen, or five hundred, or fifty."

Lea. "You and I can understand, so we can surely help them understand it also."

Daize. "What is the point of that? Wisdom's no precious, rare, widely distributed ore you accumulate only from numerous mines. It's a clarity born of a ripened and orderly calm—so's more commonly found in the sole individual, less in cacophonous crowds. Even three people—two—even one person sometimes must dally and dither. Why multiply muddle, inflicting on everyone else your uncertainty?"

The two laughing workers reenter.

Worker. "Oh, right, the meeting. Sorry." They exit.

Daize. "When you're explaining, they listen—because you are better informed, more experienced, et cetera. But then they await, often vainly, your guidance, your reasoned opinion. I won't resurrect my old arguments why we officially, formally ought to appoint you director. However, I'll say this much only: they want your direction, Lea—want to be told how to vote! Why then force them to vote at all? Rather, just tell 'em post-facto what you have decided—and why, if you must. They would thank you, I'm sure."

Lea. "Maybe, but I cannot work that way, for it'd violate collectivism's principles: I mean non-hierarchy—anarchy; transparency; democracy. —Often I recall that second day, the day we really took control, the morning after Sid walked out. That morning I let Matheson persuade me equalizing wages—fifth of our demands—would prove too radical, unpopular, extreme, would be defeated if we put it to a referendum, and for all the reasons he adduced: that people more fear change than evil that's familiar; that we gauge our value only, know our stature only, in comparison with others, and would rather be untall than in a heightless world, would rather be a nobody in midst of somebodies than merely be an anyone, an everyone; that every vote entails a modicum of chance, of risk, and equal wage was too important to be left to chance; that people can't be trusted to discern and choose what's best for 'em."

Daize. "That's an assertion I wouldn't expect from a populist."

Lea. "All my faith's the opposite direction, with enlightened self-determination. Only blinders, ignorance, and barriers prompt our wrongly choosing. Wealthiness and privilege are insupportable with open eyes. There's few could eat an apple, less enjoy, beneath a starveling's gaze. The sight of suffering others, their dejection, their abasement, doesn't cheer or puff us up, but only sickens and dispirits us—and sickens most who benefit the most. The high, no less than low, would gain if lowliness with highness were, in one sharp blow, eradicated. You and I, for instance, had our wages lowered; now there's none resent us, none whom we despise. We're better off. And aren't the shop-floor workers?"

A knock at the door, which they ignore.

Daize. "Matheson Church has a different opinion these days, it seems."

Lea. "Proof that autocratic, unilateral, oligarchic governance, when even well-intentioned, poisons hearts of those who govern. Half I blame myself for letting him eschew the vote. The only hope for lasting true community of loving and cooperating souls is perfect parity of income—that's my creed. But I betrayed my faith by implementing it by fiat. I had hoped that ends would expiate for means. Decrees, however, even those decreeing equal freedoms, do perpetuate a hierarchy, which is always built on caste, obedience, inequality. By that same token, every democratic vote, including those relinquishing democracy, do cultivate equality, respect, and freedom. We were lazy shepherds, building sheepfolds; we were nervous, fearful parents nurturing polite propriety with muzzles. Now, today, I'd rather let the factory make joint mistakes than foist on 'em by force or stealth the right decision."

Daize. "Doesn't seem different from Sid's abdication for spite—no offense."

Lea. "Had he done it for the proper reasons, I'd have said it was heroic." A knock at the door. "Crying heaven, what d'you want?" The male janitor half enters. "Get out! And leave that door unopened till the meeting's started! Please and thank you!" The janitor closes the door. "When's this stupid meeting going to start? And where is Matheson? Or doesn't he think union members have a stake in things like fiscal quarterlies, which only are our lifeblood's laboratory test results? No, why should anyone find any interest in 'em? Matheson! The problem with decrees personified, is Colleague Church! Beginning from day one, they like a savior treated him, and now he's all-too-willing master. What the hell does a collective need a union for still, anyway? Without a management, what labor-management relations can there be? There's no exploitive bosses left to fight! But he continues with his reckless windbag rhetoric, a child repeating witlessly a once-precocious cuss which drew a startled laugh when fresh. A warrior chieftain, he continues rattling spears long after battles have been won, bemused by peace, and loath to yield authority. I wouldn't doubt this bonus business only's something meant to keep him grandly busy."

Daize. "Full-time crusaders require crusades."

Lea. "So, a tethered dog, he digs and paws to mud his own backyard. I understand what people mean by saying a successful revolution's first concern is getting rid of revolutionaries. Sometimes I could wish we had a guillotine—but he'd have used it first on us, undoubted."

Daize. "Let me return, at the risk of displeasing you, to the directorship—which, I believe, in your hands, could be power to neutralize Matheson. He like an enemy treats you already; he's calling for war. Well, an army needs generals."

Lea. "No, no leaders! That's a crucial tenet. I renounce that, I'm as bad as he is."

Daize. "Sometimes to save your abode you must leave it."

Lea. "But you don't protect your valuables by smashing them upon the burglar's head. I know it's me who started metaphoring, but let's stop. They carry us away. This isn't war or home invasion, and the union's not a junta—yet. There are no enemies here, only baffled friends. And I'm no leader. I despise both leaders and, increasingly of late, the led."

Daize. "What more desirable trait in a leader? Those feelings prevent your corruption, prohibit your power's abuse."

Lea. "Let it be. This revolution will be saved without inverting or debasing or betraying it; or else we'll let it die a sinless infant's death. —Well, look who's come to join us!"

Matheson, entering. "Hello. I hope I'm not too late to vote."

Daize. "What are we voting on?"

Matheson. "Whatever. Always there's so much to vote on, isn't there? Today I come prepared. I'm representing eighty-seven of our union members. Here's their signatures."

Lea. "What is this? The maximum allowed a deputy is five deputed votes, and only then when the deputers cannot come themselves, for whatsoever reason."

Matheson. "They've all good reasons: either they're asleep, at work, or at the union hall."

Daize. "Meaning the pub!"

Matheson. "And, point of fact, I only represent these five deputers, as you call 'em; but themselves they represent five others each, which transfer with the deputation; then, those twenty-five in turn are deputies for fifty-some, whose votes all transfer with the transfer of their own."

Lea. "Transfers aren't subsumed that way; your limit absolute is five."

Matheson. "We tweaked that rule. We thought the language was ambivalent. Three words inserted, one removed, was all it took. We'll find this more efficient, don't you think? And comfortable. It's always hard to shoehorn everyone inside this room. But now, how little space our eighty-seven voters take—with you two, eighty-nine."

Lea. "Don't be flippant. We have barely managed quorum for two months now."

Matheson. "A flattering adversity: it shows the faith of our constituents. The price of able governance is apathy."

Daize. "Anyway, changes to charter amendments aren't valid unless you've got supermajority."

Matheson. "We held a meeting—I'm surprised the two of you weren't there—and changed that rule as well."

Lea. "But you cannot change those regulations lacking absolute two-thirds majority!"

Matheson. "A simple two of every three, in fact, of those both present and allowed to vote."

Lea. "You're precisely wrong; it's absolute: two-thirds of all who're eligible. Also, you are obligated to announce all meetings that pertain to charter changes one week in advance, by bulletin board, and by post, or telephone, or leaflet."

Matheson. "We also changed those rules, which wasted time."

Lea. "None of this is legal. All these things the charter quite explicitly prohibits."

Daize. "What'd I tell you? He's staging a coup."

Matheson. "Inaccurate. We're asking only that our eighty-seven votes be recognized."

Lea. "You keep mentioning a vote. But what vote?"

Matheson. "There isn't always votes? You do so love 'em, I assumed there'd be at least a few. But if, however, your agenda's blank, there is one little matter we could put upon the table for discussion's sake."

Daize, studying the signatures. "This is more signatures than your whole membership."

Matheson. "It actually's our total membership. We lately've grown significantly more."

Daize. "Carmihhal Palst is support staff! Edwina van Sowt and Alfredo Mafal are receiving, and Ben Yi's a foreman!"

Matheson. "He's called a supervisor now, and feels a bit disgruntled by the loss of his prestige, and pay, and power. Nor is he alone in that, a feeling widely shared."

Lea. "You dismay and bewilder me. You court the very same support staff formerly you vilified, enlisting to your cause the disaffected victims of your cause! You're playing pharmacist to those you've poisoned!"

Matheson. "We're widening the revolution's scope and draw, while staying true to principles."

Lea. "Nonsense! You are buying their allegiance; you are bribing them with promises of bonuses—that is, return to wages being stratified. Let's never mind a moment it's a Ponzi pyramid, in which the earliest comers only profit; my concern's its diametric treason to those very principles so glibly you espouse—i.e., equality in everything, especially in wages. That was our foundation stone, our flagship—fifth of our demands, but first important."

Matheson. "I'm grateful that you bring that matter up, that our agendas have some overlap; the bonuses were just the thing I thought perhaps we'd vote on. Let me rectify a misconception first, or titivate a frowzy memory. I never felt that equalizing wages was a real objective, for it seemed impractical, and probably impracticable, and, like your beloved plebiscites, belike to spark invidious division, too."

Lea. "That's what happens under different wages!"

Matheson. "Your disagreement rather proves my point. The question's still contentious, as I knew it would be then. But I permitted its inclusion—"

Lea. "You permitted!"

Matheson. "I advocated its inclusion for that very reason. Its exorbitance precisely was its pricelessness as chip for bargaining: a thing ostensibly held sacred which, surrendered, might exact some valuable concessions. You'll admit, we never really dreamed that Sid would grant us wage equality! When haggling, start by always asking double what you want."

Lea. "You're rewriting history. You never wanted equal wages? Why insist we push it through without a vote, then?"

Matheson. "That's proof I never thought it popular. Perhaps enthusiastic victory beguiled my judgement. When resistance of a sudden disappears, you sometimes lurch a farther forward step than your intent. We were condemned by unforeseen success to occupy each fortress we'd besieged, or risk appearing insincere. The air then crackled with excitement of reform, remember; many were electrified, and surely would have been dissatisfied with any less than too much. Were it not for wage equality, they might've asked for five-day weekends, or to retrofit the factory to manufacture doggie treats instead."

Daize. "Stunning. You open your mouth saying one thing, and close it concluding the opposite."

Matheson. "I'll clarify. That moment, I thought wage equality was likely popular enough to pass if voted on. Although I'd reservations, I could see no way to squelch it while still saving face. I thought it better then to force it through without the factious, fractious ructions votes foment."

Lea. "But you didn't say that at the time, then."

Matheson. "Not sharing your besotted love of ballots, I may have primped and pruned my words to please you better. Trying as I was to make you seize the very thing you most desired, I felt no guilt at using rhetoric. I would have *shared* if I had aired my doubts to you. Your tragic flaw— and virtue too—is balance, Lea. It keeps you upright— and immobile, for to walk one has to fall a little forward, intermittently. Excessive open-mindedness will make the mind a clangorous bazaar; and too much evenhandedness makes maladroit, undextrous hands. To spare you anguish and deliberation, I presented you the coin's most shiny side alone. I do the same thing with the union, and they thank me for it. More than for alternatives or choices, people yearn for certainty, for passion—for direction. Man's a horse who's skittish out of blinkers. Face it, Lea. If we'd've voted on the equal wage, the first thing you'd've done is candidly enumerate the disadvantages!"

Lea. "All this rationalizing tortuously's needless. All your 'rhetoric,' which I'd call disingenuous manipulation, is explained more well by greed than kindness. Your supporters' wages then were mostly underneath the mean. They wanted money then, they want more money now. You promise it."

Matheson. "And what's so wrong with wanting money? Shame, with equal justice, plants for wanting soil, or fish for wanting ocean, birds for worms or cats for milk or cows for hay, as shame a person wanting money, which is food to them and drink, and air to breathe, and clothes to wear, and bath and bed and home. Money's earth on which to stand; and it's the fulcrum and the lever we uproot the mountains with. Yes, money's freedom, possibility, potential. Money is the harnessed fire of sunlight, which bestirs our dust. It is the effervescing creativity of dreams, the fructifying kernel sown in richest chaos. Breaking hackneyed chains of habit, it's the smeared uncertainty emancipating quantum particles, the coil of flurried energy asleep in hidebound atoms. It's the sultry wind of agitation howling through the caves of frigid matter. Money is the will ascendant, soul triumphant, spirit regnant. The universe without it is a void, a barren clockwork prison winding down deterministically to entropy. The lack of money is paralysis, disease, decay, and death."

Lea. "Who now lacks? We've all a living income."

Matheson. "We less want more than chance for more. A pay unchanged, unchangeable, is like a dole or pension granted, and for granted taken—by very regularity unfelt. To seem reward, a wage must fluctuate, or threaten to at least, contingent on performance. Opportunity for more implies its opposite: the same will seem like less, and everyone will toe the line more sprightfully. A floor for wages does more damage to morale, in honesty, than even ceiling, since it guarantees the slacker equal recompense to all, and saps the motivation either through complacence or resentful bitterness."

Daize. "Who is a slacker? We turn out more product than ever before; we're not selling it fast enough."

Matheson. "That revolutionary fervor wanes, or will before too long. Our victories, like constant temperature, or sight or noise unvaried, also fade from consciousness. Each little bonus will to whom receives it seem a little revolution won."

Lea. "Tell me, by and large these revolutions all will go to union members, won't they?"

Matheson. "They'll go to those by union members deemed the most deserving: those who hardest work, whose work is hardest, who most earn respect assisting and inspiring colleagues, and whose efforts seem essentialest to all."

Lea. "How perniciously unequal wages lead us back to classism and status hierarchies! Who here's inessential?"

Matheson. "We all have roles to play, of course; but can a factory spare manufacturers and be a factory? And is it fair a worker on the shop floor, toiling hunched above a noisy, sweltry, greasy belt conveyor should be paid the same as one who sits, legs crossed, in comfy offices, and answers phones, or taps with polished nails a calculator's buttons all day long?"

Lea. "Do you glorify or denigrate our sedentary paperwork? If we're so lucky, cozy, spoiled, then why don't shop-floor workers volunteer for more rotation?"

Matheson. "Because we'd feel uneasy in such ease; because we'd lose our coworkers' respect."

Lea. "If you think our work is so distasteful and ignoble, then it's we who surely should receive the greater pay for putting up with it. And idly tapping buttons!—that's your understanding, is it, of the work performed by Daize and I? You ninny! When's the last time you were on the shop floor? What exactly is it that you do here, Colleague Matheson? Collectives don't need unions! Why don't you get back to real work!"

Matheson. "I see how much the union's needed, when I see how little's changed. You sound like Sid."

Lea. "You're the one who sounds like Sid!"

Matheson. "And you have never worked a single day upon the shop floor, Colleague Pensilby."

Lea. "Not for lack of willingness. If only I had time, if others could be trained to take my place, I'd gladly work with hands for once instead of head! To turn a crank, pull levers, heave a handle, lift a weighty box, become myself machinery: how pleasant, for a change! To come home aching from exertion, neither stiff nor cramped from immobility! Variety's as good as holiday, and I would welcome any break in my routine. I'm sure my desk, or Sandy's phones, or janitorial broom, would offer you the same relief. And when at last we're doing one another's jobs, we'll value and be valued by each other as we now ourselves each value."

Matheson. "I'm sorry, but you couldn't do what we do; and my men and women wouldn't want to do what you do—push a mop or paper. And there's an end to your utopian dream of sharing jobs like sisters sharing skirts. Besides, it's inefficient! Factories replaced the cottage industries because a congregated group could mass-produce more quickly by dividing labor up."

Daize. "Sometimes there's droplets of sense in his verbiage."

Matheson. "Degrading specialists to generalists not only blunts the worker's skills, negates his individual talents, in effect erases his unique identity; it also rewrites history—denies the revolution called industrial, and thus is anti-revolutionary."

Daize. "Soon, though, they're carried away by the floodwater."

A knock at the door, and Sid enters.

Daize. "Keep that door shut!"

Sid. "I'm unable to otherwise enter, my dear."

Matheson. "It's Sid!"

Daize and Lea. "Sid!"

Sid. "I'm relieved you remember my face."

Lea. "It's been three months only."

Sid. "But undoubted oblivious, memorable months. I imagine them heady with challenge, adventure, and expansion of self. You look ruddy and lithe and well-rested and supple, like heroes afoot at a world-building dawn, when the best is brought out of the commonest folk. How's the company doing?"

Matheson. "We're in the middle of a quarterly."

Sid. "I'd be happy to join you. It's open to all, I suppose?"

Lea. "Currently employed employees only."

Sid. "But there's some of those waiting outside in the hall."

Daize. "Leave that door shut."

Lea. "It's a subcommittee meeting, sort of."

Sid. "Subcommittee or quarterly meeting, which one?"

Matheson. "A caucus, representative, we thresh apart the coarsest chaff and grain before we all together do the winnowing."

Daize. "If representing a current employee—or eighty— you're welcome to stay, but not otherwise."

Sid. "Representative only for one am I: me."

Matheson. "You quit."

Sid. "A vacation recuperative—doctor's command. Here's a note for your files."

Lea. "You resigned!"

Sid. "You must misrecollect. When I left, there was no resignation officially, nothing in ink. Without signing, I can't have resigned. Nor did you ever send me a notice of being dismissed."

Lea. "What about that check we sent by courier!"

Matheson. "You sent a check? For what!"

Daize. "Don't be a turnip. For salary owed, and for holiday pay he'd accrued. Not a penny more."

Sid. "I admire the changes you've made to the place. It's a lounge for employees? It has that aroma."

Daize. "Whether or not you received it, we sent you a letter of severance. We've copies."

Matheson, to Lea. "We really did?"

Lea, to Matheson. "We're as capable as him of frowzy memory, if necessary."

Sid. "How are sales?"

Matheson. "They've never been so good."

Sid. "Yet the stockrooms, I noticed, are chock to the brim."

Matheson. "With orders placed and ready to be shipped."

Sid. "He's more knowledgeable than before of such things. A promotion? —Of course not: you're all, so I've heard, on a level these days. 'No more masters,' correct?"

Matheson. "We've instituted job rotation, so we all know more about most everything."

Lea. "Who's been letting you inside the stockrooms?"

Sid. "There's a few still around of my faithful old friends, a few loyal, obedient daughters and sons. They admitted, did some of them, under their breath, as if sadly accustomed to spies, that they thought that the changes around here'd been carried too far."

Matheson. "While others feel we haven't yet gone far enough. So what?"

Sid. "It's a taste, though you're none of you managers now, of the manager's foremost dilemma: you can't ever please all your workers at once."

Matheson. "That credo, like all pessimistic faiths, does guarantee itself. But every day we're nearer still to pleasing everyone—much nearer than you managed, manager!"

Daize. "Since you've no business here, please be so kind as to leave us to ours."

Sid. "I neglected to mention receiving a call from Ottavia Farr-Mp in the morning today."

Matheson. "Who's that? And wha'd she have to say to you?"

Sid. "Representing the owners, she'd little to say that was nice—rather poured the hot grease in my ear, I'm afraid. But the owners apparently think that this plant has still got a director, you see."

Daize. "They are mistaken in thinking it you."

Sid. "Is that so? You perhaps have forgotten to send 'em a putative copy of putative letter?"

Daize. "How could it matter if even we had? It's not going to work, what you're up to."

Matheson. "What is it that he's up to? What's the scheme?"

Daize. "Ten or more people here heard you resign; and two dozen more witnesses watched you walk out; and a hundred and thirty will swear that you haven't set foot for three months in the factory. Prudently, our constitution addressed absenteeism: regular workers have contracts which terminate after a ninety-day unexplained leave. You've been gone ninety-one. And in any event, it is thirty days only for absent directors, whose title devolves to the old vice-director then."

Matheson. "Was that not you?"

Sid. "Convalescent, I told you, not absent . . ."

Daize. "Prove it in court. In the meantime, you'll find that you've lost your authority, squandered your eminence. Captains their ships don't abandon, commanders their troops, or they cease to be captains, commanders. A leader's who leads; and a ruler who abdicates denigrates not just himself but his throne, and all royalty ever. A boss should be seat of a company's consciousness; quitting's lobotomy, psychical suicide, self-vivisection—the treasonous head that secedes from the body. You've forfeited all of your rights, be they moral or legal, to leadership. No one'll still take your orders here. Many in fact will be ready to swear that you're trespassing even. Reality's formed by consensus, and you're the minority."

Matheson. "Our new director's Daize! How nothing's changed."

Lea. "Shush! It's only a formality."

Sid. "But you misunderstand me. I offer to help."

Daize. "We have been doing just fine on our own, thank you."

Sid. "You call nine ninety-seven just fine!"

Lea. "That's a market blip, and well within the range of normal fluctuation."

Sid. "There's no need for assuming this martyrdom, Daize. An ideal is no thing that exists in the world, but idea—or a poltergeist haunting the brain's lumber-room, which makes move without sensible cause limbs, eyes, tongue. Why give tribute to phantoms, or make yourselves victims for sacrifice unto unseen and unseeable gods? And this combative stance that you take's inappropriate. Please understand, I'm not scheming, or creeping, or weaseling in. I am willing to make you all partners, or if you prefer, vice-directors. You've shown yourselves apt and ingenious, committed and plucky. But still, you're no businessmen, nor businesswomen. And Daize, you're correct that I hadn't a right to let fall on your shoulders the burden that rightly was mine. I'm for making amends, and reclaiming my risk."

Matheson. "The only risks we run are freedom's risks: enlightenment, responsibility, mistakes which earn us wisdom, not regret."

Sid. "I refer to the owners' year-end ultimatum."

Daize, to Lea and Matheson. "We are expected to reach ten point five percent profit by end of the year, says Ottavia."

Lea. "What! Since when?"

Matheson. "'Since when'! So what?"

Sid. "Did you fail to inform them? Collectives can't thrive in such secrecy, Daize."

Daize. "If we do not, they'll appoint a director who's able to."

Lea. "Meanwhile, fire the old—whoever that should happen at year-end to be."

Matheson. "They cannot do it. We now run the place."

Sid. "But they own it, you nozzle."

Daize. "That's why there can be, there will be, no bonuses—nor for that matter the costly rotation of jobs. We'll be needing each dollar that's coming in."

Matheson. "Could someone tell me please, not him, why we should care what ultimatums or demands the owners make? No longer do we have or recognize directors. Let them fire which one of us they wish; we'll hire 'em back. Let them appoint whomever they desire; we will ignore 'em, flout ' em—go on strike!"

Sid. "The perennial solution, the nostrum you dote on."

Matheson. "And why are you still here? Our colleague asked you several times to leave."

Daize. "Some new director can disarrange everything, Matheson: reinstate wage differentials, or outlaw collectives, or even dismantle the union; demote or dismiss the whole mass of us—probably will, when they learn what's been happening."

Matheson. "We'll stay and work, regardless who they sack."

Daize. "Work without pay?"

Matheson. "Unless they pay us, we'll refuse to work."

Sid. "How hermetically sealed is his system of thought!"

Daize. "What if they sell it, or close it, the factory?"

Matheson. "We'll lock ourselves inside!"

Daize. "They can arrest us. It isn't our property."

Matheson. "We'll fight the cops if they don't take our side! We'll start a civil war, oppressed against oppressors!

Fuck the owners, fuck the law! And fuck this messenger and lackey, who returns with promises to save us from his bosses by becoming boss again!"

Lea. "Don't you get it, Matheson? They own the factory. Unless they get their profits, they're within their rights to wrest from us its management. Consider it like rent: we pay, or else we'll be evicted. One, or all of us, the end result's the same: our revolution limping to a standstill."

Matheson. "You're all colluding, all the same! As soon as your own neck's beneath the tyrant's heel, you turn collaborationist, and stoop and scrape, and lick the polish from their boots! You're sell-outs, all of you, without a bone of revolution in your skeletons! You're welcomed back, sir, Mister Babcock. We'll resume the conversation where we left it ninety days ago. The union, you'll recall, was on the verge of striking. Now we strike. These thugs of yours have been apprised of our demands. Until you recognize our eighty-seven votes, and institute our bonuses, there's no machines will run, and no machinists pass inside the gates. We'll reckon now accounts, and learn who's least dispensable, and who most otiose. Enjoy paralysis and impotence! Good luck increasing profits with no staff! Be sure to send the owners our hello!" Matheson exits.

The male janitor enters.

Lea. "Go away! The meeting's over!"

The male janitor exits.

Sid. "It's a tough situation you're in. But I know what I'd do, were I you. Should I tell my idea?"

Daize. "Thanks, but instead I'll tell you what you should've three months ago done. With the layoffs you should've gone through. Yes, we'd planned to lay off a few people. Just think: he permitted their threat of a walkout to frustrate his lockout!—a toddler who covets a toy till it's given him. Matheson Church is now offering twice the same gift. We'll accept it with gratitude secretly; openly, though, with bad grace. We allow him to think that this hurts us. Our pride has been stung. So we dig in our heels, set our teeth, cross our arms, make provocative show of not yielding an inch. If they're starting to weaken too early—they can't have much cash in their strike fund—we rile 'em with insults, aspersions, inflame 'em with threats of replacement, arrest, litigation, thus keeping the picket line bristling, and Matheson ever declaiming. If lucky, we'll pare from the payroll two hundred and seventy months workers' wages, which betters the hundred and eighty we'd hoped for from layoffs. Then next year, we'll bring in some scabs who are young and unskilled, who we'll get at half price; while the overpaid uppity strikers, we leave them to wither and freeze—taking none of 'em back whatsoever, not ever, not even as scabs. There's another of Matheson's gifts to us: death of the union. We meanwhile with skeleton crew keep the factory running at idle. We offer support staff and fore-men a raise, or a token reversal of equalization, with promise of more in the future. We minimize output; we've plenty in stock, Sid's correct, that needs selling. We give away cases at fifty, even dump 'em at loss if need be—while committing to no guarantees for the new year. Shut up; I'm not finished. We naturally cancel all purchasing, let our supply contracts lapse, at whatever the penalty; we'll renegotiate everything after year-end. The annealers and crimpers in need of replacing, we sell 'em for scrap, and buy new ones next year. We offload to the city that parcel of foreshore, postponing those upgrades for now to the docks. As a matter of fact, we sell everything isn't nailed down. We'll find buyers, and dictate our price, since we'll promise to buy it all back in the new year at profit to them. We can even start pawning the windows right out of the walls, for the chattels need never change hands. As for next year, it's gonna be hell; but for us, for the moment, the future has no real existence; our profit in short-term is every-thing. Drowning, a swimmer can't think of conserving her breath. But we'll make it to shore; we'll survive. Let the new year take care of itself. —So you see, Sid, you've nothing to teach us, and nothing to bring to the feast but your mouth."

Sid. "I perceive that I should have allowed you more power."

Daize. "No, for I always had plenty of that. It was only esteem that I lacked; but it's lacking no longer. For everyone, since your departure, now knows who exactly is running this company, who in the past ran it for you: your secretary, and your accountant."

Lea. "Flattering."

Sid. "Could you really have thought that I didn't esteem you? How paltry our glances, our handshakes, our words. We're 'the animal gifted with language'? Pfuh! Man is the beast that communicates least. Let me mend my ineloquence. Daize, I esteem you. Rehire me. Allow me to work underneath you, beside you—whatever. I need to come back to work. Home, and this uniform structureless holiday, kills me. D'you know what it's like, to so suddenly slip from the engine of life, like a cog from its axle? The machinery, horribly, runs on without you. Where yesterday a hundred and thirty and more individuals needed your stewardship, help, and largesse, there's today only one estranged wife who depends on largesse. There were yesterday phones that were ringing at three in the morning; today, none at noon. You were piloting industry then, and were serving the nation by saving from crime our metropolises; now you're as good as a ghost in society—giving as little, as much still desiring. There danced through your banking accounts many millions of figures each week; but today, numbers dribble, excreted like wind from a sack, from your personal savings. I feel as if sloughed. But I'm full still of blood and sensation! I want to come back. Take me back. I esteem you. I need to get out of the house or I'll shrivel and die."

Daize. "Pleading with me is no use. The dictatorship's over. We now make decisions collectively. Lea, what do you think?"

Lea. "Me? I only work here."

Daize. "Lea is abstaining. I vote that we cannot this moment afford an expansion of staff. And with no other voters with eligibility present, the motion is carried. I'm sorry, Sid. Surely there's many more factories, companies eager to garner experience like yours. If you're sick of your home, try your wife's for a change, maybe."

Sid. "I am waiting to hear still what you have to say, Lea. We always together worked well, did we not?"

Lea. "I agree with Daize, Sid. You're redundant."

Sid. "Then I'll leave." Sid exits.

A pause.

Daize. "Nothing was personal. Never were you what I wanted to oust, but your doctrines. And never was I what I wanted to save, but the factory. I've no belief in anarchic equality. People don't know what to do with equality, Lea. Look at Matheson: never content. When you flatten the landscape, the hills feel belittled, and stomach it badly; the valleys enjoy being raised, and want higher to rise, even higher than mountains were formerly. That is the nature of humans. We constantly measure ourselves by the people around us. We scarcely can stand at a mirror without our comparing the sight to the image we hold of ourselves in our minds. There was something that demagogue, Matheson, said that I thought not entirely inapt: that they wanted the chance to get more. It's the chance, not the more, that is valuable, whether in money or power. The rich aren't more glad or more blessed than the poor, but the poor won't believe it: they need the exemplary fable; their hope of acquiring that wealth is what makes them the gladder and blesseder truly. What's equalization—of wages, position, or rank? Simultaneous snuffing of hundreds of dreams. We should, arrogant in our satiety, hesitate robbing from others their stimulant hunger. I started as typist here, lowly and scorned, but impressed my superiors' superiors, and proved my ability, step after step, until finally, seven promotions and seven years later, I found myself working so closely with Sid that my hands seemed to come out his sleeves. When I watched you dismantle the ladder I'd climbed, I felt hobbled, afflicted, negated: my history, all my accomplishments canceled, erased! Yet I never intrigued, never sabotaged. Always I gave you the benefit of my experience. I couldn't do less. Situation impossible: wanting your system to fail, but you, Lea, to succeed; helping the factory prosper, but hoping its management foundered. Two unreconcilable aims, incompatibly clashing inside me, their dissonance loosing, untuning my nerves. Only now that I speak do I sound my distress to its depths. What relief to let air in by letting air out! I'll yet turn politician, provided I'm always permitted to talk cleansing truth. But you're silent—upset and annoyed with me. Say something."

Lea. "Not upset, only thinking."

Daize. "Thinking of what?"

Lea. "That you're right."

Daize. "Right? What about?"

Lea. "That abodes can be returned to, vases be repaired—and generals retired. —I'll be director, I've decided."

Daize. "Oh. I'm surprised."

Lea begins rummaging in the filing cabinet. "If there's seventy percent of staff that needs to permanently be laid off—but lied to first, manipulated, used, then flicked aside like dirt—I'd rather it was me than you, an epigone of Sid's, who did it to 'em. But if we achieve, by miracle, that ten point five by end of year, I stay director—calling when I please for votes or meetings; maybe hiring back the union members who defect. The grudges that a rift will sow, emotions it'll rouse, will better serve to crumble and to bury Colleague Church's tainted congregation than a noble, proud, and unified defeat. I'll take whoever's desperate, broken, and repentant back—which they will have to be, to take scabs' wages. But we've little choice; that's what we'll have to pay 'em. For we'll be in even direr trouble next year: having sold the windows out the walls, we're due a shivery winter; also, after getting ten point five, the owners might as well demand eleven. But we'll weed those thistles when they've sprouted. First comes first, and second second. Here's the form I'm looking for." She withdraws a paper from the filing cabinet. "Your name was on it all along. I thought I knew each file, what every drawer contained. This job begins to overrun one person's shallow brim. We might in January— fate allowing—contemplate the hiring, or the training, of an aide. Sign here, and here, and here too."

Daize. "Do you believe it is possible really to reach ten point five?"

Lea. "Almost definitely not. The risk, though, should be mine. We can't afford to lose your expertise, now can we? And the blame is mine as well, and shall adhere to me and me alone for every, each dismissal."

Daize signs. "Don't be too hard on us. This will need witnesses. What could we otherwise do, after all, colleague?"

Lea. "Nothing." She puts the form in her pocket. "I will have it witnessed later. Now, my first decision as director— almost our collective's first: You're fired."

Daize. "That's the directorly spirit. You're serious?"

Lea. "As a gravestone. I can offer two weeks' severance pay, but not two weeks', two days', two hours' work. I don't intend offense, but I would rather have you not around. Your influence is bad for me, I reckon."

Daize. "If I repudiate, challenge you, fight this thing?"

Lea. "That would hardly be what's best, now would it, for the company? By splitting us, you're splitting our minority supporters, guaranteeing full ascendancy to Matheson, and making certain that we fail to satisfy the ultimatum, there- fore burdening the factory with some unknown and callow new director."

Daize. "So, I'm to choose between tyrants familiar and strange; one a plebeian, one a patrician; the one wants to fire me, the other might possibly not. A decision I shouldn't find difficult."

Lea. "That's not quite how I perceive it. If you want to fight, I'll get the union on my side by telling them your schemes. If somehow you survive the next three months, the owners will replace you anyway. There isn't any future for you here, no more for you than Sid. You're out of allies, Daize. Your only choice is whether I'm allowed to implement your plan in peace. And if you quietly resign, perhaps I'll write a reference that you can show employers."

Daize. "Maybe I'll make the identical threat to you."

Lea. "Keep in mind this paper in my pocket, which at my discretion can be copied or destroyed. That means that I decide whose neck lies at year-end beneath the saber."

Daize. "What if I take from your pocket that paper?"

Lea. "Try. We'll learn who's stronger."

A pause.

The laughing coworkers enter. "Hey, good news! We're going on strike!"

"Smash the system! Fuck the owners!"

They exit.

Daize takes a step towards Lea, and holds out her hand. Lea shakes it.

Daize. "I have decided I'm sick of this place. There's no need for a duplicate autocrat, anyway."

Lea. "Or, I hope, for even one much longer."

Daize. "Maybe I'll come to the shareholders' meeting to see how you've done at year-end. I'll be curious." Daize exits.

Lea withdraws the form from her pocket, and buries it deep in the filing cabinet. Then she too exits.

BUZZING OF THE intercom, followed by knocking at the door. The female janitor enters with a vacuum cleaner, which she puts to use.

The office has reverted to its former tidiness. The desk is back in use, and the poster is gone.

Knocking at the door. The male janitor enters. The female janitor turns off the vacuum cleaner.

Female janitor. "Look who crosses the picket line!"

Male janitor. "Aw, don't start. —She around?"

Female janitor. "Ain't seen her. You got something to say to her?"

Male janitor. "Think she'll be around?"

Female janitor. "There's some meeting starting soon. Might as well pull yourself a chair up and wait." She resumes vacuuming.

Male janitor, sitting briefly. "Do you think she'll . . ."

Female janitor, turning off the vacuum cleaner. "What?"

Male janitor. "Never mind."

Female janitor. "She might." She resumes vacuuming.

Male janitor. "Might what?"

She stops vacuuming. "What?"

Male janitor. "You said she might."

Female janitor. "What's the question?"

Male janitor. "Aw, cut the corn. Think she'll give me my old job back?"

Female janitor. "If she does, it'll be at half pay."

Male janitor. "That's all right. I expected that. I just need something coming in, or my sister's like to toss me out the house. Half's more anyway than the union's paying."

Female janitor. "I thought the union was out of strike fund."

Male janitor. "That's what I'm telling you."

Female janitor. "She'll make you sign a paper."

Male janitor. "Shit, I'd about sign a hot turd right now, if'd help."

Female janitor. "Making you promise not to join up to any more unions."

Male janitor. "And wha'd any union ever do for me but rile me and mix my brains about and lose me a perfect good job?"

Female janitor. "And get you equalized, and trained, and a little more respect. No, nothing much." She resumes vacuuming.

Male janitor. "Sure, before all them latecomers jumped onto the bandwagon and spoiled things for the rest of us. Before Church started making deals with the foremen and managers."

She turns off the vacuum cleaner. "What?"

Male janitor. "Never mind. Just that I wouldn't be surprised if Matheson Church was in the boss's pocket after all and all along."

Female janitor. "I thought so too for a while. But that's just the moth calling poison what the caterpillar called cabbage. Matheson's only stupid and stubborn, and too in love with his own voice. Straight how: you don't call a strike in the midst a recession." She resumes vacuuming, while the male janitor paces. She turns off the vacuum cleaner. "Why don't you take over?"

Male janitor. "Me?"

Female janitor. "Maybe she'll be more inclined favorable if you're already doing the work."

Male janitor. "Bless your whole heart."

Female janitor. "Don't go getting sticky. I could use the help. To me you're just free labor."

He vacuums while she dusts and tidies.

Lea enters. The male janitor plies the vacuum cleaner with increased gusto.

Lea picks up the phone, shouting over the noise from the vacuum cleaner. "Sandy? Tell Faraj I'll call him back at seven his time. Make it seven-thirty . . . Move tomorrow's lunch to two, and have the taxi meet me at the restaurant at quarter after three . . . If possible, an aisle seat . . . You will have to talk to Palst. Be firm: 'Decision's final,' and the rest. He's brought it on himself, and half expects it . . . You've as much authority as I do, or as anyone. Remember that. You've my complete support . . . Let's leave Renfrento till I'm back; I know how best to handle him . . . Review the lading from last year; it shouldn't come to more than thir-ty-seven hundred, I should guess . . . Just sign my name. That's right . . . She's here, in person? Send her in. And bring an extra copy—make it three or four—of those financials. Sandy: thank you."

Daize enters, holding copies of the financial reports. "Must I congratulate you?"

Lea. "Check the final page; the summary's there."

Daize puts the reports on the conference table. "Now there's no need. Invitations so prompt prove a homeowners' pride. My sincerest of compliments." They shake hands.

Lea. "Good to see you."

Daize. "Didn't I promise I'd come to the shareholders' meeting? —These janitors still have the shock-brigade fer-vor. But couldn't they pause for a meeting's length?"

Lea. "They've their work to do, like you or I have."

Female janitor. "That's okay, Miz Pensilby. We're finished now. I said, we're finished now!"

Male janitor, turning off the vacuum cleaner. "That's right. All done. Everything slicked and squared, sheveled and ruly."

Lea. "Then your own authority discharges you. But first, my thanks." She shakes the male janitor's hand. "We'll speak tomorrow."

Male janitor. "It'll be an honor, Miz Pensilby."

Lea. "Don't forget to take the garbage with you."

The janitors take the garbage and exit.

Daize. "Even 'an honor, Miz Pensilby'!"

Lea. "Yes. It's awful, isn't it? Some honor! He will beg, and I'll bestow his job back, but at half his former pay. A teacher, parent, or policeman must have sometime made him grovel for a favor. Now it's second nature. All society, all upbringing's our enemy. To think, I used to think it Sid! —But how have you been?"

Daize. "Though there's a petty and rancorous part of me still that'd like to declare that you ruined my life, it'd be an untruth. I am excellent."

Lea. "Then that cookie factory did hire you?"

Daize. "No, but another. Your letter was helpful. That 'supervised over a hundred employees' was most what impressed them, I think. I now supervise, anyway, over two hundred—and earn more than double what Sid at his highest munificence deemed I was worth. Not that money is everything."

Lea. "No, but as the lazy person's index to importance, income is the closest thing to praise most unimaginative bosses have to give. I'm pleased to hear you're valued—and that you, where Sid collapsed, have fallen firmly on your feet, and bounced back."

The intercom buzzes.

Daize. "Maybe because I'd less distance to fall than him."

A knock at the door. Matheson and Sid enter, followed by the receptionist.

Receptionist. "I'm sorry, Lea. They said you were expecting them."

Lea. "Sandy, thank you; that's all right." The receptionist exits. "A lie, but all the same, uncanny. I've not said nor thought your name but once in ninety days, and that was half a minute prior to your entrance, Sid. Perhaps you were expected—never, though, with Colleague Church beside you."

Matheson. "You're right to quail: your monocratic reign of terror lies upon its bed of death; its final breaths are numbered fewer than the hours in a winter's afternoon."

Lea. "Did I quail?"

Sid. "Let's not start, Colleague Matheson, thumping our chests. It's delightful to see you, Miz Pensilby, and a surprise wholly welcome to find here Miz Glied. You are both looking splendid as ever. I trust the appearance expresses the inner content?"

Daize. "If it were so, your expression would seem to be that of a snake that has swallowed a cockatoo."

Sid. "If you see what I feel, it is gratitude here on my face. If I thought that she'd take it, I'd give Lea my hand and congratulate her. Ten point five by year-end! Now the new year begins with no need for the owners to send a replacement director."

Lea. "I begin to sniff your plot's malodor."

Daize. "Lea is director; there's documents proving it."

Sid. "I have seventy-five faithful friends who'll attest that they're forgeries; more, that I never resigned."

Matheson. "You glower now, but I'm inured to that. Perhaps you should've made concessions; showed some willingness to compromise, or yield; negotiated, not neglected all our deadlines and ignored all our demands."

Lea. "Just like Sid did—or have you forgotten?"

Matheson. "He now perceives the proletariat's might."

Sid. "That's a fact."

Matheson. "Besides, a lion's less repugnant than a lamb that roars. He never was a traitor."

The intercom buzzes.

Sid. "And this lion, moreover, is learning to bleat."

A knock at the door. The receptionist enters, followed by Ottavia Farr-Mp.

Receptionist. "Miz Farr-Mp is here for the meeting, Miz Pensilby." Exits.

Ottavia "Good afternoon, all. Why don't we begin? This shouldn't take long." She sits at the head of the conference table.

Matheson. "We can't begin until the owners come."

Lea. "Miz Farr-Mp's their delegate. And Mister Church here is, or represents, the union."

Sid. "Introductions are needed, I see, all the more since there's been some confusion of late with regard to our various roles at the factory here . . ."

Ottavia. "That will not at all be necessary. I'm here today in courtesy only, on behalf of the shareholders—or the former shareholders, I should instead say. As of midnight last night, the factory has been sold to a conglomerate, the name of which will mean nothing to any of you, I'm sure, but suffice it to say they have controlling interests in a score of industries, a thousand companies in every market all around the world. Congratulations. You're part of a much larger family now, a syndicate of corporations, one whose sales in the aggregate exceed the gross domestic product of many small countries, and whose owners are among the richest and most powerful people anywhere today."

Matheson. "You sold the factory?"

Ottavia withdraws a page from a folder. "Naturally, the new owners have chosen to appoint their own director; I bring a list of what he needs from you Monday." Ottavia stands.

Sid. "But we did what you asked! We achieved ten point five!"

Daize. "You!"

Sid. "I said 'we'! It's an outrage, in any event."

Lea. "I suppose you always meant to sell it?—that the boosted profits only meant to make it more attractive for the purchase?"

Ottavia. "I cannot divine what my clients, the former shareholders of your company, intended or did not intend to do. But they didn't break any promise: They said they'd replace your director if ten point five wasn't reached. They never said they'd keep him if it was."

Sid. "What a mouthful of cowshit! A warning implies a condition, a chance of escaping its threat, or it ceases to be ultimatum, but harm guaranteed. It's like saying our laws let us lock away criminals *and* law-abiders in jail. It's like shooting a man for not burgling your house. It's a joke; it's a punchline. It's crap."

Matheson. "We weren't consulted, so we won't comply."

Ottavia. "Their actions need no justification; but supposing that they did intend to sell all along, you hardly helped them raise the price with this strike and these picketers thronged outside your gates. Every time I step inside them, this place seems upon the verge of self-combustion. If you can't control your staff, it's little wonder you cannot control your profits. I would hardly blame anyone, old or new owners, if they tore this building down and sold it for scrap. But nobody asks me my opinion. Gratuitously I squander it here. My words, I see, fall like rain on desert, so I'll waste no more. Good day—and good luck making your good luck."

Matheson. "Until we come to some agreement, till we're granted what we're asking, no one leaves."

Ottavia. "But this matter no longer concerns me." Ottavia exits.

Matheson. "She will return, or, rather, be returned."

Lea, looking at the page on the table. "Shouldn't I have somehow seen this coming?"

Sid. "What contemptible, underhand treatment. From Glen and Rebecka and Tonio I'd never expect it."

Daize. "How is it worse than what you'd meant to do to poor Lea?"

Sid. "I was only reversing what you'd done to me!"

Daize. "Don't you remember? You quit—half a year ago!"

Matheson. "That never happened. Nobody resigned, and nobody was fired. Hell, there was no strike. If she can sell the factory, impose on us some dictatorial new director, we can then impose on her the past that we prefer—and future too. Before she's back, let's get our story straight." To Daize. "Do you, for instance, work here still—again?"

Lea. "The financial statements and reports will take all weekend to compile alone. And look! He wants a list of all employees, with their past and present salaries, too."

Matheson. "You see! We draft our own reality."

Sid. "So this upstart can better dismantle it. Sure, he'll sack first who he deems to be most overpaid."

Ottavia enters, escorted by two workers.

Workers. "This one wants to talk to you, boss." They exit, standing guard outside the door.

Matheson. "You're ready to negotiate now terms?"

Ottavia. "You're the hooligan responsible for this enormity? I'll see you're thrown in prison for this, with your hired ruffians, before the day's end."

Matheson. "I told you: no one leaves until we reach together some agreement mutual."

Daize. "What're you doing, sequestering us forcibly?"

Ottavia. "There's a cordon of armed hoodlums around the factory; we're being held hostage. Do you have any idea who I am?"

Matheson. "Some big-shot owners' representative? We never properly were introduced."

Lea. "When you say that they are armed, you mean they're . . .?"

Ottavia. "Armed! With guns and knives, like vigilantes!"

Daize. "Now we know who has been raiding the stockrooms."

Lea. "Matheson, this isn't safe. One spark, and . . ."

Sid. "I had nothing to do with this, any of this. It's important that everyone realize that."

Matheson. "Don't fret. I've given firm instructions not to shoot inside the gates—unless provoked. But no one will provoke; you're too outnumbered. Today we see a microcosm here, in fact, of macroeconomics: one or two exploiting profiteers, and scores of workers, human livestock, burden beasts, the many who by few are milked till dry. Acculturation's slow hypnosis, a philosopher once said. It must be; what but mesmerism, magnetism, mind control, and lies could else subdue the herd, which could betrample anytime their herders? Today we break the trance, and demonstrate the might that's dormant in majorities."

Ottavia. "I will not submit to any speeches. You can kidnap, shoot me, knife me, beat or rape me, but you can't force me to listen to you bloviate socialist claptrap."

Lea. "Matheson, your quarrel is with only me. These others have no part in all this."

Matheson. "No, everyone is implicated now, the highest chief executive down to the lowliest of janitors; and no one leaves until we've built a better world."

Ottavia. "Fevered lunatic! The world makes people, and not vice versa. The flora in your guts have as much chance of changing you as you changing the world. You confuse for wholes what are only parts. Trust the whole to know what's best for itself. The only thing the world wants from you is for you to pursue your own interests—*that* is what makes *it* strong."

Matheson. "The cancer cell thinks he's the highest purpose—"

Ottavia. "I'm not debating! How much do you make—your yearly income? I can guess. I don't allow my socio-economical inferiors, still less my abductors, the privilege of contradicting me. I've heard it all a thousand times before. But have you, any of you, ever known, ever even met a real rich person? I don't mean any millionaire, but a mogul, a tycoon, a fiscal sun round which there orbit a million millionaires like doting planets; I'm talking about the superrich, whose wealth exceeds your dreams' imagination. Of course you've never, or for the status quo you would have more respect, because you'd realize it's based on meritocracy. The superrich rule the world because they're super clever, wise, and energetic, supremely nimble, staunch, fervid, and strong. They're healthier and lovelier even than average people; they're superhuman. When once you've met a truly rich person, the poor appear like lank imitations, pallid specters, mere dry offscourings, dust. Instead of being grateful that the rich exist, instead of praising them, thanking them for stirring your lumpen listlessness to some semblance of life, for carrying you about on their heels like pollen, you curse their weightiness and anathemize their interference!"

Lea. "What a lot of nonsense she does prattle."

Sid. "Let's not anyone provocate anyone else, and remember this all's a big misunderstanding."

Ottavia. "This cow's uprising you preach is but the hallucination of a parasite who thinks he'll survive without any host."

Matheson. "The idle owner is the parasite!"

Ottavia. "You call them idle! They who orchestrate economies, who steer corporations, who engineer and doctor the commerce that keeps us alive! They who'd die of shame before they'd so shirk their obligations to humanity by hunkering down on a picket line!"

Matheson. "They suck the marrow from the workers' bones!"

Ottavia. "And if they do, the more should you thank them for stimulating, enlivening, and whetting and honing you with the rough rasp of adversity—for putting before your eyes the image of a better life, indeed, a better you."

A gunshot is heard.

Sid. "What the fuck! That was down on the floor!"

Matheson exits, and Sid goes to the window.

Ottavia. "You'd be plutocides, and kill off the rich, but in the process you'd exterminate your own potential; you'd excise your own organs before they're even fully grown. You'd topple trees like termites, but from spite, not need— when you could yourselves become trees!"

Daize. "Everyone can't all be plutocrat millionaires."

Ottavia. "Doesn't that make it more desirable? By narrow roads one gets to high places; worthwhile things are won with difficulty. What value would jewels have if they adorned every décolletage? Who'd cherish gold if our streets were gilded, or pearls if pearls were common as pebbles? I would rather make precious things more scarce, therefore more precious, than dilute their worth with ubiquity. I would concentrate vaster fortunes in even fewer hands. I would have richer rich and poorer poor! More giddy heights and more abysmal depths! Let us undergo every experience the human frame can support, play every note that the human instrument can sound. Let's have women and men span the gamut from base to noble, from mud to ether, from insects to gods."

Matheson enters. "A false alarm."

Sid. "We'll be killed by your dogshit alarms."

Ottavia, lifting the telephone from the desk. "Did the universe, the creative force, lift itself from ooze primordial and differentiate, individuate, distribute itself in countless discrete parcels, but so we could undo its work? Your insurrection's metaphysical, not political. You cannot have light without shadow, wave without particle, pleasure without pain. Your attack on the rich is an attack on disparity and imbalance, which is the force that drives, the ambidextrous engine that propels the cosmos onward. You're worse than Satans! You'd depose the Tao, unweave the tensile fibers of the stars!"

She strikes Matheson over the head with the telephone. He collapses.

Daize. "What are you doing!"

Lea. "Matheson!"

Sid. "What the fuck!"

Ottavia. "You'd wage war against individuals, and boil this many-flavored earth down to insipidest pap. The only freedom's individual freedom; you'd use yours to demolish the very system that gives it to you. The alternative to free and open competition's not utopia, but totalitarian police-statism. You'd bloat government till each citizen's her own probation officer, a bureaucratic functionary in charge of her life-file. You'd make an anthill of society; of men and women, robots who'd never spurn their programming."

Matheson gets to his feet. "How dare you hit me in the head."

Lea. "Take it easy."

Daize. "How do you feel? If you're dizzy, you'd better sit."

Matheson. "My brains feel curdled, like a bowl of words."

Sid. "He's all right."

Ottavia. "In the end, you're steeped in hypocrisy; you embody it. 'Equality''s your battle cry, but how poorly paid are your waitresses and maids, your babysitters and your hairdressers? Do you know or care who makes your shoes, or what their profit is? Do you support your children's teachers' strikes? For that matter, how much allowance do you give your children for cleaning your homes and washing your clothes? You think you're livestock; do you ever ask what quality of life your livestock and meat animals have? Indeed, you endorse the food chain and the paramount place you hold in it every time you swat a fly or eat a fine cheese. The fact is that life feeds on other life. You cannot clear a pleasant path through the forest without your massacring scores of ecologies. Well, the rich eat the poor; be happy to feed your superiors." She throws open the door. "Your leader is hurt. I'm going for help." She exits.

Worker. "Boss?"

Matheson. "Oh, let her go. She's quite insane." The worker closes the door. "I can't believe she hit me in the head! That proves, if proof were needed, that the ruling class is doomed, and knows it: they'll defend themselves like cornered vermin, rearing, hissing, tooth and nail—and telephone. The powers that be will soon have been the powers that were. That day can't come too soon for me; I'm suddenly quite tired. But first: the war that fumigates them from their filthy nests and corridors of backstairs influence and leaves the world pristine again, and disinfected, new. I'll get me to the gates. The flunky cops will be here soon. We'll see who's better armed. To think that she called *us* totalitarians!"

Lea. "Matheson, you're still a bit unsteady, in your walk and in your thoughts. As far as I'm concerned, the strike is over, ended with your total triumph, every one of your demands fulfilled. You'll have your jobs back Monday, at whatever wage you think is safest, bearing our new management in mind; I even am inclined, before I'm fired, to write you checks for three months' back pay, since this whole commotion was incited by the ultimatum fraudulently foisted on us by Ottavia and the former owners. Sid and Daize by rights are welcome to their old positions too—or let them take whatever title pleases them. We might as well be all directors or all presidents, to make the new one's task of sifting us more difficult. But stand your little army down, and hide your weapons quickly. We will vouch that Miz Farr-Mp assaulted you quite motivelessly. Also, you should have a doctor check you."

Sid. "You could have a concussion, it's true."

Matheson. "All right. I do feel rather strange." He sits at the desk. "We won?"

Lea. "Yes. It's over."

Matheson. "That's good." He faints.

Lea. "Call an ambulance." She opens the door. "You both come in here."

The workers enter. "What happened?"

Lea. "Mister Church was wounded by that woman."

Sid. "He has probably got a concussion, we think."

Daize. "Telephone's broken. I'll use the receptionist's." She exits.

Lea. "He's in need of medical attention, which will soon arrive. Before it does, for crying heaven, ditch your guns. Or better yet, go home. The strike is done; we gave you everything. You work again on Monday."

Worker. "Thank God."

Other worker. "I told you it would work."

Worker. "Still, I wish I could've shot this baby once." They exit.

Sid. "I'll escort them outside, and make sure that they leave, and in safety. —You mean what you said 'bout my job?"

Lea. "What's it matter anymore what I say?"

Sid. "But you'll tell the director I never resigned?"

Lea. "If you like, sure."

Sid. "And that equalization of wages still holds?"

Lea. "Sure. Your salary's as low as mine is."

Sid. "Then you're still my accountant, the best that there is. We won't lap any shit from this asshole. We'll stand all together, support one another. Without us, he's nothing. He can't run the place by himself."

Lea. "If he gives us any fuss, we'll strike him."

Sid. "That's the stuff." Sid exits.

Lea touches Matheson's head.

Daize enters. "Shouldn't be long till the ambulance gets here. He's bleeding a bit, but we shouldn't compress it, in case there is swelling. Some ice would be harmless, though."

Lea. "You should go. What's left to do, I'll handle."

Daize. "Call me if ever you need other witnesses."

Daize exits, shutting the door behind her.

Lea opens the door. Then, consulting Ottavia's paper, she removes files from the filing cabinet and, as the sound of a siren grows louder, tears them to shreds.

FROM THE BEGINNING, Burris felt that there was something wrong with Oxley. His birth had been violent, and had caused him bruising, swelling, and a fractured clavicle, but there was much that it could not account for. His eyes were different sizes, and his ears weirdly misshapen. His feet both pointed to one side. Sometimes individual knuckles in his fingers moved independently of the others. His skin was at first too pink, then yellow; then, after a few weeks, it turned a purplish blue. His scalp was both flaky and oily, and his hands were cracked and peeling. In the first half-year of his life, he broke out in a series of rashes, each different from the last. He coughed a lot, cried when he was not coughing, and slept poorly. His stools, from the very first, were shockingly strange.

His mother saw no cause for concern in any of this. Rachel was simply enthralled by Oxley's existence, and found proof, even in his screaming, of his uncompromising vitality. Also, because she was with him all the time, she was better able to chart the subtle variations in his fussiness, and to recognize in his calmer moments something not unlike contentment; sometimes, usually after pooping or puking, he even smiled. Every day he learned something new: how to lift his head; how to stick out his tongue; how to track a moving object with his eyes; how to clap his hands; how to sniff things before putting them in his mouth; how to spot her in a mirror, though her voice was behind him. Together they conversed in tones and inflections. She could watch him eat, or sleep, or make faces like a troubled executive, for hours. Time, which during her pregnancy had seemed like all the sunshine falling on a baking plain, now contracted to the cozy, fascinating flame of a single candle. Her son, warm and vital in her arms, was beautiful, clever, and dynamic, and she could not believe that he was unwell.

To Burris's annoyance, all the doctors that he spoke to agreed with Rachel. Oxley's symptoms, they said, were common in newborns, and would clear up in due time. He was only colicky, they said. Try not to worry so much, they said.

This blithe advice brought back to Burris all the feelings of impotent rage that he had experienced at the hospital, when his wife, after two days in labor, had been whisked away to an operating theater that he had been prohibited to enter. Left standing in the corridor, clutching the consent form that had waived his right to object if Rachel or their baby died, unable to imagine what was happening and powerless to do anything about it, Burris had resorted to prayer—a wordless prayer in the form of a bargain: if only Rachel lived, the baby could die.

It was the thought of a moment, and soon forgotten; but some small, unconscious part of him still gnawed on remorse.

"Have you been feeding him too much?" he would ask Rachel. —"I don't think so."

"Don't let him lie on his tummy; it's not safe." —"No," she would agree.

"You are overstimulating him. No wonder he can't sleep." —"Yes," she said. But in fact, the only thing Rachel really worried about was Burris's smoking in the house.

At last, when Oxley was eleven months old, Burris found a pediatrician who was willing to countenance the possibility that the boy was not perfectly healthy. Doctor Rubenand was dismissive of Oxley's head-banging, teeth-grinding, copious drooling, and fear of strangers, but became pensive at the mention of his awkward crawling.

"Can you tell me, was there birth trauma?" —"What do you mean?" —The doctor looked at Rachel. "Was there any difficulty during the birth?"

"Well, his shoulder got stuck coming out," said Burris. He was reluctant to discuss the matter in front of Rachel, who still cursed in her sleep and jumped at the sound of supermarket cash registers, which beeped like fetal heart monitors. Oxley's birth had certainly been the most painful and debasing experience of her life, and Burris wanted, for her sake, to draw a line under it—to move forward and never think of it again. But he realized for the first time that it must also have been the most terrible experience of his son's life.

"It was my fault, I guess," murmured Rachel. "I kept pushing when they'd told me not to." —"Nonsense, darling," said Burris. "His position was wrong." To Rubenand he said, "Anyway, they tried the vacuum, and they tried twisting him out."

Rachel did not say that Doctor Paschava had cut her perineum, or that he had had, at one time, both hands and most of a forearm inside her. Nor did she say that Paschava had intentionally fractured Oxley's clavicle to try to make his shoulders narrower. —"Finally," Burris said, "they had to push him back in, and do a C-section." For some reason this too had failed, and the doctors had at last resorted to reaching in through the cesarean incision to manipulate him out her pelvis. Rachel did not say that most of this had been done without anesthetic, the anesthetist being sick at home. Nor did she say that eventually someone, misreading her chart, had given her nitrous oxide, the one kind of pain relief she was allergic to, and that she had vomited into the mask and nearly suffocated. And she did not say that she had been able to see everything the doctors were doing reflected in the chrome operating light overhead.

"In any event," said Burris, "he must not have been getting enough oxygen for some of this time, because when they finally got him out he was blue, and they took him straight to intensive care."

Doctor Rubenand opened his mouth audibly, and put down his pen. "That," he said, "is what I meant by 'birth trauma.'"

Rachel held Oxley more tightly, as if they were crossing a busy street.

Doctor Rubenand prescribed some tests, which Rachel forgot or feigned to forget to take Oxley to. Burris was bemused and irate. "You are toying with our son's health!" —But Rachel did not see it that way. The tests were only diagnostic, and she did not believe that anything was wrong with Oxley anyway. When Burris threatened to rearrange his schedule and take Oxley to the appointments himself, Rachel yielded. "Oh, there's no point in our both going."

None of the tests were conclusive, but Burris was nevertheless convinced that he now had the complete picture. Through negligence, disorderliness, conceit, callousness, and unprofessionalism, Doctor Leahy, Doctor Paschava, and the staff at the hospital had subjected his wife and his son to birth trauma. Gradually he arrived at the decision that, to teach them a lesson, and to prevent such a thing from happening again, it was his duty to sue.

The lawyers he interviewed were grandiose and discouraging. Hospitals, they said, had formidable legal departments; dozens of people would need to be deposed, thousands of pages of records and policy subpoenaed; the lawsuit could drag on for years, with no guarantee of victory. They all demanded sizeable retainer fees and a free hand; and Burris could not bring himself to commit.

At last he appealed to a cousin's brother-in-law, a man by the name of Lucrenzo Tabbat, who was reputed within the family to be a splendid litigator. He had carved out a successful practice representing himself against large corporations, who usually found it simpler and less costly to offer him a quiet settlement. He did not consider these nuisance suits, for he was a man who was genuinely and personally affronted by shoddy products, misleading solecisms, and implicit promises unfulfilled. Burris told him their story, and Lucrenzo's interest was piqued. After all, doctors had deep pockets, and there was no question that the Kornoreks had a good case; if this wrong had been done to him, he would have chewed on it for years. The size of the undertaking was no deterrent, either, for vanity made him industrious. He asked for no retainer, but worked the only way that he knew how: by adopting Burris and Rachel's cause as his own.

Rachel did not cooperate with the lawyer, because she did not like him. He was scrawny, and wheedling, and had a face like a dried fig—and, as her friend Chelsea pointed out, he was a man: "Until women support women against the system of patriarchy that oppresses them, nothing will change, and justice, when not an outright travesty, will remain a mirage." Rachel agreed; she did not approve of the lawsuit because she could not see how money changing hands between a few men would improve the lot of women or of babies. It would be far more effective, surely, to educate the pregnant woman directly, and empower her to take control of her own body and birthing. As for Lucrenzo, she felt towards him what she felt lately towards most men: an amused impatience, as if all their frantic exploits were only a kind of dirty frolicking in the garden, or building of model airplanes on the kitchen table—high-spirited but irrelevant and obstructive busywork. She secretly, and only half consciously, felt that no man, however vigorous, could have withstood the ordeal that she and every other mother had undergone.

And though she felt the same kind of tolerant exasperation towards Chelsea, Alexis, and her other childless friends, she began again to attend their feminist rallies and their consciousness-raising sessions. The other women no longer treated her as a wayward pupil, but solicited her opinions and deferred to her experience. It was not just the presence of Oxley at these meetings that accorded her this authority, but something new in her face and bearing. She looked older than they remembered.

Perhaps too she was less wayward than she had been. Certainly there was much in what the feminists said that, with the jargon removed, she could agree with. And though she might doubt the universality of this or that blanket denunciation, she needed only to picture Doctor Leahy or Doctor Paschava to admit that it applied to some men at least. When the others talked about "the system," or "patriarchy," or "the oppressors," she brought to mind the hospital, or substituted for these abstractions the abstraction of the medical establishment, and in this way could participate in the conversation and share in the indignation.

She enjoyed the storytelling portions of these meetings best. Although a few of the women used personal anecdotes to glorify themselves, to monopolize the floor, or to preface a political harangue, most of them were modestly and ingenuously candid as they described their power struggles at work, the double standards they encountered at school, the outmoded attitudes of their family, and the harassment they braved every day simply walking down the street. Rachel was both appalled and galvanized to discover that no relationship between a man and a woman, or indeed between a boy and a girl, was without its inequalities and exploitations.

From the awkward, unwanted first kiss to the traditional postures of sex, and from the proprietary language of wedding vows to the patrilineal inheritance of property and name, the very fabric of society was woven from the symbolic or actual domination of the male over the female.

She grasped this truth at arm's length, not realizing that it applied also to her own life, until one night, awed by the soft-spoken courage of a young woman who had been raped, she felt compelled to share a story of her own. She intended to talk about Oxley's birth, but found it necessary first to talk about the pregnancy, and could not do that without telling about Burris and how they had met. She and Burris had told this story many times; but tonight it did not sound funny or charming. She stumbled, repeated herself, and apologized. The more lightly she tried to treat the facts, the more heavily they weighed: An older man, in a position of trust and power, had used that position and that power to inveigle her into a romantic and then a physical relationship. "It's not as bad as it sounds," she said. "I was actually quite smitten by him." But she recognized, even as she uttered them, that her protestations were the more incriminating, because they more starkly revealed his influence over her. Her tale was unique only in how literally Burris had hypnotized her. In the end, she did not need to say, and no one needed to point out to her, that she too had been raped.

She did not confront Burris with her discovery; indeed, by the time she returned home that night, she no longer quite believed it. But a seed had been sown.

Rachel suffered toothache for a year because, as she explained to her roommates, she was afraid of dentists. "I don't like pain," she confided; and she was allergic to painkillers. The last time she had visited a dentist, years ago in high school, she had vomited into the anesthesia mask. Her mind did not remember the terror of asphyxiation, or the claustrophobia of being drugged and hemmed in by bristling instruments of torture—but her body remembered. Now, only when the pain of toothache became less bearable than the anticipated pain of treatment did she finally, with a convulsive effort, make an appointment with a new dentist chosen at random from the phone book. She was too mortified by her last ordeal to ever return to the old one—whose receptionist still sent yearly checkup reminders to her mother's address.

Doctor Burris Kornorek was dapper, formal, confident, handsome, and foreign. He was tall but he stooped slightly, as though from courtesy. He had the velvety voice and enunciation of a radio broadcaster. He moved with an attentive deliberation that his patients found reassuring. He was an excellent dentist, in fact, and he knew it. Unfortunately for Rachel, his clinic in no way betrayed this excellence. His waiting room was demoralizing, his examination rooms were bleak and cluttered with equipment, and his assistants, who were both in love with him, were curt and unwelcoming to young women. After having her mouth disparagingly inspected by one of these, Rachel asked to use the washroom, and fled.

An hour later, she was lying in bed, clutching her jaw, and mentally composing an apology, when the telephone rang. Chelsea brought her the handset and whispered, "I think you've won something."

"Is this Miss Rachel Gibbons speaking? This is Doctor Burris Kornorek calling. I understand that you had to leave our office today rather suddenly, and I simply wanted to make sure that you are quite all right."

Moved by his concern and shamed by her fear, Rachel offered to pay for the missed appointment and to book a new one.

"I can fit you in tomorrow afternoon, but what guarantee do I have that you won't abscond again?"

Rachel made a full confession. At the mention of her allergy, Burris felt a jolt of excitement.

"To dislike pain is very natural," he reassured her, "and very healthy. Suffering serves no useful purpose, and moreover is avoidable. There are, thankfully, alternatives to medication." —"Okay," said Rachel. —"For instance: though it is strangely disesteemed in this country, studies have shown, and my own clinical experience confirms, that in about eighty percent of people, hypnosis can be quite effective." —"Okay." —"You would like to try?" —"Sure. I mean, if you think it will work." —"Excellent. Then I will see you tomorrow at four o'clock."

Only after she had hung up did she begin to worry that she was one of the unsusceptible twenty percent, and that this would only be discovered too late. Her anxiety persisted until four o'clock the next day, when Doctor Kornorek greeted her in the empty waiting room, and with a warm guiding hand ushered her in to his private office.

"Here we will begin," he said, sighing contentedly. "Here we will be more comfortable." His equanimity was contagious. Even as he outlined the upcoming procedure, Rachel felt that they were discussing someone else; she felt more like his collaborator than his patient.

"Very well. First we will try a simple relaxation exercise." —"Sure."

He told her to close her eyes, to breathe deeply, and to relax. He counted slowly, and with many soothing asides, down from ten. He told her to hold out an arm, to lower it, and then to open her eyes. His smile showed that he was satisfied, and she felt a flicker of complacence.

"We will have no difficulty," he said. —"I'm hypnotizable?" she asked. —"In fact, you are hypnotized."

This surprised her, but she did not betray her surprise. She had imagined that hypnosis would feel somehow different—like being asleep, or wrapped in a fog, or submerged in a warm bath. Nevertheless, she had no reason to doubt him; he was the expert. While he spoke, she probed gingerly in her mind, trying to determine how exactly her new consciousness differed from her everyday state.

"In the examination room, we will take you even deeper, and then we can begin. You will be aware of everything happening, but will experience no discomfort, pain, or distress. You will remain altogether comfortable and relaxed throughout. If by some chance at any time you *do* feel a little twinge of pain, just raise your left hand, and we will pause again to settle you. There will be no hurry. So. Are you ready?"

"I'm ready," she said—and was relieved to notice that her voice was rather husky . . .

She followed Doctor Kornorek to the examination room, sat in the reclining chair, and closed her eyes. Again he counted down from ten; she strained to concentrate on his voice, to let it enter and subdue her. She heard his assistant enter the room and begin moving tools around on a plastic table. Doctor Kornorek put a gloved finger in her mouth. She could smell his aftershave. He prodded her bad tooth and a spark of electricity shot through her jaw, causing her to curl her toes. But she did not make a sound, and she did not raise her left hand.

"Here is the culprit. We will start by tidying him up a bit."

Now her mind was racing. Had it worked? *Was* she indeed hypnotized? She no longer felt relaxed; should she speak up? However, he had said that she would feel everything, but not be distressed by it. She felt distressed now, didn't she? Perhaps—probably—it was her own fault. Before she opened her eyes and embarrassed them both by admitting that she was not hypnotized at all, she should try first to calm herself, and to return to the state of detached and trusting calm that she had experienced in his office. Silently she counted down from ten, and then, when he began scraping her tooth with a pick, again from twenty.

No discomfort, she repeated to herself; he had promised *no discomfort*. So whatever this feeling was, it could not be discomfort.

She should have said something earlier. By not objecting or raising her hand when he had first touched her tooth, she had disclaimed any pain, and had in effect signed the contract agreeing that she was hypnotized, as Doctor Kornorek supposed. She could not renege now without making them both look foolish.

She decided that she would wait till she could bear the pain no longer, then she would raise her left hand—only that. After all, he would not have given her that instruction unless he thought it might be needed. She could raise her hand and still be hypnotized.

She realized then with dread that of course she was hypnotized. Never could she have submitted to this torture—having the rotten enamel scraped from the surface of her toothache with a metal pick!—without being hypnotized. All this fevered introspection and uncertainty was part of being hypnotized, perhaps an indispensable part: her mind was indeed, after all, colluding with the dentist to restrain her body. Painlessness had never been the goal; he was only concerned that she lie still. And she was cooperating. She would not, could not, lift her hand, any more than she would ever scream or kick or claw his face. She was trapped, entangled in the skein of her own impotent thoughts. She felt the presence, somewhere near but out of sight, of a vast, eternal, suffocating horror . . .

"And spit," said Burris cheerily. If only, he thought, the editors at the Northeastern Journal of Dentistry could witness this triumphant vindication of his method! For the moment, he did not even feel any bitterness, only satisfaction. He might never be recognized by the Association, might never win a single disciple; but let fate only bring him a regular supply of such perfect subjects, and he would be happy. He paused briefly to admire her supple stillness, her prompt responsiveness, and the strong, steady heartbeat evident in her carotid artery. Indulging in a whim of dominance, he lightly pricked the tooth's nerve, and marveled again at the young woman's total submission.

Later, Rachel told Chelsea and Alexis that she could not recommend hypnosis. But as the days passed and her toothache faded, her recollection of the event mellowed. Nevertheless, she feigned illness when the day of her follow-up appointment arrived, and wriggled out of scheduling another. She avoided the dentist's solicitous phone calls, which became less frequent after a month. But then, in the middle of exam week, he appeared at the door of her apartment when both her roommates were out. Bemused, she invited him in for tea.

Burris had been unable to stop thinking about her. Fate had not brought him any new patients, and he had been unable to interest any of his old patients in hypnosis—not even after increasing the cost of anesthetic. His hygienist, Melinda, was happy to let him practice on her; but her teeth were immaculate, and provided no scope for his power over her. He daydreamed of Miss Gibbons, and mooned over her X-rays, which revealed to his hungry eyes countless opportunities for preventive intervention. As the weeks passed, his movements became less assured, and his stoop became a slouch. Formerly he had relished meeting his patients in the street or in the grocery store, deriving a secret, pleasurable superiority from his intimate knowledge of their oral cavities; now he scarcely cared to acknowledge them outside his clinic, seeing in each of them only an unsuitable subject for hypnosis.

She was as lovely as he remembered. Her crinkled eyes, her uncertain smile, even the way she stood—legs crossed at the ankles, supporting an elbow with one hand and clutching her lapels with the other—all attested eloquently to her suggestibility. For five minutes he stifled his yearning with small talk; at last he inquired after the tooth.

"It doesn't hurt at all anymore," she said. —"I am quite happy to hear it. Of course, very few complications ever arise from a filling. Those few that do, unfortunately, can be extremely subtle. You might not yourself know anything was wrong until it was too late." —Rachel apologized for missing the appointment and offered to reschedule. "I'll be much freer next week, once my exams are over." —Burris pontificated upon examinations for a while, deploring their restrictiveness, conceding their usefulness, and beseeching Rachel to not be unduly intimidated by them. "Even professors make mistakes. Some exam questions can be very poorly worded . . ." Eventually he allowed himself to drift back to the matter of Rachel's oral health. "Probably there is no need for you to come all the way to my clinic. After all, I am here now. If you have a few minutes to spare . . ."

"Yes, of course," said Rachel, taking an involuntary step back.

"Excellent," he said, and produced a pair of gloves.

"But," she stammered, "I should probably put these tea things away first, don't you think?"

Capitalizing on her unease, he suggested that although this would be only a simple examination, perhaps she would be more comfortable after a relaxation exercise.

"Sure. Okay. All the same, I think I'll tidy up a bit first . . ."

"Please sit down." —She did.

She closed her eyes; he counted down from ten.

There was nothing new to see and nothing to be done in her mouth, but he spent several minutes poking about inside it with luxurious thoroughness, like a child appraising a new hideout. He uttered soothing and congratulatory sounds—and Rachel was soothed. There would be no pain; and pinioned as she was by his fingers in her mouth, there was nothing for her to do or to say. Her toes uncurled, and her breathing slowed. Even her exams seemed far away.

The inspection complete, Burris sat back and watched her breathe for a minute. Then, unwilling to break the spell, he began to give her posthypnotic suggestions: that she would awake feeling relaxed and contented; that her teeth and gums would grow healthier daily; that she would excel at her exams; that she would find success and fulfillment wherever she searched . . . His suggestions became more expansive, melancholy, and valedictory, but still he could not bring himself to sever the connection. At length it occurred to him that this need not be the end. Guilty exhilaration made him fidget as he planted the final instruction.

"Two weeks from today, you will go shopping, at noon, at Holman's Foods. When you awake, you will not remember my saying this; but in two weeks' time you will feel, and follow, an overwhelming urge to shop for groceries at Holman's Foods. And now, as I count to ten, you will become more and more wakeful . . ."

After Doctor Kornorek left, Rachel did feel relaxed and contented, but also puzzled, for she remembered quite clearly what he had told her to forget. This seemed to prove conclusively that she had not, in fact, been hypnotized. Nevertheless, after two weeks of speculating and deliberating, a mixture of embarrassment, consideration, and curiosity carried her to the rendezvous on time. After all, she rationalized, she needed milk and bread, and Holman's was not far away.

They each feigned surprise when they met in the dairy aisle; and each concealed their surprise when, in the checkout line, Burris asked Rachel out to dinner, and Rachel accepted.

For years, Rachel had been the feminine holdout among her feminist friends. She had enjoyed their proselytizing, and withstood it the more effectively because she enjoyed it. They used her as their sounding board, honing on her their diatribes against the injustice of patriarchy, the manacles of marriage, and the myth of beauty. Rachel had perhaps been inoculated against such iconoclasm by her mother, a flustered, doting single parent who blamed all her ineffectualness on men. But Rachel, deprived of them, grew to adore men—especially manly men, men with thick wrists and square jaws, men with swagger and composure. She adored women too—especially womanly women; and she felt that the genderless world that her friends were fighting for would be an impoverished one. If she was, deep down, a feminist, she was equally a masculist. She could not even wholeheartedly deplore sexist inequality, because it seemed to offer her friends something to undermine and overturn. For her own part, when a man in a three-piece suit and a gold watch stopped to watch her pass in the street, she felt like a spy, an infiltrator, a sorceress. All this drama, all this conflict, all this story would be lost to human experience if not for the sexes, and sex.

So she was disappointed that her roommates were not more disapproving of Burris. They seemed to forgive him his male chauvinism, as if it were only to be expected from someone of his age and heritage. At last Rachel decided that they simply liked him and saw how much she liked him. When she told them that she was pregnant, they were as delighted as schoolgirls, and never once alluded to the prison of motherhood.

She had always dreamed of a large, lavish wedding, but Burris convinced her that this would be an unwarrantable extravagance. So they were married by a functionary in a drab office; Burris took only the morning off from work. She defended him later in the restaurant to which her mother and friends took her to celebrate, but grew tearful as they grew nostalgic and maudlin over their drinks. Rachel was not allowed alcohol—or cigarettes, or coffee, or antihistamines, or peanuts, or fish. Nor was she permitted exercise, mental strain, or melancholy.

"Burris's doctor is very good," she sobbed, guiltily.

Doctor Leahy was, in fact, the best obstetrician in the city. Burris had interviewed several best obstetricians before him, but had disliked all of them for various reasons. One was harried and dismissive. One seemed to have nothing else to do but answer his questions. One was a proponent of "natural" childbirth—which sounded to Burris as absurd as a dentist advocating better dental health through neglect. One was a woman. A few seemed perplexed by Rachel's absence, as if unaware that the husband's role was to shield the wife, and the unborn baby, from as much stress as possible. Doctor Leahy understood this. About Burris's own age, with a thrusting manner and a firm handshake, Doctor Leahy treated Burris more like a coworker than a client; he even called him "Doctor." His most reassuring credential was his willingness to disparage his colleagues. He scorned doulas, dimly lit birthing rooms, and warm baths, and championed the full array of medical interventions, including pain-easing epidurals, tear-preventing episiotomies, and life-saving cesarean sections. Though he called himself a conservative, he spoke like a crusader, and Burris recognized in him a kindred spirit—a fellow individualist.

Leahy was candid about Rachel's morning sickness. "We could draw a quart of blood and do a battery of tests, each more costly than the next; and we might, in the best case scenario, find that she is in fact deficient in, say, calcium; then we could give her a supplement, and maybe it would help. Then again, it might not. Or we might find nothing. Because in nine cases out of ten, in my experience, there is no cause to be found. Pregnant women expect to feel sick—so they feel sick."

He gave Burris a prescription for a bottle of expensive vitamins. These only made Rachel feel worse, which seemed to corroborate Leahy's implication that the nausea was not physical but mental. Burris's tactful paraphrase of this was that she was worrying too much.

Her mother, on the other hand, maintained that morning sickness was natural and healthy: the body instinctively purged whatever would be bad for the baby. She belittled the doctor's diet, too, and urged Rachel to obey her cravings. "Your stomach knows better than your brain what you need."

But Rachel had no cravings; she hardly had an appetite. Everything she ate made her feel bloated and precarious. Torn by contradictory advice, she felt alternately that she was poisoning and starving the baby. In self-defense she blamed the victim, and developed an image of the fetus as a fickle, whimpering parasite. So she ate with defiance, and vomited defiantly. No one had warned her that pregnancy was an illness.

She suffered too the boredom and isolation of illness. Chelsea and Alexis rarely visited; her mother thought it best to give the newlyweds their privacy. Alone in Burris's house all day, Rachel was required to do nothing but to ripen and to grow fat. She tried from time to time to read his periodicals and old textbooks, but found that she could no longer grasp the purpose of abstract learning. She still daydreamed of careers that she might pursue after the baby was born, but as a wife and mother, she felt that school was now behind her. She leached the hours from the day with herbal tea, naps, cleaning, trashy magazines, and the small, recurrent tasks of grooming. She brushed her teeth and brushed her hair, changed and washed her clothes, polished and removed polish from her toenails, and weighed herself before the mirror. She portioned out these rituals like a castaway conserving food. On especially bleak days, she saved her second bath till evening, just to have something to look forward to.

When Burris came home, he cooked elaborate, spicy meals for her, which she struggled to ingest. After washing up the dishes, he joined her on the sofa, where they listened to music and he told her about his day. Wallowing in the sound of his voice, she would remove his wristwatch, comb the hair on his arms into rows with her fingernails, and feel for an hour or two almost normal.

She complained of heartburn, and he brought home antacids, which, she said untruthfully, helped a little. At night she experienced heart palpitations, and he brought home a portable cardiac monitor, which she cradled like a hot-water bottle for a day. The heart trace, submitted to a laboratory, proved "inconclusive."

Then she had a problem that he could not mediate—a pain in her uterus that was accompanied by bleeding. Burris, as scared and queasy as she was, drove her first to the emergency room, then, on second thought, to Doctor Leahy's clinic. He went with her into the examination room, but looked out the window while two muttering nurses put her in stirrups and palpated and scanned her. Burris, who found menstruation disquieting, was horrified by his first sight of a gynecological table. Rachel wrested her hand free of his grasp and stroked his arm, soothed by the act of soothing him. She did not care what happened, and even welcomed the pain as a prelude to some end.

After awhile they were left alone; Burris, embarrassed for her, lowered her skirt. Eventually one of the nurses returned to tell them, as if they should have guessed it, that everything was all right. The scans were all normal; anyway, there was nothing to be done. "You might still miscarry, but you probably won't." Rachel began to sit up. "Oh no you don't! The doctor still needs to examine you." Half an hour later, Leahy came in and positioned himself between her legs. His greeting seemed addressed to her vagina; in any case, he did not look at her face before putting two gloved, lubricated fingers inside her.

"Oh, sure," he said. "This'll be fine. Good size, good spacing, and good position. I wouldn't worry." He pulled the gloves from his hands with a wet snap. "It's a bit early, but let's schedule that ultrasound for next week. We'll do the amniocentesis while we're at it. Talk to Grace on your way out. Good to see you again, Doctor."

Leaving the clinic, neither of them knew why they felt stiff and ashamed. Outside on the pavement, a few anti-abortion protesters held placards. One of these showed a photograph of an aborted fetus. Bloody, alien, and the size of a dime, it inspired in Burris and Rachel neither pity nor tenderness, but only repugnance. Was that the thing growing inside her? Were they responsible for that?

During the ultrasound and amniocentesis, Burris stayed in the waiting room.

The ultrasound technician was warm and gentle. "There's the spine, and there's the big healthy head. See?" But Rachel could discern nothing human in the snowstorm of pixels. "Do you want to know the sex?" —"I don't know." Would

Burris want to know? They'd never discussed it. She wished he were here. "No," she said at last. —"Good for you. You'll love them whatever they are."

When Burris asked her whether it was a boy or a girl, she realized her mistake. "A boy," she blurted, and was hurt by his look of relief. Yet her disappointment in him proved that she too had been guilty of hoping—but for a girl. As time went by, the bluff acquired actuality, till it no longer seemed a bluff, but the intuited truth. She was carrying Burris's baby boy.

That night, she asked him about the amniocentesis. "What do they do with the amniotic fluid?" —He didn't know, but said, "Only some tests to make sure the baby is fine and healthy." —"And what if the baby isn't healthy?" —"Don't be silly. The baby will be fine." —Then why bother, she wondered, with the tests?

Burris wondered the same thing, and worried. What would they do if the baby proved abnormal, defective, or deformed? Could they love it? Should they be expected to? Would they be encouraged to keep it—or to terminate it? When weeks passed without Doctor Leahy or anyone from the prenatal diagnostic center calling, Burris assumed that the tests had been negative, and expelled the worry from his mind.

One day, she felt a strange new discomfort—an irregular throbbing in her abdomen. Because it came and went and was not very painful, she said nothing about it to Burris. Then one night a sharp pang awoke her, and she knew that it was the baby kicking. She was startled and embarrassed, like someone discovering that she was being watched. Tentatively, she placed her hands on her belly. When another kick came, she felt a jolt of affection and awe as she realized that the two of them actually shared the same body. The kicking was a protest against the same discomfort that she'd imagined she had been suffering alone.

From that day on, she moved more daintily and with more pride, like a curator through a museum. She ate more, and withstood the nausea with greater stoicism—taking her cue from the baby's stillness, or venting her frustration vicariously through his kicks. She spoke to him silently, complaining or sympathizing as to an adult peer. She had found a secret ally, and from that alliance she derived, for a while, a secret strength.

One night, too tired to cook, Burris took her out for dinner. Rachel spent an hour selecting her clothes, titivating her hair, and applying make-up. Earlier that week at the pharmacy, a horrible woman had asked her how far along she was. Tonight she was determined not to look or act pregnant.

The restaurant was owned by distant relatives of his, who prepared for them the same meal he would have made at home. Rachel simulated an appetite so convincingly that Burris was aroused: he had always liked to see a lover stuff herself before intercourse. He was attracted too by her little swollen tummy, which her dress only accentuated. He told her, "I'm so glad finally to see you eating for two!" But this seemed to be the wrong thing to say; for the rest of the dinner she was sullen. Later, in the parking lot, when he tried to signal his desire by caressing her belly, she slapped his hands away.

At his next appointment with Doctor Leahy, he asked in a roundabout way whether pregnant women could still enjoy themselves . . . —"You mean sexually?" said Leahy. —"Well, yes, for instance." —"Tremendously. Oh, yes. Some of them become quite nymphomaniacal. And the best part is: you don't have to worry about birth control!"

But whenever Burris made advances, Rachel scoffed. She did not feel sexy, and did not believe that he could find her so. For as she grew larger, she received less and less attention from men, and more and more from older women, who praised her and put their hands on her, like veterinarians admiring a heifer.

Burris allowed himself to be discouraged, secretly agreeing that there was something perverse about lusting for a pregnant woman. But he felt irritated, too, to have been confronted with this fact—and, in effect, criticized—by his wife.

Five weeks before the due date, Rachel called Burris at the clinic, interrupting a crown installation. "I think I'm in labor." —His mind went white, filled at once with every color of thought. "Are you sure?" —"I don't know, but I've had eight contractions." She did not say that each of them in succession had been the most painful and frightening event of her life to that point. —"What about your waters? Have your waters broken?" —"I'm not sure. I think maybe they came out while I was peeing."

At the hospital, while a clerk took Rachel's information with maddening methodicalness, Burris phoned Doctor Leahy's clinic. The receptionist did not even transfer the call. "Oh, those are Braxton-Hickses." —"I beg your pardon?" —"The contractions. Unless they're coming regularly and getting closer together, they're just false alarms. Sure, a lot of women get them." —Three hours later, after a cursory examination, a midwife told them the same thing. —"But they're agony," Rachel protested. —The midwife smiled, too fatigued to snort in derision. "Just wait till the real thing."

During the ride home, Rachel squirmed in her seat, shaking her head and mouthing disbelief. "I won't be able to," she muttered. "I just won't be able to . . ."

Burris, humiliated and resentful, said nothing to console her. How could she know so little about her own body?

The next week, Rachel entered Leahy's clinic prepared to demand some help. In addition to the heartburn, nausea, and contractions, none of which had gone away, her breasts were sore; her scalp was tight and sensitive, and her hair was falling out; her back always ached, though most when she tried to sleep; perhaps due to exhaustion, she had lost fine motor control in her fingers; she was often dizzy and afraid to use stairs.

But Leahy appraised her at a glance in the waiting room, zero-
ing in on her primary complaint. "You're getting humongous,
aren't you?" He clapped her shoulder, and said that if the baby
had not arrived by week forty plus one day, he would perform
a membrane sweep. Rachel thanked him, but had to ask one
of the other women what a membrane sweep was. —"They
massage your cervix to kick-start your body. It's the first step
of inducing labor." —"Oh," said Rachel. "Thank God."

On the morning of the due date, Burris watched her
quizzically, and left for work reluctantly. The next day, she
packed an overnight bag and he drove her to Leahy's clinic.
But the procedure—which seemed no different, only more
painful, than a regular examination—was quickly finished,
and to their surprise they were told to go home again.
Frazzled by suspense, they wanted only to do something,
to have something finally happen. —"But what do we do
now?," Burris asked, and Rachel gave him a grateful look.
—"Now," said Leahy, "we wait and see." Eventually Burris
extracted the information that if labor had not started in
a week, Leahy would admit Rachel to the hospital for an
induction. —Burris opened his pocket calendar. "So, next
Tuesday?" —"Sure," said Leahy, "thereabouts."

On Tuesday morning, Burris called Leahy's clinic.
—"Right," said Leahy. "Tomorrow afternoon at three
o'clock. Sound good?" —Burris consented helplessly. At
two o'clock the next day, when they were about to leave, the
receptionist called. "So, it turns out that tomorrow morning
will actually work better for Doctor Leahy. Is that all right?"
—"What time?" asked Burris. —"Eight o'clock?"

They arrived at the hospital the next morning at seven; by
nine Rachel had been officially admitted to the maternity ward.
Burris told several people about their appointment with Doctor
Leahy, and was finally informed that the doctor would not be
in till the afternoon. "Not that there will be much for him to
see by then!" —"But, you know, he has scheduled us for an

induction." —"Yes, the midwife will be by at 11:30. But then the drugs usually take several hours to have any effect. Don't worry! We know where to find Doctor Leahy if we need him."

Because the prenatal ward was full, Rachel was given a bed in the large communal postnatal ward. The other beds were occupied by wan, disheveled women, some of whom cradled or breastfed newborns. Several had visitors, who spoke in murmurs. The room was not cheery. The bisque- and daffodil-colored walls were peeling; the garish overhead lights buzzed; a television news program that no one was watching contended with piped music that no one was listening to. But Rachel and Burris did not admit their disappointment, afraid to give dismay a foothold so early. They settled down, sighing and smiling bravely, as though to a meager picnic.

While waiting for the midwife, Burris moved the car from the short-term to the long-term parking lot.

At 10:30 a nurse came to take a blood sample. Burris said, "We took care of all that when we were last here." —The nurse shrugged. "I guess these are different tests." —Burris asked what tests they were. The nurse named some of them; they sounded familiar. "Those are the same tests." —"Well, I guess we're doing them again, just to be safe!" —Rachel put her hand on Burris's arm.

At 12:30, while Burris went in search of food, the midwife arrived with the pessary. She was affable and gentle, but the way she teased Rachel about the tightness of her cervix made her feel guilty, as if she were wasting the staff's time. She wondered too how many more people whose names she did not know would put their hands in her vagina by the end of the day.

The midwife then attached an elastic belt to Rachel's abdomen, and connected it by cables to a printer, which began to slowly produce a paper record of the baby's heartbeat. The midwife watched it for a couple of minutes, then turned it off. "All systems go," she smiled. "Now, we shouldn't expect much change for twelve hours or so." —"Right," said Rachel, dissembling her surprise. —"So make yourself comfortable. Read a book, go for a walk, get a bite to eat. I'll be back to check on you regularly, but do press that call button if you feel the contractions starting."

Burris returned with juice and sandwiches. Rachel felt uncomfortable eating in bed, and suggested they go for a walk. —"What about the midwife?" —"Oh, she came and went. She said it was all right. Nothing's supposed to happen for twelve hours yet." —Burris looked at her suspiciously. —"I think that's normal," she said. —He gestured at the monitoring belt. "What about that thing?" —"It's not turned on. I guess I could take it off for a while . . ." —Burris looked doubtful. —They stayed where they were. When Rachel needed to use the bathroom, she plugged herself back in to the dormant machine on her return.

Time passed. Burris and Rachel watched the doctors, nurses, orderlies, and midwives dash to and fro, talking mostly to one another and giving most of their attention to their patients' charts. One young resident, like a border guard scrutinizing a passport, looked from Rachel's chart to Rachel and back again, then walked out shaking his head. She did not see the midwife who had inserted her pessary again.

Burris bought a newspaper, and together they attempted the crossword, lingering over the most difficult clues, in no hurry to finish. Rachel, tethered to the monitor, sat or crouched in various positions on and beside the bed; every position was uncomfortable, but lying on her back was intolerable. Burris, believing pain a sign of progress, urged her to remain supine as much as possible.

The woman in the next bed awoke, and gazed at Rachel with groggy tenderness. "First time?" she asked. —Rachel nodded. —"Don't worry about a thing. It's much easier than they tell you. When the time comes, you'll know what to do. Take me, for instance." And in the same tranquil, reassuring tone, she told them a phantasmagoric tale of pain, blood, danger, and fear, whose moral seemed to be that whatever happened, it was all for the best. —"And your baby . . . ?" —The woman made a dismissive gesture. "Eight pounds seven ounces. She's with her daddy and grandma. They're around here somewhere. *She's* fine." Then she became earnest, and offered advice. "Screaming helps; don't feel bad about screaming. Also, you have a lot more blood in you than you might think. And whatever happens, don't let anybody talk you out of an epidural. I don't know what I would have done without mine." She laughed reminiscently. "I really thought I was going out of my head for a while there." —Rachel expressed her regret that she was allergic to painkillers. —"Oh. Well." The woman's eyes lost their focus. "Anyway, you'll be okay."

At six o'clock, a midwife turned on the fetal monitor for a few minutes, made a sour face, and asked Burris if Rachel would be wanting an epidural before the anesthetist went home for the night. —"No. She is allergic." —"Because I would get one now, if I were her. She might not be able to get it done when the contractions start in the middle of the night, when we're short-staffed." —"I understand that, but she has an allergy to pain-relieving drugs. It's on her chart. See?" —The midwife seemed offended. "I was just asking. It's her decision. It's all the same to me."

Leahy visited briefly, evidently on his way somewhere else. He did not examine Rachel, but congratulated her on her progress and promised to start her on a synthetic oxytocin IV drip first thing in the morning. "It's too late today. Get some rest if you can, and have happy dreams of that cervix opening." He shook Burris's hand and was gone. Nevertheless, they both felt reassured.

At eight o'clock, the hormone began to take effect. Without warning, she was racked by a wave of pain that began in her lower back and reverberated up her torso before slowly draining away. It felt as if her spine were vomiting, as if her vital force were shaking itself free of her body. "Good, good," said Burris, and set the timer on his wristwatch before pressing the call button. —"What's the matter, sweetie?" asked the nurse. —"The contractions are starting." —A midwife they had not seen before was called to examine her cervix. "Well, you're effaced, but not dilated at all yet." She explained, with a wink, "Still a long way to go. Now, can I get you something for the pain?"

At 8:45, the television was turned off, and Burris and the other visitors were informed that they must leave. He was astounded. "I was told I could stay with her the entire time." —"Yes, in the delivery room, or on the prenatal ward, but not here. These women have just given birth; they need their rest and their privacy." —He asked if there was nowhere in the hospital he could spend the night. —"There's plenty of public areas, but you won't find them very comfortable. You might as well go home and sleep. You won't be allowed back in here till morning, even if anything does happen." —Swallowing his anger, he spoke to the nurse at the desk, who promised to call him if Rachel was moved to a delivery room during the night. He thanked her and went home—where he dozed fitfully on the couch, harassed by nightmares of traffic jams and full parking lots.

At ten o'clock, the piped music was extinguished and the overhead lights were fractionally dimmed. All around Rachel, machines hummed and beeped, babies gasped and cried, and new mothers sought relief from soreness in creaking beds, while hospital staff bustled back and forth in the hallway, and from farther away came the sounds of alarms, rattling carts, and the mewling and groaning of a woman in childbirth. Rachel could not sleep. In between contractions, she paced the perimeter of her bed or nibbled on the food that Burris had left behind. "I wouldn't do that," said her neighbor in the next bed. "If they have to sedate you for an operation, you might throw up and choke on your own vomit." —Rachel reminded her that she was allergic to painkillers. —"Still."

When Burris returned in the morning, nothing seemed to have changed, except that his wife looked more haggard. He massaged her feet and helped her remove the monitoring belt until it was needed again. He asked at the desk if Rachel could join him for breakfast in the cafeteria. The nurse was appalled. "Certainly not. She's scheduled for an IV insertion at ten o'clock." —He pointed out that this was an hour away. —The nurse made self-absolving gestures. "If you want to risk missing your wife's induction, and maybe having to wait till Monday morning, please be my guest." —He went alone to the cafeteria, and brought back sausages and eggs. Rachel, mindful of her neighbor's censure, said she wasn't hungry; and indeed, whenever the contractions came or she rolled absent-mindedly onto her back, food was far from her mind.

At ten o'clock a young resident, who introduced herself as Doctor Fulhill, gave the curtain around Rachel's bed a symbolic tug, then examined her cervix. Her expression clouded over. "Where is this woman's pessary?" —No one knew. The resident examined her again, more roughly, then invited first a nurse, then a midwife to try. —"It's not there anymore," they agreed. —"Did *you* take it out?" —Rachel shook her head. —"You sure?" —She nodded. —They all searched the bedclothes and the floor, but the pessary was not to be found. Doctor Fulhill's irritation, which Rachel imagined directed at her, made her feel like a child. Too late, the doctor tried to console her. "No matter. These things happen. I was only going to take it out anyway. We'll get your IV started now, and things should get moving again." —The nurse, imagining that the doctor's irritation was directed at her, chided Rachel for removing the monitoring belt, and told her that once the IV was in place, she would need to stay put—"So we can keep a close watch on baby's heartbeat." —"What about going to the bathroom?," Burris asked. —"Oh, we'll put a catheter up her for that."

Rachel lay still and silent on her back, listening to Burris's voice murmur soothingly, while these things were done.

By noon the contractions were stronger and coming more frequently; she had to remind herself to breathe when they were at their height. She would have liked to moan or bellow, but was conscious of the other women and their families. She promised herself that she would holler her head off when she was moved to the delivery room. That time, however, still seemed ages away. Every hour now her monitor was turned on and the interval between her contractions measured (these measurements deviated somewhat from Burris's, for Rachel did not always tell him, and could not always distinguish, when one contraction ended and another began). The midwives wanted to see peaks every two or three minutes; but Rachel's contractions were still irregular, and sometimes ninety seconds, sometimes ten minutes apart. So, every hour, they increased the percentage of hormone in her IV drip.

At three o'clock, Leahy came by to wish them luck; he was leaving town for the weekend. They were both flabbergasted. Burris managed to stammer some words of protest. —"Don't worry," said Leahy. "I'm leaving you in the very capable hands of Doctor Paschava. I believe you met him at the clinic?" —They had not. —"Well, that's the way of childbirth. You never know just when it'll happen, and we can't be everywhere at once. That's why OBs, like birds of a feather, flock together." Before leaving, he asked Rachel if she would like an epidural. "Sometimes it helps speed things up."

Burris almost sobbed. Collecting himself, he took Doctor Leahy aside. "We discussed this the very first day we met: my wife is allergic to painkillers." —"Oh," said Leahy, "I doubt that very much. Tell me, do you use opiates much in your practice, doctor? Then you know that they can cause itchiness and nausea, certainly, but never a full-blown immunological allergic reaction. After all, there are opioids produced endogenously in the brain." —All Burris could do was splutter; he did not understand why Leahy had waited till now to tell him this. —"What precisely is it that she's supposedly allergic to?" —Burris told Leahy what Rachel had told him: that she had once vomited after inhaling nitrous oxide. —"Also not an allergic response," said Leahy. "And besides, N$_2$O has nothing to do with opiates." He gave a conciliatory smile. "If it makes you feel better, I'll put a note here on her chart that she's not to be given air and gas. And we'll start her out on a small bolus of morphine to see how she likes it. All right?" He showed Burris the amended chart: *Allergic to pain relief (nitrous oxide only).* "All right?" —His mind in turmoil, Burris capitulated.

Holding his wife's hand, he watched her closely while a nurse injected the morphine into her IV line. Her brow smoothed, and her eyes softened. Nothing else.

He felt like a fool and a failure. All this time, he could have spared her much pain.

Rachel said, "I feel a little better all of a sudden. I must be getting my second wind." —"Excellent, darling. That's excellent."

In the late afternoon, a doctor, evidently not Paschava, because a woman, arrived to perform an artificial rupture of the membranes. —"An artificial what?" said Burris, standing in her way. —"An amniotomy. We want to break her waters. Often it helps the labor along." She showed him a thin plastic utensil like a crochet hook. "We put a little tear in the amniotic sac with this guy, and the amniotic fluid comes out, which sends the signal to the uterus to really start squeezing."

Burris said, "Shouldn't she have an epidural first?"

Rachel was too exhausted to object. The morphine had worn off and her back was in constant pain, which even the contractions could scarcely augment. Her hands trembled, her eyelids fluttered, and tiny muscles in her face twitched. When she closed her eyes, grains of fatigue exploded in her skull, and the fragmented hubbub of dreams crowded in upon her thoughts. She only intermittently remembered that she was giving birth; most of the time, she thought she was sick and dying. She wished that the doctors would hurry up and cure her or put her out of her misery. Perhaps the epidural would do one or the other.

"This shouldn't hurt," said the doctor, "but I can send the anesthetist over as soon as I'm done here." —"All right," said Burris. "Thank you." —"Thank you," echoed Rachel.

A midwife changed her catheter bag, then helped her lie down. Her arms were strapped to perpendicular armrests, the foot of the bed was lowered, and her legs were spread and lifted into stirrups. A bolt of pain, as though from a bastinado, shot up her spine from her sacrum; she gripped the armrests and clenched her face and neck to keep from screaming.

"May I . . . ?" said Burris, gesturing at the curtain. —"Of course," said the doctor, who had already begun the procedure. —He drew the curtain, and found himself on the other side of it, grinning fatuously at the neighbor's infant. "What an adorable little nipper." He went to the nursing station for more ice chips, which was all that Rachel had been permitted to eat since that morning.

When the doctor had finished, she gave Rachel's arm an exhortative squeeze. "Now you've really got to get cracking, love. Without the amniotic fluid, the baby's at an increased risk of infection. So I want to see you push that little one out in let's say under twelve hours—or else we might have to resort to a C-section, which would be a shame after all the hard work you've done." —This ostensible pep talk had on Rachel a decidedly astringent effect. She feared a C-section, but did not know how she could labor any faster. She succumbed to a moment of self-pity, tears streaming down her cheeks. Why could no one help her?

By nine o'clock, the end of visiting hours, the anesthetist still had not appeared. Burris refused to leave, demanding instead that Rachel be moved to a delivery room. A nurse referred him to a midwife, who referred him to a doctor, who examined Rachel and referred him back to the midwife. The midwife shrugged. "She's only five centimeters dilated, so it's a bit early. But the room is available now. I really don't care."

A gurney was fetched, but Rachel asked if she could walk. The midwife, who had other patients in more advanced stages of labor, suppressed her impatience. "Of course, dear. It might even be helpful. Let gravity do some of the work, you know." The monitor belt was removed, and Burris and the midwife helped her to her feet, out of the damp, stained bed that she had occupied, with only brief breaks, for thirty-six hours. She shuffled down three long corridors, the midwife supporting her, Burris rolling her IV pole, amniotic fluid trickling down her thighs, but the pressure on her spine so reduced that she felt almost revitalized.

The delivery room was not entirely private; it was shared by another woman, separated from Rachel by a collapsible screen. She emitted deep, lowing moans, as of perpetually renewed revulsion. Rachel at last felt free to let loose a grunt or two herself; but whenever she did, the groans on the other side of the screen faltered and paused.

Shortly before midnight the anesthetist burst in, looking as harried as a fugitive run to earth. He had just come from the operating room, where his patient had suddenly and unaccountably expired. Though her death had not been his fault, his colleagues' sullenness had left him feeling implicated, and he had taken refuge in a stance of defiant disgust. He looked at Rachel's chart and said, "Where's your scalp electrode?" —"I don't know." —He turned to Burris. "Why hasn't she had a scalp electrode inserted? Jesus." He walked out before Burris could reply. He returned fifteen minutes later, and explained that he could not administer the epidural without a fetal monitor in place, and that, since Rachel's amniotic sac had been ruptured, it might as well be the more reliable scalp monitor. Burris started to apologize, but the anesthetist made an interruptive gesture. "Forget it. I'll be back in an hour, if you care."

Burris, gritting his teeth, went to inform the midwife that, according to the anesthetist, his wife needed a fetal scalp monitor before she could be given an epidural. —"Oh, fiddlesticks. He's just being difficult." Nevertheless, she agreed to placate him, and inserted the electrode herself two hours later. After studying the printout, she congratulated Rachel on her progress. —"How far dilated am I?" —"Nearly six centimeters!" Seeing Rachel's disappointment, she added, "But your contractions are getting a lot closer."

Finally, at four in the morning, the anesthetist reappeared, looking much refreshed. He had Rachel lie on her side, and opened the back of her gown. She felt a first needle, then a second that entered much more deeply, into the very core of her lower-back pain. He told her to stop fidgeting. "There," he said at last, helping her roll supine again. "That must feel better." —She did not know. The pain was still there, crescendoing with each contraction, but its texture and position had changed. It seemed to have split in two, most of it sinking a few inches, as if into the bed, while a sharply defined box of it remained behind, a free-floating throbbing ache that she could almost dissociate herself from. She could not have described this sensation, so said only that she felt a little nauseous, and itchy. —The anesthetist scowled. "Should I take it out?" —"No, please. Thank you. I do feel much better." —He handed Burris the button for the pump, and left. The midwife, called in, explained that he could press it whenever his wife started hurting again. "And don't worry about pressing it too often. The machine won't let you overdose."

He sat at her bedside, watching her face, and pressed the button every fifteen minutes, whether she seemed to need it or not. At five-thirty they drifted together into a brittle, priceless sleep—from which they were soon propeled by a nurse who came bounding in to check the fetal monitor. "Your electrode has come loose!" she cried. She rectified this ponderously, like one wading through another's crimes, and chastised Rachel for tossing and turning too much. "Your urine bag is nearly full, too," she said, and did not offer to empty it. This Burris did, with the midwife's guidance.

At seven, Doctor Paschava entered with knitted brow. He studied Rachel's chart and the fetal monitor with many signs of dissatisfaction. Finally he pronounced his verdict: "This is taking altogether too long, I'm afraid." He ordered compression stockings for her legs to prevent embolism, restarted her IV drip at a higher concentration, and told Rachel that she must focus. "Our anesthetist has called in sick, so there can be no emergency cesarean sections. You must get this baby out by yourself, and you must do it today. No more dozing on the job!" —But she was too tired to muster either guilt or resolve; all she could manage was angry despair. She wanted to die, wanted the baby to die, wanted Burris to die, wanted the doctors and nurses and midwives all to die, wanted the hospital and the entire city to crumble to ashes in a flaming earthquake. "Fuck this," she sobbed softly.

Feeling useless, Burris asked her, with none of his old confidence, if she would like to do a relaxation exercise—something he had not suggested since they were dating. —Rachel laughed through tears. "Oh, honey, what good would that do?"

At nine, the midwife came to wish Rachel luck; after sixteen hours and four babies delivered, she was going off duty. "You're almost there, dear. You're doing great; you're such a strong woman. It won't be much longer now." —Rachel wept, and the midwife embraced her. Overcome with gratitude and love, Rachel refused to let go. She felt something opening and releasing inside her. "It's coming," she whispered. "The baby's finally coming." —The midwife extricated herself. "Not while I'm here, sweetie!" On her way out she notified the day staff that Number Seventeen was transitioning. —In fact, Rachel had only defecated. A cheerful nurse gave her a sponge bath in full view of Burris and the new midwife, unwittingly stripping her of her last shreds of adulthood. Even the woman on the other side of the screen stopped groaning for a few minutes, as though aghast.

An hour later, however, the midwife announced—by this time, to everyone's surprise—that Rachel was at last fully dilated. Rachel's relief was short-lived. "Now what happens?" —"Now you can push, love." —But she didn't know which muscles to push; she'd thought she had been pushing all this time. She wailed, "I'm only starting labor *now?*"

She fell into a shaking, shivering delirium; she dreamed that the ice chips in her mouth were Burris's fingers, that the box of pain in her back was an infant's coffin, that the analgesia button was the trigger of a dentist's drill that had been driven into her spine by her tormentors; she dreamed that she was giving birth to a brood of hairy, sluglike spermatozoa. She looked down at herself, and saw blood everywhere. She started to scream.

"This won't do," said Doctor Paschava. "You've got to save that energy for pushing." —"Please shut up," said the midwife. —She stopped screaming. —Immediately, the woman on the other side of the screen began screaming more loudly. The doctor sighed and the midwife rolled her eyes humorously for Rachel's benefit, then they stepped around the screen to investigate. A minute later, the midwife rushed out, a strident electronic alarm began to peal, and the screen was pushed aside to make space for all the new staff and equipment entering the room; Burris was jostled to the far side of Rachel's bed. He asked Doctor Fulhill, the resident who had started Rachel's IV the previous morning, what was happening. She shushed him, then shrugged and said, "Fetal heart rate just crashed." The doctors and nurses were exclaiming in code; Paschava was asking for "ventouse"; a nurse was calling for anesthetic; someone kept saying, "We need to get her into an OT," and someone else kept saying that it was no use, there were none available. The midwife returned to say that operating theater six had just cleared. Unaware of Rachel's fingers clawing his arm, Burris watched through a shifting forest of white coats as the fat, half-naked stranger was heaved onto a gurney and rolled, trailing carts of equipment, from the room.

Stricken, he gazed down at his wife without recognition. "Call the doctor," she gasped. He leaned over to soothe her. "I need the fucking doctor!" she screamed. "It's happening!" She was thrashing, and her gown had ridden up to her waist. For a horrific moment he thought she was splitting open; then he realized that the pale and bloody, hairy and wrinkled membrane bulging from her groin was in fact the baby's head. He raced down the hallway after the gurney and its train, and grabbed the midwife's elbow. "The head," he said. "The head is coming out." —She shook him off. "Well, for goodness' sake, tell her to stop pushing! I'll be there as soon as I can." —He ran back, only a little more slowly, and hesitated only slightly on the threshold. The head had emerged no further, and seemed even to have retracted slightly. "You're to stop pushing," he said, "till they get back." And, like a man entering a burning house, with arms extended and face averted, he stepped boldly forward, prepared to prevent her from pushing the baby out onto the floor.

"Okay, all right," said Rachel; but she was not about to stop pushing now. The last dose of anesthesia had worn off, and she could feel quite clearly, as if outlined in phosphorescent pain, the position of the baby in the birth canal. Moreover, she knew just which abdominal muscles to flex. She believed that in straining these muscles now, she was probably ruining her physique forever. She didn't care. The hospital staff had abandoned her; Burris was ready to positively interfere; she was in charge now. She would not let them kill her. She would push, if need be, till she burst.

"Darling, bring him to the toy, not the toy to him."
—"What difference does it make?" —"Well, you'll spoil
him." —"I'll spoil him just as much by carrying him around
everywhere."

For months, Burris had been attributing his wife's mood-
iness, lethargy, and frigidity to birth trauma and to post-
partum depression. He did not know to what to attribute
the contrariness that she now began to exhibit. It seemed
he could not make the most benign suggestion without her
resisting it.

"I don't think all this baby talk is good for him. He
needs to learn the right words for things." —"What's the
big rush?" —"You don't want him lagging behind his peers."
—"Who cares? It's not a competition."

This behavior was exasperating enough at home, but in
public she was even more outspoken. One day at the park,
she went so far as to chide him for hovering over Oxley.
"Let him alone; let him explore with the other children."
He was ashamed, and ashamed for his wife. When he tried
later to explain this to her, Rachel denied that she had done
anything wrong. "The other parents thought it was funny.
Anyway, you're always correcting *my* parenting." —"It's

different for a husband to a wife." —"Not anymore, it isn't," she muttered.

One evening, he asked her to turn off a violent television program. —"Don't worry," she said. "He's not even watching." —"But he may be listening." —"So what? He can't understand it." —"He understands more than you give him credit for. He understands harsh noises, and scary music, and angry voices!" —Oxley began to cry, and Rachel went to soothe him. To Burris she serenely said, "So whose voice is angry?"

He began to worry that she was not merely being perverse, but sincerely believed that children could learn to express and comport and protect themselves, by themselves. If she was this negligent when he was present, what must she be like when he was at work all day?

In fact, Rachel's nonchalance did not come naturally; she deliberately adopted it as a counterbalance to Burris's fretfulness. She too was alarmed and sickened by what she saw on television. Indeed, since Oxley's birth, she found most programs as distressing as a drive down the highway, for she now watched them (and the highway) with her son's defenseless eyes, seeing for the first time with psychedelic vividness how crass, manipulative, and vicious they really were. But a parent, she felt, must never betray her disgust, worry, or unhappiness. Indeed, a parent's duty was to instill fearlessness and self-reliance—not through instruction, but by example. She worried that Burris's example was teaching Oxley that words were medals, that strangers were invisible, that playgrounds were malevolent, and that even make-believe was dangerous. And the lesson underlying all his anxious protectiveness was that the world was full of bad things from which Oxley, feeble and helpless, needed protecting. She protected him better, surely, by showing that no protection was needed.

They argued too about the domestic chores. Burris, who had been working one less day a week at his practice since Rachel took a job at the cooperative bookstore, felt that he had already made a sacrifice and was contributing more to the household than any other husband he knew. Rachel was less concerned by how little he did, than by how poorly he did it. She found it faster and easier to pack a day bag, get Oxley dressed for the park, or clean the bathtub herself than to have Burris do it, because she could not rely on him to do it conscientiously or correctly. —"But we each have our own areas of expertise," he objected. "For example, I cook." —"Yes, but you like to cook." —"And you do not! So what's the problem?" —"How many of the things that I do do you think I enjoy?" —"But if you are better at them . . . ?" —"You mean because I'm a woman?" —"Because you yourself admit it every time you criticize my attempts!" —"So do things better!"

"The fact is," he said, "you have more time than I do." —Rachel did not bother to refute this. "If you don't have enough time," she said, "then work less hours." —"You know I cannot." —"Why not? We'd save money on daycare." —"Nowhere near the money I'd lose from patients!" —"So your job is more important than mine because you make more money than I do." —"No, my job is more important than yours because I have been doing mine for nineteen years; because I perform an essential service in the health industry; and because mine is a career, and yours is a part-time job, taken for pocket money we don't need and for prestige among your man-hating friends." —"Well, it's nice to finally know what you really think of the most important work I've ever done in my life. Thank you." —"The most important work of your life is raising your child. And all this shouting and strife cannot be good for him." —"What's a lot less good for him, I think, is having a selfish, outdated, chauvinist pig for a father."

"All right, all right! So I will do things better. I will clean the bathtub better, and take out the garbage better, and fix the pram better, and babysit better. Will that make you happy?" —"*Babysit?*" —Burris threw up his hands. "I will not get into a semantic debate," he said, and left the room.

He went into the nursery, where Oxley was wailing. He plucked him from the crib and put him down on the floor, but the boy collapsed in a heap and screamed more loudly. "Oh, shut up," said Burris. He did not believe that his and Rachel's argument had caused this outburst; in fact, at the moment, he did not really believe that anything the two of them ever did had the slightest effect on Oxley's tantrums, which were as violent, implacable, and senseless as thunderstorms. He reminded himself that the boy had suffered an injury at birth, and was not responsible for his behavior. At the moment, however, this did not seem an extenuating circumstance, but an aggravating one. Whatever was innate and unchangeable in the boy was also intrinsic, an essential part of his character. "You wouldn't be acting like this if your mother were here." To refrain from throttling him, Burris spanked him and put him back in the crib.

He grew less tolerant of Oxley's illnesses too. It seemed the boy was constantly, as if willfully, suffering from a cold, flu, or upset stomach. Rachel decided that he was the victim of allergies, and fed him herbal and holistic remedies recommended by her friends. Burris soon tired of contesting this regimen, and in any case could hardly advocate the orthodox medicine that his lawyer was busy trying to discredit. Indeed, both he and Rachel had now begun, if only half consciously, to distrust and eschew doctors, with the result that they neglected to obtain all of Oxley's vaccinations.

When he was twenty months old, Oxley developed a fever that was worse than usual. He vomited, refused to eat, and screamed ceaselessly for a day and a half before Burris wondered whether a doctor shouldn't examine him. —"He'll be fine," Rachel said. "It's only a little temperature." —"We won't know what it is unless we have a doctor look at him." —"We can't take him to a doctor every time he bruises a knee or gets a runny nose." —"No, I suppose not . . ."

The next day, Oxley was no better, so Rachel took him to her mother's. "Give him a cool sponge bath and lots of liquids," she suggested. "He'll come out of it all right." Rachel stayed the night, to avoid a confrontation with Burris.

The next morning, she took Oxley's temperature; it was a fraction of a degree higher than it had been the previous night. She solicited her friends' advice. —"Have you tried cream of tartar?" asked Chelsea. —"I always make raisin tea," said Alexis. But nothing helped. That night, feeling restless and apprehensive, she phoned Burris. —"All right. If he's not better tomorrow morning, we'll take him to a clinic, first thing."

He was not better, but he was no worse; so she kept him at her mother's. By this time the weekend had arrived, so Burris did not protest; but on Monday he drove his family across the city to a clinic they had never visited before, and which he therefore did not yet distrust. —"It's only a little temperature," said the doctor. "Keep him dry and cool, and mix an ibuprofen into his juice to keep the fever down. If it doesn't clear up in three or four days, we'll take another look." —On the drive home, Burris pounded the steering wheel with his fist. "The man is obviously a moron. It's already been three or four days! We'll take him to someone else tomorrow." —Rachel was silent.

That night, she stayed awake at Oxley's bedside, replacing the damp washcloths that he swatted from his forehead, and pleading with him to be healthy. Shortly before dawn, he began to convulse.

She picked him up and put him down several times. She tried to get him to drink. She removed his pajamas and dabbed him with water. She rolled him gently back and forth. "Oh honey, don't," she murmured continuously as she paced the room on her toes. "Oh honey, oh honey, please don't." At last, with a gesture of tearing herself free, she wrapped him in a sheet and carried him across the hall to where Burris was sleeping. "Should we call an ambulance?"

"Oh, God," he said. He reached out for but did not touch his son. After a moment of anguished indecision, he said, "No, it'll be faster if I drive."

She did not put Oxley in the car seat, but held him in her arms. "Take the freeway," she said. —"I know, I know."

The seizure had stopped by the time they reached the emergency room. After a nerve-racking hour's wait, a tired nurse told them that they had done the right thing bringing him in, but that there was nothing to worry about: febrile seizures were common and harmless in children under five. Meanwhile, a better-rested resident noticed that Oxley's abdomen was tender, and that he was guarding it with raised knees. "Before you go," she said, "let's do a few tests, just to be safe." —"What kind of tests?" asked Rachel. —"Oh, just a urine test, a blood test, and maybe an X-ray." —"Why is that necessary?" —"Simply in order to rule a few things out." —"What things?" —"Well, appendicitis, for instance." —"Would that be serious?" asked Burris. —"Let's just say that we'd want to address the problem as soon as possible." —"But really," said Rachel, "what are the odds that it's appendicitis?" —"We won't know that till we've done the tests, I'm afraid." —"They're just tests," Burris told his wife. —The nurse, who was rebuking herself for overlooking the child's abdominal pain, said shortly, "You really don't have a choice."

With Oxley thrashing and screaming, the resident found it impossible to insert a catheter into his urethra. So she asked Rachel and Burris to hold him still while she took the urine sample directly with a needle through the abdomen. Feeling like monsters, Rachel and Burris pinned his wrists and feet as Oxley alternately choked and shrieked with rage. "Super," said the resident, though the sample was small. "Now for the blood test."

Forty minutes later, the resident, a radiologist, and a surgeon ushered them into a consultation room and explained in subdued voices that they wanted to operate. "It doesn't appear to be appendicitis," said the resident, speaking to Burris, "but the abdominal cavity is infected and the peritoneum is inflamed. We can reduce the inflammation and attack the infection with antibiotics, but we need to know what the underlying cause is. The urinalysis and the blood work do not show the kind of bacteria typically found in a primary spontaneous peritonitis." —"I don't understand anything you're saying," said Rachel. —The radiologist said, "We think we see something on the X-ray that might be a tiny perforation in the large intestine." —The surgeon said, "We want to fix that, and while we're at it, wash all the bad bacteria out of the abdominal cavity. All right?"

"How dangerous is this procedure?" asked Burris. —"It's much, much less dangerous than not doing it." —Rachel stifled a moan. "Can we stay with him?" —"Not in the operating room, no. But you can wait right outside, and we'll keep you updated."

They sat in the corridor holding hands; but as time passed and each pursued their own thoughts, their hands came slowly apart. Burris kept expecting to recognize or be recognized by one of the many doctors, nurses, and midwives whom Lucrenzo had named in the lawsuit. Would they make him leave when they discovered who he was? Would they refuse to treat his son? —Rachel, to combat remorse, and clinging to the future as to a talisman, made indistinct resolutions: From now on . . . Never again . . . I promise you . . . —Burris, in contrast, wallowed in remorse: I should never have sued the hospital; I should have spent more time at home; I should have been more firm with her;

I should have hired a nanny . . . —As far as Rachel knew, a perforated intestine was an ulcer, and ulcers were caused by stress—by fear and worry. Who but Burris had taught her baby to worry and to fear? —Gradually the anger and frustration that Burris dared not direct at the hospital staff began to settle upon his wife. She should have taken the boy to a doctor three days ago. —From now on, thought Rachel, things will be different . . .

Two hours later, the resident emerged from the operating theater to say that the worst was over. Two weeks later, Rachel and Burris were finally allowed to bring Oxley home from the intensive care unit. And two years later, there was still no one who could tell them the cause of these tiny, recurrent leaks.

MARVA LEEHAVEN, THE director of Shady Tree preschool, had never seen as unhappy a boy as Oxley Kornorek. He screamed when his mother dropped him off, he screamed when she came to pick him up, and he screamed for most of the interval. He would not nap. He pinched the other children and scratched himself. He would not let anyone help him go to the toilet, and invariably made a mess. He went into trances. He stole and hid the same snacks that he refused to eat when they were given him. He interrupted. He did not share. He was always taking off his clothes. He was pale, puffy-eyed, and sniveling, and one of the teachers had noticed that he was spotted with bruises. But most alarming was the bleakness of his imagination. Describing a picture he had drawn of his family, he had pointed at the figure of his father and said, "He's trying to kill me with a knife." Asked what his mother was doing, he'd said, "Running away."

Marva called a meeting with Oxley's parents. His father, an eminent dentist, was unable to come, but his mother quickly put Marva's mind at ease. The boy, she explained, suffered from a rare gastrointestinal disorder that poisoned his blood. "They think that's what causes his fits." She apologized for not informing her sooner; it had been such a hectic month. "If you like, I can get Doctor Ghernan to call you; he explains it much better than I do. Or I can make you a copy of the letter he wrote to our last daycare. Or both."

Rachel Kornorek was bright, and solemn, and warm, and she was patient but firm with her son, who sat fidgeting but uncomplaining in her lap for nearly five minutes before wriggling free. When she warned him not to leave the room, he slammed his head on the doorknob and slumped to the floor screaming. Without interrupting the conversation, she returned him to her lap and stroked his hair with absent-minded affection.

Marva suggested that perhaps it would be better, after all, if Oxley waited outside in the play area. —"All right. Hear that, bunkie? You can go play." She put him down and opened the door for him, but now he did not want to leave. Groping for some justification, he moaned, "Elsie hates my shoes." —"That's okay. You hate her shoes too." —Marva frowned; but Oxley seemed mollified. He ventured past the threshold, then lunged hollering towards some indignity being done to a toy he considered his own. Rachel shut the door softly on the altercation.

The director's manner became informal, and Rachel knew that she had made a good impression. When the talk turned to Burris, she was pleased to praise his calm, his strength, and his commitment as a parent, feeling more judicial with each judgement she delivered. It did her no harm to commend him; she could afford to be generous.

"Your husband works full time?," Marva asked. —Rachel laughed. "And then some." —"Do you work as well?" —"I used to help out at a bookstore occasionally, but lately there hasn't been time. Oxley's kind of a full-time job." —"Are you getting enough help? How's your support network?" —"Oh, great. My mom is always around, and some of my best friends have had babies recently, so we prop each other up. And then there's you folks. I can't tell you how helpful it is to have these two extra afternoons a week to catch up on my grocery shopping. For some reason, the fluorescent lights and the cash registers just make Oxley crazy."

"I'm glad to hear we're of assistance. Of course, our mission as a preschool is not just to provide childcare, but to prepare and equip these children to integrate themselves into the larger society." —Rachel agreed readily, and asked if there was anything she should be doing differently.

Marva had some ideas, which she shared. At the end of the meeting, Rachel seemed grateful and resolute, and Marva, gratified, felt that they had accomplished much.

Oxley, however, was not ready to leave. He had just craftily and efficiently demolished another child's block tower, and was exulting in a rare sensation of power and success. The mere sight of his mother was enough to remind him of his usual abjection. The transience of joy, the perpetuity of misery, the fundamental hostility of the world to all his wishes, were revealed to him with crushing clarity. His understanding had no words with which to contain these felt abstractions, so it rendered them in images: he saw himself in chains, being eaten by snakes and spiders, and burned by flaming swords, eternally. He let loose a belly howl of outrage and despair.

Marva watched Rachel pick him up and carry him out the door, writhing and clawing like a cat. Gravely she uttered her verdict: "Poor boy." —"Poor mom," said a colleague. —Marva conceded that the child was a handful.

When at last they were on the road, Rachel said, without reproach, "Well, you certainly made mommy look bad today." Oxley's cries subsided as he puzzled over this. Had something happened to his mother? Did she look bad? Had he done it? He strained to see her in the rear-view mirror, desperate to confirm his fears before they could grow worse.

Rachel stopped at the pharmacy for Oxley's and Burris's prescriptions, made an appointment for herself and Oxley with the hairdresser next week, delivered a box of Oxley's old clothes to Alexis, swapped a bag of magazines and children's books at the library, paid the telephone bill, and bought herself a coffee and Oxley, for his patience, an ice cream bar, which he had disseminated across the backseat by the time they arrived home. She gave him a banana to eat in the bathtub while she tidied the bedroom; she dressed him and let him undress himself in the kitchen while she made two curries, one for him and one for Burris; then she put him in his old car seat with a newspaper, a crayon, and a new noise-making toy car, which he tore, ate, and dismantled, respectively, while she fixed the broken shelf in the refrigerator.

Burris came home in a good mood, having successfully hypnotized two patients that day. To vent his happiness, he hugged his son, gave his wife advice, and, with a voluptuous profligacy of dishes, utensils, and spices, cooked himself a fresh meal, which he sat down to and enjoyed like a prince amid the cozy clutter of his palace.

"Are those my socket wrenches he's playing with?" —"No," said Rachel. "They're mine." —He raised his eyebrows. "Since when do you have socket wrenches?" —"Since today. I don't like yours. And now we both have a set." —He chuckled. "I cannot in good conscience approve such extravagance."

He put Oxley to bed, and over his protests read him a story. Then, while Rachel puttered in the kitchen, he sat in the den, listening to music and dreaming of one young woman's teeth.

"Sorry I missed that meeting," he said, when at last Rachel joined him on the sofa. "I couldn't get away." —"That's okay. I covered for you." —"What did she have to say?" —"Oh, just that he's a pain in the neck." —"Did she give you a hard time?" —"No. She was quite nice, actually. Maybe too nice." —"What do you mean?" —"I don't know. She was a little too pragmatic." She paused and hunted her thoughts. "I guess I'd rather be blamed for some things than absolved of everything." She tossed her head and laughed. "That must be my upbringing."

She recounted for him the director's suggestions: positive reinforcement, timeouts, consistency, and exercises in visualization, verbalization, and sharing. —Burris put his arms around her. "Maybe what he needs is someone to practice with." —"Like who?" —"Oh, like a sibling, maybe." —Rachel grinned. "It's funny you should say that." —"What's so funny?" —"A coincidence. Guess who I visited this morning." —"I'm sure I have no clue."

"Doctor Leahy."

He gave her a searching look.

HIGH GROUND. —SERGEANT MONTAZO wriggled on her belly to the crest of the ridge and surveyed the valley below through her field glasses. She had never seen landscape like this before. The gaunt and ragged mountains were smoothed in spots with shelves of snow; the rolling foothills were checkered with cottony groves of trees and swaths of furze; a stream twisted like a child's scribble through pastures splashed with wildflowers; a dirt road divided cultivated fields that from this height looked no larger than patches on a quilt; and a village, asleep or abandoned, lay nestled in the blue shadows like an heirloom in velvet. The sky was slowly filling with infinitely gradated dawn—colors that, she would swear, did not exist back home—and even as she watched, a sliver of sun topped the horizon and poured its pearly warmth across the valley floor. Overcome, she lowered the field glasses, and the scene dissolved into daubs of colored light. She resolved to return here someday, with a camera, hiking shoes, a pipe, and a companion. No part of her would admit that nothing could ever again carry her halfway around the earth from home to a comfortless mountaintop at daybreak, or that for this exquisite moment she had the war to thank. To relieve her emotions, she decided to drop some shells into the valley.

She beckoned to Culverson, the new radio operator, who joined her on the ridge. She gave her a lesson in artillery observation. A good observer with high ground and a radio, she said, was more powerful than even a battalion of rifles, for she could rain down ordnance on any position in her view. "So," she asked, "if you were the enemy, where in this valley would you place your observatory?" After some thought, Culverson indicated the same unobvious vantage point that Montazo herself had selected. Montazo grimaced. "All right, wiseass, but why?" —Culverson shrugged. "Good field of view both up and down the valley. Overlooks the village, and that crossroads down there." —Montazo raised the field glasses again. There was indeed a crossroads in the distance. Scowling, she said, "Okay, sure, sure. Let's assume that's your target. What're you going to tell your arty?" —"To shell it." —"I mean, what are its coordinates? How far away do you think it is from our position?" While Culverson considered, Montazo added, "It's not something you can teach, distance estimation. A person's either got it or they don't." —"I'd say twenty-two, twenty-three hundred yards. Add maybe seventy elevation."

This was so accurate that Montazo, exasperated, said nothing more. Muttering, she made some new estimations, did some calculations in her notebook, then grabbed the handset off Culverson's back and dialed the field artillery frequency. She gave them coordinates, and requested a full concentration.

After a minute, the shells came shrieking down from the sky and landed with elegant precision, in little puffs of smoke and debris, inside the village. A moment later came the reverberant rumble of the explosions. Two buildings had received direct hits. Montazo, had she not been prone, would have placed her fists on her hips.

"Isn't that a civilian village?" asked Culverson. —"It's abandoned." —"Oh. I thought I saw smoke from the chimneys. Yeah, look, there's people coming out into the street." —Montazo glanced through the field glasses. "This is a free-fire zone. Anyone still in that village is either enemy, or abetting the enemy."

"Oh," said Culverson. "Should we hit them again?"

Sergeant Montazo did not reply. She crept back down the ridge and climbed into her funk hole, where she opened a packet of curried beans and awaited the counterattack.

SNIPER BAIT. —LATE in the afternoon, Speed Bumps, intoxicated with coffee for want of anything stronger, took her idea to Pschaw and Smith at the communication dugout, which had been harassed the past few days by an unseen sniper. "I'll stand on the roof and draw fire; you watch for the muzzle flash." —"That sounds like a bad idea." —"Don't worry. They can't hit me if I keep moving." And she was certainly moving. She shuffled from side to side, rubbed her hands, wagged her eyebrows, and rolled her shoulders alternately in a cajoling manner. Smith and Pschaw doubted whether they could have hit her at point-blank range. They agreed to the plan. It might be fun.

She climbed onto the sandbagged dugout, hollering and waving her arms. Then she began to writhe and spin and lunge about. She leered, and guffawed, and bowed, and sobbed, and hopped in place. She made ugly faces and vulgar gestures. She cocked a hip and tossed her head like a model; she flaunted herself like a saleswoman displaying an irresistible product. She soon drew an appreciative crowd; even Smith and Pschaw crawled out of the post to watch. She began to feel invincible, as if her body were composed of air.

The sniper watched too, but refused to take a shot at the crazy woman. She was, in effect, a casualty already.

Later that night, Smith was shot in the face through the loophole. The bullet passed through one cheek and out her open mouth, doing little damage. She finished the word she was speaking, but not the sentence. She'd been telling Pschaw about her parents' upholstery business.

STILL ALIVE. —Sunachs monitored her fear like a blackout warden, lest any glimmer of it be seen by her comrades. This hypochondriac self-consciousness only aggravated the inevitable effects of insomnia, malnutrition, danger, and caffeine, so that her teeth were always on edge, her heart felt strangled in her chest, perceptions poured through her like radiation, and her nerves jangled constantly, like telephones ringing just below the threshold of hearing. To prevent her hands from shaking, she kept them busy cleaning her rifle or shuffling cards; to camouflage the starts and flinches to which she was prey, she flexed her shoulders and wagged her head like a pugilist; and her trembling lip she concealed behind a sneer. No one but she suspected that she was a coward.

She coped best when under fire, because then all her idle wits and muscles were enlisted to hug the ground, or to hold her weapon still and squeeze the trigger. For this reason, she usually volunteered for patrols. She was perhaps happiest when crossing a minefield or skulking through the enemy's positions, because it was only at such times that her inner turmoil seemed balanced by, even justified by, the ambient threat.

Volunteering one night for a retrieval patrol, she discovered within herself a new, unfathomed fear—the residue, perhaps, of childhood ghosts and bogeys: she was, it seemed, terrified of dead bodies. As the patrol crept noiselessly through the moonless valley, every rock appeared to her a smirking skull, and every shrub, every log, every shadow appeared a writhen, putrefying carcass. But when at last Vrail found the body they were looking for, lying twisted and limp in a puddle, its mundane lifelessness was puzzling, and somewhat frustrating, to Sunachs. Under the pretense of checking it for booby-traps, she put her hands all over it, searching for some justification for her earlier dread. But this thing was just clothes and cold, sticky meat. Not even the cavity in the back of the skull, nor the dry eyeball under her thumb, could explain her horror. This body was just a body—one that bore no resemblance to the corpse that poisoned her dreams. It proved, too, to belong to an enemy, so, after stripping it of its boots and its buttons, they left it where it lay.

In an effort to exorcize, or at least erode, her newfound fear, she undertook to study the dead around her—to scrutinize them with one eye turned inward, as it were, to record her own reaction. Taking advantage of a canteen halt one day, she dropped into a bomb crater where a dead peasant lay festering in the sun. This time she felt no fear or awe, but only an understandable revulsion. The stench, for one thing, though horrible, was not horrific: nothing that smelled so much like rotting garbage could be uncanny. And the blotched and bloated face, which the gases of decomposition had distended and discolored, was too garish, too inhuman, to be frightening. She peeled back the man's lips to reveal the teeth, the visible part of the skeleton; but still she experienced nothing but distaste.

Formerly she had been too squeamish to loot the dead for souvenirs, but now she began to make a point of it. Each time, the approach was the dreadful part; she trudged toward the crumpled heap as toward some inconceivably gruesome evil; but each time, the horror, like fog, dissipated as she came near. She concluded that old rotting corpses were not what bothered her—and she resolved to confront a fresh one.

One morning she heard that a member of Third Platoon had been crushed by an airdrop crate that she'd been trying to dislodge—had finally dislodged—from a tree. But by the time Sunachs arrived, the body had been carried down out of the hills by stretcher-bearers. A group of soldiers stood around the blood-splashed spot, grumbling. A piece of hairy scalp adhered to the intact crate, just below its PINEAPPLES IN OIL stencil. The sight did not much affect Sunachs—because, she supposed, she had not known the woman.

A few weeks later, when the company was back in the rearward positions, her good friend Gedge was killed by the concussion from a shell. Sunachs spent half an hour with her body in the aid-station dugout. There wasn't a mark on her, aside from some caked blood at the corner of her mouth. Sunachs felt desolate and angry but not afraid. Days later, when she permitted herself to think about it, she decided that Gedge's death had been too sanitary to evoke any terror. Whereas the other bodies had looked too dead, Gedge had looked too alive. Sunachs had been unable to see her as a corpse.

After a while, Sunachs forgot about her fear of dead bodies, and abandoned her study of them. She neither avoided them nor sought them out; she took only their banknotes and valuables; she dreamed of them only occasionally. But when Lieutenant Farl was killed, the night they attacked the enemy outpost on Hill 68, Sunachs's fear returned in a flood. Here was someone she loved, and his death was not sanitary.

Farl, standing on the parapet and shouting to his troops below, was drilled in the torso by a burst of machine-gun fire. When, ages later, Sunachs and Vrail reached him, he was screaming silently, blood spurting from his mouth, his eyes as large as eggs. He kicked them with the force of a mule when they tried to put him on a stretcher. In the ghastly, spastic light of the flares, they did not realize at first that the lieutenant had been cut in half. When his body came apart in their hands, Sunachs recoiled in every muscle, and fell to the ground retching. This was the corpse of her nightmares. This corpse was still alive.

Weeks later, Boorq came across Sunachs hacking at an enemy corpse with her bayonet. "I think they're dead, buddy." —Sunachs slowly backed away. "Just making sure," she said.

AN EPITAPH. —FOURTH Platoon were removing spikes from a railroad. It was slow, back-breaking work, for which, as usual, they had been given no reasons. Presumably they were rendering the track unusable for the enemy, which meant that a reverse must be expected or a retreat planned—both dispiriting prospects. And this particular form of destruction afforded no opportunities for catharsis; it had none of the zest of burning down churches, booby-trapping basements, smashing valuables, or poisoning wells. Also, they had been provided with tools ill-suited to the task, they were constantly being interrupted by the trucks of a munitions column that continued to use the railway as a road to the main area of conflict, and it was midday, and hot.

Fidget, shirtless and sweating and cursing, had been working on a single spike for ten minutes, and had nearly succeeded in prying it free with her corroded entrenching tool when a supply truck, tired of waiting, began blaring its horn at her. She ignored it, her brain meanwhile throbbing with the compound rage of the exploited laborer, the righteous martyr, and the lowly pedestrian harassed by the lordly motorist. At last she threw down her tool and tore her pistol from its holster; she would have begun firing into the windshield, but the driver had already descended. They faced each other for a moment; then their grimaces broke into grins, and they fell to grappling and yelping. They had been at the training depot together.

Fidget and Tsetse had not been close friends, but basic training was the nearest thing to an upbringing that two soldiers could share. Each reminded the other nostalgically of home, and, erroneously, of peacetime. Smoking and teasing and marveling, they crouched in the shade of Tsetse's truck and exchanged news, while the other drivers gunned their engines, craned their necks, and sighed.

"Did you hear about Doakus?" asked Tsetse suddenly. —Fidget laughed, at the mere mention of this name, as if an old burden had been unexpectedly shed. "Don't tell me she's an officer!" This was a joke; but a charming absurdity adhered to Fidget's idea of Doakus, making the joke seem not at all unlikely. The truth, however, was more absurd, and all too likely: Doakus, of course, was dead.

For the rest of the day, Fidget groped irritably through a fog. Doakus dead. How could that be? Fidget had seen friends wounded, probably fatally; she had seen the corpses of animals, of locals, and of soldiers unknown to her; before the war, she had attended the funerals of her grandmother, a cousin, and a schoolmate; but she had never before felt so vividly the proximity and indiscriminateness of death.

Joan Doakus had been husky, robust, and good-looking, but so altogether without guile, conceit, or indeed introspection that everyone who met her liked her. Even her famous laziness was endearing, for it had no root in weakness, but on the contrary seemed the natural product of her implacable good humor. She could, when pressed, and as it were for a lark, double-time up a mountain under full kit; but it was more pleasant to lie atop one's gear in the valley—so why pretend? There was something inspiring and almost invigorating in her lassitude; she took the path of least resistance

as a sail takes wind. Because she never doubted her place
in the universe, she had no need of a personal providence;
indifferent to omens, curses, and godsends, she accepted
both windfalls and setbacks with amused equanimity, track-
ing the flight of her own fortunes like a birdwatcher. Her
serenity was contagious, and baffled and balked even the
drill sergeants, who found it impossible, or perhaps pointless, to punish her. Fidget still recalled in amazement the
only time they ever heard Staff Sergeant Haoubess laugh.
Having found in her locker a contraband letter and photograph from Doakus's boyfriend, he had berated her viciously
for ten minutes, denigrating her patriotism, her intelligence,
and even her taste in men; he had concluded, like a jealous
parent, by forbidding her to associate with such a feeble,
pimply, sloppy young man. Her reply from any other recruit
would have drawn a court-martial. "Unfortunately, sir, I
doubt I'll ever get me as nice a man as you."

But in general, there had been few transgressions to punish, for everyone in the unit helped to cover for Doakus and
to keep her squared away. She was for them like a pet, a sister, and a daughter. They made allowances for her; they were
proud of her; she brought out the best in them.

Her eyes blinked asynchronously. She denied that she
snored. She could throw a knife with great accuracy. She
was proud of her bowel movements, which were "as regular
as sheet music." She confessed to incestuous feelings for her
brother, who was a lawyer and a married father. She was a
born debater, and was always playing devil's advocate—to
provoke others, but also to challenge them. "No one ever
got very far on one leg," she liked to say. She believed everything, and so could question everything—especially orders.
She did not smoke, but she sucked on a pipe, and liked
to punctuate her pronouncements with its moistened stem.
She knew one line of poetry, which she recited at every
opportunity. She was twenty-one years old. She was dead.

That night, Fidget awoke in the dark to a feeling of suffocation. She thrashed free of her sleeping bag, then lay there gasping, her mind racing haphazardly. She felt that Doakus was a problem that needed solving, but one from which she could not stand back sufficiently to even see. She slogged through a mire of repetitious platitudes: *such a shame; before her time; her poor family; a better place . . .* She was trying to glean something from her friend's death, a lesson or a moral; she was searching for a vantage from which to view it, or a frame in which to place it. When at last, just before dawn, she fell back asleep, she had arrived at no conclusion; but the troubled part of her mind had exhausted itself, so that she felt an illusory repose, as of satisfaction. Probably everything is all right after all, she thought, and her thoughts went no deeper.

But in the morning, she seemed to be in possession of the answer. She recalled what Tsetse had said when asked how Doakus had died. "Who knows? Probably a shell, like everybody else." Then she had offered in extenuation this fact, which Fidget now saw as the woman's epitaph: "She wasn't much of a soldier, I'm afraid."

That day the First/Fourth replaced the spikes they had removed the day before. No one knew or wondered why.

THE COOK-UP. —AFTER three days of footslogging through tangled forest concealing treacherous terrain, C Platoon lost radio contact with command. Lieutenant Ryyss called a halt and conferred with Culverson, the radio operator.

"It's because we're down in the valley," she told him. —"We were in a valley yesterday," Ryyss observed. —"Yes, but there was cloud cover then." —Ryyss said nothing, betraying neither understanding nor failure to understand. —Gently Culverson explained, "The transmission bounces off the clouds, which extends your range."

Ryyss looked at the sky resentfully. He had been a lieutenant, and platoon leader, for only five days, and he felt the disconnection from higher authority as keenly as a severed thumb. For three days he had received orders every eight hours to continue marching for another eight hours. Now, in the absence of new orders, was he to stop, or to go on? Of their ultimate objective he knew only that they were to rendezvous with D, E, and F Platoons somewhere near Burzgao, still two or three days away if they maintained their current speed. He could send Culverson and a squad back up the hill to reestablish radio contact, but if anything happened to them, if they got lost, he would be without a radio, without orders, several days' march from a friendly position, and at two-thirds strength—less, in fact, for they were already seven soldiers short of a full platoon. Alternatively, he could lead everyone back up the hill, but that would mean a delay of five or six hours. If the sky were to become cloudy in that time, he would actually do better to stay put. He was reluctant, however, to order a rest. New to command, he did not feel that he was doing his job unless his troops were active—which was why they had marched so far, and slept so little, in the last seventy-two hours.

Privates Kellek and Tolb came forward to ask permission, if there was time, to pick some berries they had spotted in the vicinity. —"You've identified them?," Ryyss asked. "They're edible?" —"Yes, Lieutenant," said Kellek. "That is, I performed the combat-pragmatic edibility test on them." In fact, Kellek had curtailed this test, which normally required two days and involved gradually increasing one's exposure to the potential food source, from handling to tasting to holding in the mouth to chewing and finally to swallowing. What Kellek had done was eat a handful of the berries the day before; today she felt fine, or in any case no worse.

The request gave Ryyss an idea. He knew that everyone was fed up with the ABC rations, which some joked had not just Already Been Cooked, but Already Been Chewed—or even, in the case of the despised pineapples in oil, Already Been Crapped. Florze, their de facto field cook, had subjected the nutritious but flavorless contents of the zippered packets to a variety of preparations: she had stewed them, fried them, boiled them, cooked them down to sludge or to cinders, made soup or tea from them, and roasted them on skewers over burning plastique; she had requisitioned for spice or seasoning every available substance, including rifle grease, antifogging gel, malaria pills, aspirin, shaving cream, and the faintly perfumed antiseptic napkins from their first-aid kits; and she had combined the rations every way possible, in every permutation and in every ratio: she had mixed coffee with sausage, brandy peaches with pork noodles, curried beans with carrot cake, sugar and cinnamon dumplings with fish balls, and, on one memorable occasion, all the above fried into a massive omelette. No preparation, however, could alleviate the monotony. And the monotony had only been exacerbated by the latest airdrop, which, due to an oversight or to whimsy, had contained nothing but pineapples in oil.

Lieutenant Ryyss called the platoon together. Placing his hand on the trunk of a tree, he said, "This is platoon HQ. Be back at HQ by thirteen hundred—that's a little over two hours. Bring back whatever food you can find. This is not an exercise. This is victualing in the field. Travel in pairs or small groups. Remember: Leaves of three, let them be. And, uh, no toads or snakes. That's all. Don't get lost. Dismissed."

Within five minutes, the woods all around were crackling with rifle shots, and Ryyss realized that he should have imposed fire silence. He did not think that there was enemy in the area, but one never knew. Popping a week-old quid of tea leaves into his mouth, he pulled out his maps and studied them moodily, and needlessly.

After firing their rifles a few times to relieve tension, the soldiers fanned out, for the most part singly, to each pursue their own private act of foraging, hunting, or leisure. Osini spent an hour constructing a snare with communication wire, and an hour peacefully watching it. Laskantan climbed a tree and, no other prey being visible, followed the movements of her fellow soldiers through her sights. Vrail discovered a deer run, which she followed on tiptoe for several miles, knife in hand. Culverson sat in the shade and peeled a hundred sumac shoots, most of which she ate. Sunachs, Raof, and Klipton, independently, found secluded dells in which to masturbate and nap. Sergeant Montazo, a few steps at a time, stalked a pheasant all the way to its roost; then, lowering her field glasses for the lunge, she blindly seized a stone instead. Frustrated, she tossed a grenade into a pond, and collected as many of the dead fish that floated to the surface as she could carry.

Others had some success too. Kellek and Tolb returned with several quarts of berries. Sergeant Gijalfur, covered in gore, came back with some animal's antlers, in lieu of any more edible part, for there had not been time to drag the carcass back to the headquarters tree, and no mere piece of meat would have done justice to the beast's size. Solzi succeeded in netting two chatty, brightly plumaged birds, which she refused to let Florze butcher. Pannak and Boorq, grinning triumphantly, brought back nine bludgeoned hares on a string. But the most popular catch proved to be Narran and Alcott's bucketful of worms and beetle grubs, which, crushed to a paste and flavored with some of the gingerroot and laurel leaves that Florze had found, made delicious burgerlike patties.

By the time they had finished eating, it was late afternoon and the sky had clouded over. The radio was working again, and Lieutenant Ryyss received his orders to continue marching towards Burzgao. The platoon had to admit that, though he would never measure up to Lieutenant Farl, Ryyss was not such a bad guy after all. He even allowed them to sing a little, till they began the ascent out of the valley.

> "We've got tanks for shooting guns and guns that shoot
>   tanks;
> We've got bombers that drop bombs on anti-aircraft.
> But a gun that riddles hunger I'd wield with thanks,
> Or a bomb that blasts fatigue or boondoggles daft.

Weapons galore have we got in store
For friends and for good jobs well done;
Imagine what fun inventing a gun
That kills loneliness, fuckups, and war!"

At dusk they walked into an ambush.
Pannak, Vrail, Florze, and Culverson were killed.
Ryyss blamed himself, and the cook-up, which had made
everyone lax and complacent.

CLASSROOM AMBUSH. —Two Words hated new fucks. She also hated generals, MPs, KPs, and journalists; she hated husbands, cooks, civilians, and all the leprous cunts of Second/Third Platoon; and she had her trademark "just two words" to say about the air force, who were "a bunch of blind and titless brain-dead cocksucking shitpigs." But for new fucks she felt a special contempt, as pure and consuming as fire. New fucks were repugnantly fresh, well fed, and spruce, and they made the old fucks look shabby and ill by comparison. They kept themselves and their gear clean and tidy, as if they were still on parade-ground. They were cocky and inexperienced, a deadly combination. On patrols they were loud and clumsy, and invariably took unsighted cover, from which they could provide assistance to no one. They accepted witlessly all the official propaganda about the progress of the war, the righteousness of their cause, the superiority of their weaponry, the gratitude of the locals, and the craven ignobility of the enemy. Worst of all, they knew nothing, cared nothing, about the soldiers, wounded and dead, that they had come to replace. Two Words curated a secret ledger of the members of First/Fourth Platoon, and, to her, each new name inscribed therein was an attack on history; each new arrival represented the desecration of a beloved friend's memory.

New Fuck Nebel was a quintessential example of her class. She buffed her boots, wore her helmet in the bunker, and stood watch with bayonet fixed. She couldn't wait to get into a firefight; she couldn't wait to blast the brains out of some invaders' skulls. Two Words, listening to this, gritted her teeth for a minute, then exploded. "What the fuck do you know about a firefight, pussy fuzz? What they tell you at basic; what you've seen in the movies. You don't know shit about shit, so why don't you shut your fucking spunkguzzler." —To avert a brawl, Christmas Tree defended Nebel. "She's just a little trigger-horny, T.W. She's got the whore's itch. She'll get over it. Give her a break." —Two Words ignored this. "And 'invaders'? What the fuck do you know about motherfucking invaders? There are exactly two kinds of enemy soldiers you're going to see in this war: the dead ones, and the ones trying very hard and very skilfully to fucking kill you. I've got exactly two words of advice for you: stay the fuck away from all of them, and you'll be a whole fuckload better off." —Nebel objected, "But it's our job. It's our duty. We're trained, and ready, and paid to kill the bitches." —"Don't even," said Two Words. "The shit coming out of your mouth makes me want to puke out of my fucking ass." —"Aw," said Nebel, "you're just scared."

This statement was so ignorant and so offensive in so many ways that it overloaded Two Words's capacity for indignation; she subsided, deflated. "Let's just hope for your own sake that you get scared too, fuck-knuckle, and soon."

A few days later, Nebel volunteered for a reconnaissance patrol—and Two Words saw an opportunity to teach the new fuck a lesson. She recruited Winky and Pschaw to assist, and brought her idea to the other three members of the patrol fireteam. Only Sawed-Off was hesitant; she asked, "Shouldn't we ask the Corp's permission first?"

—"Are you fucking kidding me?" said Longpork. "You know exactly what she would say." —Corporal Cobweb had three stock phrases: "The wherewithal and the inclination," "Drumhead," and "Waste of ammo." Sawed-Off conceded that the corporal would probably adjudge the mock firefight a waste of ammo.

They discussed practicalities. "Should we use blanks?" —"Fuck that," said Upsize. "I'm not going out on any recon without fucking live rounds." —"The area's been dead for weeks," Two Words reminded her. "Anyway, we'll never get hold of enough blank rounds. Don't worry. We'll shoot over your heads, and you'll shoot into the ground." —"What about Nebel?" —"She'll never see us." —"And grenades?" —"Don't use them." —"But what about her?" —Two Words made an impatient gesture. "She'll be too shit-scared to do anything. Trust me."

They studied a map of the patrol's proposed route. "We'll wait for you here, where the road curves." —"Sure, where the burned-out tank is." —"No, that's farther on." —"Oh, is it? Never mind." —Eventually everyone believed that they knew which spot Two Words was referring to. —"Winky and Pschaw will take the hill here, and I'll be here, beyond the ditch. Any questions?" —There was a long silence, but no questions.

That night in the mess dugout, everyone got into the spirit of the practical joke, even those who had not been coached by Two Words. They gave Nebel solemn and contradictory advice, told exaggerated or apocryphal tales of their own first patrols, and throughout feigned a struggle to restrain their feelings of pity and foreboding.

"Last time I was out that way, the whole fucking area was swarming with invaders." —"There's about ten fucking classroom fucking ambush points on that route they got you walking." —"Who's the sorry saggy-tit on point?" —Upsize, Longpork, and Sawed-Off declined the lead position. —"I guess that leaves me," laughed Nebel, but there was a catch in her voice.

"I just can't shake this bad fucking feeling," muttered Sawed-Off. "Last time I had a bad feeling like this, Doc Throb and Chop Top came back dead." —In the end, they managed to spook not just Nebel, but themselves as well.

Nebel's nervousness mounted throughout the briefing, which she scarcely absorbed, and continued to crescendo in the hours preceding the departure time, till by midnight she was certain that those around her could sense the anguish radiating from her like a stink. Her bowels were clamorous but she could not shit; her breathing seemed shallow and rapid, but any correction she imposed left her dizzy and gasping. Not until they were moving out through the camouflaged chicanes in the razor wire did her anxiety diminish, or rather find an outlet. For the first time she discovered the difference between useful and useless, active and inactive fear; and she understood why, under an artillery barrage a few nights earlier, her partner on watch had scrambled about for hours making superficial improvements to their bunker. Now, creeping daintily across the darkened landscape, her every muscle strained, her every sense afire with perceptions, she was still terrified, but at last she was doing something: moving to meet, and perhaps to shape, her fate. She seemed to have all the oxygen she needed; the air was brimming almost visibly with it; she could sip it like wine for pleasure or gulp it like water for strength. The terrain she navigated seemed familiar to her from childhood, when in imagination and in dreams she had skulked and slid and tumbled and sneaked across fields, over hills, and through shadows and forests like these.

Their progress was slow, for Nebel tested each patch of ground before giving it her weight, insisted on crawling up any rise, and frequently motioned for a stop and drop so that she could investigate a suspicious-looking twig, or stone, or signpost, or furrow. Sometimes she left the others for ten or fifteen minutes—an eternity of lying on the frozen ground, listening to the rustling of grass and trees and the miscellany of tiny stirring noises that loomed in the silence like the sounds of a soldier being stifled, subdued, and garroted. Each time Nebel returned, often from a different direction than that in which she had set out, Sawed-Off was half convinced that she was an enemy, and had to consciously refrain from shooting her.

Shortly after checkpoint two, Nebel dropped to the ground and lay motionless for a long time. Eventually, Longpork slithered forward to join her. Nebel pointed first subtly, then with increasing emphasis, at a thicket fifty meters distant. Longpork saw only the thin black silhouettes of trees standing in a pool of their own shadow. In truth, anything could have been in there. She made a questioning gesture; Nebel replied with a gesture of irate incredulity, and pointed again. Longpork looked harder, with fixed gaze, till the whole countryside seemed to be dancing with sinister motion; she was staring into a damp, pulsating tunnel teeming with glistening gremlins, then into a kaleidoscopically shifting hallway being built and dismantled by scaly self-replicating machines. She blinked and shook her head. There was a reason new fucks were not usually permitted to take point. "You're seeing things," she said.

Nebel's whisper was slow and adamant. "I saw their helmets."

Longpork did not know what to do. She did not really think anyone was there; and if anyone were, it could not likely be Winky and Pschaw, who were supposed to be waiting past checkpoint three, and not in any trees but behind a hill. Nevertheless, Two Words might have moved the site of her ambush forward due to impatience, disorientation, or other reasons she'd been unable to communicate to the patrol. Longpork switched her rifle's safety off, and, to let whoever might be there know they had been spotted, she fired a burst over the thicket.

Nebel started and nearly screamed. Her finger was on her trigger; indeed, the only thing that had prevented her from firing already was the warning she'd received earlier that night: namely, that the muzzle flash suppressors they'd been issued were useless, and that the only sure way to avoid revealing your location at night was by tossing a grenade. Now she squeezed the trigger, emptying an entire magazine into the thicket, with the desperate conviction that it would probably be the last thing she ever did. She intended to go on firing until she died; when the rifle emitted a hollow click, she cried, "I'm empty!" as if she had been shot.

"What the fuck?" said Upsize, coming forward.

Silence. No return fire. Nebel peered into the trees. The helmets hadn't moved. Either they were extraordinarily disciplined soldiers, or . . .

She loaded another magazine, set her rifle to semi-automatic, got to her feet, and loped, crouching, in the direction of the thicket, firing a round every few steps. The helmets did not flinch. Finally, from ten meters away, she saw that they were not helmets, but burls. She returned to the group without a word, and with a gesture resumed the patrol.

Winky and Pschaw, meanwhile, were growing jumpy. The patrol was far behind schedule; had something happened? The gunfire in the distance unsettled them further, and Winky crossed the road to consult with Two Words. —"Get the fuck back to your position. They're probably just doing some rape fucker." This was code, in Fourth Company's informal phonetic alphabet, for reconnaissance by fire—shooting at something to see if it shot back. "Stick to the plan. Everything's fine."

But Two Words was also unsettled. Several times she was on the verge of canceling the ambush and returning to camp; and when at last she saw figures approaching from the wrong direction, and in an untactically tight group, she panicked and tossed a concussion grenade into the road.

This frightened not only Nebel, but the rest of the patrol and Winky and Pschaw too, who had not been expecting grenades. Everyone got low and began firing at once, not bothering to aim, let alone to aim over anyone's head or into the ground. No one was hit; but later, comparing stories, each of them swore that bullets had passed within centimeters of them; and this led to counter-boasts of having sharpshot rings around one another. Back at camp, some wags said that it was a miracle nobody got killed; but in fact, as the carelessness of fright was soon succeeded by the carelessness of exultation, it probably would have been more miraculous if any bullet had met, in all that black space, a body. The only real danger came from Nebel, who, believing herself surrounded, lobbed grenades in every direction.

The firefight drew the attention of two infrapodean infanteers lying in a nearby listening post. They radioed their commander, who decided, after studying the map and communicating with other platoon leaders, that it must be an enemy field exercise. He ordered an artillery barrage, which, even before correction, landed close enough to the mock ambush to bring it to a halt. —"That's enemy incoming!" screamed Two Words, and initiated the retreat.

Not until they were halfway back to camp did Nebel realize that there were now seven of them. To Sawed-Off, who was running alongside her, she said, "Shit, were you all in that ambush too?" —"Uh, yeah," said Sawed-Off. —"Fuck; anybody hurt?" She wanted to hear that others had been hurt, even killed, for it would make the ecstasy she felt at still being alive even more acute. But she could not wait for a reply, and she prattled on: "I killed one of those fuckers for sure, maybe two. I saw an arm flying, and a boot. It could've been two. That was some extremely intense shit, huh? You ever seen shit like that before? I think it was two. It must've been two. Did you see? It was something else."

Back at camp, her excitement rendered her oblivious for a long time to her comrades' laughter and ridicule. Only gradually did she realize that the whole thing had been a joke, and that no enemy had been present. Her face crumpled and fell; she looked ready to weep. "Shit," she groaned, "then who'd I kill?"

This question was relished, and cherished, and repeated, and soon became the platoon's latest all-purpose catch-phrase. It was used as an expression of bewilderment, of braggadocio, and of hangdog complaint. And when, a month later, Albene Nebel drowned in a collapsed trench, it was as Old Fuck Who'd-I-Kill that she was affectionately remembered. Striking this name from her secret ledger with regret, Two Words added a succinct obituary: "Mud"—the cause of death.

MAIL CALL. —A bag of mail caught up with Forty-Third Company in the village of Apillnol, where for several days they had huddled in the shattered cellars awaiting orders, munitions, and food. In the bombed-out skeleton of a cathedral, C Platoon gathered around a few smoky, nause-ating heat tablets, and shared the last of Florze's illicit goat jerky. The mood, which had been dismal for days, became almost convivial. The letters were a welcome distraction from the damp and the inaction, and were savored even by those who feared, with or without reason, bad news from home—a death in the family, a debt incurred by a spouse, or a jilting by a lover. The procedure in these cases was the same as with a wound: you stared at the ceiling while some-one else surveyed the damage first; then a glance at their face told you the worst.

Only Boorq truly dreaded the mail call, for each let-ter received from her brother was another she would not answer. It was months—she dared not reckon how many—since she had last been able to write. What could she write about? The noise, the scarcity, the filth? The dismember-ment of her friends? The farmer she'd murdered? To answer Bibb's perky chatty domestic reports with a grim litany of objectives taken and lost, casualties abandoned, provisions scavenged, and landscapes and livelihoods smashed to rubble by unceasing storms of high explosives, would be obscene. Finally, she had found it no less obscene to conceal these facts behind a veil of stoic or phatic circumlocution; and so she had stopped writing altogether. Now her brother's letters, which formerly she had warmed herself by, served only to sharpen her guilt—with the result that she felt attacked by them. Of course, feeling attacked helped lessen the guilt, so she scoured his lines for reproaches, and found them even in his avoidance of any tone of reproach. The saintly way he continued to write letters exactly as if his sister continued to reply to them was surely meant to be shaming.

Today's note was no different. Two devilishly inane pages about the weather, the neighbors, the cost of yams, and another trivial milestone achieved by her toddler niece, Milu; then a perfunctory paragraph of optimism; and finally the fatuous, hurried close: "I must stop here if I am to get this off by today's post"—as if it mattered when he got it off. Why not spend a week crafting something of value, of interest? Because, of course, it was a chore, one that must be completed in a single burst of willpower. Here, too, in his exemplary performance of an unpleasant duty, she detected an indictment.

Hiding her disgust, she allowed the letter to be passed around the circle, so that those who had received no mail could project their own fantasies of home onto the screen of her brother's prose. When the letter came back to her with compliments, she scanned it once more with affected objectivity. She thought she now perceived a crack in Bibb's sanctimony; surely here, in his defense of his daughter's temper tantrums, was an overt expression of resentment: "After all, one must be patient, for the girl struggles, as we all do, with your absence." Boorq almost laughed aloud with vindicated spite. And yet the feebleness of this jab was quite pathetic.

Did he really imagine she might feel responsible for the child's burgeoning psychopathy? Besides, nothing could be easier than to turn that argument to her own use. If Milu's "struggle" gave her permission to behave badly, then how much more exonerating was Boorq's own greater struggle. Indeed, in the context of this slaughterhouse, her misdeeds were trifling. If Milu was not to blame for her tantrums, her aunt was not to blame for anything she might do while a soldier in this war, fighting, at the risk of her life, for her country against the aggressors. She had just enough strength to be a good warrior; she need not also be a good aunt, or sister, or citizen, or soul. She could steal food from the poor, destroy property, and kill with impunity. She would support her fellow soldiers; she would not run away. That was enough.

She felt a knot loosening within her, and a welling of freedom and power. Excusing herself with a grunt, she went out into the street and picked her way through the debris, humming and chewing meat, a feral animal flexing its thews.

One parcel remained unclaimed. It was addressed to Private Popatisu, a puke who'd been crushed the week before by one of their own tanks. Raof had been nearby, and had seen the body, a flatulent, quivering slab of flesh trussed up in tattered khakis. After staring at it for a minute, she had waved another tank forward, so as to mash the horrific sight more completely into the earth. When after the skirmish she reported Popatisu's death to the lieutenant, she was vague about the location, so that the graves people would not have to rummage in the carnage for her dog tags.

Raof was against opening the parcel, but she was in the minority. —"What if there's food?" —"What if there's a sexy note?" —"Or a sexy photo?" —"If she were here," said Osini, "she'd want us to have it. She'd want us to at least look." No one could convincingly deny this, for Popatisu had not been well known. When the lieutenant excused himself, he seemed to say that the army had no ruling on the matter. Osini opened the package.

What they found inside was better than food or pornography: seven pairs of thick, dry, clean, hand-knitted woolen socks. Everyone stared agape at them, each basking in her own private image of the soft, warm, sheltering human being who had made and mailed them. Then Pannak broke the spell by trying to start an auction. There were jeers: "Yeah, and who'll the money go to, orphans?" Tolb thought the socks should go to Culverson or Sergeant Costitch or the machine-gun team, who carried the heaviest gear. Burnok, untying her boots' laces, said they should go to whoever had the worst case of foot rot. Osini pointed out that the parcel had only been opened thanks to her. Finally Kellek leapt up. "We'll draw high card for them, you fartholes." —"Wait," said Pannak, "for *all* of them?" —"That's right. Winner takes all." —"I think we should have seven winners. Seven pairs of socks, seven winners." —"Aw, swallow it. If you win, you can give six away." —"Well, whatever we do, let's hurry up and draw before the other two get back."

To her embarrassment and everyone else's annoyance, Tolb won the socks. She tried to give a few pairs away, but no one but Burnok would publicly accept them. Within a few days, however, four of the remaining six pairs had gone missing from Tolb's pack.

After this prize was awarded, Laskantan plucked from the parcel the neglected letter to Popatisu, and began to recite from it. There were words she did not recognize, however, and the subject matter, when not outright inscrutable, did not lend itself well to declamation. "Here, on the matter of which particular manifestation a decision would take, I am afraid we stand divided . . . Whether circumstances will continue as they have heretofore, or whether, on the contrary, an about-face is to be expected, is not for me to speculate . . . Leaving to the side for the time being the question of responsibility, I will go so far as to say that your involvement, if pursued freely, would not be unwelcome to any party here." Laskantan groaned and let the pages drop.

"What the fuck. Was she a scientist or something?" —"Is that thing from her *husband?*" —"I think it's her lawyer." —"Look, it's signed 'Thalim.' Must be her husband." —"Must be her dad." —Everyone laughed. —Osini whistled mournfully and said, "Poor bitch is better off dead."

Sergeant Costitch alone understood that the dead woman had inherited a factory. She kept the letter, and glanced at it sometimes.

THE MINEFIELD. —THE stream through the woods that they had been following up the mountain now led out into a grassy clearing, a dozen hectares in size. Corporal Cobweb signaled a halt, and called over War Juice, Jaywalk, and H. Crap, her section leaders. They knelt around her map. "Well," she said, "this must be the minefield."

The three lance corporals lifted their heads and peered at the harmless-looking glade. This morning, at this altitude, the medipodean summer was balmy. Even Jaywalk, city dweller, who hated the filth and bristly disorder of nature, was charmed. A lukewarm breeze carried glittering pollen through the air; birds and insects chattered and whirred like children's gizmos. For a moment, the war seemed far away.

"Are they anti-tank or anti-personnel?" asked H. Crap. Anti-tank mines were deadlier, but sometimes did not explode when stepped on. —"No fucking hunch," said Cobweb. "All the map says is 'mines.'" She pointed at the map. —Jaywalk asked, "Are they ours or theirs?" Their own mines were shoddier, but their sappers tended to lay more of them. —Cobweb's face expressed pained impatience. —"Definitely ours," said H. Crap, with the conviction of pessimism. "We controlled this hill a year ago, didn't we?"

—"Can't we go around?" asked Jaywalk. —Cobweb pointed. "We're continuing up that ravine." The cliffs on either side were too steep to climb. —War Juice spat. "Exactly why we put a fucking minefield just here."

The lance corporals returned to their troops and solicited volunteers. "We just need one person to mark a route with tape." Each section looked askance at the other two, grumbling. The Colonel, who often volunteered, was disgusted and made obstinate by the assumption that she would volunteer, and by the general lack of esprit de corps. Longpork prayed that no one would volunteer, or she too would feel obliged to. Speed Bumps, who loathed mines, forced herself to stand up—but then could not speak or meet her section leader's gaze.

"All right," said Corp Cobweb, "we'll all go. We'll leapfrog in file at quadruple-arm interval. A straight line is our shortest route, so let's aim for that gap in the rockface. Stay as nearly as possible in the previous soldier's steps. I'll go first."

"Wait up, Corp," said Speed Bumps. "I'll go." —"It doesn't matter who goes first. We'll all get a turn." —"No, I mean I'll volunteer. I'll go the whole way with the tape." —"No," said Cobweb. "Too late." She walked ten steps into the tall grass, stopped mid-stride, and looked back over her shoulder. She nodded at Speed Bumps, who followed without hesitation. Addressing the rest of the platoon, she said, "Don't make your LCs determine a marching order. We share the risk, and we get across this field intact. Scrunch your tits!"

Speed Bumps, her pulse sounding in her ears, brushed past the corporal, took another ten steps, and stopped. The Colonel did the same, going a few meters farther; then Jaywalk, then Longpork, then Chop Top, followed by Two Words, Teacher's Pet, and The Professor. "All right," Cobweb called to the troops still behind her. "No need to wait till she's in position. Don't bunch up, but keep coming."

Bongo Drum was the second from last to leave the treeline. By this time, the file had reached the middle of the field. She stole from soldier to soldier, squeezing past each of them as if they shared a foot-wide gangplank. —"Stop jostling," said Christmas Tree. —"You're pushing me out of line, cunt-knuckle," said Triple-Time. —But Bongo was too intent on her footing to spare a reply. When at last she reached Shitjob at the front of the file, she clung to her for a moment, then launched herself forward. —"Hey," said Shitjob, when Bongo showed no sign of stopping, "don't get ambitious . . ."

Then she did stop, abruptly, poised like a cat burglar. Twisting her head around, she shouted, in a deep, even voice, "I think I stepped on something here!"

Cobweb winced. So much for noise discipline. "What are you spitting about?" —"I stepped on something and it went 'click'!" —Shitjob giggled anxiously. "Fuckbag, mines don't go 'click,' they go 'boom.'" —"Hold on," called the corporal. "I'm coming forward. Everybody stay put."

"I'm gonna jump for it," said Bongo. —"What the fuck are you talking about?" said Shitjob. "You heard the Corp; wait for the Corp."

"I can feel it under my boot," said Bongo, her voice becoming high and thin. A shudder of revulsion moved up her leg. "I triggered it."

"Ass-lips, mines go off when you trigger them. You probably just stepped on a fucking twig. Hey!" —Bongo flung herself to the ground.

At the sound of the explosion, Chop Top, Speed Bumps, and Helmet dove reflexively for cover—regretting it even as they fell. Shitjob was splashed with gore. Bongo Drum had leapt not off, but onto a mine.

H. Crap said, "Fuck." The mines were enemy anti-tank mines.

Doc Throb, hurrying forward, ran alongside the trodden path. Two Words grabbed her arm as she passed and pulled her back into the line. Doc Throb, not understanding the other's intention, shook her off; Two Words staggered back a step or two, and her whole body cringed in expectation of a blast. Angered, she gave Doc a didactic shove. Doc, exasperated, swung a fist at Two Words, which sent her reeling again into the treacherous tall grass. With an outraged bellow, Two Words lunged at Doc, and they fell to the ground, rolling and wrestling, each infuriated by the other's recklessness.

Jaywalk and War Juice pulled them apart. —"For fuck sake," cried Cobweb, moving back down the line, "everybody stay the fuck put." She sent Two Words forward to join Shitjob (who was covertly swigging codeine syrup), and ordered Doc Throb to take one person with her and return to company for a stretcher. Doc nodded; she understood that Bongo Drum was dead. She gestured at Helmet, who was nearby, and together they started back towards the woods.

Corporal Cobweb then turned to Christmas Tree. "C.T.," she said, "tell me you brought that fucking piece-of-shit metal detector of yours." —C.T. grinned. "Sure did, Corp." —Cobweb sighed. The detectors were notoriously unreliable on the mineral-rich medipodean soil, and useless anywhere that ordnance had been dropped. But she hoped that using the tool might restore some of the platoon's confidence. Extrapolating from her own anxiety, she imagined that the troops were on the verge of hysteria.

"Do you know how to use the fucking thing?" —"Sure, Corp. I found nearly three dollars in town last month, remember?" —"All right, lady. You got the wherewithal and the inclination to find a route across for us?" —Christmas Tree shrugged bashfully, honored by the corporal's trust. —Cobweb gripped the nape of C.T.'s neck. "Good woman. Go to."

But Speed Bumps, unable to stand still any longer, broke from the line with a strangled cry and dashed across the field at full pelt—as if she might, by sheer momentum, skim across the mines without detonating them. But it was such a relief to be running, and every harmless contact with the earth seemed such a dispensation, that soon she felt a tremulous joy swelling her throat. One course was as dangerous as the next, no step safer than another. She would either die or live, and nothing she did could make any difference. So fuck it. Half laughing, she began to leap and zigzag. She had almost reached the far side of the clearing when several things happened at once.

With a noise like sundering concrete, an unseen machine gun roared to life, and Speed Bumps fell, tumbling, into the grass; Helmet stepped on a mine, which shattered her legs and sent her torso cartwheeling into the air; and the crump of artillery fire rang out from somewhere in the hills above.

They all crouched and glanced wildly at one another.

"That's incoming!" screamed Corporal Cobweb, as the whistle of shells changed pitch and began to grow louder. "Spread the fuck out!"

Nobody moved.

EVERYTHING OKAY. —SPEED Bumps lay dying beneath the sky. She watched as a pill bug, with endearing diffidence, climbed onto a bloodied hand; the hand was as much or as little hers as the bloodied grass around it. A great buoyant relief poured through her, as if some vast, intractable problem were simultaneously revealing and resolving itself. "You're okay," she laughed; she didn't know whom she was talking to. Everything was okay.

REQUISITION MISSION. —FLORZE wanted to put together a requisition detail. Lieutenant Farl, washing his hands and face with ashes from the cookfire, paused to consider. They were currently bivouacked in a hangar on the outskirts of Lucallzo, towards which they had been marching without sleep for two days. But more than exhaustion, the platoon— the entire company—felt frustration. The siege that had been expected to last days and cost countless lives was over in hours, before they even arrived. Thus the purpose of all their exertion, sacrifice, and nerve had been negated by the fleeing enemy. No counterattack was anticipated. Meanwhile, the supply column was at least a day behind, rations were scarce as ever, and many of the troops had abandoned every nonessential item on the road. Nothing would be better for morale than a good looting; but looting had been prohibited. It was going to be a long war yet, and they could not afford to alienate the medipodeans. Some soldiers in the Fifty-Ninth had even been shot for slaughtering a cow.

He told Florze to go ahead, but to restrict herself to whatever rations the enemy had left behind. —"But won't they be poisoned, sir?" —"I doubt it. We caught them with their pants down. Bring Narran along to translate, so there are no misunderstandings with the locals. And I know our medics are short on morphine, bandages, and, um, antifatigue pills." Farl had taken his last antifatigue pill five hours earlier, just before hearing that their attack was canceled. He was already feeling frazzled. "Ask Doc Tzu if there's anything else she needs, and try to solicit some donations from a hospital or clinic, or another company's aid station." He gave Florze a score of blank and signed requisition chits, and wished her luck. "Be back by dawn."

Despite the lieutenant's blessing, Florze had difficulty finding helpers. Those who were not asleep were suspicious. "We're not supposed to loot," said Tolb. —"We're not. We're requisitioning." —"What's the difference?" —"We're not taking, we're borrowing." —"I don't think we're supposed to borrow, either." —Florze scoffed. "And we're not supposed to belch, either. —"I'll pass," said Tolb. "Bring me back something nice."

Vrail was erasing the answers from the foxed pages of the platoon's only crossword-puzzle book; Florze decided not to interrupt this delicate operation. Montazo and Burnok were again debating whether tracers had a different trajectory from normal rounds; Florze invited neither, not wanting to risk bringing along the argument too. Winurhtry was tinkering with a dud grenade; Florze kept her distance. She would have liked to ask Sergeant Costitch, who appeared to be awake and idle, but she was intimidated by the woman's rank, soldierly competence, and self-assurance. Laskantan was amusing herself and a few others with "psychological tactics": gibbering suprapodean-sounding nonsense into a captured enemy radio. Though no one could understand the aggressors' replies, their anger and bewilderment were plain, and hilarious.

Raof did not want to go; she preferred to stay hungry. She believed in a cosmic balance of pleasures and pains, and her secret strategy for survival was to remain as unhappy and uncomfortable as possible, so as not to make herself a target for nemesis. This self-denial, coupled with a natural pessimism, had made of her a surly anchorite. When cold, she refrained from wearing more clothing; she waited a week to read letters from home, by which time they were soiled almost to illegibility; no matter how thirsty, she never emptied her canteen completely; and though always ravenous, she always denied herself the last bite of every meal—and would have denied herself the first, more delicious bite, if that were possible. That afternoon, she had not even permitted herself to feel relief that the attack had been called off.

Finally, Culverson, one of the pukes, agreed to come. Though exhausted, she could not sleep; her body seemed still to be marching whenever she closed her eyes. She hoped that there would be trouble, for she had not yet been in a real, close firefight. Boorq, too, was eager to try the .31-caliber automatic rifle she had stolen piecemeal from Thirty-Second Company and lugged all the way here. Godbeer wanted to decline, for malnutrition had made her night-blind; but she thought this condition was psychosomatic and best treated with courageous disdain. They all armed themselves heavily, to Florze's disquiet.

Narran was in her sleeping bag but not quite sleeping. Since being deafened by an artillery shell three days earlier, she'd spent most of her time inside the bag, and had even wrapped it around her shoulders on the march. With her hearing gone, her skin, and especially her hands and face, had become extraordinarily sensitive, almost painfully so. A breeze now felt like ice-water, walking on gravel was like chewing glass, and shaving her head made her skull reverberate with a noise like tearing canvas. At the moment she was half dreaming, half hallucinating that her hunger was a redoubtable enemy position, that the pinpricks of sweat breaking out on her back were badly aimed shells, and that the glimmers of firelight coming through the sleeping bag's seams and zipper were falling flares and rising anti-aircraft rounds. It took Florze a few moments to rouse her, and she remained befuddled even as she got her gear together; she never felt quite fully awake anymore. She assumed that they were going on a reconnaissance or prisoner patrol. She too took all the ammunition she had.

Doc Tzurakinh had gone into town to help at a forward aid station, but they found a medic who told them what was needed. "Ethyl chloride, if you can find any, or any anesthetic, and hydrogen peroxide, or any good disinfectant." She spelled *ethyl chloride* and *hydrogen peroxide*, while Florze watched spellbound as she sprinkled maggots into a soldier's open wound. "Don't drink all the ethyl chloride on the way back," she teased. "And don't drink any of the hydrogen peroxide," she added, seriously.

They escaped the buzzing confusion of camp and began the descent into Lucallzo. After weeks of huddling in wet trenches and frozen dugouts, tramping through fields and forests, and sleeping in barns and basements, they would have found any large town magical. But the sight of Lucallzo was breathtaking, like something out of a dream, or history. Lit only by sporadic fires whose clouds of smoke were made more garish by sunset, its thousands of exotic buildings and structures carpeted the hills around a little glowing mirror of lake. All this was open and available to them. They had to restrain themselves from running.

In the air were stone dust, the ammoniac smell of cordite, and a delicious aroma of roasting meat. Godbeer's stomach turned, slightly, when they passed a team of soldiers with flamethrowers who were spraying heaps of rubble with jellied gasoline. They were burning the buried bodies before they could start to stink. This was, she supposed, preferable to waiting till the bodies had begun to rot before burning them. Hard luck for anyone still alive under that rubble, though.

Down one dim street, Boorq spotted children kicking a ball and laughing; down another, she saw adults standing around in small groups, as if gossiping on market day. She was disgusted. "Don't they know there's a fucking war going on?"

At a makeshift roadblock of furniture, an MP captain asked their unit and destination. He could not direct them to any hospitals or aid stations, but pride in his work, inflated by a long day of chaos and danger, pressed him to offer some advice. "Hug the walls," he said. "Half the resistance we met here was from local snipers, and we haven't by any means flushed all of them out." They thanked him, and with rifles at high port, continued in single file along one side of the street, gazing up uneasily at the buildings on the opposite side.

Boorq was now angry and incredulous, and looked at the civilians in the street differently. Florze was confused and dismayed. Local snipers? Didn't they realize her army had come to liberate their town from the aggressors? Godbeer began seeing, or imagining that she saw, hostile faces at windows. Narran, who had heard nothing the MP said, deduced from her comrades' behavior that the town was still teeming with the enemy. Culverson felt an urge, as inexorable as peristalsis, to fire her weapon.

They entered a wide promenade lit at intervals by burning trees. There were more soldiers here, and they felt safer. From one grandiose hotel there escaped flashes of electric light, the thrum of generators and music, and the smell of frying fish. But a glance inside revealed that only officers were being served here. The sight of so many commanders gathered in one place was tactically repugnant to them, and they hurried from it.

They were turned away at the door of another hotel by a private made truculent by guard duty; she too would have preferred to be inside and eating. "This is for Twenty-Second Artillery Company only," she said. "Find your own rations."

"Come on," said Boorq, and led them down a side street of shops and apartment buildings. "There," she said, pointing up at a window that flickered with what might have been candlelight or might have been the reflection of distant fires. "That's as good as an invitation." Finding the front door locked, she tried the next building, and then the next. —"We're not supposed to bother the locals," said Florze. —"Who's bothering anybody?" muttered Boorq. She began hammering the door with the butt of her rifle and shouting the medipodean word for "enter."

Culverson, surprising even herself, fired a round into the plate-glass shopfront. Narran started at the sound and also let off a burst. "What the fuck!" cried Florze. Some shards fell tinkling to the ground, but the window did not shatter. —"Sorry," said Culverson. "I heard a shot." Indeed, they had been hearing the sporadic crackle of small-arms fire all night, from afar. —"Come on," Boorq laughed. "Let's get out of here before we get arrested." —Culverson, realizing that she was still squeezing the trigger, released it with an effort. —"What happened?" said Narran, shuffling after them.

They walked downhill into a less affluent neighborhood. Night had now fallen, and the town was so silent that they could hear a truck being started miles away, could even track its course through the streets. Boorq stopped suddenly, punched Narran's arm, and pointed at some figures lurking in the shadows. "Ask them where we can find some food." —Narran slowly aimed her rifle at the group. —"What the fuck!" cried Florze, batting it down. —Narran was flustered. "I thought you said to cover them." —The figures, meanwhile, sputtered "Friend, friend!" and scurried away into the darkness. Boorq, like a predator provoked by the flight of its prey, sent a careless burst of automatic fire after them. The noise and power of her new weapon was intoxicating, but she noted that the muzzle had a tendency to rise. She tried again with the weapon turned sideways, and now achieved a satisfying horizontal spray of bullets. Godbeer also fired a few shots, equally harmlessly. —"What the fuck," groaned Florze.

Boorq thumped her on the shoulder and gestured at the nearest apartment block. "Come on," she said. "Let's reap the rewards of gratitude for ridding their neighborhood of collaborators."

The door was unlocked, but feebly barricaded by an overturned armoire. They pushed past this into a dark, close stairwell, in which only Narran felt more comfortable. Florze clapped her hands and shouted, "Friends, friends!" Culverson produced a red-tinted flashlight, which was supposed to preserve one's night vision, but which probably only achieved this effect by emitting little light. Boorq squeezed Narran's elbow, and gestured her up the stairs first, because she spoke the language. Godbeer, unable to see anything, came last, gripping Florze's tunic.

On the first landing, Boorq knocked politely at a door. "Friends," said Florze. The doorknob turned immediately, but there was a long pause before the door was pulled open.

A stooped and wizened man stood clutching a candle in one hand, and in the other a bedsheet whose symbolism he had forgotten. The five soldiers pointed their five rifles at his chest.

He raised his arms. "We haven't got much, but of course you're welcome to anything you can find . . ." —"Shut up," cried Boorq. To Narran she said, "Tell him we're hungry. Ask him if he's got any food." —Florze muttered that they weren't supposed to loot. —"All right, ask him if he wants to *give* us any food." —The old man said, "There's no need for guns. It's just my wife and our grandson and I and we're all unarmed. We'll cooperate, of course . . ." —"Clip the gabble," said Boorq. She nudged Narran. "Ask him!" —Narran, who thought she was being ordered to shoot, whimpered, "He's just an old man." —Boorq pushed the door farther open with her toe. "Ask him if there are any snipers here. Ask him if he's shot anybody today." —Another door on the landing opened or closed behind them; Culverson wheeled around. "Don't move!" —"I can't see shit," said Godbeer. "I'm lighting a heat tablet." —"Guys," said Florze, "this was supposed to be my detail." —A woman's voice called out from within the apartment. "For God's sake, Solley, don't block the door or you'll give them an excuse to shoot you." —The old man staggered back a few steps. —"Who was that?" said Boorq. "Who else is here?" She asked Narran, "What did she say?" —"Narran!" cried Culverson from the landing. "Tell these people to come out here with their hands visible and no clever stuff." —Boorq said, "What are you doing? We got our hands full with this situation in here." —"Oh God," moaned the woman, as Godbeer began striking matches. "They're going to burn us down." —"What the fuck did she say?" —Narran lowered her rifle with resigned defiance. "Fuck you, Boorq. You're not my sergeant. You do it." —"What are you talking about? I don't speak the fucking language!" —From a higher floor came a child's scream: "Go away! There are no bad people here!" To the jumpy soldiers, this sounded like a war cry. —Now Godbeer managed to light the heat tablet, and the stairwell began to fill with smoke and suffocating fumes, which caused her eyes to water and blinded her further. More doors opened and closed, and more voices were heard. —"Guys," said Florze, "come on."

"Hello," called a voice. "You are for wanting the booze, okay? I will show you for where to finding the booze." The owner of the voice descended the stairs slowly with his hands held out before him. His undershirt and baggy pants, his receding hair, and his cumbrous, accented infrapodean reminded Culverson of her father; she lowered her rifle in distaste.

His offer, as it was translated and circulated among his neighbors, prompted a flurry of protest. That afternoon, the fleeing suprapodeans had urged the local populace, by radio announcement and handbill, to destroy all stocks of liquor, because there was no knowing what atrocities the barbarous and bloodthirsty invaders might commit if under the influence of alcohol. The man in the undershirt did not doubt this characterization any more than his neighbors did, or indeed than the propagandists who had in good faith broadcast it. But he did not care what these soldiers did outside this building, where his children were; and he hoped that a gesture of goodwill might placate the new occupiers, drunk or not. For the past year, he had been meticulously courteous to the suprapodeans, and they had never given him cause to regret it.

"Booze, okay," said Florze, matching her diction to her interlocutor's. "But food, too, okay. More okay." —"Okay," said the man in the undershirt. "Food and booze okay. I'm for showing you. You will for following me." —"Hey, Boorq," said Florze. "Come on. This guy's taking us to get some food."

Boorq did not like to leave without having requisitioned something. Her gaze flailed about in the gloom; at last she snatched the bedsheet from the old man's grasp, tossed a requisition chit onto the floor, and hurried down the stairs after her comrades. (Later that night, after much deliberation, the old couple wrote in the chit's blank, "Twelve loaves of bread"—and added it to the stack of other IOUs, which they supposed were now worthless.) In the street, Boorq saw that it was just an ordinary bedsheet, and tossed it in the gutter.

With solicitous backward glances, the man in the undershirt led them down winding streets to the former police station. He halted on the far curb, gestured at the building enticingly, and explained that until a few hours ago it had served as a barracks and warehouse for a company of garrisoned troops. Surely it was brimful with booze.

The soldiers conferred. Was it a trap? Boorq, bridling under Florze's leadership, professed to think so. Culverson pretended to agree; she had traveled these thousand miles to escape and appall her parents, and she resented this man's meddlesome assistance, so like her father's. Godbeer pretended to disagree; she was so tired and fed-up that she positively welcomed a firefight, which at least might provide an opportunity to lie down. Narran, wrapped in her sleeping bag, shrugged.

Florze fired a few rounds into the side of the building. The man in the undershirt sank, cowering, to the pavement, but otherwise there was no response. "Combat-pragmatic reconnaissance negative," said Florze. Then she squeezed Narran's elbow and motioned her across the street first, because she spoke the language. Narran did not argue; she was still disgusted with herself for having failed to shoot the old man. She shambled up the front stairs, tucked the sleeping bag under one arm, and readied a grenade. Then, leaning heavily on the door, she slipped inside. After a few moments, the others followed. The man in the undershirt hurried home, regaining stature as he went.

The building, inexplicably, had electricity. After ascertaining that the windows were blacked out, they moved from room to room, untactically, switching on the overhead lights. Had the rooms been bare, they would have been awed by the size, age, and opulence of the building itself. But the rooms were not bare.

As excitement overtook disbelief, they scampered about opening cupboards, drawers, and boxes, and calling out to one another their discoveries. There was no need to hoard anything, for there was more of everything than five of them could carry.

"Powdered milk!" —"Sweet canned milk!" —"Bandoliers!" —"Powdered eggs!" —"Dried carrots!" —"Brand-new e-tools!" —"Actual potatoes!" —"More concussion grenades than you've ever seen!" —"Pinto beans!" —"Garbanzo beans here!" —"Peach Melba!"

—"Load-bearing vests!" —"Looks like dehydrated soup!" —"Some kind of pork jerky!" —"Plastique! Cases of it!" —"Tomato sauce!" —"Rice!" —"Boots!" —"Tuna!" —"Corn!" —"Peas!" —"Sugar! Real sugar!" —"Cigarettes!" —"Coffee!" —They shouted themselves hoarse, pausing only to plumb one another's astonishment. "Did you hear that I said *boots?*"

They found sacks of flour, tea, and salt. They found shoelaces, and runcible spoons, and stainless-steel toothpicks. They found mustard, and pepper, and onions. They found complete uniforms, in a variety of extra-large sizes, that had never been worn. They found crackers, and cookies, and chocolate. They found handguns, and rifle oil, and muzzle flash suppressors. They found, in drums that had never contained anything else, gallons of water so pure it tasted sweet. They found no alcohol, and did not miss it.

"Blankets," said Narran, pulling one from a box. It was dry, clean, soft yet sturdy, and so new that its nap was unruffled. She swaddled herself in it and subsided onto a bunk, whose squeaking mattress springs sent exquisite shivers through her body.

Fading exhilaration left Culverson's nerves jangled. To keep from crying, she tried to be angry. "Why are these assholes so well equipped? I thought they were all supposed to be so weak and hungry and demoralized. Look at all this shit. It fucking demoralizes *me*." —"Not me," said Boorq. "Think about it. Would we have retreated if we were living like this?" —"We wouldn't ever retreat," said Godbeer. —"Exactly. These bitches," said Boorq, "are a bunch of chinless sissies. We'll wipe them out."

Florze lighted a stove and began tossing ingredients into a dixie. Meanwhile, outside, the locals watched the building from a distance, expecting every minute the explosion of booby-traps.

LOVE ON LEAVE. —T.P. and The Professor lay shivering shoulder to shoulder in a bomb crater, looking up at the imperceptible but undeniable progress of the stars.

"What makes them sort of different colors?" asked T.P. —"Refraction," said The Professor. "Like with a rainbow." —After a silence, T.P. said, "Oh."

Miles away, the drumfire of machine guns and artillery ceased for a minute, and the two soldiers tensed, their senses straining and groping. When the bombardment resumed, they relaxed, and T.P. asked The Professor how far away the stars were. —"What's the longest road you know?" —T.P. named the highway passing through her hometown, which was for her a symbol of bidirectional infinity. —"Well," said The Professor, "take that and multiply it by a million." —T.P.'s lips slowly parted. "Gosh." —Solemnly The Professor added, "And multiply *that* by a million." —At this, T.P.'s imagination bridled; she felt as if she had been told that the most handsome man on earth possessed a hundred perfect faces.

Because they were on listening-post duty, they spoke in whispers, with long pauses between sentences. Consequently their thoughts had time to stray, and the conversation had a dreamy and desultory quality that reminded each of them of bedtime conversations with siblings, and which made them feel, despite the cold, almost cozy.

"Hey, Professor?" —"What." —"Does it hurt to get shot?" —"Sure as shit it hurts," said The Professor, who had never been shot. "It hurts like hell." —"But sometimes it doesn't, right? Sometimes you go sort of numb, isn't it?" —"If they hit a nerve, maybe. But if they hit muscle, or a bone, or an organ . . . Don't even." She told T.P. about a soldier from an adjacent company who had been shot in the guts, and whom the stretcher-bearers, pinned down by enemy fire, had been unable to retrieve for two hours. "The whole time, she only stopped screaming to catch her breath. She was begging us to drop a mortar on her . . . That shit was fucked."

This only confirmed the fear that T.P. had been hoping to dispel, namely, that anything, even death, even abrupt and total nonexistence, was preferable to certain kinds of pain. She tried another tack. "Well, what do you think is the best place to get shot?" —"I can tell you the worst place: the tits. I knew a woman who rolled onto a mine. Her right tit was literally vaporized. The pain . . . It just broke her mind. Like an instant lobotomy. From that day forward, she was just a baboon. Worse than a baboon. There was nothing there. She was gone." —"You mean, she was numb?" —"No, lady. The opposite of numb. She hurt so bad, her mind just ate itself. Her brain just went up in flames and never stopped burning."

T.P. persevered. "But sometimes you just pass out, right? If the pain is too bad." —The Professor's shrug was a kind of sneer. "Maybe in movies."

T.P.'s thoughts in recoil returned to her other pole of fascination. "But you can still fuck with one tit, can't you?" —"Sure," said The Professor, "but you only get half turned-on." —T.P. considered this. "But it would still feel good, wouldn't it?" —"More for you than for him," The

Professor laughed. Then she became confidential. "The fact is, men don't care so much how big your tits are. What's more important is how hard they are."

T.P. had gleaned from conversation and observation that hers were, if anything, slightly above average in size; she now resolved at the earliest opportunity to gauge, with a man's sensibility, the solidity of her breasts. She resolved, too, with a yearning intensity that was like a supplication, to fuck at least one man at least once before she died or was irreparably mutilated in combat. With all she had learned from The Professor, she felt confident that she would have little trouble seducing a man when next she saw one. Indeed, she felt that even without The Professor's advice, she would have had little difficulty. There was no mystery, really. Combat had enlightened her: life was too short for coyness. Though she had never been exactly shy with boys back home, she realized that she had not been nearly insistent enough. She now knew just the tone—confident, playful, and desirous—with which she would ask a man to join her for a drink back at her place. She was not ugly; she had if anything slightly larger than average tits; men must desire her too. All the fumbling, oversensitive equivocation that had characterized her relationship with Michal seemed to belong to a previous life. She was a woman now; she must ratify her womanhood.

A thought bothered her. —"Does fucking feel better if you, you know . . . love the man?"

The Professor was a long time replying. She did not want to belittle the brusque dalliances that constituted her own sexual history, nor did she want to dishearten T.P., who was unlikely to find love on their upcoming leave. On the other hand, she was reluctant to mock her friend's romanticism—but she felt that displaying the same weakness would be unsoldierly.

For the five months preceding T.P.'s arrival, The Professor had been without friends in the First/Fourth.

At the beginning, she had been affronted by the platoon's aloofness (which was in fact a kind of initiation that they had all been through) and offended by the nickname they gave her (which was in fact neither sardonic nor anti-intellectual, but merely descriptive: she was often seen reading books, and had been heard in unguarded moments to use polysyllables without irony). She had signed up for danger and heroism, and had been handed toil and tedium; she had anticipated pain and blood and tears, and had found only discomfort, dirt, and sleeplessness; she had expected help and camaraderie, and to her surprise discovered loneliness.

When T.P. arrived, The Professor was, unwittingly, the first to address a friendly word to her. One night together on sentry duty, she told her to switch her selector lever to burst. —"Okay, sure. Why?" —"Then you're guaranteed a tracer." —"Oh yeah. Hey, thanks." —This brief exchange established the pattern of their friendship. For whatever reason, and to The Professor's initial embarrassment, T.P. adopted her as mentor. Perhaps because The Professor was from a city, or because she was a year older, or because she wore her forage cap at an idiosyncratic slant, or because she was not a virgin, or because she was called The Professor, T.P. assumed that she knew everything there was to know about life. And T.P.—called Teacher's Pet by the platoon—was hungry to learn it all. She asked The Professor about algebra, and gardening, and jazz, and fishing, and architecture, and comparative religion, and world history, and electronics, and fashion—and men; and death. The Professor told her what she knew, and embellished it with what she could guess, what was plausible, and what would be best for T.P. to believe. She humored her, sensing that any uncertainty or confession of ignorance would surely injure T.P.'s curiosity.

"The fact is," she said at last, "that from a strict sensation point of view, every cock feels about the same—that is, equally good. But the ideas and feelings that go on in your head while you're fucking, and of course before and after, are generally, yeah, I guess, a little nicer when you actually love—actually like the man." The treacly, burdened word that she had let slip triggered a reaction: "Of course, there's something to be said for fucking sons of bitches you hate, too. You can get right nasty."

"Yeah," said T.P. But she thought, on the whole, that it would probably be best for her to fall in love. Would forty-eight hours be enough?

The night before they were scheduled for leave, The Professor gave her a caveat. "Don't feel bad if all we can find is whores. There's no shame in it. Lots of women lose their virginity that way." —T.P. nodded, determined not to settle for a whore.

The two-day leave officially started at 0900, but their train did not start moving till 1030, and then stopped frequently along the way. They had not been told their destination or its distance, and the cars had no windows. T.P., like the others, curbed her impatience with alcohol, gambling, horseplay, boasting, and making plans. When at last the doors were opened, it was mid-afternoon. A staff sergeant appeared and asked what the hell they were waiting for. The train had been sitting in the siding for nearly an hour. They tumbled out, blinking in the waning sunlight, and stretched and spat and hollered and yawned. They had been looking forward to this moment for months. Freedom.

T.P. wanted to find a room with a shower in town, but Christmas Tree and Triple-Time, with whom The Professor had been bullshitting on the train, were in high spirits and wanted to continue drinking. There were several bars nearby in the safe zone, and they would take scrip. The Professor asked T.P. what she wanted to do. It was clear to T.P. what The Professor wanted to do, so she shrugged acquiescence. "I guess we can hitch a ride into town later."

They marched from bar to bar counting cadence. They leered at the locals and saluted the staff and supply officers with sarcastic crispness; these soft and natty noncombatants made them aware of their own rough and rumpled filthiness, which they wore like a suit of honor, strutting and swaggering. Because they felt strange and vulnerable without their rifles, their talk in compensation grew more coarse and their posture more aggressive. Christmas Tree failed to pick a fight with three pilots, for whom she then devised an elaborate ambush and assassination, which only lack of a concussion grenade prevented her from carrying out. "I knew I should have brought more kit." They stole a jeep, which they crashed and abandoned at the first curve in the road. They put their fists through windows and they chewed glass. They shadow-boxed, and shadow-fucked parked cars. They howled. They laughed, puked, and passed out.

T.P. awoke the next morning wedged between two crates on a strange floor, aching with dehydration and stifled by dust and sunshine. The room she was in appeared to be a school auditorium that had been requisitioned for use as a warehouse. She stumbled outside, pissed behind a shrub, and, in lieu of mouthwash, lit a cigarette to kill the vile taste in her mouth. Her head throbbed, her skin crawled, and she stank of sweat and vomit; but worst of all was the remorse at having wasted a night. She had enjoyed herself, but she should have been looking for a man. The train back to the MAC left tomorrow at 0500. She had less than twenty hours.

She found The Professor with C.T. and Triple-Time at the post exchange, nursing their hangovers with coffee and government-issue rum. She greeted and was greeted with insults. They asked where she had disappeared to, and whether she had found any cock; she replied with a military phrase of obfuscation. When she broached the matter of going into town, The Professor said, "Operational update, lady." There was a whorehouse nearby, within the safe zone, where scrip was accepted; they were headed there as soon as they finished their bottled breakfast.

T.P. was confused and disappointed. "Isn't it kind of early for a place like that?" —The Professor, willfully it seemed, misconstrued her. "The joint is open all the twenty-four." —"It'll be quieter now than if we wait till tonight," said Christmas Tree. "We'll have our pick." —"And if we're lucky," said Triple-Time, "they'll have just done a shift change." —T.P. could not, without revealing her inexperience to the other two, remind The Professor that she'd hoped to lose her virginity to a man. She muttered, "I sort of wanted a shower first." —"They'll have showers," said C.T. "And everything else." —"Come on," said Triple-Time. She swallowed the heeltap of rum and tossed the bottle into the street. "Let's go take some fucking prisoners." —"Yeah," said C.T., "let's entrench some fucking positions." —The Professor drew a more abstruse analogy between fucking and clearing a lane through a minefield. —Eyes narrowed and brow knitted, T.P. searched her mind and her field of view for some escape.

But when she found herself in a dim and sumptuous room, surveying five sleek and perfumed women in lacy underwear, she discovered that she had momentarily misplaced her reservations. Perhaps none of them were men, but their petiteness and their exoticness made them seem exquisite and precious. She forgot about the shower, and indeed began again to exult in her grimy shabbiness. When at last she chose the biggest woman, it was with a thrill of defiant luxuriousness, like that of a grimy laborer reaching for her master's cleanest, plushest towel.

Sharlelle liked best virgins who needed to be coaxed. Being a whore, like being a soldier, was mostly sitting around waiting; and sometimes she could prolong the coaxing to an entire afternoon. T.P. was a virgin and a darling, but she didn't need to be coaxed.

Fifteen minutes later, she was back in the street, smoking and grinning and congratulating herself for having cast off her girlhood. She had perhaps not done everything possible, but she had undeniably climaxed in the intimate presence of a naked person. Surely no virginity could survive such an event. She was satisfied with herself on other counts, too. She recalled with nostalgic tenderness that Sharlelle, massaging her nipples, had murmured, "So hard." And T.P. had wasted little time; she still had eighteen hours to get into town and find love. Should she wait for the others? Leave a message? No, she was a woman now.

Her good mood evaporated on the bus into town, which at this hour carried only locals. No one sat next to her or met her gaze, and she remembered that she must stink. No one spoke or smiled, and she imagined that her very presence was constraining. She debussed too soon, and had to ask directions to a hotel. Although she knew and (she believed) pronounced flawlessly the local word for hotel, the old woman she addressed pretended not to understand her, and sent a son or nephew down the street to fetch another son or nephew to act as interpreter. This young man was gorgeous, and she mistook his amused curiosity for amused contempt and his offer to guide her for mockery. Half spitefully, she failed to hear his directions, and trudged for an hour through the cramped and odorous streets, feeling more and more alien and alone. She did not see another soldier anywhere. Hunger and hangover aggravated her unease, which released her latent racism, and she muttered derogatory generalizations (which would have applied equally well to her own country's cities) about the congestion and disorder. When at last she found a hotel room, its opulence and affordability seemed to confirm that, as a people, the medipodeans were both backward and decadent.

She undressed slowly and with ambivalence; she had not removed her socks or boots for weeks, and the sensation was both salubrious and unsettling, like removing grit from a wound. She scattered her clothes and belongings as widely as possible, then ran a steaming bath. While waiting for it to fill, she urinated and rubbed herself with urine, as she had been instructed, to prevent sexual disease. As she climbed into the tub, lappets of dead skin detached from her legs and floated to the surface, and the soap bubbles turned grey with scum. She drained and ran two more baths, shaving and scrubbing herself gingerly and with absorption. She was reminded of the epic baths she'd enjoyed as a child, with their splashings and submersions, their discovery and intrigue, and which lasted so long that they often necessitated slippery intermissions on the toilet. At last she emerged, as taut and pink as a scar, and feeling five kilograms lighter. She loped and lunged about the room, relishing her privacy and nudity. She opened every drawer, turned every knob and latch, upended every bowl and basket, inspected every bauble, sat on every chair, and jumped up and down on the bed. She lay dozing and daydreaming awhile, then reluctantly squeezed back into her uniform, soused herself with complimentary perfume, and went looking for food, and for men.

Her mood had rebounded, and where earlier she had seen squalor and clutter she now saw vivacity and plenty. And soldiers were now everywhere; restaurants, food stalls, and fruit carts were plentiful; in many alleys were open-air markets offering new and used tools, books, clothes, cloth, jewellery, appliances, watches, electronics, and weapons. She filled her belly with fried and floury things, and her pockets with handkerchiefs, pens, rings, flasks, lighters, a magnifying glass, and a bowie knife. Then she prowled lazily through the throng, belching and jingling and staring at men unless they stared back.

After rejecting several faces or bodies on grounds that seemed preposterous as soon as the face or body was out of sight, she finally persuaded herself to follow one man doing his shopping. His gait was relaxed and his hair disheveled, and she became convinced that he was spirited, passionate, and kind. This was the man. This was the moment.

She hesitated, and played in imagination a preview of her advance. It suddenly seemed obvious that confident and desirous were not qualities that this man would welcome from a stranger. Bluntness would be an insult, insistence an assault. If only she had some excuse to talk to him, some reason to approach him! She wished pettishly for an air raid, a thief, or a hawker from which she could rescue him. Even a dropped coin!

Then a miracle occurred. Retracing his steps, he crossed the street to the very fruit cart she was pretending to peruse. He smiled, drawing a smile from her that she felt throughout her body. He was perhaps ten years older than she was, and her eyes trembled in their sockets at the thought of his ripe and jaded libido. He began selecting oranges, cradling the finalists in one arm. She must say something, anything. *Good price for oranges*, perhaps? No. And *was* it a good price? For some inscrutable reason the medipodeans priced their groceries by the hectogram, and even back home she didn't really know what oranges were supposed to cost. Fatuously praising the cheapness of some outrageously overpriced oranges would hardly impress him. Looking closer, she was not even sure that these *were* oranges.

The man had noticed her following him and had decided to confront her. He saw that she was a mere girl, awkward and bashful and rather adorable; her diffidence, however, was contagious. "Not a bad price for oranges," he observed. —"Sorry," she grunted in her language, "I don't understand." —"I'm sorry," he said in his, "I can't understand you."

Reduced to mime, they felt shielded from embarrassment, for they had no choice but to indulge in the simple, silly avowals of childhood. T.P. indicated by gesture that oranges were yummy; the man replied by gesture that oranges were tart. They chuckled and shrugged; then he paid for his oranges, gave an arpeggio wave with three fingers, and walked out of her life.

Should she run after him? . . .

Should she have run after him?

Her mood suffered another reversal. Now the vivacity of the streets seemed garish, the abundance immoral. She felt glutted and spoiled, and recalled with mortification the deprivation and hardship of the main areas of conflict. She was irritated by the undisciplined congestion of the crowds; how easily one could slaughter hundreds of them with a mortar and a machine gun! She surveyed the streets with a tactical eye, choosing which walls would have to be torn down, which roofs occupied, which approaches barricaded. Yes, a single platoon could kill thousands ...

When, an hour later, she spotted Triple-Time coming out of a movie theater, it was with mingled frustration and relief that she abandoned her crucial, degrading, desperate, hopeless search. Sneaking up to her, she punched her in the small of the back and caught the cigarette that fell from her mouth. —"Hey, cunt-knuckle. Give it back." —"Hey, saggy-tits. What the fuck is this?" It was not a cigarette but a lollipop, warm and sticky in her hand. She popped it in her mouth with a moan of satisfaction that was feigned, then another that was not. "Where the fuck'd you get this?" —Triple-Time grinned and dug her elbow into T.P.'s ribs. "Come on, shitpig. I'll show you."

She too was half relieved. Agitated and unsatisfied by the massage she'd received at the whorehouse, she had left Christmas Tree and The Professor behind in the safe zone and come into town looking for sex; but she had not been able to resign herself to the submissiveness required for a quick fuck. Encouraged by Teacher Pet's enthusiasm, and for the moment free of the First/Fourth's atmosphere of competitive derision, she confided that the place to which she was taking them served ice cream too.

A few days later on sentry duty, The Professor, hurt by her protégé's silence on the subject, finally asked T.P. how she'd enjoyed the whorehouse. —T.P. shrugged. "It was all right, I guess," she said. That was all. —The Professor struggled with her emotions, and lost. "I guess you had more fun with Triple-Time," she scoffed.

T.P. was at first too puzzled to reply.

Six Inches. —At dusk, Forty-Third C Platoon sat in the dirty snow waiting irritably for air support. Kellek complained that her shell-fragment wounds were itchy. Boorq said that hers ached like arthritis. Solzi's throbbed, but only when she walked. They tallied their scars; Laskantan was the winner, with twenty-five. Osini had the ugliest scar, a ragged purple excoriation the length of her forearm, caused by white phosphorous. Tolb, everyone but Tolb agreed, had received the most painful injury: a tracer round had burned slowly through her knee. Tolb, for whom nothing was quite real unless it happened to someone else, thought she'd been lucky: unlike some, she could still walk. "Anyway, the more painful, the less deadly." —This was debated. —"Anyway," said Tolb, "nobody ever died of a bullet in the knee." —This too was debated. —"Well, anyway," said Tolb, "*I* never died of it." —This was conceded. —"But look at Sunachs," said Tolb. "Show them, Sunachs." Sunachs lifted her tunic to display a thin cicatrice between two ribs. No one could see it in the darkness. "That's the point," said Tolb. "The shard was so thin it was like a scalpel—but *this* long. It just missed her lung by half an inch." —Sunachs, embarrassed, grunted.

Burnok, to whom nothing was quite real unless it happened to herself, scoffed and said that a sniper's bullet had grazed her arm the other night and slammed into the dugout wall behind her. Everyone in earshot was able to cite a more deadly and more recent incident; but Burnok persisted. "If I'd been standing six inches to the right, it'd have gone straight through my *heart*, never mind my lung." —"Sure," said Sergeant Costitch, "and if you'd been standing six inches to the left, you'd still be fine." —"Or if you'd been standing six inches forward," said Godbeer, "or six inches back." —"Or if you were six inches taller," said Kellek, "or six inches shorter." —"Or eight inches, or eighteen." —"Or eight feet, or eighteen." —"Or if you were standing anywhere from two feet to two miles away in any direction." —"All right, all right, wiseasses," said Burnok. "What's your point?" —Sergeant Costitch was explicit: Of the infinite number of spots she might have been standing in, only one would have been fatal. Thus her odds of survival had been excellent, and she had not, in fact, almost died.

"That's why I'd rather be in a firefight than a shelling any day," said Boorq. "Bullets are small." —Godbeer agreed. "Shells are nasty." She could not be more specific, but felt that there was something eldritch and impersonal about a shelling. "At least the bullet that gets you has your name on it." Shells had no one's name on them; they killed meaninglessly and indiscriminately, like disease. —Solzi disagreed. She would by preference take her chances with a shell, because splinters and shell fragments could not be aimed. For her it was the element of human agency, felt like an eye on the back of her head, that made firefights so dismaying, and sniper fire so uncanny.

Tolb brought the conversation back to Burnok's six inches, and supported her view. "Guys, if she had taken just one more step to the right, or one less step to the left, at any time the whole night . . ." —"A fallacy," said Kellek. "Because if she'd been in a different position, the sniper would have adjusted their aim." —"You don't mean to tell me that the bullet was fated to miss her by exactly six inches, no matter where she happened to be." —"No, all I mean to tell you is that snipers do their best, and still often miss." —"No, they often *don't* miss," said Burnok.

A wide range of opinions was put forward regarding the accuracy of sniper fire. They all knew that for every casualty suffered by their own forces, two were inflicted on the enemy; but whether their snipers performed somewhat above or somewhat below this average was a fine point, which they argued from anecdote and personal experience.

"Hey," said Boorq. "If I've killed two aggressors, does that mean my number is up?" —Godbeer was distressed by the thought. "Shit, I've killed five already. That means I'm overdue?" —"Don't be snotwhistles," said Solzi. "The more you kill of them, the less there are around to kill us. We're all better off. Your odds get better, not worse." —"The more you kill," said Sergeant Costitch, "the luckier you are." By lucky she meant exempt from probability; favored; invincible. She had killed sixteen aggressors for certain, and possibly as many as twenty-five or thirty. "It's a good thing," she murmured. —"But still," said Boorq, "for every two enemy you get, they get one of us, somewhere along the line, even if it doesn't happen to be you personally." —"So what are you saying?" asked Laskantan. "We should hold fire and all be friends?" —"It's not like a baby being born every time a cicada sings," said Solzi. "It's not cause and effect." —"I think you've been misinformed," laughed Kellek. "That's not cause and effect either." —"Aw, clip it. All I mean is, it's not magic. It's just statistics." —"In other words," said Burnok, "a bucketful of air."

"All I know is," said Osini, "if it's your time to take a bullet, then it's your time, and that's all there is to it." —There were grumbles of agreement. —"So why worry?" said Laskantan, taking off her helmet and performing a crouching dance. "Trust in God, and let Him tie up your horse!" —"Piss on God," said Boorq. —"Now hold on," said Tolb. "Let's not go asking for trouble." —"Piss on trouble," said Boorq. —Laskantan adopted this phrase as a refrain in an improvised song. "Piss on trouble, or trouble'll piss on you-hoo!" —Lieutenant Farl decided that it was time to intervene.

"Listen up, troops. Let's foreshorten the horseplay and the horseshit and look vigilant. Let's drop the God-talk, too—whether for or against. The IP Infantry Corps is a secular organization; that means God doesn't enter into it one way or the other." —Boorq said, "I thought Field Marshal Renmit was God, sir." —Laskantan said, "That's right, and he doesn't enter into this war one way or the other." —Lieutenant Farl chuckled along with them, though the irreverence galled him. "Let's also nip the insubordination, shall we? Let's not forget that it's the decisions of the CFL that are allowing us to win this war. And one more thing. Osini." —"Yes, sir." —"You know better than to talk like a fucking fatalist. The only soldiers who die in my platoon are the ones who fuck up. Don't make any mistakes, and you'll be going home to your loved ones in one piece. That goes for all of you. A dead infanteer was a bad infanteer. Understood?" —"Yes, sir." —"Then keep your tuft down, eyes up, tongue in, and ears out." —"Yes, sir."

Air support, when at last it arrived, dropped its cloudburst of hundred-pounders short; the bombs came screaming down right into the midst of Forty-Third Company. Cursing infantry scrabbled for cover in every direction across the hard and barren landscape, crawling inside bare bushes, covering themselves with snow, or stretching out in depressions so slight they could only be detected with an eye to the ground. Sandstorm gusts of dirt and bomb fragments raked over them, sparking off their helmets. Kellek rolled indecisively from supine to prone and back again, her head under her pack. Laskantan crouched motionless, her hands protecting the back of her neck. Narran's fear had an astringent effect: she felt herself shrivel into a rigid ball no bigger than her helmet. Burnok heard the screech of each plummeting bomb grow impossibly louder, till it was right on top of her; she could not understand why she was still alive. Culverson, to vent her terror, shouted angry gibberish into her handset. Tolb, curled around her rifle, reflected that it was surely better for a self-respecting soldier to be under this idiotic bombardment than to be the cause of it. Godbeer, skittering on hands and feet toward a fresh crater, was suddenly thrown breathless onto her back.

There was a pain in her leg stronger than any she'd experienced, and which seemed, like intense exertion, to involve her entire body. She was afraid that she would scream, and afraid that she would never get the breath back to scream. She could feel something pouring out of her and was astonished at the pool of warmth it created. She was slowly steeping in her entrails; she was turning inside out. At last she was able to draw some air into her lungs, and soon was wheezing effortfully. How stupid! She should have stayed put, or at the very least waited to see where the concentration was falling. She'd fled aimlessly after the first explosion, like a stupid recruit. And now, to make matters worse, she was dying. She had let everyone down. The lieutenant would be disappointed and derisive. Godbeer prayed for another bomb to come down and obliterate her error. Clinging to her shame as to an elusive resolution, she slipped out and in and out of consciousness.

Her body was retrieved by stretcher-bearers a day later, when the attack, so inauspiciously begun, was rebuffed, with heavy casualties.

STRONGPOINT. —FOURTH COMPANY were being shown a movie. Corporal Cobweb stood outside the theater tent, listening to the raucous enjoyment of the troops. She decided to wait till the movie had finished to fall her platoon in and brief them. She too was enjoying what she could hear of the film, and would have been as surprised as the privates, and indeed as the staff officers who had selected it, to learn that it was an anti-war film. Certainly, many of its suprapodean protagonists died, mired in filth, and for pointless or illusory objectives; but that was war. Its ugliness was its glory, for surely no one but heroes could abide it, let alone thrive in it. In fact, the troops seemed to feel that the battle scenes should have been even bloodier, and the setting even more squalid. Cobweb heard one infanteer complain, in a tone of offended pride, "There ought to be more shit and flies everywhere. How can you believe a war where there isn't shit and flies everywhere?"

As if to prove the point, a fat fly alighted on the corporal's lapel and began to rub its legs together thoughtfully. She reached slowly towards it with an index finger. The insect fell still, as if assessing her intentions. She had nearly succeeded in touching it, when at last, after a minute of genial communion, the fly shook itself and buzzed away.

Sawed-Off, on her way back from the latrines, smiled at Corp Cobweb in passing. She would have liked to invite her inside, but was daunted by her aura of authority. Besides, she was probably standing out here for some good reason.

On screen, a grizzled soldier injected heroin into her arm and slumped into a stupor. This incited among the audience many arguments about the relative merits of opiates, amphetamines, and psychedelics. Fidget, noticing Parade-Ground's silence, began mocking her inexperience. Parade-Ground winced, as if a moral flaw had been exposed. She swore that she was no prig, and insisted that only lack of opportunity had prevented her from experimenting with drugs. Her friends decided to rectify this at once—but discovered that the only drugs in their possession at present were some dried leaves and snuff, sacred to the medipodean aboriginals but of doubtful recreational value. Nevertheless, Parade-Ground, for whom bravado served as bravery, declared that she would snort, swallow, or smoke any amount of anything anyone put before her. So, shortly before the movie ended, Christmas Tree fetched and Parade-Ground was given a quid of black leaves to suck and a pinch of green powder to sniff. The taste was vile, like mud and bitter cucumber. Her friends laughed and clapped her on the back and began to monitor her face for signs of intoxication, though these could not be expected to appear for an hour or two.

Everyone in First Platoon was surprised and appalled to learn that the corporal had volunteered them for a night patrol, but none more so than Parade-Ground. During the half hour that Cobweb gave them to get their gear together, Fidget and Christmas Tree took Parade-Ground to the next company's medical dugout, where a doctor had her swallow two cotton balls with a spoonful of castor oil. This accomplished, Parade-Ground sputtered, "Okay, now I'll be okay?" —"Now we send you to battalion, where an X-ray will confirm my suspicion of ulcers." The doctor winked. "Always good for a week or two of bed-rest." —When Parade-Ground explained that she was not interested in malingering but only in counteracting the drugs, the doctor shrugged and offered her a spoonful of baking soda.

During the transport ride to the MAC, the platoon was again in high spirits, roughhousing, boasting, and quoting, in character, lines of dialogue from the movie. Jaywalk, who was an actor back home, obscurely resented this trespass upon her domain. Unknown to the others, she had been these seventeen months playing a character of her own invention, compounded from several laconic and hard-bitten soldiers she'd seen in movies and in plays—and she did not like to think that this method of simulating courage or embodying valor was available to everyone. Now she closed her eyes and inhabited that character, Lance Corporal Jaywalk, more deeply, clenching her jaw and slowing her breath like one drawing strength from within. Then she opened her eyes, and with a cat's negligent grace, lit a cigarette, took a puff, and passed it around.

In the distance, artillery shells exploded with a strange rumbling gulp, as if the earth were swallowing itself in gobbets.

Parade-Ground was nauseated, and felt a tingling tightness that extended from her jaw through her chest to her groin. Christmas Tree methodically wrapped in tape her zippers, chains, grenade pins, dog tags, and her lucky necklace made of ration can-openers, so that they would not clink or rattle. Jimjam, hidden by the dark, raked the serrated edge of her trench knife across the scarred flesh of her bicep; and although she managed not to flinch, she knew a bullet would hurt more. Shitjob wished she had cleaned her rifle.

The truck stopped and they climbed out, subdued now. While the corporal went to recruit stretcher-bearers, a parson, backlit by an enemy flare, led the platoon in prayer. Private Privates heard none of it, for she was engaged in her own pleading, wheedling dialogue with God. God reassured her. "You'll be fine, lady. Cram the whining and the worrying. Have I ever let you down before? Just stay alert, follow the woman in front of you, and I'll take care of the rest. Okay?" Teacher's Pet used the time to piously recollect the man at the fruit cart. Sawed-Off, head lolling, continued the important work of curtailing her thoughts, banishing from awareness everything but her immediate surroundings and the present minute; she contracted her body likewise, hardening it to pain and insult. Parade-Ground, studying the intricate geometrical patterns on the back of her hand, tried in vain to decide whether her vision was more acute than usual, or whether she was hallucinating.

They spread out and lay or crouched waiting for the corporal to return. When at last she did, they waited another long half hour, no one knew why, for the time of departure. —"Fifteen minutes," said Cobweb, peering at the luminous dial of her wristwatch. —"Ten minutes." —"Seven minutes." —Two Words wanted to kill her.

SERGEANT MONTAZO BECKONED Lieutenant Ryyss and handed him the field glasses. "There," she said. "Right in that gully. At least a squad. They dropped to the ground when the flare went up." There was smugness in her voice, for only an hour earlier the lieutenant had criticized her request for another artillery barrage—on this very spot. She had at that time only pretended to see movement, in order to check that the guns were still registered on one of the most likely approaches to the outpost. Ryyss had frowned at what he felt to be a waste of shells and of the radio's battery. Now Montazo felt vindicated, and watched hungrily for signs of her officer's approval. "Repeat the last concentration for effect," she suggested, "and we'll exterminate them."

Ryyss adjusted the field glasses—his vision was much better than Montazo's—but could not see any human shapes in the area indicated. —"They're right there!" insisted Montazo, and grabbed the glasses; but by the time she restored them to focus, the flare had gone out. "Shit! Let's hit them quick before they move."

The urgency of the situation had the usual paralyzing effect on Ryyss. "What if that's our people?" he muttered. "What if that's our relief?" But their relief were not expected till dawn—if they came at dawn: they were already two days late. Ryyss observed more aptly that the flare had been white—an enemy flare. "They wouldn't expose their own patrol like that."

Montazo saw the logic of this, but wanted to shell the spot anyway, just in case; however, she let herself be persuaded to contact by wire Tolb and Boorq, who were lying out in a listening post a hundred yards nearer the gully.

Tolb and Boorq—who had been huffing into their fists and taking turns naming all the famous people, living, dead, or fictional, that they could think of—had noticed nothing, but promised to stay alert. Instantly, they began to hear the soft, intermittent sounds of soldiers creeping towards them. Tolb contacted the outpost again, and whispered inaudibly her alarm.

Ryyss ordered Tolb to challenge the patrol for the password; he reminded her what the challenge word and password were. Montazo was disappointed; but Ryyss would not be responsible for the death or injury of any more of his compatriots. Four nights ago, when first occupying the outpost, the platoon had fired on three patrols and a supply column—wasting half their ammunition. Two of the patrols had turned out to be friendly, and had suffered casualties.

At the time that he had been ordered to take and hold the two blockhouses on the little hill known as The Nubbin, a large-scale enemy attack had been imminently expected. Ryyss's commanders had hoped that an outpost deep in the CFP—or contested forward positions, where the fringes of the two armies roiled indistinguishably— might check or distract the oncoming force. Though that force had not materialized, C Platoon's position was still far from enviable. The entire area, which was less No Man's Land than Everyman's Land, was constantly being shelled and strafed and patrolled by both sides; and, as one of the few prominences in the valley, The Nubbin made an irresistible target. Its defenders had renamed it The Mailbox, for all the incoming ordnance it received, and referred to themselves as number eights, after the largest targets used on firing ranges. Their only good fortune was that they had yet to suffer a direct ground attack. Ryyss doubted they could fend off even another platoon. He had decided, in the event of a fight, to abandon the position as soon as the machine-gun ammo was spent. He was reasonably sure that his orders did not prohibit such an action; but he did not search his memory or his documents as carefully as he might have; and, except to inquire about their relief, he stayed off the radio. This uncharacteristic self-sufficiency of the lieutenant's was noted with approval at the command post—and contributed to the delays in relief and resupply.

Tolb and Boorq were reluctant to draw attention to themselves, so decided that they had heard nothing. Tolb got on the wire again to say so; but Ryyss meanwhile had been called to the other side of the outpost by Alcott and Meck, who also thought they had seen something. Montazo, in a panic because the lieutenant had taken her field glasses, advised Tolb and Boorq to keep their heads down, then told Yomi, the new radio operator, to dial the field artillery net.

Now Boorq heard voices. Tolb, who was lying half under her in the double funk hole, felt her stiffen, and went rigid herself. Then she too heard the voices. With their heads pressed together, they argued, in breathless whispers and frantic gestures of the fingertips, whether the voices were speaking their own language, or another.

Then someone called out—in their language, but not their accent—this strange question: "Are you all right, sir?"

They did not know whether or how to reply. Then Boorq, who could distinguish the telltale whistle of an artillery shell falling a mile away from that of one coming directly down upon her, screamed heedlessly, "Incoming!" and covered her head with her hands.

"Keep it coming," cried Montazo into the radio. "That's beautiful."

As SOON AS they were beyond the razor wire, Upsize felt all her brimming anxiety spill out into her bloodstream, where it was quickly engaged. A feeling of relief and recognition came over her, as if some forbidding doorway had led to an old familiar haunt. Already she recalled the anxiety of a minute ago with baffled condescension. Memories of previous patrols, ambushes, and charges came back to her indistinctly, but with a sensation of confidence. She knew how this was done.

She cursed with the others when the flare went up, but did not drop to the ground with the others. She remained motionless as a tree, and watchful as an owl. She was a tree; she was an owl. When darkness returned, she crept back to where H. Crap, her section leader, was lying, and told her what she had seen.

"You're sure it was occupied?" —"One hundred percent. I saw two heads."

Lance Corporal H. Crap resented the surprise, which seemed to her characteristic of this muddled and ill-advised patrol. But after a moment's consideration, and with Upsize's guidance, she saw that here might be a shortcut to their objective. If they could take a prisoner, there would be no need to draw fire from the outpost in order to determine the size and strength of the unit holding it; they could simply ask the prisoner. Corporal Cobweb would have to commend her initiative, if successful.

But first, it was necessary to make sure that the two soldiers in the listening post were in fact enemy; the Corp had warned them that the MAC was less No Man's Land than Anyman's Land. H. Crap was unwilling, however, to reveal her own identity by using the suprapodean challenge word; so she called out a phrase that she had heard an angry or injured invader cry out repeatedly, several days ago, while being mortared, and which she imagined meant something like, "Have mercy on us."

At first there was no reply. Then one of the soldiers in the listening post shouted some gibberish, and H. Crap gave Upsize the thumbs-up. But before they could reach the funk hole, shells began to fall exploding around them.

The only nearby cover was the funk hole. Upsize scrambled towards it, dropped a grenade in, then another, clutched her helmet, counted to five, then crawled in atop the warm, wet bodies.

SHITJOB WINCED AFRESH at each audible step. She was straining every muscle, even those in her neck and face, to lighten her tread, but the frozen earth was as crunchy as coral. The Colonel and the others seemed not to be even trying to minimize the noise they were making. The enemy must be able to hear them coming from miles away; and the rising moon was as bright as a spotlight. In these circumstances, she found that a continually renewed effort of will was necessary just to keep going, with the result that her movements felt sluggish and lumbering, like those of a giant. Her mind by comparison was dizzyingly swift and clear, pursuing a score of worries simultaneously.

It was a relief to drop to the ground at the sound of the artillery, and a sweeter relief to see the shells bursting on the southwest side of the outpost. Even after she realized that H section must be somewhere near that spot, she grimaced with spiteful satisfaction, glad only that it was someone else's turn for a change. Let them get theirs.

IN THE BLOCKHOUSE that served as kitchen, Laskantan and Sergeant Costitch were acting out a scene from the book of mythology that had been found among Winurhtry's personal effects. Raof, disassembling her rifle by feel, watched with mingled admiration and distaste. She was amused by Laskantan's clowning and impressed by Costitch's perfect elocution; but she was puzzled and irritated by the story, which told of the interference of fickle, peevish gods in a war between humans. Also, she had not expected a famous classic to be so repetitious. The book was tainted for her too by its association with Winurhtry, who was believed to have committed suicide. Raof herself had once discovered her handling an unpinned grenade in a wistful manner. That was before she began dabbling with high explosives—in search, Raof now thought, of a more certain death than a hand grenade could offer. No doubt she had been miserable. But Raof felt no more pity for her than for any deserter.

Lieutenant Ryyss appeared and ordered everyone to stand to. Raof cursed her luck without surprise, and began to reassemble her weapon. She supposed, as she always supposed, that this was the end. Whatever was coming, she would be the first one, and probably the only one, to die.

She found a place on the parapet beneath a useless, collapsed firing slit. She had forgotten her helmet. Lieutenant Ryyss told them to conserve their ammunition, to hold their fire till the attackers offered a clear target. To Raof this sounded like a call to defeat.

THERE WERE MOMENTS when Triple-Time loved the war. She loved to climb a mountain in the rain under full pack.

She loved to watch an airplane fall blazing from the sky. She loved to sit with a beer in the refectory and listen to The Professor or Jaywalk or The Pacifist lecture, better than any teacher she'd ever had, on gardening or carpentry or poetry. She loved to leg-wrestle, and win. She loved to fire her rifle on its bipod at a moving target. And she loved nothing better than to march with impunity in the midst of a full company across a strange landscape at twilight. But she hated all these chickenshit nighttime skulking platoon-sized missions. She longed for a good, honest daylight street fight, kicking in doors with bayonets fixed.

She vented her frustration on Teacher's Pet, thumping her and cursing her every time she came too close. "Stop bunching up on me," she hissed. "Maintain the fucking interval, cuntpig." —"All right, all right," said T.P., who found the hardest part of night patrols to be the feeling of isolation. "Fucking sorry." —"Shut your fucking spunk-traps back there," said The Colonel, who was, against all regulations, literally leading the section by walking point.

The Colonel had been seething since her promotion to lance corporal. She did not herself realize that she was angry; she did not permit herself introspection, but carried out her duties with rabid punctiliousness.

She had wanted nothing more than to be made section commander (and perhaps one day platoon commander), but somehow she had never imagined that the honor would come at the expense of another soldier's life. The promotion had been further spoiled for her by the ceremony, at which Lieutenant General Roseberry, in front of journalists and camera operators, had addressed her by War Juice's name, and conferred on her War Juice's medal of valor. Corporal Cobweb had quietly asked her not to make a fuss. So Lance Corporal Colonel, with opaque self-loathing, wore the medal, and became a more avid soldier than ever. The troops in her section noticed a change in her, but attributed this to the corrupting influence of power.

She waited, poised, for G section to start firing; then she leaped up, bellowing, and with a wave like a swimmer's stroke, led her ten troops forward in a short rush over the hard, uneven ground. She tossed a grenade with her whole body, then, still upright and silhouetted against the sky, let off several rifle rounds from the hip. "Come on, you shitbags! Break some fucking hearts!" She emptied a magazine before the others, taking aim from a prone position, joined in. The awe, pride, and annoyance that they felt towards their reckless leader were mitigated somewhat by the fact that there was no return fire from the outpost. Once everyone had fired a few rounds and tossed a grenade or two, they rushed back to their departure point, where they reloaded, breathless and elated.

"That wasn't so bad," conceded Jimjam.

TOLB KNEW THAT Boorq was dead. The pity she felt for her friend welled over and became self-pity, which, combined with a strange, placeless pain, convinced her that she too was dying. Outrage brought to her eyes tears that were spilled in mournful impotence. Her mind clutched at memories and unfulfilled plans, struggling in this last spasm of consciousness to impose some order upon or extract some significance from her life. She thought of her mother, and of her sister, and of her boyfriend, and, imagining their sorrow, felt sorrier for herself. She thought of all the meals she would never taste, and the money she would never spend. The franticness she felt proved that there would be no afterlife.

The shelling had ended, and now she felt Boorq's lifeless body being dragged off her, the boots scraping the back of her neck. She lay still and small, eyes closed, thoughts clamped, averting her attention from the sounds of the enemy soldiers ransacking Boorq's corpse a few feet away. She was not here.

"Look at all this shit," said Upsize indignantly. "She's got a bunch of *our* shit." —"Souvenirs," said H. Crap, handling sadly the trench knife, field manual, and captain's stripes.

—"Well, fuck," said The Pacifist. "They're no worse than we are." —"Fucking photos probably aren't hers either," said Fidget, taking them. —"This looks like this letter is written in suprapodean, too," guessed Sancty, taking it. —Upsize and Pschaw bickered over which of them would get the dead woman's .31-caliber rifle. "I touched it first," said Upsize. —"So? I touched it *last*," said Pschaw, touching it. —Meanwhile, Tinkerling and The Professor hauled the other enemy soldier out of the hole.

I'm dead, thought Tolb, going limp; I'm already dead. But as they rolled her onto her back, the fear of being stripped or maimed or hacked at for mementos made her leap up screaming, scrabbling at her web belt for her bayonet.

The suprapodeans staggered back, cursing and fumbling for their rifles. "Don't fucking move!" —"Hands the fuck up!"

Tolb, shivering, slouched in submission as pain racked her innards.

"For the love of God, nobody fire," said H. Crap, addressing Fidget in particular. "We're in a goddamn bumpkin's firing circle here."

"These devious fucking fuckers!" said Upsize. "Pretending to be fucking dead like that!" —They had all heard stories of the enemy's deceitfulness, but had not known till now whether to fully believe them. The Pacifist was most surprised; she had often argued, from the evidence of their literature in translation, that the infrapodeans were in fact more civilized and sophisticated than her own compatriots. She felt personally betrayed.

"Don't shoot," said Tolb. "I'm hurt."

"Shut your fucking spewpipe," said The Professor. —"Yeah, or speak fucking human," said Pschaw, jabbing Tolb with her rifle barrel. —"Fuck off, you guys," said The Pacifist in disgust. "Leave her alone. Can't you see she's hurt?"

"Cork your bunghole, Pacie," said H. Crap quietly. "We're taking this piece of crap prisoner."

Pschaw peered menacingly into the prisoner's face. Tolb gazed back, seeing in the protuberant brow and slack lips proof of the enemy's bestial cruelty. A whimper escaped her, less now from pain than from shame and hopelessness. And yet there was an unconscious element of craven calculation even in her weakness: perhaps if she showed herself pathetic enough, they would leave her alone. "I need a doctor," she blubbed. —"You shut your fucking bunghole," said Pschaw.

A flare went up; Tolb flinched, and Fidget fired.

H. Crap said, "Fuck."

"Shit," said Fidget. "Sorry, LC."

They crowded around the prisoner, who lay squirming on her back, one hand clawing at the frozen earth, the other clamped over her shattered, bleeding chin, her eyes liquid and bright with reflected flare. Tolb, looking up at their calm, quizzical faces, felt a huge and expanding panic, as of gas pressurizing a cracked container.

"I thought she was running." —"She wasn't running any fucking place." —"She sure as fuck isn't running any place now." —"Look," laughed Tinkerling, "she *is* trying to run away!" —Tolb, kicking out one leg, was pushing herself inch by inch along the ground.

"Someone should put her out of her fucking misery," said The Pacifist.

The dying woman was making sticky, wet snoring sounds. Her inability to speak made her seem subhuman. She stank of blood and shit. They looked away, moved more by disgust than pity.

Death was worse than Tolb had imagined; and this was not yet the worst.

A volley of small-arms fire from the direction of the outpost recalled H. Crap to her duty. "Come on, we're behind schedule." —"What about this bitch?" —"Just leave her." —"What about her stuff?"

One of the medipodean stretcher-bearers asked hopefully, "We take back casualty-casualty?" —"No."

Left alone, Tolb rallied. The pain, once she had taken its measure, was sufferable. Perhaps death was not inevitable. She decided to live. She would not let herself become a corpse—a lump of offal, exposed to the public, unowned, unowning, bereft of dignity and rights. She would not let death defile her.

From quickening breaths and slackening muscles she wove a dwindling braid of determination. Ten minutes later, she became unconscious. Her last sensations were of a presence like her father's, and a smell like mown grass.

ONLY ONE GRENADE—The Colonel's—had passed over the parapet and fallen inside the outpost. No one was hurt; but the lieutenant, leaping away from it, had dropped Sergeant Montazo's field glasses. Montazo fussed and fiddled with them loyally, but finally admitted, after many vacillating fits of hope and despair, that they were smashed to uselenessness.

"Eyes up, Sergeant," said Ryyss, brisk and unrepentant. "That was just probing fire, but they'll attack in earnest any minute now. Hold your fire till you see them coming."

Montazo peered through the firing slit, her blindness made total by emotion. She felt resentful, and guilty, and giddy, and frightened, and powerful. She felt insubordinate. The nearest she came to acknowledging this feeling was a wistful, idealized memory of Lieutenant Farl, nobly urging them on at Hill 68.

She told Yumi, the radio operator, to stay close.

"I guess this is it," said Meck to Alcott. "Hey: I love you." —"Aw, shut it," said Alcott, kindly, though embarrassed. They hardly knew each other.

H. CRAP SIGNALED that they had come far enough. The Professor lay down, propped on elbows, and readied her rifle. It was only two weeks since she had killed Winky, who, blinded by smoke, had come rushing at her screaming like an invader. She had told no one what she had done, and not even Winky ever knew; but she had vowed never again to release her safety catch. Now, the first time this vow was tested, she found herself conforming to habit and obeying orders. She could hardly do otherwise without drawing attention to herself. But she aimed harmlessly high; she would not shoot even an invader except in self-defense.

The Pacifist also aimed high, believing it a condition of her own survival that she not kill anyone in this war. The others aimed carelessly, and at H. Crap's signal, fired carelessly at the side of the blockhouse, wanting only to fulfill their obligation and retreat.

The defenders, however, keyed up by Ryyss's cautions, believed that at least a company was against them. Those on the southwest wall, led by Sergeant Montazo, fired back liberally—frightening themselves and startling those on the other walls, who also started firing, frightening themselves and startling others. For half a minute, Ryyss's screams of "Hold your fire!" went unheard, and, for another half minute, unheeded.

H section sprawled wriggling and twisting beneath the onslaught. The torrent of bullets twanging and whistling over them made as much noise in the aggregate as the roar of the machine guns and rifles. The Professor cursed in fury at what she felt was an unprovoked attack. The Pacifist was astounded and indignant. Tinkerling, a recruit, cried "Stop it!" repeatedly. No civilized person would heap such hurt and destruction upon her worst enemy; no sane person could treat even an animal this way. How could the world hold so much malice? "Look what you're doing!" she sobbed. Sancty, the other recruit, remained unshaken. She was only relieved that this, her first firefight, was no worse. She had expected something more unspeakably terrifying than what was, after all, just bits of metal flying through the air. And for the time being, there was nothing she could do; the unusual lack of responsibility was almost cozy.

H. Crap spent one pulse beat cursing herself for leading the section too near the outpost; then she became practical, calling for covering fire and a staggered retreat as soon as they could lift their heads.

Pschaw called out to Upsize. —"What?" —"Let me shoot the .31 for a while."

To Montazo, the enemy's shouts sounded like battle cries, and the flash of their covering fire, when it began, appeared to be coming from no farther than the other side of the parapet. She dragged Yumi by the radio into the blockhouse, screaming grid coordinates into the handset.

The field artillery CO was bemused. "That's your location, Nubbin. What direction and distance from you, over?" —"Zero fucking distance!" came the reply. "Put it all on us! They're coming down our fucking throats! Give it to us now! Now now NOW NOW NOW!"

The artillery XO shrugged to conceal a shudder. "Sounds like a real shitstorm. Better give it to them."

"Now WHAT THE fucking fuck?" said Corporal Cobweb. "Is that our arty?" —"That's theirs," said Shitjob. "Those're three-fifty-fours. Listen." —Jaywalk agreed. "That's enemy ordnance, all right." —"That's what I thought," said Cobweb. "So what the fucking fuck are they doing?" —No one could say.

Cobweb, muttering sighs, radioed the MAC command post to confirm that the outpost was in fact being held by the enemy. Neither of her other two sections had returned to the rendezvous, and now H section appeared to be storming the target singlehandedly. She should have known better than to volunteer for this horseshit mission with this bunglefuck platoon; but she'd decided that the only way to escape this lonely goddamn post was by demonstrating some zeal. Unfortunately, it was also a good way to get herself killed.

Staff Sergeant Ciborsck betrayed neither surprise nor uncertainty. As if it had been his plan all along to incite the enemy to shell himself, he ordered Corporal Cobweb to take the outpost as soon as the bombardment abated. "What's their strength, anyway?" —Because her troops were listening, Cobweb did not exaggerate. "About a platoon, I'd guess. At least one machine gun." —"That's what we figured. Capitalize, Corporal! This is our chance." —Through a stiff mouth, Cobweb said, "Yes, sir. Out."

For five seconds, she pondered, champing her teeth. Was there any way out of it?

There wasn't. So make the best of it.

She made a short speech, grinning grimly. In closing, she said, "I'll be honest with you. Till this moment, this was a horseshit fucking mission. But they've let us off the leash. This is it, ladies. We've got opportunity by the fuzz."

Parade-Ground was told to stay behind and wait for G section. She did not reply. She was listening in a crescendo of amazement to the twittering chorus of flying shrapnel, of which every voice was distinctly eloquent, so that the night seemed swarming with the chatter of frisky elves. Christmas Tree thumped her, and she spent a moment rediscovering her own language. "What is it?" —"If they're not here in ten minutes," said Cobweb, "rejoin us and H section. Got it?" —"Yes, ma'am. Ten minutes, rejoin us and H section."

When she began to shamble after them, Christmas Tree hissed and gestured for her to stay put. Though C.T. had misgivings about leaving her alone, she supposed that she would be safer here than in combat.

"Ten minutes, rejoin us," muttered Parade-Ground, sinking to a crouch. "Ten minutes, H section." The words seemed loaded with importance; and their importance only loomed larger as, with each repetition, their context and meaning faded to obscurity. Soon they were only a string of syllables, an ancient incantation performing itself upon the wondrous instrument of lips, tongue, and teeth. And even when she doubled over to vomit, it was to the rhythm of those sacred sounds.

KLIPTON LIFTED WOOZILY her ringing head. There was a sharp pain in her hip which she ignored, both from squeamishness and from obstinacy. The only wound bad enough to stop her would be the one that stopped her.

Without turning her gaze from the firing slit, she called out to Sunachs on her right and Raof on her left. Sunachs was fine; from Raof there was no reply. "Raof, you all right?" —"She's done and gone," called Osini. "Let her be." —Klipton spared a glance, and saw the limp body with the top of its head sheared off, bearing now no resemblance to Raof but the uniform. —"That'll come as no surprise to her," said Laskantan. —"Cover her field with me, Osini," said Klipton. "They'll be coming any second now." —"Teach a dog to shit," muttered Osini.

Solzi was moaning and calling for help.

Elzby shouted, "Aiersbax!"; "Elzby!" shouted Aiersbax. —"You're all right, you farthole?" —"Nip it, you snotwhistle. I'm fine."

Meck was hit. "I'm hit," she bawled. Her tunic was wet with blood, glistening like oil in the moonlight. At least it wasn't day; in daylight her blood would be red. She was afraid to move, afraid to probe the damage. There passed over her a cloud of horror at her own body, as if it belonged to someone else. —"Where are you hit?" asked Alcott. —"I don't know." —"Well, where does it hurt?" —"I don't know." —"Then swallow it," said Alcott. "You're okay, for God's sake. Look vigilant."

"I'm out of tracers," cried Burnok. "Does anybody have any more tracers?" —"Forget tracers," said Kellek. "Does anyone have any goddamn ammo at all? I'm down to half a mag here." —"That's half more than I've got," said Sunachs, pumping her cocking handle in demonstration. —"Then go scrounge some the fuck up for us." —"Don't move," said Sergeant Gijalfur. "Throw a grenade. Throw rocks! Use your bayonet if you have to. Just nobody move!" —After a moment, Sunachs asked if anyone had an extra grenade. —"Goddammit," said Gijalfur. "Here." She slid a flare gun towards Sunachs. "Just hold your goddamn position."

"Fuck all you fucking guys!" cried Solzi.

"Conserve your ammunition," said Laskantan, in a chiding singsong. —"Where's the lieutenant?" asked Osini. —"Over and out," said Gijalfur, gesturing towards a child-sized mass of torn flesh in an adult's torn tunic, lying like trash against the wall of the blockhouse. —"Shit," said Kellek. "Where's Montazo?" —"Hurt pretty bad," said Yumi. The blockhouse they'd been inside had taken a direct hit. The concussion had knocked them both to the ground, dazing Yumi, but rupturing something inside Sergeant Montazo. Currently she lay unconscious or dead, bleeding from the ears and mouth. "Radio's busted too," said Yumi; this was her way of asking for orders. —"Congratulations, Sarge," said Laskantan. "I guess that leaves you in command." —"First of all," said Gijalfur, "Costitch was sergeant before I ever was, and second of all, never the fuck mind who is in command right now, just keep your eyes up and tongue the fuck in, this attack is about to get imminent any fucking second now, and third of all, *stuff your fucking tuft, Solzi!* You're not the only one hurt!"

"Fuck you, Sarge! I'm in fucking excruciation here! I'm fucking dying!"

In fact, Solzi felt pain more hurtingly than most people. She couldn't know this, but she suspected it, and felt bitterly sorry for herself. The conviction that her present suffering was worse than anything her comrades would ever know filled her with contempt and absolved her of all modesty. Screaming with hatred made the pain a little more tolerable, too.

H section, on the opposite side of the outpost, paused in their withdrawal, and even The Colonel, leading I section back to the fight, hesitated in her step at the sound of Solzi's caterwauls. Farther away, Parade-Ground hugged her knees, vibrating in sympathetic agony.

"Dammit, Solzi," shouted Costitch, "shut your face! That's an order!" —When this had no effect, Gijalfur threatened her with a court-martial—also to no effect. —Others began to threaten, cajole, or advise Solzi. "Can't you give yourself a shot of morphine?" —"I can't find my hands, let alone my first-aid kit!" —"Goddammit," said Gijalfur, "would someone help give her a shot of morphine." —"Can't reach her, Sarge," said Osini. "She's on the other side of the parapet." —"Solzi! What the fuck are you doing outside the OP?" —Solzi didn't know or care, and again told them to hurry up.

Klipton made a decision. She felt only disgust for Solzi's suffering; she dared not soften so far as to pity in others what she must not allow in herself. But she believed superstitiously that she had only survived till now by helping her comrades, especially when at her own risk. She asked Sergeant Gijalfur for permission to leave her post long enough to find Solzi and give her a shot of morphine. —Gijalfur grumbled. "Goddammit. Ask Costitch. She's in command." —Costitch's own superstition was that she must kill as many enemy as possible to stay alive, and she was afraid that accepting command of the platoon would hamper her in this pursuit. Her flamethrower, too, was almost empty, and she thought that she could do more damage outside the walls, in close combat. "Come on," she said to Klipton. "I'll help." —"I'll come too, Sarge," said Sunachs, brandishing the flare gun sarcastically. —"Sure. With one more, we can bring her back inside." —Aiersbax raised her hand. —"Don't be stupid," hissed Elzby. —Laskantan whistled, grimaced, and wagged her head. "Shit mountain without a Sherpa," she said. "I guess I don't want to be left out of all the fun." Her own belief was that the safest place to be was the one that seemed most dangerous, and the most dangerous place the one that seemed safest.

They climbed over the wall and dropped out of sight. Moments later, rifle fire began to be heard on all sides. —"Spread out and fill those gaps!" cried Gijalfur. "Here they come!" The de facto platoon commander fired a few shots, then retreated from the firing slit, the better to direct and exhort her troops. She shouted and stamped and waved her arms in rage. "This is it! No more conserving ammunition! Kill the filthy bitches!"

Meck reloaded her rifle, whimpering. At least she would die honorably.

TWENTY MINUTES LATER, what remained of First/Fourth Platoon succeeded in taking possession of Strongpoint E15, known informally at MAC command as The Nipple. Corporal Cobweb, breathless, exhilarated, and bleeding, contacted Staff Sergeant Ciborsck by radio to tell him of their feat.

He cut her off. "Pull yourself together, Corporal, then call me back." —Cobweb was stunned. She thought she had been relating the facts calmly, in a succinct and orderly way. She closed her eyes, and for the first time in two hours turned her attention inwards; glimpsing there a clamorous chaos of anxiety, pain, and remorse, she quickly opened her eyes.

"Here," said Jaywalk, offering her a canteen. "But take it easy. Looks like they're out of water, too." —Longpork confirmed this. "They were using piss to cool the machine gun. You can smell it." Her face was stiff and unfamiliar, her voice flat; she had shot in the face at close range one of the women operating the gun. —Cobweb poured some water in her mouth and held it there without swallowing; nevertheless, it was somehow gone in a minute, leaving her feeling drier and thirstier.

Upsize came in to say that a third survivor had been found among the carnage in the other blockhouse, where the defenders had made their last, useless stand. —"Okay," said Cobweb. "Thanks." —"What do you want us to do with her?" —"Does she speak any suprapodean?" —"I don't know. Since coming to," Upsize snickered, "she just cries over her dead buddy. I thought these bitches were all supposed to be so tough." —"And smart," said Longpork. —Cobweb shrugged. —"So what should we do with her?" The battle was over now; even five minutes earlier, Upsize would not have asked this question. —"She hurt?" —"Pretty bad, I guess." —"If she lives, she lives," said Cobweb. "We'll need all our first-aid gear for ourselves." Then she ordered everyone out, so that she could be frank with Ciborsck.

". . . And fifteen unaccounted for, presumed wounded or dead. We don't have enough uninjured troops to send out rescue parties." —Ciborsck sounded pleased. "You've done excellent work, Corporal. This is going to change the face of the war in E grid. Just hold on till noon for those reinforcements. In the meantime, use your stretcher-bearers to round up your casualties. That's what they're there for!"

THE PROFESSOR LAY balanced upon a rock, looking up unseeing at the stars, and concentrating on her breath. If she shifted her position or inhaled too quickly, she choked on salty blood. The pain was tremendous, but it imposed focus. She felt no resentment or fear, but rather a bemused and contingent joy. She inspected this feeling gingerly, with the occasional spare drop of attention, and realized that she was happy because she was alone. She had not experienced solitude for many months, and had forgotten how precious it had been to her. —When the stretcher-bearers arrived, she scowled and hid her pale face behind her arm. "Leave her," said one of them. "She doesn't want to be looked at now."

Private Privates tossed and twisted her body incredulously. She could not find the wound, and she did not seem to be bleeding, but the pain in her chest, at the very pinpoint core of her, could not be alleviated. How could you let this happen? she asked God. How could you let it hurt this much? I did everything you told me to! —But God was silent. His silence was contemptuous, and she withered beneath it.

Shitjob lay sprawled in a ditch, cursing and shivering. She was not hurt, but did not know where any of her comrades were. She dared not call out or raise her head.

"Does it hurt?" asked Triple-Time, binding the gory, shattered shin. She was disgusted by the anxiety in her voice. —"Nah," said T.P. In fact, it hurt like hell, but she realized that crying or complaining would make no difference; the pain would come whether she took it or not.

Jimjam was pleased almost to pride by her wound. It had stopped bleeding, but was painful enough to prevent her from walking. Perhaps she would be sent home! She snuggled into herself, and waited luxuriously for the stretcher-bearers and the medics to do their jobs.

IN A SHELL crater at the base of the outpost, Laskantan murmured soothingly to Solzi. Solzi, with two shots of morphine in her, had mellowed from screaming rage to hissing disdain. "Fuck you, Laskantan. I'd like to see how you'd fucking bear it if you were in my place. I'm fucking dying." —"Maybe so, but you'll die a whole lot faster if they hear you out here." —"Fuck them." She lifted her head an inch in defiance. "Let them come and put me out of my fucking misery, the fucking bitches!"

Laskantan breathed deeply to deflate a rising bubble of hilarity. "What if I gave you something to chew on, would that help?" —"I'll chew your fucking eyeballs, you fuck." —Laskantan laughed out loud a little.

"Laskantan," said Solzi, her eyes focusing with seriousness. "Give me a grenade." —"Can't. I'm all out." —"Then give me your trench knife." —"What's wrong with yours?" —"All right, give me my fucking trench knife. Put it in my hand." —Laskantan did. "All right, hero, now what?" —Solzi held the flat of the blade briefly to her neck, then let out a feeble sob. "Fuck you, you fuck. I'll fucking stab your fucking guts out and see how you fucking like it."

Laskantan patted Solzi's cheek. "I guess I wouldn't like it any more than you do, sweetheart. Now, do you think you can zip it for ten minutes while I go find someone to help me carry you out of here?" —"I'm dying!" cried Solzi. "I don't fucking want to live anymore!"

A burst of automatic rifle fire from the parapet churned up the dirt around them.

Grinning, Laskantan pressed her face into the icy earth.

PARADE-GROUND FOUND THAT she could walk only if she let walking happen by itself. Her body, formerly solid and uniform, had crumbled into a congeries of ill-fitting parts, a disorderly stack of overlapping maps. There were maps of touch and friction, of heat and cold, of the position of her limbs, of the loosening and tightening of her muscles, and of the aches in her bones and the burbling turmoil in her guts. To collate all this data and deploy all these systems for movement would have required a staff of intent geniuses; but there was only her, and her mind was as thronged with fragmented ideas as her body was with sensations.

The river of her thoughts flowed wide and wordless, except for occasional phrases that broke like spray from the wave, became crystallized, and finally melted into meaning-lessness beneath the spotlight of her fascinated attention.

Sometimes she sank to the cold ground and marveled at the symphony of light and noise crashing across the valley and sky. Even lying flat on the earth, she felt precarious and unstill, as if she might at any moment roll out of the trough of her body.

Soon, without having decided to, she was on her feet and walking again, clanking and stumbling over herself like a battalion retreating in disarray. She did not know if she was moving backward or forward. She only knew that she must not stop; there was something she was trying to catch up to, or stay ahead of. She looked behind her, became disoriented, and struck out again—and again—till she did not know if she was chasing or fleeing. "Desultory vexa-tion," she muttered—the term for untargeted shelling of an area presumed to be occupied by the enemy. She could taste her teeth. When she swallowed, there was an echo. Colors leaked out of the backs of her eyes. Emotions poured through her, stirred by some music too rapid or refined for hearing. "Dildo vagina." She'd better hurry. Ten minutes. H section. Desultory vagina. Scrunch your tits. Uproot those feet, soldier. No lily-dipping. Her name was Lily. "Lily." They'd named her Parade-Ground because she brushed her teeth. Not anymore. Toothbrushes were for cleaning rifles. Teethbresh. They told me not to binge drink. I bange drank. I'm bunge drunk! She giggled, smitten with vice. What would her mother say? But the thought of her mother was one of the things she was trying to stay ahead of. Onward.

"Lily. Li-lee." What a foolish name! Her parents might as well have called her Flip Flop or Gewgaw, or Pell-Mell or Nitwit, or Pish-posh or Hubbub or Ragbag or Flimflam or Claptrap or Knick Knack or Mishmash or Hodgepodge! Or Jimjam. Why had they called Jimjam Jimjam? Because she was anxious? What was her real name? She was reminded, for some felt but inexplicit reason, of her childhood friend Dulie, with whom she had built the Mantrap—a kind of caltrop made by nails driven through a board and camouflaged with mud. Their parents had been livid, their victim amused. She could see his wry face.

A score of forgotten faces and playgrounds of her childhood flashed within her. She felt a bittersweet nostalgia; and the conviction that she had forgotten or failed to do something was intensified.

Her bowels were as squeaky as wet plastic. Was she hungry? Digestion seemed obscene, as exploitative as the invaders' colonialism.

She became mesmerized by a frozen moonlit puddle, rough and smooth in arabesque variegation.

When she fixed her gaze, her peripheral vision congealed into a tactile ring of marching, sliding patterns that faded to an all-encompassing obscurity; she became a watchfire in a little clearing around which danced serried hordes, citizens of a vast civilization of emotion and sensation. She laughed out loud to discover that this whole world could be laid to waste and a new one built with a flick of her eyes.

She unearthed the wisdom in every hackneyed proverb, discovered the calcified poetry in every idiom and cliché. You can't have both the bottle of wine and the wife drunk. Children grow looking at their parents' backs. Old crabs tell young crabs to walk straight. It takes less time to drench the boot than to dry it. The sinner makes the better saint. You could use her shit for toothpaste. Teethpawst.

Every returned thought gave her a delight of synthesis. Everything suggested everything else, and her associations and intuitions seemed the more profound for remaining vague.

She saw the interdependence of all opposites, how every ostensibly separable thing formed the ground of some other thing's figure.

Humility was a form of vanity. Charity was selfish.

Dissonance accentuated harmony—was in fact harmony, in the same way that sound was only structured silence.

Her shoulders supported the sky. The moon was within arm's reach; closer.

Twelve months, but thirteen moons in a year?

Empty space did not exist. The universe was gelid ether, all its gravities balanced.

Sparks spat fresh sparks before falling to cinders.

No drop could fall out of the ocean.

The large wave swallowed the little wave and was forever changed.

The prerequisite for this little fingernail? All that ever was!

She cringed reflexively at the demented screech of howitzer shells, a sound which could not have been made more terrible by design, and which filled her more with awe than fright. The war too was a contingent miracle, every bomb a triumph of technology. Near this thought, however, there lay in wait something unpleasant, and she shied from it.

She shivered extensively, every fiber within her stamping its feet and rubbing its hands for warmth. Her body too was a triumph, even when poisoned. Indeed, every thought, however trivial—even this one!—represented the culmination of millennia of evolution.

She felt in touch with every jagged, tattered part of herself. Every cell and nerve was hollering for attention. She could feel her feet in her boots, and the weight of her rifle—no longer a part of her—in her hands. Tides swished and soughed in her empty ears. This was her true self. Reality was fevered, good health a smooth, dissembling coat of varnish. But habituation provided leverage. Otherwise one would flounder about, steeped in stimuli all day long. Nothing would get done. And something needed to be done. She tripped over a soldier's corpse—

And was flooded at once with all the discomfort and guilty thoughts that she had been skirting: She had a duty to her mother to stay alive; but she also had a duty to the memory of her father, a good soldier, to be a good soldier, and a duty to her brother, a good officer, not to embarrass him. She had a duty to Lance Corporal Jaywalk and to her section; she had a duty to Corp Cobweb and the rest of the platoon—but she had abandoned them, and ignored her orders. She had a duty to Fourth Company; she had a duty to her battalion, her brigade, her division, and to Generals Roseberry, Elrust, and Abgrusck—but had she done one heroic thing to help win the war? She was guilty of having killed, and guilty of not having killed enough. She owed allegiance to her homeland, but she owed allegiance to her home, too. She had responsibilities to her person, and she had irreconcilable responsibilities to the planet; she had duties to the cells and nerves of her, and she had duties to God. Above all, she had a duty to her fellow soldier—and she had shirked her duty. She remembered that on the night of the long march out of Burzgao she had stumbled over such a soldier as this, lying wounded, wan and resentful, on the lip of a shell crater. She had given the woman a sip of water and had promised to send a medic for her. But she had forgotten to send anyone.

How could she forgive herself? Why, when the time came, should anyone help her?

What had she made of her miraculous life? What good had she done with her inheritance, those millennia of evolution? How had she earned a mother's love and worry? This corpse too, its face buried in frozen mud, had a mother, who was perhaps still anxiously writing it letters and baking it cakes. The acid nausea, the gob of phlegm in her throat, and the bloat in her bowels racked her like recriminations. Nearby shouts and rifle fire could add nothing to her shrinking horror, and she fled into an unbombed grove more to escape herself than to save herself.

She soon regretted this. The trees closed over her like a bog, screening the lightning and muffling the thunder of combat. But the wood was neither dark nor silent. She could hear it growing, breathing, creaking, reaching, gnawing; and moonlight dribbled through the foliage, and the very shadows swirled and shimmered like grease on water. Every plant was awful, trembling with life as with suppressed laughter. Every tree was a slow-bursting firework of branching bristles. Predatory animals and enemy soldiers crept continually out of sight. Snaking vines twined round her; venomous thorns abraded her skin; unblinking owls' eyes peered through her. She turned in circles, whimpering and clutching her rifle to her chest. She shut her eyes and shook her head, but the scene did not disappear; indeed, she could see it more clearly, and from all 360 degrees. Panic-stricken, she peeled wide her eyes, to no effect. The forest grew larger and denser, crushing her beneath its churning mass to an infinitesimal insignificance. All the weight of the universe was rolling over her; she tried to lunge free, and only threw herself the more fully beneath its wheels. Every good and vibrant thing was moving irretrievably away from her at an ever-increasing rate. At last the thread of her fear snapped, and she collapsed groaning in defeat—but there was nowhere to go; no drop could fall out of the ocean. Her bottom opened to an abyss, and she emerged from a nightmare into a vaster nightmare. Now dissonance subsumed harmony. War was fundamental: even light was at war with itself. The quintessence of the universe was raw terror, from which God hid in creation. Even this was not the worst or final truth: countless times that night she awoke to a worse one. Susceptible and exposed, she rode a recursively cresting wave of hideous revelation.

Thus hours passed like eras, and it was not until the first glow of dawn that exhaustion finally dulled her misery. Weeping with relief, she hobbled out of the grove (she had

not penetrated it deeply) and surveyed the scorched landscape, which was softened to beauty by morning and mist.
Not ten meters away, one of the strange local deer stood on
its hind legs, placidly grazing. In the distance, a procession
of refugees trudged across the valley, leaving in their wake
scattered detritus: mattresses, broken-down carts, trunks and
cabinets and cases that had proved too heavy. At this sight of
her fellow creatures, Parade-Ground's heart reopened, and
she started towards them, smiling tenderly.

She was back inside her skin, and the earth was again firm
beneath her foot. Already little more remained of her night's
ordeal than a loose and wrung-out feeling—she supposed
that she had been enlarged, even improved by her suffering—
and an unpleasant but unshakable conviction of a *something*
lurking beyond everyday sense. However, the ideas that had
plagued or delighted her now seemed mere paradoxes, or
trivial, or false. Nor was she aware of any irresolvable inter-
nal conflict. She would find First/Fourth Platoon; she would
write a letter to her mother; she would help to rid the medipodeans of the invaders. Her nerves and cells were again quietly working; she too would do her work quietly.

"Who are you running from?" she asked one of the
refugees. —The man shrugged, and said in his language,
"Soldiers." —"Which army? Like me, or not like me?" She
indicated her uniform. "Same, or different?" —"Same like
you," said the man in her language. —She thanked him, and
began walking against the stream.

THE RELIEF FOR Forty-Third C Platoon arrived at dawn.

Though surprised to meet resistance from The Nubbin,
Fifty-Ninth D Platoon were well rested, better equipped,
and more numerous than the suprapodean troops. They
expulsed the aggressors quickly, suffering few casualties.

Staff Sergeant Ciborsck and MAC command never
attempted to retake Strongpoint E15, but they remained

convinced that First/Fourth's possession of it for one night had permanently improved their position in the area. Corporal Cobweb was posthumously promoted two ranks. The Colonel was posthumously awarded the very medal of valour that she wore when she died. Their mothers had little choice but to be proud.

GRAVE RESERVATIONS. —PRIVATE Shyve had again been
assigned to a graves-registration fatigue—which, due to a
mental snag, and with no witticism intended, she called
Grave Reservations. This was, in Thirty-Second Company, an
unpopular duty, and was usually handed out as an unofficial
punishment. Shyve, however, though careful not to show it,
relished the work. It was unsupervised, and no officer seemed
to know how long it should take; no doubt they made allowances for its grisliness. Shyve found that she could drag her
feet, smoke, and take rests without ever being told to hurry
or reprimanded for loafing—an unheard-of luxury. And the
handling of corpses did not bother her. Indeed, she took pride
in her intrepid callousness—just as she had done as a school-
girl, loitering solitary in lush cemeteries. With two plugs of
garlic up her nose, she didn't even notice the stench.

But the great unspoken perk was that she could keep any
valuables she found on the bodies. To date she had acquired
necklaces, bracelets, rings, wristwatches, pocket watches,
lockets, knives, pens, eyeglass frames, a cigarette holder, a
cigar cutter, a magazine loader, and other tools and devices of
fine craftsmanship whose purpose eluded her. She was hoard-
ing all these treasures in her bunk, for she was contemptuous

of the local currency and distrustful of the mail service. Most of the photos and letters that she found she honored as "personal effects" and wrapped up with the soldier's dog tags to be shipped home. But occasionally one caught her eye.

"Dear Premli, This is the third time I have written this letter. The first two I was ordered to self-censor by Captain Dowz, and simply tore up. To censor one's own letters somehow seems pointlessly destructive—just like this war, in fact. Anyway, God knows what precisely in them crawled up his ass. Nothing but my usual screeds against incompetence and wastefulness, nothing that should surprise anyone. There: I suppose this letter too is already unsendable. So I might as well get a few things off my chest . . ."

Shyve stuffed this into a pocket for later reading, and continued rummaging. A few minutes later, she sprang upright, holding at arm's length a notebook written in code. She had to show this to Iargus. On her way to the quartermaster's dugout, she told two privates and a sergeant that she was just taking a latrine break.

Her friend quickly disillusioned her. "That's not code, you farthole. That's suprapodean." —"Oh. Well, it could still be important, couldn't it? Maybe it's intelligence." —Iargus riffled the pages skeptically. "It doesn't look like intelligence to me." —"What do you know about intelligence?" —"A lot more than you." —"You don't even know what it says." —"I know what it doesn't say," said Iargus oracularly. —"Oh yeah? What's that?" —"Everything." —Shyve made a gesture of suffering.

But Iargus had a friend with a suprapodean dictionary. This friend, in the midst of an artillery barrage that twice blew out her candle, laboriously translated a few lines. Shyve was disappointed.

Helmet: mine.
Bongo drum: mine.

Fast bumps: machine gun.

Cut the top: hundred-pounder.

Doctor ache: strafed.

Who I killed: mud.

Winker: rifle shot.

Smith: infection.

Juice of war: hand grenade.

"WHAT THE HELL? Is it poetry?" —"It's intelligence," teased Iargus. "Hey, take your intelligence!" —"Keep it."

On her way back to Grave Reservations, she told the sergeant and two privates that she had been delayed by diarrhea. They stared at her in blank wonder.

The heap of corpses had received a direct hit. Bloody hunks of flesh lay scattered everywhere. Shyve drooped— not at the gore, but at the disorder, and at the responsibility of cleaning it all up.

"We thought you were in that mess!" said one of the privates. "We thought you were dead for certain."

Shyve laughed at the idea. She rolled up her sleeves, spat in her palms, and got to work. Dead flesh was just dirt, and once you were completely dirty you had nothing more to fear. Indeed, she soon discovered that the explosion had greatly simplified her labor. There was no longer any way of identifying or even counting the corpses; she shoveled into the pit any five limbs, or any two torsos, or any three heads, or any hundred pounds of meat, and called it a person. She was whistling at her good luck, and plucking three gold teeth from a disembodied jawbone, when a section of pukes passed by her, gawping and aghast. She grinned at their image of her, and waved, as if to reassure them that war was not so bad, provided you had a sense of humor, and a little brains.

AT 12:51 P.M. ON TUESDAY, March 16, President Trifenia Radil capped her pen, turned off her dictation machine, and asked her caller to hold. She stared at her door in baleful disbelief as the noise in the hallway swelled to a cacophony of stomping, chanting, shouting, and song. Then the door burst open and seventy or eighty students, some brandishing placards, flooded into an office that, though large, had never before accommodated more than ten people at one time.

"What on God's green earth is the meaning of this?"

No one heard her. She tried to stand, but the crowd penned her in. Impotence made her furious. She had returned to work only the previous Thursday from a week of convalescence following a quadruple coronary bypass, and she was in no mood to sit idle. She had been busy ratifying or countermanding all that had been done in her absence by Vice-President Martin, whose mistakes were all the more galling for being elusive. She resented the students' interruption, but resented even more their boorishness: they had not so much as knocked. Also, her sense of smell had been unnaturally keen since the operation, and the odor of seventy post-adolescent bodies in a confined space struck her with the force of an assault. Someone bumped a photograph of her children off the desk.

"What in fuck's sake do you want?" she screamed.

"I lost my head a little at first," she admits.

Several voices told her what they wanted, when they wanted it, and how they intended to get it.

"One at a time. I can't make out a word you're all saying."

"Hey, *shut up!*" someone yelled in real rage. The room quietened briefly, but the hubbub in the hallway and the atrium beyond only grew louder by comparison. At last President Radil realized the significance of what was happening. Not just seventy or eighty but several hundred protesters had occupied Founders' Hall.

She told her caller that she would have to phone them back—not realizing that they had already hung up.

THE ORGANIZERS OF the Parks Not Parking Lots protest rally, scheduled for noon, had been disappointed at first by the turnout. Of 14,565 full- or part-time students enrolled at the university, only about a hundred showed up to protest the expansion of Lot M, which would involve the razing of four hectares of campus parkland. And those who were in attendance seemed disengaged; most chatted with friends or munched the free cookies baked by the Undergraduate Birders Group.

"I counted about fifteen placards," says Sylvie Reinhardt, treasurer of the Outdoor Activities Club. "And half of those were held backwards, or upside down, or were being used to shield people's eyes from the sun."

Says Edward Xin, photographer for the student newspaper, *The Weekly Beacon*, "At the beginning it was more like a lawn party than a demonstration."

But at ten after twelve, Nolan Forntner, chairman and one-fifth of the membership of the local chapter of Students for the Protection of Urban Natural Spaces, climbed onto Speaker's Rock and began to speak. A change came over the crowd instantly. Forntner's indignation was contagious. "This is bullshit," he cried periodically; and those hearing him agreed that it was bullshit, and those overhearing him came nearer to learn what was bullshit.

Forntner had been fighting the expansion of Lot M for six months, since its discreet announcement by the Campus Development Office in September. His campaign had begun modestly, with letters, petitions, and informal meetings with administration in which he appealed to their humanity and good sense. Far from being ignored or obstructed, Forntner's entreaties were received each time with sympathy and encouragement.

Says Barbara Eisniz, public relations officer for the CDO, "It was impossible not to respect Nolan's passion and commitment. And from the beginning, I believe we were all in fundamental agreement as to principles. We too prefer parks to parking lots. In my experience, it is generally not the big questions on which people differ, but the minute details. We all share much the same ideals, but we may have very different notions about how best to achieve them, or approximate them, in the actual everyday helter-skelter of conflicting interests and compromise which is any large institution."

Forntner and his associates began to feel that they were being humored. They adopted a more adversarial stance, seeking the aid of lawyers, conservation agencies, and the Ombuds Office.

"Everyone told us that it could be done," says Forntner, "and showed us just what to do. We followed their advice— and nothing was done."

The growing membership of Parks Not Parking Lots spent hundreds of hours submitting grievances, filing injunctions, and canvassing community support. By January, Forntner had dedicated himself full-time to the cause, and was facing suspension from the university for incomplete coursework.

Thalia Undine, a founding member of PNPL, says, "Nolan was one of the few people I had met who not only believed that the world could be improved, but actually did something about it. It didn't matter what you did, as long as you did something. For him, the choice was not between saving the world on the one hand, or turning your back on the world and cultivating your own garden on the other; cultivating your own garden—fixing the little problems in your own backyard, neighborhood, or community—*was* improving the world, one acre at a time. But everything about our experience fighting Lot M only undermined his faith. If we could not prevent this one little evil, maybe no evil could actually be prevented; maybe the world was getting irreparably worse. Some people called him an extremist, a fanatical tree-hugger. But I think he was defending less this one copse of trees than his own idealism. This was his stand. He threw his whole self into the fight—and met only setback, hindrance, frustration, and failure."

By March, the sole concessions made to Forntner's half-year campaign were the relocation of some of the parkland's more conspicuous wildlife, and the proposed planting of twenty-nine ash trees on the median strips of the new lot. Construction was scheduled to begin on Friday, March 19, with the bulldozing of the trees. Forntner slept little that week, planning and advertising the Tuesday protest rally, at which, desperate and irate, he spoke so effectively.

"People would rather save twenty minutes' commuting time than save a tree that has been alive for a hundred and fifty years! People would rather pour poisonous carbon monoxide into the atmosphere than let that tree do its work, putting fresh, clean oxygen out into the air we breathe! People are such idiots that they would rather have a place to put their car for a few hours a week than a place to walk their dogs, a place to smell flowers, a place for their children to play for the rest of their lives! It's fucking bullshit!"

This was met by a roar of endorsement from the now doubled crowd.

"It was exhilarating," says Forntner, "and terrifying. I felt that all these bodies were extensions of my body, that all these people were thinking my thoughts. It was like finding yourself in a strongman's body: you feel an incredible urge to flex your muscles. It crossed my mind—*our* mind—to just march across campus en masse and start tearing the construction site to pieces. All I had to do was say the word; I almost *didn't* have to say the word. It was scary."

Among those affected by Forntner's speech was Langdon Bellhouse. "I hate politics and politicians and all that shit. I didn't know who this guy was or what he was about, but it just went through me, this anger at all this stuff he was getting at: cars and pollution and all that garbage. And skyscrapers and traffic jams, and jackhammers and gas-powered leaf-blowers, and no place for kids to play. I really got that. All this stuff I wanted to destroy—here was somebody finally saying, you know: Go out and destroy it."

Meanwhile supporters of another protest, conflictingly scheduled for 12:30 in the same spot, had begun to gather. Suresh Arjmand, one of the organizers for Reinstate Professor Reid, decided to move his rally across the common, and asked Forntner to make this announcement. Instead, Forntner graciously stepped down from Speaker's Rock, introducing Arjmand as "someone else who has a gripe against this university."

Arjmand was greeted by cheers and applause, which he tried in vain to curb. Someone improvised a chant, rhyming "four" with "Professor," and "eight" with "reinstate." With a shrug, Arjmand delivered his address to a much larger and more impassioned audience than he had anticipated.

At about the same time, Suz Palombo was delivering much the same address to the Special Committee reviewing the nonrenewal of Hiram Reid's contract for the fall. Reid himself was not present at this hearing, and had in fact dissociated himself from the advocacy group formed in his name.

"I never asked anyone to intervene on my behalf," he says. "And I think the whole movement had very little to do with me, actually. Most of these kids who signed the petition had never been to any of my classes. They were doing this for their own reasons—to flout authority, or what have you. And just pragmatically speaking, I had no confidence that they would accomplish anything. The so-called Special Committee was obviously just a sop. It didn't have any power."

The committee did not have the authority to overturn the Department of Physics and Astronomy's decision; at most they could pass along a "recommendation" that the decision be officially reviewed—a recommendation the Department would not be obliged to follow.

Suz Palombo, who had never attended any of Reid's classes, had spearheaded the petition that had led to the convening of the committee—which comprised six faculty, two administrators, and four students, including Palombo herself. A tireless and ubiquitous activist on campus, Palombo was Student Union Director of University Affairs, councilor-at-large to the Student Life Center, deputy political editor at *The Weekly Beacon*, and student liaison to several administrative councils, including Communications and Marketing; Security and Safety; and Scholarships, Awards, and Prizes, among others.

Arjmand's and Palombo's speeches argued simply that Reid was a much loved teacher, and that in dismissing him the university was showing a flagrant disregard for the will of the student body.

"In calling for Professor Reid's instant reinstatement," said Palombo, "we are also calling for greater self-determination for students in constructing their own educational experience."

"What a nightmare," says Professor Anton Rimmer, who was on the Special Committee. "Let the undergrads hire and fire their profs by popular vote! It would be the end of what little academic distinction this university still retains."

Claire Yaremko, assistant dean of the department, had been present at the original meeting at which Reid's contract had been let lapse, and was also on the Special Committee. She was bemused by Palombo's arguments. "First of all, as was clearly pointed out in the memorandum provided to the committee, quality of instruction had played no part in our decision to let Doctor Reid go. Our primary concern had been what we perceived to be a lack of commitment to the department—an insufficiency of what you might call *esprit de corps*."

"He was not a team player," says Rimmer.

"They fired me," says Reid, "because I wasn't a joiner. They made that fairly clear. I didn't attend their cocktail parties, I didn't sleep with any of them, and I didn't sign the little petitions they passed around at departmental meetings—which had less to do, I felt, with saving polar bears or dismantling nuclear weapons than with congratulating one another on how very enlightened and righteous we all were."

Although Reid's teaching was not at issue, Yaremko and some of the faculty had nevertheless prepared themselves for the Special Committee by listening to audio recordings of his classes—recordings made by a disgruntled student who resented that so many of the professor's exam questions were drawn not from the textbook but from his lectures. ("This," says Yaremko, "amounts to a kind of blackmail. It has been known for years that not everyone learns best *in situ*. Therefore it is arrogant, autocratic, and discriminatory to insist on perfect classroom attendance.") Nothing that Yaremko or the others heard in those recordings seemed to justify Palombo's claim that Reid was an extraordinary instructor.

"His pedagogy was positively medieval," says Rimmer. "He simply stood there and *lectured* for fifty minutes. No discussion; no questions from students; no interaction. He just reeled off facts—as if there even are such things as facts!"

"Science is in a perpetual state of growth and ferment," says Professor Eldridge Shimkus, who was also on the Special Committee. "To state dogmatically that something is *so*, or that such and such is *true*, is to harden a young mind against future development or innovation. We must not say we know; the most we can say is we *think*."

But Reid's willingness to state facts was just what some of his students liked most about him. "I'm so tired," says junior Karin Channing, "of professors hiding behind open-mindedness to avoid committing themselves. You have no idea how refreshing it is to be able to ask someone point-blank, for example: 'What about the redshift controversy?' and have them tell you point-blank: 'It's nonsense. There is no controversy. The universe is expanding—end of story. Never mind about it; don't waste your time.' Every other prof at this school is only too happy to let you waste your time chasing down every false lead—all in the name of independent learning."

Yaremko points out that Reid's didacticism deprives students in the classroom of the very thing that Palombo was demanding outside it: self-determination. "The best way to understand any scientific discovery is to rediscover it for yourself. You cannot do that if you have some figure of authority telling you in advance what you can or cannot find, or what others have already found. That lofty imparting of wisdom leads only to rote and superficial learning—encyclopedic, not organic knowledge."

And finally, Yaremko denies Palombo's claim that Reid's classes were especially popular. "His feedback ratings from the three previous semesters were slightly below the department average, and significantly below the university average."

Palombo and the other organizers of Reinstate Professor Reid had intended to prove to the Special Committee that Reid was indeed popular, by having Arjmand lead the protesters to the Whitethorn Building, where the hearing was being held. "We never planned to go inside or to disrupt the meeting," says Herman Triem. "The idea was simply to stand outside the window and show our support."

However, Arjmand, following his address, was not sure how to propose this march, and was moreover reluctant to annex the Parks rally. He went so far as to make generic calls to action, and to decry apathy on the one hand and bluster on the other, before Forntner, sensing his uncertainty, relieved him on the Rock.

"Are we going to put up with this?," Forntner asked. —The crowd cried, "No!" —"Are we going to let the bigwigs dismantle this university tree by tree, professor by professor?" —The crowd cried, "No!" —"Are we going to stand for any more of their bullshit?" —The crowd said that they would not.

"I had no idea what to do next," Forntner admits. "All I knew was that we mustn't lose the momentum we had built up. We had to *do something*, and we had to do it before people started losing interest, before they began to disperse. So in between all the pep talk, I just started thinking out loud, brainstorming our options."

"We *could* smash those bulldozers," he told the crowd. "We *could* go on strike against our shitty classes. We *could* march over to the radio station and take over the airwaves. We could do all these things. Or we could do none of these things. We can do anything. It's up to us! So what are we going to do?"

"Smash the bulldozers!" —"Go on strike!" —"Take over the radio station!" —"Burn the library!" —"Hold the president hostage!" —"Take over Founders' Hall!"

Philosophy graduate student Angelik Huaraman says, "I wasn't the first one to say it. I'm sure I heard people saying it all around me. I may have said it *louder*, at first; but then other people took it up, and were shouting it a lot louder than I had."

"I think a lot of people had the idea at the same time," says sophomore Jacqui Urribarri.

Langdon Bellhouse says, "That was my idea."

Nolan Forntner thinks it was his idea. "It was one of many suggestions I made, but it was the one most enthusiastically embraced by the crowd."

A chant was taken up: "March on the president! Take over Founders' Hall!"

Professor Bertrand Laing watched the protest from the sidelines with mixed feelings. "They were steeling themselves, I guess," he says. "The noise became deafening. This went on for what felt like several minutes. I began to think that they weren't going to do anything after all, that they were just howling at the moon. Then—I don't know what changed—they were on the move. It was like a flock of birds all taking flight simultaneously."

About three hundred students marched across campus from Speaker's Rock to Founders' Hall. Some latecomers followed the crowd out of curiosity. Some went along to criticize and to heckle. Some, sitting in stuffy classrooms, watched the boisterous group pass by the window, and felt left out and lonesome. Others put their heads out the window, and were exhorted to join the revolt; some did. About four hundred people altogether—including by now a few faculty, staff, and visitors—climbed the marble stairs and entered the ornamental front entrance of Founders' Hall.

Kinesiology major Oreggio Ballenby recalls the moment he entered the Hall. "My friends and I had been treating the whole thing as a lark till then. Everyone was having fun; it just seemed like a big joke, or a game. But then, actually going inside . . . Without becoming any less fun, it suddenly became a lot more serious. I mean, we came striding right into these huge, beautiful rooms that most students never even get to see. And the rooms were divided into all these offices and cubicles, and dozens of people were working there. And they all just dropped what they were doing and stood and stared at us. I felt like a trespasser—but invulnerable. It was wild."

For economics major Hifan Hwan, the experience was exhilarating and revelatory. "We just walked in. No one tried to stop us. No one could have stopped us. And I realized that everything is like this. No one can stop you from going anywhere you want to go. This ritzy old building was just like any other building. It was made of walls and windows and doors. And you can walk through the doors. And if you want to, you can smash the windows. And the walls are just ordinary walls. And most walls, actually, are only in your mind. You can go anywhere."

The administrative staff working in the front offices reacted in a variety of ways to the students' arrival; but most felt at first only a benign curiosity, as towards a school play, and paused to watch the action unfold.

"I remember thinking quite clearly," says Esther Dentonne, "that someone had, as usual, forgotten to tell us about this. In other words, I assumed that this parade—right between our desks!—was something scheduled, authorized, sanctioned. I welcomed the interruption—or would have—but at the same time resented the lack of forewarning."

Dan Altengood felt mild irritation. "No one ever uses those doors, and I wanted to tell them to go back out and around and come in the right way."

Albert Nhizhdin was also unimpressed. "I was in the middle of running numbers for a report to the trustees. I wondered how long this thing was going to take."

Only a few felt trepidation or fear, and these emotions were conflated with excitement.

"I felt exactly the way I'd felt last year during the earthquake," says Phoedre Montez. "Like the fabric of everyday reality had torn open a little."

Delilah Johannes, to her own surprise, and to her later embarrassment, let out an instinctive whoop of delight, "like a kid welcoming the circus to town."

ALLISON ZIEGENKORN WAS eating lunch in the basement office of *The Weekly Beacon* when she was visited by Edward Xin, who informed her that protesters had occupied Founders' Hall.

"What are you doing here?" she cried. "Go get pictures!"

She raced across campus still chewing, and juggling a pen, notepad, student press card, and voice recorder. She found several students milling about at the top of the stairs, some still pushing their way in, some hanging back uncertainly. She grasped the elbow of the tallest person standing at the threshold and asked him what was happening.

Dunkan Tomlinson did not know what was happening, for he had joined the crowd only recently. However, not wanting to discredit the protest, and feeling the flush of importance that comes from being interviewed, he spoke as though he did know. "Us students are plain fed up," he said, "and we're not gonna take it anymore." He said that lectures were boring, irrelevant, and often taken verbatim from textbooks. He said that textbooks were too expensive, and that unnecessary new editions were forever making last year's books obsolete and worthless. He said that the plastic knives in the cafeteria were too flimsy to cut through a baked potato, and that garbage cans all over campus were overflowing by Monday morning. —"What are your demands?" asked Ziegenkorn. —"Everything! All of it! We want *everything* to change, and we're not leaving here till it does!"

Tomlinson suddenly found himself at the center of a circle of supporters who could not understand why their spokesperson was not with the vanguard. They began to clear a path.

PRESIDENT RADIL, MEANWHILE, was searching desperately for a spokesperson among the roiling, jostling, chanting crowd in her office. "The only thing worse than fighting a beast with a bunch of heads," she says, "is fighting a beast with no heads at all."

"Dialogue!" she cried. "Haven't any of you ever heard of dialogue? I can't hardly negotiate if I don't know what it is you want."

"We *won't* negotiate!" someone shouted. —"*Nobody* knows what we want!" someone else shouted, in accusation.

"You, with the sign," said Radil. "Tell me what all this callithumping hullabaloo is about."

This was freshman Ethan Hendry's first protest rally. Taking his cue from those around him, he had been stomping, hollering, and clutching his "Parks Not Parking Lots" placard like a talisman. He was having a good time, and did not want it to end. Now, addressed by the president of the university herself, he felt a dizzying, dangerous freedom, as if he might as easily have told her to fuck off as that he loved her. He drew himself upright, raised the sign over his head, and hollered, "March on the president! Take over Founders' Hall!" Others joined in.

Some interpreted this absurdity as strategic obstinacy, a refusal to enter into that dialogue demanded by the enemy. Following this supposed lead, they contributed to the chaos with more noise, nonsense, and reflexive contrariety.

"Dismantle the machinery!" —"The machinery is your disease!" —"The disease is the status quo!" —"The status quo has got to go!"

Law major Rennie Jarabal says, "I don't know what I expected to happen when we got in there, but it wasn't happening. All my joy, all my optimism that we were really about to change something—it just turned to ashes." In desperation, she began singing "We Shall Overcome" at the top of her voice. Others joined in.

"All right, all right," said Radil. "Go on and blow off some steam. But would someone at least do me the kindness of opening a window? It's thick as beef stew in here."

"Open your own window!" —"Oh, don't be an ass! Open a damn window for the lady!" —"Who are you calling an ass?"

Eleanor Fitzhugh-Larman, among others, felt that the hysterical stonewalling was only damaging the protest's credibility. Raising her arms, she pleaded for some quiet and order.

"Quiet is the prison of the spirit!" shouted someone, joking. —"Order is the tyranny of the oppressor!" shouted someone, not joking.

Her friend and secret admirer, Tedi Wuat, gave an ear-splitting whistle and told everyone to shut up. "You're all giving me a goddamn headache."

Clark Dalerow, who had been impressed by Dunkan Tomlinson's speech on the front steps, was able to push no farther than the hallway outside Radil's office (leaving Tomlinson somwhere behind). Here the crowd was impenetrable, and cantankerous. "People were snarling and throwing elbows just to get a little breathing room," he says. "And everybody was telling everybody else to shut up and move back, while all the time trying themselves to creep a little closer to the door to hear what was going on inside."

Dalerow began to ask himself, then others, why those students who just happened to be in the president's office were privileged to bargain on everyone's behalf. Various chants to this effect were tested—"Democracy means everyone" and "No more decisions behind closed doors" eventually giving way to "Who the hell elected those assholes?"

The students inside the office took up these cries too, assuming, naturally, that they were directed at the university administration. Finally, the disgruntled fringe resorted to physically pulling people out of the room and into the hallway. Anyone going inside to bring someone else out instantly became a target themself—and not without justice, for indeed many used the ensuing melee as an opportunity to secure themselves a better position nearer Radil's desk.

"It was great," says Sylvie Reinhardt. "Just like a punk rock show."

"It was awful," says Rennie Jarabal. "People were behaving like animals. Every muscle in my body went tense with disgust and misanthropy."

Literature major Carla DiAmbla clenched her fists, closed her eyes, and screamed. Nearly everyone froze.

The short-lived scuffle, in which no one was seriously hurt, had one productive result: a more widespread desire for calm and orderliness.

Psychology grad student Winston Prajda says, "It seemed like everybody at the same time took a deep breath, took a look around, and realized that this thing wasn't working. We had to get ourselves organized, or we'd implode."

In the lull that followed, Tedi Wuat signaled Fitzhugh-Larman to proceed. She began to summarize for the president the speeches given by Forntner and Suresh Arjmand. She was affiliated with neither rally, and spoke clearly and dispassionately. She did not get very far before she was booed. Bellhouse, from the back of the room, asked who had put her in charge. Others succinctly accused her of grandstanding, sycophancy, and self-aggrandizement.

Fitzhugh-Larman tried to apologize to the crowd. —"You're still talking!" —Trembling and blinking, she looked about her. "I didn't mean to . . . I just thought . . . If we don't tell her what we want, she can't . . ." —"Shut up, bitch!"

Now President Radil finally managed to stand. "What you all want to do," she said, "is go on back outside, where everybody can see everybody and everybody can hear everybody else, and you want to elect maybe one, maybe two, maybe three representatives. Then send them on back in here, and then we can talk."

There were objections, but no one could offer a better solution. —"If we don't consult everybody," said Clark Dalerow, "we're no damn better than *they* are."

Despondently, the crowd shuffled out of the office. "We're having a meeting; pass it on." —"Move back to the atrium!" —"Everybody to the atrium!"

"It was depressing," says Rennie Jarabal. "I don't know why, but it felt like we'd lost."

"It was certainly kind of anticlimactic," says Ethan Hendry. "We went from taking over the university to—having a meeting." He left his placard behind.

Bellhouse was no happier about the retreat. "We were just a bunch of damn sheep, doing what we were told to do by the big boss-woman."

Angelik Huaraman said, "Shouldn't someone stay behind and make sure she doesn't, you know, escape?" No one volunteered, so Huaraman assigned a couple of undergrads to guard duty.

"Fuck," said Bellhouse, "who died and made *you* queen?" —"It's okay," said Troy Rosswind, one of the delegates. "We don't mind." —"You'll miss the meeting," someone said. "What if there's a vote?" —"Will *you* vote for me?" asked Rosswind shyly. —"Bullshit!" cried Bellhouse. "Nobody gets two votes!" —Dalerow agreed: "Everyone needs to be at the meeting, or it defeats the whole purpose of having a meeting."

In the end, President Radil was left alone and unguarded in her office. The room was soiled and disarrayed—footprints and litter on the floor, handprints and smudges on the windows and walls—but, aside from one slogan inscribed on a bookcase ("Being—Not Buying!"), no damage had been done. She closed the door, opened another window, and returned her children's photograph, its frame cracked, to the desktop. Then she lay on the floor with her legs up the wall. Breathing deeply, she allowed the blood to trickle down into her brain. A minute later she sprang to her feet, rejuvenated. She smashed her fist down onto the telephone handset, catapulting it out of its cradle, and caught it in the air with her other hand. She dialed the dean of students' extension. It was 1:15.

"She asked me what I knew about Professor Reid," says Dean of Students Dean Hanirihan—known to the students as "Dean Dean" and to his colleagues simply "Dean." "I told her what I knew. She told me to have Leopold McRobins, the chair of the Special Committee, call her as soon as possible. She said it was urgent—she told me to interrupt the hearing—but then everything had been urgent since her return. I certainly had no idea, she certainly gave me no clue, that Founders' Hall had just been occupied by several hundred protesters. I found that out from one of my students, a few minutes later."

Radil put her finger on the cradle just long enough to sever the connection, then dialed the extension of Jabbar Shah, dean of campus development—who was not in his office, having gone to investigate the takeover of Founders' Hall. President Radil dialed another extension irritably. She could not prove it yet, but she felt sure that somehow all this kerfuffle was Vice-President Martin's fault.

AT 1:20, SECURITY Officer Gary Holdona received a call from Albert Nhizhdin at Founders' Hall, who told him that the building was being occupied illegally by trespassing protesters who refused to leave. For half an hour, Nhizhdin had watched in dismay as the students made themselves more and more at home. "They took our chairs, used our phones, stole our pens," he says. "Some of them were kicking a soccer ball around—in one of the oldest buildings at one of the most venerable institutions of higher learning in our country!" The last straw for him was the sight of several students sitting on the floor of the atrium, passing around a cigarette. "The building has been nonsmoking for years."

Holdona could hardly hear what Nhizhdin was saying over the noise in the background. "Then," he says, "a second individual came on the line and asked me who I was. I identified myself, and asked them who *they* were. I received in reply a coarse insult, and was hung up upon. I immediately radioed Chief Pedersen."

Elea Bukarica, who snatched the telephone from Nhizhdin, recalls, "I told that pig to fuck himself, this was a legal protest."

Nhizhdin denied this, and was able to cite the pertinent clause in the campus constitution, which he had helped draft. "A permit is required for any demonstrating assembly larger than fifteen people to enter any building."

Bukarica was enraged by Nhizhdin's pedantry, but far more by his calm and eloquence, which seemed calculated to provoke. "If someone's shouting in your face," she says, "it's much more offensive to reply in a normal tone than to shout back in their face. Staying cool and rational is just a way of belittling the issue and deprecating their emotion."

She shouted in his face: "We just took over the university, you fascist prick! Your shitty Nazi bureaucracy doesn't apply anymore!"

Nhizhdin remained infuriatingly impassive. Biochemistry major Wil Partlingover took Nhizhdin aside and suggested that he might be safer outside the building.

"That," says Nhizhdin, "was the most chilling threat I've ever received—the implication being that I was about to be lynched by a frenzied mob."

"I certainly didn't mean it as a threat," says Partlingover. "I just thought that someone should point out to him that maybe it wasn't the smartest thing to stand there, in the middle of a hundred excited protesters, after you've just ratted them out to security, and tell them they're breaking the law."

"What's happening here?" asked Allison Ziegenkorn, holding out her voice recorder. "Are you being ejected from the building?"

"Eject them from the building!" —"Throw them out!" —"If they're not with us, they're against us!"

Says Delilah Johannes, "Personally, I never felt threatened. I was jostled a little, maybe; but it was enough just to say, 'Okay, I'm with you guys, I'm on your side,' and they left you alone—even welcomed you."

Nevertheless, Nhizhdin and about twenty other staff members took this opportunity to exit the building. —"Are you going against your will?," Ziegenkorn called after them. —"Most certainly," said Nhizhdin. "As you can see, we are being physically and forcefully ejected from our workplace."

"What a laugh," says Bukarica. "Nobody laid a hand on any of them till they were already on their way out. And then it was only a gentle, guiding, escorting hand."

"We were pushed out the door," says Dan Altengood. "Esther nearly fell down the steps."

In Room 204 of the Whitethorn Building, Professor Leopold McRobins found himself mechanically transcribing onto his notepad a long list of two-digit numbers being mechanically read aloud by Professor Shimkus. His colleague, Andrea

Scholt, leaned over to whisper that he probably did not need to write this down, since Shimkus was reading from Item 38, of which they had all received a copy. McRobins acknowledged her advice with a reproving nod—he did not want anyone to think that they were conspiring—and continued to transcribe for a few moments before raising his hand, clearing his throat, and finally interrupting Shimkus: "My apologies, Doctor, but perhaps, in the interest of time, we could all simply refer to the printed data, and save you the trouble of reading them to us?"

Shimkus acknowledged this suggestion with a similar nod, and explained the significance of the figures: the mean grade given by Professor Reid on midterms last semester was lower than both the departmental and university-wide means. Burt Hayle asked for a copy of the statistical analysis. Shimkus told him that it was a simple average. Val Perdemertonich also wanted a copy. McRobins was about to step in when Dino Varlew, one of the student committee members, moved that everyone receive a copy; Suz Palombo seconded; the motion was passed. Shimkus asked if for the time being and for the sake of argument his statistics could be taken as correct. This was deliberated.

McRobins followed these proceedings as mindlessly as he had transcribed Shimkus's numbers. "I'd agreed to act as chairperson," he says, "because I'd anticipated strong emotions and bitter conflict, and felt myself to be impartial; but I'd forgotten how numbingly dull all such committee meetings actually are." He had failed too to foresee how fully that moderating the discussion would remove him from it. And the coffee was burnt, and the lunch had been cold. He had already decided to vote for reinstatement—everyone deserved a second chance—and so the endless hairsplitting, jockeying, and deliberation held for him neither interest nor suspense. Inevitably, his tactful interventions and paraphrases became fewer and farther between, and the conversation, without his realizing it, grew long-winded and fractious.

At 1:35, Dean Dean Hanirihan burst into the room panting, and asked to speak privately to Palombo and McRobins. Apologizing, he assured them that the matter was urgent. McRobins was flustered by the untoward interruption, and at first told the committee to carry on without them, but Palombo rightly objected. He suspended the hearing and joined Dean and Palombo in the hallway.

Dean led them into an alcove and told them what had happened. He spoke in a strained whisper that did not do justice to the event or to his emotion.

"My immediate reaction," he says, "was heartbreak. I couldn't believe that my students had done something like this. Why hadn't they come to me first?"

He turned his hurt incredulity on Palombo. "What are they thinking, Suz?"

Palombo replied sadly, before her own surprise or anger could show, "I was afraid something like this would happen." Instinctively, she steered a course between feigning full knowledge, which could have made her culpable, and denying all knowledge, which would have made her an outsider. She told Dean and McRobins about the rally's planned march to the Whitethorn Building, and speculated that Arjmand had got carried away. —"Or this other rally carried him away," said Dean. —"Maybe. There are a lot of hotheads in our group. I foolishly thought I could control them, or at least channel their energies more constructively. I'm sorry, Dean."

Palombo was one of the few students who called him "Dean." He wished he could explain to her that "Dean Dean," rather than being his formal title, was, like any rhyming or repetitious nickname, actually a term of affection. But some things were spoiled if stated explicitly. And perhaps, he thought desolately, she knew just what she was doing. Perhaps he was not as close to any of the students as he'd imagined. "It's all right, Suz," he said. "It's not your fault."

Bafflement and anxiety caused McRobins to sway on his feet. "But what shall we do? Should we adjourn the hearing?"

Dean felt that their first priority must be preventing damage, injury, expulsions, or arrests, and that the best way to do this was by ending the occupation as quickly as possible. Palombo agreed, and volunteered to liaise with the protesters.

"Then we should postpone the hearing," said McRobins.

"Not necessarily," said Dean. "Depending on the outcome, the decision could help defuse the situation."

McRobins stiffened. "I'm not going to push the committee towards reinstatement just to placate some hooligans!"

"Of course not. But *if* the committee arrived there anyway, by itself—well, it could help. Tell me, both of you, without prejudice: which way are things leaning?"

"I honestly couldn't say," said McRobins. "We have yet to vote."

Palombo was more willing to speculate. "Rimmer, Yaremko, and Shimkus aren't going to budge; but I thought Hayle, Scholt, and Perdemertonich were coming over to our side. I was optimistic."

She was no longer. "I was afraid," she says, "that the committee would see the takeover the way McRobins had: as a bunch of hooligans trying to intimidate them. I thought they very well might vote No in defiance."

She did not phrase it that way to McRobins. "I'm only worried that now," she said, "even if the committee does vote for reinstatement, the department will ignore the recommendation, saying it was made under duress."

Gradually, McRobins saw what he must do: sequester the committee and guide them to a speedy but honest and unadulterated decision. Dean and Palombo wished him luck; they all shook hands solemnly.

"But what should I tell them happened to you?" he asked Palombo.

She shrugged. "Family emergency. And oh: if they'll allow a vote in absentia, I vote for reinstatement."

McRobins returned to Room 204 with trepidation and resolve. Despite everyone's best intentions, the discussion had gone on without him. Val Perdemertonich asked to see the official departmental grading guidelines. Yaremko said that there were none in print. Perdemertonich asked how Reid could be censured for failure to comply with nonexistent guidelines. Rimmer said that there were unwritten guidelines, as the memo of September 15th from Dean Ulgrave proved.

"It is not the student's but the teacher's fault if the student fails to learn," said Rimmer, "and grades reflect only this. Professor Reid's excessively harsh grading, especially for spelling and grammar on midterms, is unjustifiable elitism that discriminates against foreign, underprivileged, regional, rural, and other minority students."

While McRobins waited to interrupt, the departmental secretary came in and told him to call the president, who had been taken hostage by several hundred protesters occupying Founders' Hall.

"Thank you, yes. I've already been apprised of the situation by Dean Hanirihan."

So he had no choice but to tell the committee about the takeover. After much astonished deliberation, they voted to sequester themselves until a decision was reached. Dino Varlew, who, unlike McRobins, had greatly enjoyed the free lunch, broached the possibility of ordering supper. —"I think," said McRobins, "that that is a bridge we can cross if and when we reach the river." —"Right, no problem," said Varlew, but suddenly he felt famished.

THE LARGE MAJORITY of those who'd entered Founders' Hall had not proceeded any farther than the atrium, or had retreated there from the overcrowded hallway outside the president's office. This majority felt itself to be the real core of the protest, the occupying force, and some of them were bemused and vexed by the calls to order from the returning vanguard.

"I didn't know who these guys were," says sophomore Tonja Salanitro. "They came in shouting, 'Meeting in the atrium.' Well, we were already having a meeting in the atrium. They said that we needed to figure out what our demands were. Well, shit. Dunkan Tomlinson, Nolan Forntner, Daenil Polotz and I had been outlining our demands to Professor Falck and the dean of admissions for the past twenty minutes. We were already in negotiations."

"They were discussions," says Gloria Chisholm, dean of admissions, who, like Falck, had an office in the building. "We had no authority to negotiate. We were just asking them questions."

Oreggio Ballenby too did not welcome what he thought of as the "political" group. "Sure, we had been screwing around: kicking the soccer ball, dancing in a conga line, shouting out the windows at passersby, wrestling. And then the politicos came back and said we needed to get serious, needed to get organized. But if there's no room for fun and games during your revolution, there's not going to be any fun or games in your new regime, and you'll be just as bad as what you're replacing."

Others, like general studies major Sanders Brand, welcomed the meeting. "I was so sick and tired of the laziness and apathy of the people at that school, that when we first marched on the Hall, I was really excited: 'All right! Finally we're *doing* something—not just talking about doing something!' But then nothing more happened; we just milled around beaming at one another, congratulating one another. 'Okay,' I thought, 'we took over a building. Good for us. But now what are we going to *do* with it?'"

"We don't need a meeting!" cried Nolan Forntner reflexively, then turned this defensive cry into rhetoric. "We know exactly what we want already! We know our demands! Haven't we been making them for months, for years? Haven't we been fighting for what we want all our life? Ask anybody here; they'll tell you. Do we want to preserve our green spaces? —That's right. Do we want to keep our good profs and throw out the bad? —You bet we do. Do we want

to be listened to when we speak? —Hell yes! So you tell me:
What do we want?"

The atrium rang like a bell with replies. Dunkan Tomlinson
wanted free textbooks. Sanders Brand wanted the old textbooks to be donated to poor nations. Langdon Bellhouse
wanted an end to lies. Angelik Huaraman wanted a crack-
down on campus muggings. Sylvie Reinhardt wanted a ban
on plastic bottles, Daenil Polotz on advertising. Elea Bukarica
wanted all experiments on animals stopped. Troy Rosswind
wanted smaller classes. Langdon Bellhouse wanted to fire-
bomb his literature survey course. Carla DiAmbla wanted
corporations to be taxed more. Many wanted the popular
singer, Glade Lufiz, acquitted of his manslaughter charge.
Sanders Brand wanted an end to world hunger. Clark Dalerow
wanted to abolish prudery, Oreggio Ballenby monogamy,
Tonja Salanitro gender. Some wanted freedom, some power,
some self-actualization; some poetry, some magic, some love.
Langdon Bellhouse wanted all telemarketers killed.

"You see," said Forntner, "we already know what we
want!"

"I want a meeting," said Rennie Jarabal.

Diana Pirales proposed a vote. A middle-aged returning
student with three adult children, Pirales was accustomed to
mediating arguments at home, and to leading discussions
among her less confident, less outspoken classmates. (Says
classmate Paula Earleywine, "She was one of those students
who thought out loud, and who couldn't seem to absorb
any information without first speaking it.") Wil Partlingover
refused and urged others to refuse to vote; he did not want
to be bound by the outcome, or to validate the system by
participating in it. Yet the vote was held. "Everyone who
wants a meeting," said Pirales, "put up your hand." About
forty percent raised their hands. "And everyone who doesn't,
put up your hand." Another forty percent, not exclusive of
the first group, raised their hands. —"And who doesn't give

a shit if we have a meeting or not?" shouted someone. About sixty percent raised their hands. Nevertheless, the meeting was underway.

"We have to confine ourselves to reasonable demands, or we'll only discredit the movement." —"I disagree. If we don't overshoot, we won't leave any room to haggle." —"No, we mustn't haggle; it shows weakness." —"On the contrary, refusing to negotiate, to make any compromises, will only make us look like crazy fanatics." —"We *are* crazy fanatics!" —"If we confine ourselves to what *they* would say is reasonable, we're defeated before we've begun." —"No compromises! They do what we say now; we're in charge." —"I agree. If we go into this prepared from the beginning to compromise, we're liable to gobble up the first bone they throw us." —"Anything they're willing to give us is, by definition, not hurting them much, and therefore isn't good enough. We want to make them pay!" —"Okay, but pardon my obtuseness, but how are they to blame for Glade Lufiz, or world hunger?" —"Everything is connected, and everything boils down to poverty. Without poverty, there is no exploitation; without exploitation, there is no wealth; without wealth, there is no oppression, no inequality, no competition, no bitterness, no greed, no destruction of natural resources . . ." —"Exactly: natural resources! Because everything boils down not to poverty, but to the exploitation of nature, which is the only form of wealth we have, and which must be preserved and shared equally by everyone. Every other evil stems from the evil of ownership, the evil of property." —"Nonsense. Poverty subsumes property: if everyone had money, we would all have property." —"Bullshit. If everyone has the same amount of money, you have in effect abolished money." —"All right, calm down. We're all on the same side." —"No we're not! This artificial concern for other people's supposed hardships, in some abstract country far far away, is only a distraction from the real battles we need to fight here. This fashionable abstract humanism is nothing but a trick of the ruling class to divide and co-opt and dissipate our energies. The real enemy is and always has been capitalism." —"You've got it exactly backwards! 'Capitalism' is the abstraction; anticapitalism is the distraction. Anticapitalism betrays the poor!" —"But even if what you all say is true, how is the administration of this university, just pragmatically speaking, supposed to grant an end to capitalism, or to property, or to poverty?" —"This isn't just about the administration of this university; it's about the administration of this government, this country, this planet!" —"That's why we've got to tear down the whole system. It's corrupt through and through, so to fix one part of it is only to improve its overall functioning and therefore exacerbate its total corruption." —"And that's why we mustn't compromise. Every concession is just another link in our chains. They enslave us with their compromises, the same way a factory owner better enslaves his workers with little token raises and slightly improved working conditions from time to time." —"But what the hell are we even doing here, if we're not going to let them consent to our demands?"

CHIEF OF CAMPUS Security Radner Pedersen was eating lunch in his patrol car, parked behind the stadium, when Gary Holdona called him on the radio. He swallowed before answering, for the same reason that he ate his meals clandestinely: he believed that the dignity of his office, upon which discipline depended, would be undermined by the image of him relaxing.

He had been brooding about his son, and at first the news of the takeover seemed only a continuation and amplification of his thoughts. "I could imagine all too clearly," he says, "an army of Delrons loping into Founders' Hall, slumping down on the desks and the floor, and slowly filling the air with their fug, like toxic plants turning oxygen and light into sweat and smoke." They would bring their girlfriends along too—lissome, pliant girlfriends—and transform the building into one big fetid bedroom.

Indeed, Chief Pedersen could not think about his son without his thoughts turning to Sandria, the boy's rangy, large-eyed girlfriend. She was seventeen, the same age as Ronnie, and though she dressed like a boy and laughed like a child, there was no question that she was sexually mature, and that together they were sexually active. The idea angered Chief Pedersen for reasons so numerous they remained tangled and obscure. He objected to their youth, which was, after all, so much more puerile than his own (sexually active) youth had been. He objected to their frivolity, their lassitude, their immoderation, and their depravity. He blamed his son for all this; towards Sandria he felt only a sad, disappointed protectiveness.

The scene at Founders' Hall infuriated him for as many, and many of the same, reasons. A large crowd of the curious and the more cautiously supportive had gathered outside, and the mood among them was festive. "They were running this ostensibly serious political protest like a carnival," says Chief Pedersen. "They were having too damn much fun."

Chief Pedersen radioed Holdona back. "What happened to 'Julius'?" —"I don't know, Chief. He's not answering his radio. He must have gone in." —"All right. Here's what we're going to do. Get Elio and Alban to fill the truck with barriers and drop them off behind the Hall, that is, on the south side, away from the crowd. We're going to cordon off the building. Send Nevis and Lo over for traffic control: let nobody else in. Pull Charles and Réal from the library, too. Everyone in yellow vests and full kit. Got that?" Full kit meant truncheons, handcuffs, and pepper spray, and was usually reserved for night patrol. —"Got it." —"Then you get on the horn and call everybody on day crew and tell them we have a Code Eleven." —"Code Eleven, Chief?" Code Eleven was a bomb threat. —"Just to get their attention and get them down here. While you're doing that, have Lois wake the night shift and put them on standby." —"All of them?" —"Everybody." —"This thing's pretty heavy, huh, Chief?" —"Not yet it's not. We'll try to keep it that way."

Holdona told Pedersen that President Radil had called. —"Tell her I've got my hands full at the moment." —"She's still inside the building." —"Well, maybe I'll see her in a minute." —"You're not going in there alone, Chief?" —"No," said Pedersen. "'Julius' is inside, too."

"Julius" was Security Officer Darren Kolst, whom Chief Pedersen had sent to keep an eye on the Reinstate Professor Reid rally. Because the sight of security officers was known to sometimes inflame protesters, Kolst had gone incognito. He was not much older than the average student on campus, and could have passed unremarked in any of his civilian clothes; but this was his first undercover assignment, and he had taken great pains with his disguise. He had torn his pants, chafed his shoes, mussed his hair, and borrowed his girlfriend's eyeglasses, which rendered him purblind. But he had labored most over his alias, finally adopting "Julius Arbuston" after an hour of making studious, ingenuous, and irate faces in the mirror. He had tested the name on his girlfriend and colleagues, and they had all deemed it plausibly namelike. He had been silently rehearsing it all that morning, and indeed through much of the rally, until it was so ready on his lips that twice, joining in a chant or a cry, he had nearly shouted his pseudonym instead.

Kolst was somewhat surprised to find himself shouting anything, having intended only to observe and smile sympathetically or, if necessary, discouragingly. But, afraid of being exposed, he reflexively matched his behavior to that of those around him. He reasoned that he was building credibility, which he could draw on should he need to intervene. Soon he began to take pleasure in this performance, a pleasure that was partly the thrill of deceiving, partly the satisfaction of exercising a newfound skill, and partly the intoxication of playacting—a feeling of liberated invincibility that was only enhanced by exaggeration.

He felt a tremor of disquiet when the rally entered Founders' Hall; and he came fully out of character for a moment when Nhizhdin and the other staff were ejected from the building. "I felt in that moment," he says, "not professional disapproval, but the isolated vulnerability of the minority, and a fear that I hadn't experienced since a child, attending a new school." He quickly recovered the armor of his alter ego; but, twenty minutes later, it was with some relief—which he was careful to mask with derision—that he saw Chief Pedersen making his way through the crowd and into the atrium.

Kolst was not the only one to welcome the appearance of the Chief of Security, in his yellow vest and paramilitary cap, and carrying at low port a bullhorn whose trigger he squeezed whenever he encountered an unyielding back, and which gave off a frightening crackle. Protesters got out of his way with sarcastic deference, but they got out of his way; and soon the room spontaneously quietened, without his needing recourse to the bullhorn.

"I can't explain it," says Rennie Jarabal, "but the sight of the chief made me feel optimistic—like things were finally about to get underway." —Says Ethan Hendry, "I let out a sigh when I saw him, and felt myself relax—the relief of the criminal when he's finally arrested, maybe." —Elea Bukarica says, "It was time for a showdown."

Allison Ziegenkorn was the first to speak. "Are you here to kick everyone out, Chief Pedersen? Will you use force if necessary?"

"I am here," said Pedersen, in his deep, clear voice, "to ask everyone who is not here on official business to please vacate the premises immediately. If you leave now, no trespassing charges will be laid."

"This is official business!" —"We don't recognize your authority!" —"You're the one trespassing, Chief!"

The jeers that met his ultimatum were, for the most part, amused and playful; but levity was more outrageous to

397

Pedersen than anger or defiance, because it showed no respect for his person, his position, or the institution he represented.

"You have ten minutes to disperse. Anyone still here without good reason at 1:55 will face the consequences of their actions."

"How about pollution? and theft? and injustice? Are those good enough reasons for you?"

Pedersen had turned on his heel to leave, the better to underscore his threat, but he could not resist a reply. "If you have legitimate complaints, you should lodge them through the proper channels. You're not gaining any sympathy for your cause by behaving like a bunch of ruffians."

Now the protesters grew angry. "When we go through proper channels, fuck-all happens!" —"Who's the ruffian, threatening to arrest us?" —"Unlike you, we're unarmed. This is a peaceful protest."

Chief Pedersen pointed out that they were holding the building and several people hostage. —"They're free to leave anytime!" —Pedersen reminded them of the staff whom they had ejected and who were not free to return to their work, an obstruction which, as surely as vandalism or theft, was costing the university time and money. —This argument elicited so many objections, factual, economic, and ad hominem, that Pedersen had to resort to the bullhorn to be heard over the uproar.

"What you're doing here makes absolutely no sense. You might as well protest the price of potatoes by kidnapping the grocer's wife. If you don't like the system, you've got to work within the system to change it. Otherwise you're just renegade delinquents. You don't gain prestige by shoving people around, and you don't get into a position of power or influence by hijacking buildings! It boggles my mind that grown adults need to be told such things!"

Elea Bukarica snatched the bullhorn from his grasp, to resounding cheers. Darren Kolst tensed, preparing himself, he believed, to leap to the chief's aid. But Pedersen, his heart clenched in wrath, exited the building without another word. "I felt like I'd been mugged," he says, "by a beggar I'd just given food. I should have known better than to try to reason with a pack of animals."

The bullhorn was passed form hand to hand till it reached Sanders Brand, who used it to repudiate the chief's speech. Langdon Bellhouse, standing nearby, found Brand's amplified voice much more abrasive than Pedersen's, and wrested the bullhorn away from him. He handed it to Nolan Forntner, who had again taken charge, and was calling for volunteers to guard the doors and stand watch at the windows.

President Radil, who had emerged from her office at the sound of the bullhorn, pursued Pedersen outside. Having spent the last half hour mostly failing to reach anyone on the phone, she rebuked him first for not returning her calls.

"I've been busy," he said, and illustrated this statement by hailing Holdona on the radio and requesting an update.

Radil now told Pedersen what she had been trying to tell the Special Committee, the Campus Development Office, and the board of trustees: that the protesters were confused and poorly organized, and that, given a little time, she was sure she could persuade them to disperse before anyone got hurt. "But you make the job a lot harder for me when you go in there and stir up hornets' nests."

"And you make my job a lot harder for me," said Pedersen, "when you treat unlawful trespass like a bargaining chip. As far as I'm concerned, anyone who hasn't come out of that building in six minutes is not a protester but a criminal—and will be treated accordingly."

"And as far as I'm concerned," said Radil, "it's you who'll be trespassing if you come in and start pushing those kids around."

After another minute of fruitless argument, President Radil strode back up the stairs, but was stopped at the entrance by a couple of zealous sentries. "I'm the president of this university," she said. "I'm here negotiating. I've been here the whole time. I just stepped out for a moment." —The sentries conferred by gaze, and shrugged. "Sorry, lady. Can't let anyone in who isn't a student." —Eventually Radil tried another door, where she had more luck.

About a dozen people, some with their hands raised over their heads, emerged from the Hall by Chief Pedersen's deadline; but over the same period of time, and by various doors, another forty or fifty people had entered—including Professor Givcha Lura's entire local history seminar. "This was history in the making," says Lura. "I decided to hold an old-fashioned teach-in." Most of her students were delighted by the break from routine, but some, like Jallica Ingledew, were consternated by the unorthodox field trip. An ambitious academic and assiduous conformist, Ingledew navigated the vagaries of university bureaucracy with anxious complaisance, and could be thrown into a state of panicked self-reproach by a last-minute room change or an unintelligible exam question. She too, like Chief Pedersen, was repulsed by her first glimpse of the protesters, who struck her as a rambunctious mob obviously breaking any number of rules; but at the same time, she could not believe that Professor Lura was wrong to invite her to witness and in effect join the takeover. Trembling with a mixture of apprehensions, she quickly began to devise justifications for her presence there, arriving eventually at a stance of judicious sympathy. In retrospect she says only, "I didn't necessarily agree with their methods, but I did share many of their concerns."

Suz Palombo, too, was appalled by her first sight of the takeover. Following Chief Pedersen's warning, most of the protesters had spontaneously broken into small groups to prepare for the raid, which they expected imminently. Some groups built barricades or armed themselves with unlikely bludgeons; some planned passive resistance, and discussed the relative merits of going limp and going stiff; some, expecting tear gas and nightsticks, pulled their shirts over their faces and crouched under desks; others linked arms and braced themselves for martyr-dom. But when Pedersen's ten minutes and another ten min-utes had elapsed, the would-be defenders became restless. To vent their nervous energy, they deconstructed or improved for-tifications, threw objects and insults out windows, and roved throughout the building, looking for acts or symbols of oppres-sion to thwart or destroy. Slowly, and by small increments, the cost of damages done to university property rose from the price of a restaurant dinner for four to the price of a used car.

It was this scene of frazzled lawlessness that Palombo found when she entered the Hall. She went hunting for Arjmand, but found Allison Ziegenkorn first, who gave her a colorful if fragmentary summary of the past hour's events, one which seemed to absolve Arjmand of any real respon-sibility for the takeover. Palombo was somewhat mollified, but could not share Ziegenkorn's enthusiasm. "Xin has got some gorgeous photos. It's a real coup, Suz!"

She found Arjmand in the atrium, where President Radil was urging the protesters to elect their representatives. Several people nominated Forntner, who nominated Tonja Salanitro, Daenil Polotz, Sylvie Reinhardt, and Thalia Undine. Clark Dalerow nominated Dunkan Tomlinson, who nominated Clark Dalerow. Elea Bukarica, Sanders Brand, and Rennie Jarabal nominated themselves. Palombo nominated Arjmand and Herman Triem, and accepted their nomination for her. Radil nominated Dean of Admissions Gloria Chisholm and Professor Vaglaf Falck to represent the administration and faculty. Diana Pirales, by commenting on the election for everyone's edification, inadvertently nominated herself.

Says Radil, "It was a larger group than I would have liked, but I hoped that the large net would catch all the largest fish, and that no one would feel neglected."

"It was not an ideal election," says Jarabal, "but we didn't know how much time we'd have—so we acted quickly. And since no one objected, and there were no more nominations, we felt that everyone who wanted to be part of the decision-making had been included. Of course that wasn't true."

Clapping her hands ceremoniously, Radil invited the sixteen members of the newly formed Occupation Committee to convene in the boardroom. Nolan Forntner wanted to make a parting speech, but most of his audience had melted away, and he could think of nothing to say. On his way out of the atrium, he took Langdon Bellhouse aside and handed him back the bullhorn. "Protect the building," he said. "It's all we've got."

As soon as the negotiators had left the room, voices of cynicism and dissent were heard. "Shit, whatever happened to 'No more decisions behind closed doors'?" —"Yeah, who the hell voted for those assholes?"—"You know they're just going to sell us out, don't you?" said Wil Partlingover. —Angelik Huaraman agreed, noting how readily they had accepted the president's nominations. —"Yeah, they were kowtowing to her already. What a joke!" Most of those present were content to wallow in their validated pessimism, but Partlingover was angry and wanted to do something. "Man, let's take over this fucking takeover!"

Bellhouse pointed the bullhorn at him menacingly. "Shut up," he said.

Oreggio Ballenby pleaded for faith and patience. "Let's give them the benefit of the doubt. We should at least wait and see what they negotiate before we tear the place down." Others agreed, and helped pacify Partlingover.

Carla DiAmbla turned to Troy Rosswind and said, "Well, what do we do in the meantime?" —Rosswind suggested shyly, "I've got drugs . . . ?"

As NEWS OF the takeover spread across campus, hundreds of curious students migrated to Founders' Hall to see it for themselves, while most of the staff and faculty sought one another out to discuss its significance and debate its merits. "Most everyone you talked to," says biology professor Ajay

Nutter, "was against it. Without even knowing what it was all about, they reflexively assumed that the students must be in the wrong. It was disconcerting, to say the least, to see all my ostensibly liberal and progressive colleagues side instinctively with the defense of the status quo."

Says Assistant Dean of Humanities Kimsun Poon, "I was dismayed, to say the least, that virtually everyone was automatically on the students' side. There is a deplorable culture of youth worship at this university—an unwritten code that the pure and innocent student intuitively knows more than his corrupt and flyblown teacher. Without even understanding the issues at stake, most of us took it for granted that the university was to blame, and that the protesters had a good case."

Vice-President Yusef Martin, however, felt no compulsion to discuss the takeover, or indeed anything else, with his staff and faculty. A week as acting president had left him with a strong distaste for committees, conferences, and meetings, and for arbitrating disputes and reconciling discord. He longed only to return to his paperwork, letter writing, and congenial, one-on-one business lunches. But his colleagues would not let him alone, and congregated anew in whatever room, in whichever building, he escaped to. They had again made him arbiter, and had come to tell him, in a dozen contradictory voices, what must be done.

"We've got to stop this thing now, before it gets any more out of control." —"On the contrary, if we stop them now, they're just going to start up again somewhere else." —"Not if we give out suspensions to the ringleaders." —"There's a thousand people in there; you'd have to suspend hundreds of them. Then you'd really have a revolt on your hands." —"I thought there weren't more than a few hundred protesters." —"Whatever the exact number, it's more than enough to start a riot, if we act foolishly or precipitately." —"What do you suggest? Let them have their fun today, then carry on tomorrow as though nothing happened? We've got to suspend some of them, or we set a precedent of implied permission, and this sort of thing starts happening all the time." —"Nonsense. It hasn't happened before; why should it happen again?" —"It happened not fifteen years ago!" —"That was completely different." —"I say let them get it out of their system." —"What if they get a taste for it?" —"I hate to think how this is going to affect enrollment next year," said Charity Meerquist, one of the trustees. —"I still think we should wait awhile. These movements quite often fizzle out on their own." —"On what are you basing that generalization?" —"Listen. If we go in there like strikebreakers and bust up their demonstration, not only do we look like brutal reactionaries, and probably incite a whole new legion of demonstrators in the process, but we actually become opponents of free speech; real oppressors of new ideas; stranglers and snuffers-out of creativity, discovery, and dissent. When surely, I'd have thought, one of the things we strive to inculcate here, at an institution of higher learning such as this university purports to be, is freedom of expression, liberty of opinion, untrammeled and independent thought. It's the only way knowledge progresses, for God's sake. If we shut down this protest, we might as well shut down the university, because it will be a crime against science, against education, against humanity." —"Look. To tolerate this insurrection, and it is an insurrection, is to condone and indeed support it, and the university cannot support and encourage its own overthrow. The free and open university is a tradition that too often in this country we take for granted, but let us recall what it really means: opportunity for self-improvement and advancement; access to the combined wisdom and knowledge of history; the production and development of new forms of knowledge; and liberty of thought, yes, and liberty through thought. But those who attack the university are not fighters for freedom, but enemies of the very freedom that the university represents. For my part, I find this rebellion painfully reminiscent of the anti-intellectual attacks of certain fascist and repressive political regimes—not least the one I fled in my youth. I should be disconsolate were a similar evil to arise here, in my adopted homeland. If history has taught us anything, it is that such cancers must be extirpated early, and swiftly." —"What bugs me is how little historical perspective these young people have. I mean, good Lord, do they not realize how much better things are today than when we were their age? What do they even have to complain about, really?" —"Oh my God. Enough talk; let's *do* something—anything."

Vice-President Martin sighed. "Where's the president?" No one knew, and no one but Martin really missed her. A week of working with her tactful, self-effacing, and obliging surrogate had made them all starkly aware of President Radil's contrasting traits. There was a rumor, corroborated more than not by the security bulletin from Chief Pedersen, that she was being held hostage.

Martin's first decision as acting president that day was to appoint an Ad Hoc Committee to decide what was to be done.

"Oh, shit," said Meerquist, standing at the window. "The press is here."

DENISON SUNDHI AND his video crew arrived first, and set up on the lawn in front of Founders' Hall, where the light was best. "No way was I going inside," he says. "The information we'd received was about a bomb threat at the university. That didn't seem to be the case—surely the security personnel there would have evacuated the building if it were true—but I wasn't taking any chances." Sundhi, a new father, had become more cautious in the weeks since the birth of his son. "One day shortly after Nibbu was born, we were racing across town to get to the site of a car crash. I suddenly realized how crazy that was. And I started having panic attacks in the news van whenever we drove above about forty kilometers an hour, or whenever traffic got heavy. I just kept seeing myself mangled in a fiery wreck, and Nibbu growing up without a dad. No way was I going inside the Hall. Anyway, we got a lot of great footage outside."

Meanwhile, Naumi Orambe and her crew, who were half a generation younger than Sundhi, and childless, entered the occupied building without hesitation. Orambe interviewed several protesters, who were posed negligently against a backdrop of somber splendor. None of them were alarmed by the bomb threat. "That's obviously just a ploy by the powers that be to scare us out of here," said math major Jerme Carpintieri. "We're not budging till we get what we want." —Said art history major Midge Hasan, "I don't know if there is or isn't a bomb, but I'll tell you one thing: if those fat cats don't give us what we want, it's gonna be a hell of a lot more than explosives that blow up."

Allison Ziegenkorn, overhearing, tried to interview Orambe, who parried by interviewing her. —"Can you confirm or deny that the bomb threat is a ruse of the administration of this university to curtail this peaceful demonstration?" asked Ziegenkorn. —"Are you able to confirm or deny," asked Orambe, "that the bomb was placed by protesters, in the hope of strengthening their bargaining position with the university administration?" —"Perhaps you would care to comment on the perception of the protest among the privileged professional class in the community?" —"Is it your opinion, then, that the demonstration is motivated in part by the antagonism felt by students towards the locals?" —"What do you say to critics who claim that your past coverage of campus politics has been heavily biased towards the administration, who have well-known ties to the operation of your news organization?" —"Do you find it difficult here, as a student, to maintain journalistic objectivity? That is to say, are you strictly an observer and reporter of today's events, or are you also a participant?" —"No comment," said Ziegenkorn, shutting off her voice recorder and walking away.

With growing disgust, Langdon Bellhouse watched the news crews roam through his building. They were doing no harm, perhaps, but they were clearly outsiders: they belonged to the world of alienation, noise pollution, and machine-made junk. They should never have been let inside; should he eject them? After many minutes of tumultuous vacillation, which took the form less of inner dialogue than of a series of abortive gestures and half-steps in various directions, he at last resolved to ask Forntner for guidance.

Imagining the tension in the boardroom to be directed towards him, he felt small, out of place, and resentful. "The news is here," he said.

Sanders Brand volunteered to be interviewed; Suz Palombo nudged Suresh Arjmand; but Forntner, unexpectedly, put forward Diana Pirales. "We would all have been happy enough," says Forntner, "to get rid of Brand or Bukarica, who were obstructing and filibustering every issue we came near to deciding." (Says Bukarica, "It became clear early on that, as the only real activists in the room, we would need to be extra steadfast." —And Brand says, "If the president seemed inclined to accept one of our demands, we changed our minds and demanded something else. Remember, our goal was nothing less than the complete collapse of the whole rotten system.") "However," says Forntner, "if the takeover was going to continue for any length of time, I didn't think Brand would be the best public face for it." Pirales, he observed, was articulate, presentable, and self-possessed; and, referring to her age, he said, "I think it would be good to show the world that this is not just some children's crusade."

Pirales was touched by the testimonial, and accepted the delegation. She handled the reporters with an aplomb that later amazed her husband and children. "I had never seen her like that," says Chamela Pirales. "So fervent, and yet so calm and dignified. I was really proud of her." —Says Pirales, "I'd finally found my niche. For six months at that school, I didn't know what I was doing; I didn't know who I was. I'd enrolled with the highest hopes. This was to be nothing less than a new chapter in my life. But the reality was so different from my dreams. The coursework was monotonous, the lectures perfunctory; the other students were all half my age, and even the profs seemed to resent my presence. With the takeover, I finally found what I'd been looking for: community, purpose, and opportunity for growth."

Bellhouse was flabbergasted. "I didn't think old people should even be allowed inside the building," he says, "let alone be allowed to talk for us." Nor was he satisfied by the draft Nine Demands that Pirales read before the cameras, and which seemed to him neither numerous nor far-reaching enough—though he could not have said exactly what was missing.

Rennie Jarabal was also dissatisfied with the Nine Demands, but because they struck her as being altogether too inclusive. "So much of what they were asking for," she says, "was either already in reach—I mean the food bank, and classes for the community—or was not actually in the university's control—hazing, for example, which is obviously a tradition perpetuated by the students themselves."

Suz Palombo was more troubled by the president's willingness to negotiate beyond her authority. For instance, Radil objected at first to Demand Three, "No more muggings," claiming that there was no money in the budget for increased security patrols; but eventually she relented after the students agreed to drop advertising from the agenda. But, as Palombo points out, "Advertising revenue is the purview of the Communications and Marketing Council, and patrols are the purview of the Security and Safety Council. They have nothing to do with each other, and you can't simply reappropriate funds from one to the other by diktat. The same goes for the reinstatement of Professor Reid, or the expansion of Lot M. These are decisions that can only be made by the Department of Astronomy or the Campus Development Office—not by the president."

Gloria Chisholm, the dean of admissions, admits to having similar reservations. "I didn't know what game Trifenia was playing. I thought maybe she was just stalling for time, or trying to coax them out of the building with false promises. I went along with her, but I did realize that none of what we were consenting to would stand."

Says Radil, "I didn't concede anything that wasn't possible. I knew roughly the budgets involved, and how far they could be stretched; and I knew all the key players, and exactly how far they'd bend. I didn't grant anything that I wasn't confident could be ratified. If we'd had more time, I'm sure we would've made a dinner everyone could sit down to."

Forntner tried to reassure Palombo. "We've got sixteen witnesses here," he said. "President Radil knows she can't revoke anything when this is over—or we'll just take the building back; or, at the very least, publicly shame her into resigning. And getting the president to resign is a hell of a lot more than any of us ever expected to accomplish today."

Palombo did not think Radil would resign over a few broken promises made to a handful of trespassing students; nor was Palombo content to aim so low. "We should be negotiating with the real policymakers," she said, naming some of them.

Forntner shook his head. "I'm tired of groveling at those people's feet. Right now, here, in this room, *we* outnumber *them*. Let's capitalize."

"It was clear to me then," says Palombo, "that Nolan had lost his perspective. He'd made the matter personal. Who were 'we'? Who was 'them'? Was Professor Falck 'them'? Was Elea Bukarica 'we'?" She adds, "I think all Nolan could see was that he was in negotiations with the president of the university. He imagined he was being taken seriously—that he was important. And at that moment, I believe, he was more interested in playing out that drama than in saving trees, or reinstating Professor Reid, or any of the rest of it. That's why I left."

"All right," said Forntner, patting her on the shoulder like an affable supervisor. "See what you can do out there; we'll keep fighting the fight in here."

At 3:36, Dean Dean Hanirihan, sent on behalf of the Ad Hoc Committee, interrupted Hiram Reid's Cosmic Radiation class. In the hallway, he told Reid about the take-over, omitting for the sake of speed and clarity any mention of the Occupation Committee's other eight demands. —"That's got nothing to do with me," said Reid. —"I think you'll agree," said Dean, "that we must stop this thing before anyone gets hurt. Whether you like it or not, they'll listen to you." —Reid declined, and returned to his class; but when the class was over, he decided to visit Founders' Hall.

He heard the protest long before he saw it. He thought he could discern one refrain amid the clamor of catcalls and chants: "Doc-tor Reid! Doc-tor Reid!"

The Hall was engulfed by a crowd of several hundred people held imperfectly at bay by Chief Radner Pedersen's security cordon. The thought that all this commotion was in his honor made Reid's throat constrict. Then he realized that the crowd was actually shouting "Fuck the pigs! Fuck the pigs!"

Says engineering major Chanson Gearie, "The security guards were lined up facing us, motionless and expressionless as robots. Half of them wore sunglasses, and seemed to stare right through us, as if we weren't even there. They had their hands on their hips and their chins in the air, like they were inviting us to try something, just daring us to do something. Even their posture was vain and contemptuous and provoking." —Says Security Officer Nevis Kalhil, "The protesters never stopped trying to incite us. They screamed insults, made rude faces and noises, and writhed about with a kind of aggressive obscenity, like prostitutes mocking our virility. They *wanted* us to hit them—so they could start hitting us back, I guess."

Reid pushed his way through the crowd to the barricade, where he spoke to Security Officer Réal Doloron. Reid identified himself, but received no reply. "I'm supposed to be inside," he said. "I've been asked to speak to the students." —"No one goes in," said Doloron, made obstinate by fear.

Reid was tapped on the shoulder and directed by a young woman to the east side of the building. "Just wait till they're not looking and hop over the barrier." —Reid thanked her, then paused to ask why she didn't go in. —"Oh, I've been in there," she grinned. "It's funner out here."

In fact, he did not need to wait or to hop, but simply squeezed through one of the gaps in the cordon that the security officers were too beleaguered to fill. Inside the east entrance, a gang of student sentries accosted him. Again he identified himself, again with no effect. "I'm the Professor Reid they're trying to reinstate," he elaborated. —"Oh yeah," said one, with clouded recognition. "I guess he's cool." They let him pass.

Reid wandered dumbstruck through the Hall. "I've never seen anything like it," he says. "It was as if an army of gypsies had been living there for a week. There were mattresses and blankets and even tents. Food was being eaten or prepared in every room, in some cases on portable butane stoves. The air was thick with smoke and grease and perfume, as well as more human smells. The students were dancing, playing instruments, and singing. A mock wedding ceremony of some sort was taking place in the atrium, and a young woman in a toga and paper crown was conferring bogus degrees in the president's office. Some fellow was tossing lit cigarettes to a dog, who caught them in its teeth. In some rooms I found some of my colleagues conducting a kind of educational burlesque—aimless, interminable rap sessions in which everybody at once talked about their feelings. Several groups were writing manifestos. Some were painting ungrammatical slogans on bedsheets, which they hung out the windows. I saw kids kissing and fondling in alcoves, and

I believe I overheard at least one couple having sex. And everywhere, everywhere, were bottles and pills and pipes."

Says undeclared major Valba Ghurraine, who sneaked into the Hall half an hour earlier, "It was the best party I've ever been to."

Says Carla DiAmbla, "I realized that the universe is an involuted cataract of energy, a boundless torrent of overlapping and interfering patterns of vibration. I saw that energy is both movement and stasis, vibration being impossible without both on *and* off, crest *and* trough, and that therefore 'death' is meaningless, since it is but one pole of the eternal pulse, and no more detrimental to life than blinking is to sight. I understood that 'the universe' is not, as I had imagined, everything outside me, but in fact both the observed and the observer, myself and not-self, inextricably. I was an eddy, a ripple on a wave on a swell, which could in no way buck the stream. As part and substance of the stuff of the universe, I contributed unfailingly and effortlessly to the dance of the universe. I sat back in myself, as it were, and rode my nervous system, my personality—that masterful orchestration of every influence I had ever known—like a schooner under full sail. All my motions, all my actions, however trifling or important, hackneyed or strange, were liquid and unhesitating, like the brushstrokes of a practiced artist. Existence was play, and I played exuberantly—not like a child, who forgets she is playing, but like an actor, in complete control of her instrument. It was fun while it lasted."

Says Troy Rosswind, "I felt excruciatingly thin-skinned. Everything happening was high tragedy. Sensation fell upon me like a suffocating cloud of dust."

Says Hifan Hwan, "It was a different world. People were holding eye contact, and smiling at strangers. Everyone was introduced to everyone else. The woman who'd sat next to you silently all semester suddenly greeted you like an old friend. Distinctions of class and age and clique evaporated. Every face was beaming with friendliness, goodwill, and laughter—laughter because we'd all discovered how easy it was. The answer had been there all along. We just had to open our eyes to it. Life could be like this always. We'd figured it out. We'd won."

By 5:15, THE Ad Hoc Committee, convened across the commons in Room 410 of the Law Tower, had accepted six of the Nine Demands: hazing would be outlawed; a food bank would be established in the Student Union Building; unfilled courses would be opened to locals, free of charge; a committee would be appointed to investigate alleged clear-cutting by certain scholarship donors; to help prevent muggings, the Security and Safety Council would solicit student volunteers to escort pedestrians after dark; and Jaromir Ulgrave, dean of the Physics and Astronomy Department, promised to abide by whatever recommendation was given regarding Professor Reid by the Special Committee, still meeting in Room 204 of the Whitethorn Building. In exchange for all this, Suz Palombo had abandoned Demand Six, "No more animal testing," agreeing that it was impracticable at a university so invested in the sciences.

Only two items remained contentious. Jabbar Shah, dean of campus development, refused to discontinue or postpone the expansion of Lot M; and a few committee members, led by Albert Nhizhdin, were opposed to Demand Nine, "Amnesty for all protesters."

The stalemate was finally broken when Chief Pedersen entered the room, his face haggard and his yellow jacket smeared with blood. He spoke briefly to Vice-President Martin, who had been lurking at the back of the room, and who now made a gesture of renunciation.

"I don't know! You'll have to ask the Committee. They're in charge now."

Without meeting any gaze, but with head held high, Pedersen addressed the assembly. He said that the situation had deteriorated all afternoon, and was now nearly out of control. Though his men and women had fought the tide valiantly, they were frankly outnumbered and would soon be overwhelmed. He alluded to injuries, and everyone in the room stared at the blood on his jacket (which actually belonged to a student who had failed to hurdle a barrier). He said that he had been in communication with Chief of Police Les Dugul, who had two hundred officers trained and equipped and ready to deploy.

"Oh God," said Dean Dean, standing suddenly. "You're talking about sending in the riot squad." —"This is a crowd-dispersal unit," said Pedersen. —"What is this equipment they'll be using?" asked Shah. "Tear gas?" —"I was referring primarily to personal protection: helmets and shields and so forth that we simply do not have." —"Will there be arrests?" asked Hofman Walchalm, one of the trustees. —"That would be at Chief Dugul's discretion. My understanding is that arrests would only be made if necessary to expedite dispersal." —"Oh God," said Dean Dean, sitting suddenly.

All of them, even those who had most strongly advocated punishment, were chastened by Chief Pedersen's proud, battered solemnity, and appalled by the thought of riot police invading their campus.

"What choice do we have?" asked Sacha Frean, dean of security and safety. "We either bring in Chief Dugul, or we surrender the Hall to the protesters."

"Put it to a vote," suggested Martin. But no one wanted to vote. —"This should be your decision," muttered someone.

At last Suz Palombo stood. "We must reach an agreement. Now."

"Well, what do you offer?"

"We could, perhaps, restrict the extent of amnesty . . ."

"To whom?"

"To the fourteen student members of the Occupation Committee—for example."

Nhizhdin made a seething sound and slumped in his chair. "In exchange for what?"

Everyone looked at Shah. —"It's impossible," he said. "We have a very clear mandate from the board of trustees to increase the parking facilities at this institution by no less than 3.5 percent over the next two years to keep pace with enrollment."

Everyone looked at the trustees, Hofman Walchalm and Charity Meerquist, who looked at each other, and shrugged.

Sirens were heard in the distance.

Shah closed his eyes and placed his hands on the conference table. "We can—we will—reduce the area of expansion to eighty percent." He opened his eyes. "Seventy-five percent! Three hectares. It cannot be less."

"Okay," said Palombo, and hurried from the room.

The members of the Ad Hoc Committee all stood and began talking at once, like a class of schoolchildren whose teacher has been called away. Said Chief Pedersen, unheard at the window, "That's no police siren."

IT WAS DETERMINED later that the fire started somewhere in the southeast corner of the basement, where the permanent records were stored. The crowd outside, who were in a better position to see the smoke begin to billow, cheered the arrival of the firetrucks with cries of "Yay, pigs!" Many of those inside, however, annoyed by the shrill alarm and smelling at first no smoke, decided that this was another ploy to oust them from the building. "Stand your ground!" shouted Wil Partlingover; and Langdon Bellhouse, at last brimming over with anger at the soulless, gimcrack modern world, stalked from room to room crying, "Protect the building! Let it burn!" while smashing fire annunciator panels and pull stations with the butt of his bullhorn. Dozens of people fled the building when the sprinklers turned on, but hundreds rushed to the windows and doors, taking up defensive positions against the onslaught of firefighters and

security officers, who screamed at them in incredulous outrage to clear a path. "The place is on fire, you idiots! Move!"

As the Occupation Committee broke up in chaos,
President Radil ran to her office to retrieve the photo of her
children, then descended the fire escape. Nolan Forntner
trudged aimlessly through the brawling throng, numb
with dismay. Tonja Salanitro removed her shirt and bra
and waved them over her head. Allison Ziegenkorn tossed
a newsperson's camera out a window. Darren Kolst, a.k.a.
"Julius Arbuston," helped Elea Bukarica push a filing cabinet down a staircase. The cost of damages rose exponentially.

Outside, a firefighter's forehead was split open by a flying
paperweight. Students, staff, and visitors alike were clubbed
and pepper-sprayed. The crowd was quickly polarized by the
violence, and rushed into the fray to render justice or exact
revenge. Fire Chief Fenton Glaslum gave the order to turn
the hoses on the protesters. "By that point," says firefighter
Linda Thule, "you couldn't tell protesters from bystanders;
everyone was a protester."

President Radil met Chief Pedersen hurrying across the
commons. After a brief colloquy, she told him to call in
Chief Dugul's crowd-dispersal unit.

"It's my decision," she said. "I take full responsibility."

Then, feeling a strange pain in her chest, she sat down on
the grass. She had eaten nothing all day.

THE FIRE WAS soon extinguished, but the firefighters, denied
free access to the building, were unable to ascertain this by
the time the police arrived at dusk.

Says Chief Dugul, "We were moving into a building 23,000
square feet in size, filled with an unknown number of violent
demonstrators, and possibly on fire. Naturally we were a little
keyed up." —Constable Lafcadio Stusdal says, "It was disgusting—a bunch of spoiled brats who'd never done a real day's
work in their lives behaving like they were the victims of some

kind of horrible injustice." —"The place looked like a fortress," says Constable Kennett Labron. "There were crowds of people at every window. They were throwing rocks and bottles and heavy books at us before we could even get out of the vans." —Sergeant Gladiola Kjesbu says, "For most of us, this was our first real action outside of field exercises. We had no idea what to expect. It was worse than any of us could have imagined. The demonstrators were behaving like crazed animals."

Many of the occupiers were equally intimidated by the sight of the police. Says Sanders Brand, "When I saw the cops, in all their armor and carrying rifles, get into formation at the bottom of the front steps, I knew that was it. We were doomed." He left the building by another door.

In fact, protesters outnumbered police by about five to one, but they did not realize it, scattered as they were throughout the building.

Dugul's force, inexorable behind shields and gas masks, entered Founders' Hall at 6:17, pushing back the protesters as far as the atrium. Then, as much due to congestion as to defiance, the crowd retreated no farther.

Chief Dugul, speaking through a bullhorn, ordered them to disperse or risk being fired upon. None knew that the rifles aimed at them were loaded with plastic bullets. A panic infected the crowd, composed half of fury, half of terror. Says Oreggio Ballenby, "I really thought I was about to die. I couldn't breathe."

Constable Coary Harbitz could not wear his eyeglasses under his gas mask. Sweat stung his eyes. "All I could see was the back of the guy in front of me," he says. "And him I couldn't even hear over the screaming of the protesters, the thud of projectiles raining down on our heads."

Chanson Gearie threw a brick, but it fell short, walloping a fellow student in the head. This made her even angrier at the police. "In a way," she says, "it was their fault."

Several voices pleaded for negotiations. "Haven't you pigs ever heard of dialogue?"

At 6:23, twelve rounds were fired into the crowd. Chief Dugul denies issuing any command, but does not condemn his officers for opening fire. None of the seven constables who discharged their weapons that day believes they were the first to do so, and all of them are certain that they aimed at the floor or over the protesters' heads, in accordance with their training. Nevertheless, four students were injured, and one, taking a direct shot to the eye, was instantly killed.

The crack of gunfire, the wail of screams, and the sight of blood sickened even the most ardent protesters. The crowd dispersed.

Says Constable Harbitz, "They charged at us. We had no choice."

"EVERY GENERATION HAS its monsters to slay," says linguistics professor Bertrand Laing. "The problem with this generation is that, though they feel the itch to slay, they do not know what their monsters look like, or where they live, or how to find them. This frustration only makes them more violent and indiscriminate. They don't know what to lash out at, so they lash out at whatever's nearest. In the past, the enemy was much more manifest. You had a definite target."

Says Assistant Dean of Humanities Kimsun Poon, "The fact is that higher learning in this country and in this era has become altogether too wishy-washy. We educators today have all swallowed the liberal dogma that truth is merely a social construct—that which would be best for us to believe, as William James put it; our as-yet-irrefutable errors, as Nietzsche said. We are so afraid of being called elitist that we refuse to exalt one idea over another, or praise one book before another, with the result that everything combines into a porridge of mediocrity. I believe the takeover was nothing less than an instinctive revolt against this bland, mealy-mouthed relativism. The students, perhaps only half consciously, realize that what's needed is a return to good old-fashioned elitism and exclusivism. They crave a firm hierarchy of values, such as we had in my youth. They crave authority."

Dean of Donations Jelke Beiersdorf believes that the extended adolescence is to blame. "In the past," he says, "teenagers rebelled against their parents. Today, steeped in luxury and ease, children grow up more slowly. By the time they are ready to rebel, they are at university, where they find only proxy parents to attack."

Administrative assistant Esther Dentonne believes that such uprisings are bound to happen from time to time. "Every intelligent young person gets to a point in their life," she says, "when they realize that everything is fundamentally a lie. Language is an arbitrary code; morals, like manners, are a convention; politics is show business; science is a tottering patchwork of makeshift hypotheses; the economy is a collective hallucination; even personal identity is a phantasm. Indeed, realizing that everything is a lie could be said to be the hallmark of adolescence. The hallmark of adulthood, on the other hand, is realizing the usefulness of lies—understanding that, though all our castles are built in the air, they are not therefore any the less majestic, or any less delightful to explore."

Philosophy professor Nifel Niesbundsun, paraphrasing Schopenhauer, says, "Young people are generally dissatisfied, but they ascribe their dissatisfaction to the state of things, and not, as they should, to the vanity and wretchedness of human life everywhere, which they are for the first time experiencing."

Says local resident Margit Strummel, "Kids will be kids."

Says Suz Palombo, "The takeover occurred for at least nine very good reasons."

Langdon Bellhouse says, "Just look around you."

THOUGH THE CAUSES and significance of the takeover were long debated, public opinion was soon agreed that the death of undeclared major Scott Pollen, aged twenty, was a deplorable and avoidable tragedy. At his memorial service three days later, he was universally eulogized. Those who spoke remembered him with rough fondness as an ebullient partygoer and womanizer, an irrepressible clown, a free spirit who daily seized the day. His attendance records and grade point average verify the portrait of a young man who had come to university not to mellow in stuffy classrooms but to cultivate friendships and celebrate life. Of the dozens of mourners who celebrated his life that day, not one turned his death into propaganda or used the platform as a soapbox.

"I hated him," says Nigel Garff, his roommate. "For six months I hated him passionately. He was the worst roommate imaginable. He made noise at all hours; he left filth everywhere. I hated his clumsy card tricks, his dumb jokes, and his silly pranks—tossing lit cigarettes to his dog, or making himself faint by holding his breath, or sneaking up behind you and draping his penis over your shoulder just to get a rise out of you. Most of all I hated him for his many friends, and his constant parties, and the countless women he brought home—and blithely offered to share with me. I hated that everyone liked him. I hated the way he made life seem a lazy Sunday stroll. I hated him as we only hate the better self we're too frightened or habit-bound to become. I hated him; and I never told him how much I loved him."

Elea Bukarica, for one, is critical of the public outpouring of grief. "All this sentimental pity for some dead rich kid that most people never even knew is simply a distraction from the real tragedies of poverty and hunger, which kill untold thousands of people every day."

Chief of Security Radner Pedersen says, "It is not a tragedy when a criminal is injured while committing a crime. It is unfortunate, and it is to be regretted, but it is not a tragedy. When you break the law, you run a certain risk."

THE LAST ACTION of the Ad Hoc Committee was to appoint a disciplinary committee, dubbed the March Sixteenth

Committee. After weeks of deliberation, this committee, feeling that popular sentiment was still on the side of the occupiers, decided not to suspend, expel, or otherwise punish any students. They did recommend that certain clauses of the campus constitution be rewritten to help clarify which demonstrations and rallies would be condoned, and which would be considered unlawful.

The Security and Safety Council requested and received funds to hire thirty more security guards. These were deployed not at night to deter muggers, but in the day to discourage spontaneous assemblies.

A tribunal was ostentatiously convened to determine whether the police who fired their rifles had been negligent; after months of investigations and hearings, they were quietly acquitted.

Trifenia Radil resigned as president of the university, citing health concerns.

The Department of Physics and Astronomy, adhering to the Special Committee's recommendation, offered to renew Hiram Reid's contract. Reid declined the offer, and is now teaching in Canada.

The Campus Development Office bulldozed three hectares of parkland, but, following a massive campus and community protest led by Sanders Brand, the area was never paved and Lot M never expanded. No shortage of parking spaces was noticed the following year, for enrollment did not increase at the expected rate. Today the trees and plants have largely returned, but the boundary between the old growth and the new growth is still perceptible.

Contents